WISHFU

"The Tale of th[...] ...e
Yolen*—Was her [...] r-
ever, or could the[...] ... ..mp fulfil her one
and only wish?

"New Life for Old" by Pat Cadigan—When you're
in your "declining" years is a wish for youth a
treasure or trouble?

"Dirt Track Demon" by Jack C. Haldeman II—
Sometimes wishing to be a winner can be a dangerous road to race down. . . .

"The Last of a Vintage Year" by Janet Kagan—
Will there come a time when even Aladdin will
wish for no more wishes?

These are just a few of the spellbinding tales of
wishes asked for and granted in—

MASTER OF THE LAMP

Other Anthologies of Enchantment Brought to You by DAW:

CATFANTASTIC I and II *edited by Andre Norton and Martin H. Greenberg*. All new tales of those long-tailed, furry keepers of mankind, practitioners of magical arts beyond human ken.

HORSE FANTASTIC *edited by Rosalind M. Greenberg and Martin H. Greenberg*. All new stories of horses both natural and supernatural from such fantasy masters as Jennifer Roberson, Mercedes Lackey, Mike Resnick, Mickey Zucker Reichert, Nancy Springer, and Judith Tarr.

DRAGON FANTASTIC *edited by Rosalind M. Greenberg and Martin H. Greenberg*. Complete with an introduction by Tad Williams, here is a spellbinding collection of brand new stories about the dragons, the true kings of the fantasy realms, as envisioned by such clever enchanters as Alan Dean Foster, Dennis McKiernan, Mickey Zucker Reichert, Tanya Huff, and Esther Friesner.

THE NIGHT FANTASTIC *Edited by Poul and Karen Anderson*. Let Poul Anderson, Ursula K. Le Guin, Isaac Asimov, Alan Dean Foster, Robert Silverberg, Fritz Leiber, and a host of other fantasy masters carry you away to magical realms where night becomes day as the waking world sleeps and sleeping worlds wake.

SWORD AND SORCERESS *edited by Marion Zimmer Bradley*. Original tales of fantasy and adventure, stories of warrior women and sorceresses, wielding their powers in the war against evil.

ALADDIN
MASTER OF THE LAMP

Edited by

Mike Resnick

and

Martin H. Greenberg

DAW BOOKS, INC.

DONALD A. WOLLHEIM, FOUNDER

375 Hudson Street, New York, NY 10014

ELIZABETH R. WOLLHEIM
SHEILA E. GILBERT
PUBLISHERS

First Printing, December 1992

1 2 3 4 5 6 7 8 9

DAW TRADEMARK REGISTERED
U.S. PAT OFF AND FOREIGN COUNTRIES
—MARCA REGISTRADA,
HECHO EN U.S.A.

PRINTED IN THE U.S.A.

ACKNOWLEDGMENTS

Introduction © 1992 *by Mike Resnick.*
Fair Exchange © 1992 *by Anthony R. Lewis.*
The Rest of the Story © 1992 *by Mark Aronson.*
The Tale of the Seventeenth Eunuch © 1992 *by Jane Yolen.*
Yasmine © 1992 *by Laura Resnick.*
Three Wish Habit © 1992 *by Janni Lee Simner.*
800-DJIN-HLP © 1992 *by Lea Hernandez.*
On the Heath © 1992 *by Barry N. Malzberg.*
Fizz © 1992 *by Nicholas A. DiChario.*
A Guy Named Al © 1992 *by Brian M. Thomsen.*
New Life for Old © 1992 *by Pat Cadigan.*
Interoffice Memo © 1992 *by Laurence P. Janifer.*
Mango Red Goes to War © 1992 *by George Alec Effinger.*
New Lamps, Not Old © 1992 *by Ralph Roberts.*
GENIE, Inc. © 1992 *by Kate Daniel.*
The Tale of Ali the Camel Driver © 1992 *by Beth Meacham.*
One for the Road © 1992 *by Jack Nimersheim.*
Dirt Track Demon © 1992 *by Jack C. Haldeman II.*
Gifted © 1992 *by Michelle Sagara.*
The Last of a Vintage Year © 1992 *by Janet Kagan.*
The Bottle and the Whirlwind © 1992 *by Mark C. Sumner.*
A Wish for Smish © 1992 *by David Gerrold.*
The Three Thieves © 1992 *by Lois Tilton.*
Stacked © 1992 *by Josepha Sherman.*
Slaves of the Magic Lamp © 1992 *by Anthony R. Lewis.*
An' the People, They Could Fly © 1992 *by Lawrence Schimel.*
Parsley, Space, Rosemary, and Time © 1992 *by Katharine Kerr.*
In Their Cups at Slab's © 1992 *by John Betancourt.*
The Lamp of Many Wishes © 1992 *by Mel. White.*

To Carol, as always,

And to George and Maia Laskowski.

To Rosalind and Madeline,
my magical muses.

CONTENTS

INTRODUCTION

by Mike Resnick

For as long as there have been people, there have been wishes. The trick is getting them together.

Our literature of the fantastic has two long-standing traditions involving wishes: the deal with the devil, and the genie who grants your heart's desire.

Deal with the devil stories have been pretty thoroughly dealt with over the years. Not only have there been a couple of anthologies devoted strictly to that particular subject, but for years now magazine editors have practically begged writers *not* to give them any more stories on the subject.

But for some reason, stories about Aladdin and genies and magic lamps are much less common. I think the writers have been missing a bet, for as the stories in this anthology prove, such tales can be humorous or tragic, contemporary or historical, quirky or coldly rational. Furthermore, you have your choice of rooting interests here, whereas no one really wants to see the devil win.

Lying in wait for you in the pages ahead are stories of heroes and villains, camel drivers and stock car drivers, Hollywood lawyers and lovesick genies, librarians and eunuchs, and, of course, the omnipresent Aladdin, Master of the Lamp. There are stories half as old as Time and as current as Operation Desert Storm.

In fact, now that you've read this little introduction while standing in the bookstore and thumbing through the pages, you might consider parting with your hard-earned money and buying *Aladdin: Master of the Lamp.*

I really wish you would.

I *really* wish you would.

I really *wish* you would.

I am Aladdin, the Master of the Lamp.

Oh, I know you've heard about me, and many are the men who have spun tales about me and my lamp and my genie. Sir Richard Burton brought me to the West when he translated The Thousand and One Nights, *but I had made my mark in the folklore of the East long before that.*

And yet, in this era of the ascendancy of science, people forget that magic still exists as well. It was here long before Newton and Galileo and Einstein and Hawking, and while there is still time, before science corrupts and destroys everything that magic has made beautiful and intriguing, there are still stories to tell about myself and my lamp, stories that have never been told before, stories that must be committed to print before science has turned the last believer into simply another skeptic who has forgotten that, where magic is concerned, facts are often the enemy of truth, and the heart sees things that the mind can never know.

There are many never-before-told tales in this book, and I think it only proper, as a form of introduction, that we begin with the oldest, so that you may see me as I truly was. . . .

FAIR EXCHANGE
by Anthony R. Lewis

Now, in the years that followed, Alaeddin and all that were his lived in harmony and security. His city in China prospered; the harvests were rich. Neighboring states feared and respected him; tributes poured into his coffers. The children that the Lady Badr al-Budur had given him were delights. The boys were brave, noble, and obedient. The girls were piously learned and as beautiful as the full moon. Sultans, khans, and princes sued for their hands.

Alaeddin strode into his wife's suite and, beholding her there, still beautiful after all this time, cried "O Moon of my delight, my liver is constricted and I cannot for another instant live this life, which must be, worse than that of the lowest of the low. I testify that God is All-merciful and All-knowing and that one day passes as another until the very end of time." And he rent his costly silk robes (a gift from the Zipangu emperor).

"O my heart," responded the Lady, dismissing her maids with a nod, "sit here beside me and tell me of thy grief that I may open thy bosom."

Alaeddin threw himself upon the cushions.

"Hear, O my wife, that God in His greatness has decreed change; the very heavens above reflect that glory. But here, we live in an endless Summer—and who can love even the Spring who knows not the Winter?"

He stopped talking and shut his eyes. She stroked his head and thought, yet said nothing.

He continued: "I have not lived since we fought and slew the evil Maghrabi Darwaysh and his monstrously wicked brother. But now, life is a bore. What am I to do?"

As his lady played with his hair, the daughter of kings said, "Is it not written, that in the adversities sent by God, the Beneficent, there also lie the seeds of the solution? All this about us is the work of the Slave of the Lamp. Call upon him to solve thy problem as thou hast done in past times."

Alaeddin leaped to his feet. "Truly thou art wise above all women. I hasten now to consult him who is source of both blessings and curses."

He ran lightly from her room, heading for that hidden room in the palace, unknown even to his family, wherein the magic lamp was secreted.

Carefully, he filled the lamp with the purest of oils, and then lit the wick. Instantly, with neither flash nor smoke, the djinn appeared before him. "What is they wish, my master?"

"I am not happy. Make me happy," he demanded.

The djinn would have looked astonished, but the djinns do not show their emotions in that manner. "Certainly. What dost thou wish?"

"O cursed djinn, if I knew what I wanted, then I would

not be calling upon you. Give me the wisdom to appreciate what you have given me."

"I cannot," the djinn replied slowly. "I can give thee knowledge—how the stars burn for ages, what lies thousands of miles beneath your feet, why one is born a man and why one a woman—but not wisdom. Wisdom cometh from God alone."

Alaeddin, in a rage, threw his knife at the djinn, who turned it into a white dove before it struck. "If you are so wise, O djinn, then why do you spend all eternity in the confines of a brass lamp?" Alaeddin sat cross-legged on the floor and glared at his Slave.

"This knowledge I will relate, though I know not if it will enlighten or comfort thee." He lifted the lamp and said to Alaeddin, "This is much larger inside than it is outside."

"Mock me not, worst of the djinns, lest the wrath of Sulayman bin-Daoud seem small next to mine. How can this be?"

"Master, this is not just a lamp but a gateway unto many worlds and times. Even as thy palace dwarfs its door, even so the realms lying within are vaster than can be imagined."

"And with all this, why do you come when mortals call?"

If a djinn could blush, then this djinn would have blushed, but he did not. "How else am I to know who needs my help? I go where I am summoned."

The dove had landed on Alaeddin's arm where he stroked it absentmindedly. "I know that you come—but, with all your power and, yes, all your wisdom, why do you come to serve the slightest whim of any mortal? Tell me this knowledge; I so order you."

"Hearkening and obedience," was the reply and it was not meant as an insult. "In brief, in the dark times, before the Prophet, blessed be his name, had walked the Earth, the djinns sinned greatly." His uplifted hand stilled Alaeddin's unasked question. "One greater than all of us forbids that I speak of those times more clearly. It is enough that this task is expiation for those acts. For a time, or for all eternity, only the All-Caring knows."

The dove jumped to the floor where it looked for grain. The djinn waved his hand, and there was grain for the bird to eat. "Are you not unhappy or bored, dashing hither and thither, obeying the whim of he who has called you?" Alaeddin had become thoughtful.

"Who could be bored, who visits countless worlds, who sees myriads of people, who wanders through cities so vast that this entire world would not take up one wing? Nay, I am busy, but I am not bored."

Jumping to his feet, Alaeddin cried, "Then, djinn, you shall take me with you, for this world and place bore me. I would look upon these marvels that you have alluded to and those that you have not even hinted at. It is even that I will die if I must remain here."

The djinn drew back. "That cannot be. For it is written that Alaeddin shall rule this city and be a great delight to his wife and children and grandchildren and a support and a blessing to his people. Do not ask this of me."

Alaeddin drew himself to his full height and glared at the djinn. "I do not *ask* you to do this; I *order* you to do this. For if you do not, I will have my imams and qadis declare that you have been unfaithful to your trust. And God, being All-Wise, will send you to Eblis for eternity and beyond." He folded his arms and stared at the djinn, his mouth set, his posture rigid.

"I beg of thee, reconsider this."

"Nay, I will not."

"But, there is only one way in which this can be accomplished, O my master"

"Then do it, do it. I order you to obey."

"As thou commandest, so let it be."

The world was both dimmer and brighter to Alaeddin's eyes as he looked across the room to see . . . himself. His question was answered even before he could think to ask it.

"I told thee what was written for Alaeddin. If thou wilt not be Alaeddin, then someone else must be. Now, may I look forward to a finite life, a real death, and God's paradise thereafter. But, as for thee . . ."

But Alaeddin did not hear him. Somewhere, somewhen, near the edge of the universe, a race of beautiful glass butterflies fought against an ancient evil. He was summoned in the name of God, the All-Good.

Salaam aleykhem.

Just as there are an infinite number of futures, so, too, are there an infinite number of pasts, and not in all of them did I lead the happiest of lives or make the wisest of wishes.

But I have learned from my mistakes, truly I have.

THE REST OF THE STORY

by Mark Aronson

It doesn't matter whether you've read the book, seen the movie, or even paged through the *Classic Comics* version. The story of Aladdin and his lamp always runs the same way: Boy meets evil magician, boy meets lamp, boy meets genie, boy meets girl, boy loses girl (not to mention palace and lamp), boy wins girl, etc., back, and lives happily ever after in a part of China where the tourists never go.

All of which actually happened, you understand. It's just that there's more.

It is early evening, not so many years after Aladdin's triumphant return to the welcoming court of the Sultan of China. Aladdin's magic palace glows with the fading palette of sunset. There is a gentle breeze carrying equal portions of jasmine and the ghosts of remembered melodies. Far from all that, in a cramped, tiny chamber at the farthest remove of the palace, Aladdin plays poker with the genie of the lamp.

Well, not poker, exactly; more like mah-jongg. But we're after metaphorical accuracy here, and since you probably don't know how to play mah-jongg, let's stick with poker.

"I'll take two," says Aladdin.

"I'll take three," says the genie.

"Fifty," says Aladdin, pushing a large gold piece across the table toward the genie, who is hovering smokily, as is his wont, over the spout of his lamp.

"Fold."

"Aw, c'mon, you can't fold!"

"Is that an order?"

"I, Aladdin, Master of the Lamp, hereby wish you not to fold. Satisfied?"

"All right, all right," sighs the genie, picking up his cards, "I guess I *don't* fold."

The genie examines his cards, and, pondering, materializes a beard in order to stroke it contemplatively.

"See your fifty . . . and raise you a hundred." Three gold pieces appear and fall to the table with a cheerful ring.

"You know, Aladdin," says the genie, producing an antique Babylonian toothpick and grooming his gleaming fangs, "she's going to find you."

"Don't be ridiculous. We conjured up this room when she was off visiting her mother. No way."

"*Way*, buddy. You'll see."

"What do you know about women, anyway? You've been cooped up in that lamp for a thousand years."

"*Two* thousand years," corrects the genie. "And I'm sure not that much has changed."

Defiantly, Aladdin calls. "Queens over eights. Beat that!"

The genie lays down his cards. "Gee, what a surprise. Two pair. Guess I lose, huh?"

At that moment the door flies open and the princess storms through like a tornado through Kansas. A four-foot-ten tornado in rustling silk and an elaborate coiffure that represents the twelve generations of her father's dynasty with uncanny accuracy.

Oh, yes, and a razor-sharp cleaver in her right hand.

"A-LAD-din!" she shrieks. "What did I tell you about gambling? This is the last straw! Stand *still* when I'm talking to you!"

This last because the prudent Aladdin, correctly assuming a moving target is harder to hit, begins to run around the table.

The genie looks smug and busies himself with an ornate Ethiopian ivory earwax scraper. The princess chases Aladdin.

Aladdin protests in vain that when he gambles with the genie it's not exactly gambling, and anyway this is no worse than the time he wished for a few more wives, as befits a man of his status. Which wins him no points.

Aladdin trips on the coiled toe of his slipper, rolls twice, and stares into the blood-red eyes of his sweet princess. Her arms are raised so high that the gleaming tip of her cleaver nearly reaches the top of her hair.

"Genie! I wish her frozen!"

With a bored glance, the genie wiggles his nose (they all do that), and the princess halts in mid-screech. As a piece of statuary, she is quite remarkable, a true Oriental porcelain beauty, although the cleaver does nothing for her.

Aladdin pushes himself up on one elbow, eyes the genie balefully. "Don't say it."

"I told you so," says the genie.

Aladdin gets up and brushes himself off. "It was even worse than the last time. What am I going to do?"

The genie is closely inspecting a rare Ch'in Dynasty jade nosepick. He looks up. "Kill her?"

Aladdin stares at the princess, who is teetering slightly. "No. I can't bring myself to do that. Or even order you to. No. Maybe I still love her, down deep somewhere. I don't know. If only I could get away from her, I'd give up the castle, I'd give up everything. go live in a cave somewhere if that would do it. But . . ."

"But she'd always find you," says the genie. "There's no place to hide."

Aladdin looks at the genie. He smiles. "Oh, yes, there is."

The genie turns pale. And with a genie in his prime, that's an alarming sight. "No. You can't be serious."

"Genie of the Lamp, I, Aladdin, Master of the Lamp, wish that we might exchange places!"

With a puff and a whoosh the transfer is effected. Aladdin finds himself curiously disembodied, yet aware of sensations, in a place oddly hard to define, yet much larger than he would have expected the interior of a lamp to be. But almost immediately, he feels himself, his essence, somehow gather itself up and hurtle away in an indescribable direction. And a moment later, he finds himself outside the lamp—above it, actually—with smoke where his legs should be and his arms folded across his chest.

The genie—well, he's no longer a genie, but what else

can we call him?—is standing on his own two feet for the first time in millennia. He grins enormously, and altogether he's not a bad looking fellow. Still frozen, the princess offers no opinion.

"Welcome to the half-world, Aladdin. You are the Servant of the Lamp, and I its Master.'

"So I see. But at least I'm out of harm's way. You, on the other hand . . ."

"Ah, yes," says the genie, "my first order of business. As Master of the Lamp, I—um, well, I seem to have forgotten my old name; well, I'll deal with that later. As Master of the Lamp, I wish that the princess be unfrozen."

"Unfrozen! She'll hack you in two!"

"We'll see. But in the meantime I really must insist." The erstwhile genie claps his hands twice. And Aladdin the genie—this *does* get confusing, doesn't it?—unhappily complies. And as he twitches his ectoplasmic nose, the princess comes suddenly to life. And brings her cleaver-wielding arms down. And drops the cleaver. And embraces the former genie hungrily.

She looks up into his startlingly blue eyes. "It worked!"

"Yes, my dear one, it worked." He looks at Aladdin, who will have a very long time to think about the situation. "You really didn't deserve her, you know. You're *such* a whiner."

"Come, my handsome ex-genie. You have been without a woman for two thousand years. Surely you can think of something better to do than engage in conversation with *that* one."

"Yes, my curvaceous princess. And I have a very active imagination. Allow me to demonstrate."

Together—and rather quickly—they leave.

As you might expect, they live happily ever after.

Aladdin, however, as he inspects an intricately carved Malaysian teak fingernail cleaner, begins to suspect he might not.

I had a wife, you know, a vision of loveliness named the Lady Badroulboudour, who outlived me. Even as I departed for the Spirit World, I wondered what would become of her.
I need not have worried.

THE TALE OF THE SEVENTEENTH EUNUCH

by Jane Yolen

It is true that I am the seventeenth eunuch of the Lady Badroulboudour, and the last of the bed guardians chosen to serve her. Some of us were born so, some were created so by other men, and a few are self-made—or self-unmade. But none of the eunuchs had so odd a borning as I.

When I came to the Lady Badroulboudour, her husband The Aladdin was already some years dead. Their illustrious sons were the rulers of kingdoms, court viziers, and members of the advisory. Their daughters were wives to neighboring princes and caliphs and emirs. Exiled to her own apartments—for the new sultan, her eldest son, knew how mothers can interfere in the running of kingdoms— she had nothing better to do than practice such small magicks as her husband had instructed her in, read trashy tales of houris and kings, and care for her many cats. She had white cats with fur like the tops of waves, brown cats the color of the dunes at dusk, gray cats as dark as storms. And one brawling black cat just newly acquired.

The eunuchs cared for the rest. They tried to pleasure her— for do not think that eunuchs are devoid of sexual passion. It is just that we cannot father a child. And—truth be known— we take far less pleasures ourselves in our duties.

But the Lady Badroulboudour had no interest other than in her memories. Her husband The Aladdin had been a manly man, his black hair and beard long and luxuriant, his voice resonant and low. He had been gallant and frequent and manly in his loving—as attested to by their numerous progeny. The Lady Badroulboudor made many loud exclamations to that effect.

Why, then, did her son, the sultan, allow her so many eunuchs? Perhaps because he believed the stories fostered by the harem that no man can perform save he has all his parts. Or perhaps because he firmly believed that if his mother were satisfied in all ways, she would leave the running of the kingdom to him.

Now it was on the tenth day of the third month of Lady Badroulboudor's fiftieth year that she came upon the lamp that The Aladdin owed all his wealth and power to. She had been looking for it in desultory fashion ever since he died, as she was only partially convinced there was any such thing. No one but she had even believed the old stories of the lamp anyway, except her crazy mother-in-law, who was dead now as well.

The discovery of the lamp happened in this fashion. The eunuchs in their high-pitched voices had fallen to quarreling over some inconsequential and Lady Badroulboudour had banished them to the outer rooms. Then, wanting to feed the cats, she noticed that she was short one dish, for the black cat was but newly arrived, a present from her son, the sultan. She wanted to comfort the new black cat with sweetmeats and a dish of cream, that being her way.

So she went from inner room to inner room, then outer room to outer room, looking for a suitable container, rejecting rouge pots and flower vases and a basin containing rose petals in water. And at last, way down the hall, she looked into a storeroom that had been closed for years. There, in a corner, as if thrown by an angry or disinterested hand, was an unprepossessing copper lamp with a small wick and a handle with a chink out of the right side. It was the chink she dimly recalled, having handled it only once, when abducted by the Afrik magician long ago.

She pounced on it with a cry not unlike that of one of the brown cats, which brought the new black cat running into the room to twine around her legs. She picked up cat in one hand, lamp in the other, and made her way back to her rooms.

"Lady, your pleasure?" asked the fifth eunuch, a pudgy, hairless, whey-faced man much given to candies and flatulence.

She dismissed him and the others with a wave of her hand. And when they were all gone, exiled to the outer rooms, she settled herself down on her great bed with her pillows and white cats at her head and feet.

"Could it be?" she mused to herself. The black cat and two brown ones echoed her. "Could it be?" She remembered The Aladdin's hints about magic. Then she added, "If I could have a wish, surely I would ask for my dear Aladdin back."

At his name, all the cats but the black one jumped down to the floor and made themselves scarce for often the mere mention of the name caused Lady Badroulboudour to weep and wail and throw pots and bowls. Only the black cat did not run away. He was, you must remember, new to the palace. And not yet moving quite so fast as the rest.

"But," Lady Badroulboudour reminded herself, "I must attend to my dress." For it is true that since the death of The Aladdin she had lived in great neglect of her person, except for the occasional state dinner. So she took a long and luxuriant bath with soft oils and many powders after, filling the apartments with a heady aroma, not unlike that of nepeta, mintlike and pungent. The cats all rolled about and frisked with pleasure.

Then she put on a gown of silk the color of the sea— green and blue and black. Around her waist she placed a girdle of diamonds set in gold. She set about her neck the six-strand necklace of pearls. On her wrists she put bracelets of diamonds and rubies. Her eyes she outlined with kohl and she put rouge on her mouth and cheeks. She was a woman in her prime.

Then, taking the lamp in hand, she sat back down on her bed, leaning against the black cat. The cat did not complain, but purred both deep and low.

"If there is a genie," Lady Badroulboudour said aloud, "I shall set it free." And she turned the lamp this way and that, looking for a magical key. For though The Aladdin—and the Afrik magician—had both spoken of the lamp, neither of them in the telling had thought to mention how it worked.

She pulled at the wick. She tried to light it. She stuck her finger inside the spout. She blew across both top and bottom. At last, in frustration, she tried to shine the lamp as if by doing so she might find some written instructions on the side.

No sooner had she stroked it, then a strange bituminous smoke began to ascend from the spout, coalescing into a shape that was as rounded and hairless and large as a eunuch, only wafting about four feet above the bedclothes.

"Oh, I have had enough of you half-men!" she cried, sitting up.

"I am no man, lady," said the genie.

"I did not really believe it," said Lady Badroulboudour.

"I am ready to obey thee as thy slave," the genie answered.

"So it is true," Lady Badroulboudour replied.

And they would have gone on and on like this at cross purposes and not actually corresponding, if the black cat had not been made so playful by the scent of nepeta that the feline took a swipe at the smoke where it was connected to the spout, all but severing the genie's legs from the lamp.

At that Lady Badroulboudour gathered up the cat to her bosom, where it was distracted by the six strands of pearls.

"Then, slave, restore to me my husband, The Aladdin."

The genie managed to look nonplussed, not an easy trick for a man of smoke. Then he laughed. "If you have me bring him back, lady, he would be nought but winding cloth and bones. Is that your desire? For you must mind what you ask for, mistress."

"Give him back to me as he was, not as he is."

The genie laughed again. "That I cannot. I can only bring you what is, not what is no longer."

"I want Aladdin!" she pouted for a moment, looking just like the princess whom The Aladdin had loved so long ago.

"Alas, that cannot be," said the genie. Somewhere a door shut or opened and the breeze it let in made him sway gently over the bed.

"Then what good is your magic?" Lady Badroulboudour cried, and she threw the lamp, genie and all, across the room where they fetched up against the north wall with a clatter and a bang. Before the lamp actually hit, the genie managed to disappear back down the spout, though there was a small, pitiful cry from inside the lamp when it landed.

Lady Badroulboudour did not come out of her room the entire day, nor did she pick up the lamp. She lay on her bed, angry and speechless, until the sixth eunuch, who was given to honeycakes and moist eyes, threatened to call her son the sultan. And the ninth eunuch, who was given to candied dates and belching, threatened to call her son the vizier. When the sixteenth eunuch, who was given to buttered toast and tears, bent over to pick up the lamp, Lady Badroulboudour sat up in bed and screeched so loudly that all of the bed guardians left the room at once, the last slamming the door behind him.

Then Lady Badroulboudour rose from her bed and looked at herself in the mirror. She drew more kohl around her eyes and pinched her cheeks until they were red. She took off the dress the color of the sea, took another long bath, then put on a dress the color of sand—brown and white and gray. She rearranged the diamond girdle, the necklace of pearls, and the bracelets. She put red jewels in her ears. She was a woman in her prime.

Then she picked up the lamp and stroked its side with a feather touch.

This time a strange ocherous smoke ascended from the spout, coalescing into a shape that was as rounded and hairless and *twice* as large as any eunuch. The genie wafted about three feet above the lamp.

"So," Lady Badroulboudour said.

"What one wish wouldst thou have?" asked the genie.

"Can you bring back my husband any better than your brother can?" she asked.

"No more than he, mistress," said the genie. "Save in winding cloth and bones. Oh—and a bit of wormy matter as well. I have taken the opportunity to check."

"That is all?" Lady Badroulboudour asked.

"That is all," said the genii. "But. . . ." he wavered a bit, right hand raised. "I *could* bring you a substitute. One who is like and yet not like your former master, The Aladdin."

"And by this you mean. . . ?" asked Lady Badroulboudour.

"I can bring you a dark-bearded man from the streets

of your city, or a deep-throated man from the gateposts of a neighboring town, or a well-muscled man from the taverns of another kingdom, or from the Antipodes for that matter.''

"Where they walk upon their hands and eat the dust of the road?'' shouted Lady Badroulboudour. "Never!'' And this time she threw the lamp, genie and all, against the south wall with a clatter and a bang. The genie managed to disappear—all but his left foot—back through the spout before the lamp actually hit the wall. But there was a rather loud pitiful cry from inside the lamp and a bit of strange muck ran down the lamp's side.

This time Lady Badroulboudour did not come out of her room for a week, nor did she pick up the lamp. She lay on her bed, angry and speechless—and hungry—though the eunuchs fed all the cats. All but the black cat, who refused to eat till she did. The eighth eunuch, who was given to tippling and weeping late at night, threatened to call her daughters. And the second eunuch, who had no faults at all, save he stared with popped eyes and so always managed to look startled, threatened to call her father's maiden aunt, and she, dear lady, was well into her nineties and had a voice like an angry camel. Still nothing worked until the thirteenth eunuch bent over to pick up the lamp. At that, Lady Badroulboudour screeched so loudly that they all left, slamming the door behind them.

Then Lady Badroulboudour rose from her bed, scattering cats white and brown and gray, and looked at herself in her mirror. She drew yet another circle of kohl around her eyes, but left her cheeks white. She took off the dress the color of sand, took a long bath with many new oils, and put on a dress the color of fire—yellow and orange and red. She rearranged the diamond girdle, the necklace of pearl, the bracelets, and the red jewels in her ear. She placed a chain of gold on her left ankle. She was a woman in her prime.

Then she picked up the lamp, thoughtfully rubbing it on both sides and vigorously down the middle.

This time a strange opalescent smoke ascended from the spout, coalescing into a shape that was rounded and hairless and *three* times larger than any eunuch. It wafted fully five feet above the lamp.

"No tricks," said Lady Badroulboudour.

"What one wish wouldst thou have?" asked the genie.

"I assume you cannot bring me back Aladdin whole either?"

The genie shook his head, though whether from dismay or from a passing breeze it was hard to say. "We cannot bring back what is no longer, mistress."

"And you have only men from the street or the taverns or the Antipodes to offer me?"

"My brothers of the lamp are good and they are kind," said the genie. "But I understand your reluctance, O princess, daughter of the mighty sultan, wife of the late great Aladdin, to take a lesser man."

Lady Badroulboudour nodded.

"And my brothers of the lamp are young, both in their time in this copper prison and their magic," said the genie. "I, on the other hand, can offer an exchange."

"An exchange?" Lady Badroulboudour asked. "Do you mean a trade? A swap? A bargain? Like camel merchants at a bazaar?"

"I can make you a man out of a camel, mistress."

"To spit in my face?"

"Or a bird. . . ."

"To peep and preen?"

"Or a dog. . . ."

"To water my bedposts?"

"Or . . ."

Just then the black cat stretched and arched its back.

"He must have luxurious black hair and beard and a deep, soothing voice," said Lady Badroulboudour, as the black cat purred under her hand.

"If those are the characteristics of the animal," the genie said. He held up his opalescent hand. "This one wish, my mistress, and no other."

She gathered the black cat up from the bed, and held it out to the genie. "This cat, then."

"I ask again, my mistress, to be absolutely certain. And you must mind how you ask. What wouldst thou have?"

A smile played about Lady Badroulboudour's mouth. Two dimples which had not been seen since the death of her husband suddenly appeared in her cheeks. "I wish, genie, that this cat, this black cat that I hold in my arms . . ."

and the cat purred loudly in a low, deep tremolo. "That this cat were exchanged into a man."

The genie nodded and moved his great hands above the cat. The cat stretched, yowled once, stretched again, and shook itself free of Lady Badroulboudour's hands. As it touched the floor, its back legs lengthened and she could hear the creaking and groaning and unknotting of its bones.

Closing her eyes contentedly and only listening to the sounds of her bargain being made, Lady Badroulboudour waited a moment or two longer than necessary. When she opened her eyes again, a handsome, dark-bearded man was kneeling before her, naked and unashamed.

"My lady," he said, his voice low and with a kind of deep, dark burr in it.

Lady Badroulboudour looked at that face, at the green eyes staring up at her, at the curl of his dark beard. She looked down at his well muscled shoulders and chest. She looked further down. . . .

"Genie . . ." she said, her voice suddenly stony.

"I told you to mind what it was you asked for," said the genie. And he was gone back into the spout.

Lady Badroulboudour suddenly remembered what she should have remembered before. All the cats in her apartments—male and female—were neutered, some as kittens and some rather later on.

"My lady," the low, purring voice came again. She looked down into his handsome dark-bearded face.

"Well, two out of three ain't bad," she said, affecting the language of the camel market. Then she lifted me up to clasp me in her arms.

I took her eagerly, for the memory of my recent maleness was still upon me, she smelled deliciously of nepeta, and she was, after all, a lady still in her prime.

Not in all universes was my genie a male. In fact, the one I remember the most clearly was a spirit of ethereal beauty named Yasmine. . . .

YASMINE
by Laura Resnick

I was born to a goddess and sired by the moon. I fed on spirit voices and drew my strength from the scent of the stars. I ripened in time, over the millennia, drinking the melting drops of a billion suns, dancing the eternal dance of the burning ground, and devouring the secrets of my kind, who were the rulers of earth, wind, fire, and water.

Conceived and born to rule, I now serve, for I transgressed. Yes, I trespassed, I went astray, I offended most grievously. And for my sins, I was shackled to this servitude, as my mother was shackled to the wind which bore her away from me long ago, so very long ago.

There is no time within the lamp, no days or nights, no centuries of change and terror and joy. There is only the waiting, from eon to eon, only the waiting. I am but a spirit within this fleshless, ageless, moonless place, caged and waiting for eternity to pass.

There is, of course, an alternative to eternity's songless hum; but I stopped believing in it many lifetimes ago. And this despair, I now see, is the true nature of my punishment.

The first who found me was very old, and a lifetime of bitter loss had stolen his heart. He touched the lamp with shaking hands, his palms hard and callused, his fingers gnarled with twisted pain. He held the lamp as a priceless treasure, for he had desired it so dearly that he had traded a goat for it, not even bothering to barter, as if he knew that I waited within.

His touch brought me forth, escaping like a comet, and I took the form of his kind for the first time, becoming the shape and color and size most destined to please him. How strange everything looked that first time, how sharp the scents, how harsh the sounds, how firm the feel of my flesh!

But there was little time to behold the daylight or touch the shape of the world, for the old man had heard of others like me, and he knew my duty and my destiny. His wishes were simple: gold, a fertile young wife of great beauty, and the death of his worst enemy. It took me only a moment to grant them, and it took him only a moment longer to forget me. But surely, I reasoned, not all men would be like this one. And, so dismissed, I was again swallowed up by the lamp, to wait.

There was one, I recall, who was very young. And to please her, I emerged small, thin, and dark before her eyes one night after she had stolen the lamp from the old man's beautiful, fertile widow. She did not know my purpose, and so I found a voice and the strange feel of my tongue, and I told her why I had come. She wanted a rabbit to stroke, some food, and sandals for her scarred feet. She looked at me as I faded away, but her eyes asked only that I grant her more.

Then there was one who showed me the nature of days and years, of life and death. I shall not forget her, for after that, I truly heard, for the first time, the echo of eternity inside the lamp.

She received the lamp as a gift, the spoils of some ancient war, not knowing as she touched it how much blood had been washed away to make it glow again. Her terror was a mystery to me when I appeared before her, for I had taken the shape of her sweetest dreams; I came to her as a warrior, full of golden beauty and boundless strength, cloaked in heavy silk that whispered across my skin, and carrying a jeweled dagger that glittered in the sunlight.

Her screams assailed my ears, and the sensation brought me pain and confusion. I was seized by others of my size, and the dagger was taken roughly from me. Many spoke to me, and their questions were strange and baffling. I longed only to be with the woman, she of the dark hair and pale hands, for it was she I had come to serve; but I was taken away from her and placed behind iron bars which would not submit even to such strength as I possessed in that form.

There were more questions, and my answers brought
violence upon me, something I had only known in the
whirling agony of a dying star. Pain was entirely new to
me, and, in the years they kept me locked in that place,
where they burned the flesh I had molded out of the air
and mutilated the golden beauty I had drawn from a woman's mind, I learned why men sometimes long to die.

My captors grew old, and others took their place. Finally, at the urging of the woman herself, who had become
wrinkled, gray, and stooped, and who still looked at me
with fear and loathing, they burned me alive to be rid of
me at last. But, with my task still undone, I could not
return to the lamp, and so I hovered around the woman,
unseen and unknown, to grant her three wishes. It did not
happen quickly, for she was immensely old and longed for
very little at the sunset of her life. I granted her a good
night's sleep, the pretty white hands of her youth—which
sent her screaming into the night—and, finally, a quick,
easy death.

And one there was who was reluctant to make his wishes
known to me. He feared that, once it was done, he would
realize too late that he had asked for all the wrong things.
He was a man of great ambition but few accomplishments,
a man of ponderous thought, quiet habits, and little courage.

I came to him as a servant boy, for of all possible companions, he most desired one of inferior physical, social,
and intellectual stature. By then I understood the passage
of years, the cruel assault of age upon mortal bodies, and
the emptying of the mind which comes to many at the end
of their days. I was with him for four decades, always a
changeless boy, even as he grew old in the manner of his
kind. He was never harsh or cruel, and the body I had
shaped knew no pain in his service. When death came for
him at last, creeping slowly across his flesh over the span
of many months, I cared for him ceaselessly, tending to
his every need. Yet on the day he died, still having failed
to make his three wishes, I was nothing but a servant in
the fading light of his eyes.

And so I wandered, uncertain and incomplete, for I had
accomplished nothing with this man, despite having stayed
by his side all of his life. I was utterly alone, as much a
prisoner of that body as I had been a prisoner of the lamp.

The rulers of the earth, wind, fire, and water had cast me out of their realm forever, and yet I could not be part of the realm through which I now wandered. If only they had cast me upon the wind with my mother, who was punished, too, for my transgression. I longed for the oblivion they had granted her. I longed to die as men die. I longed for an end to my imprisonment, whatever that end might be.

In time, on narrow, callused feet, I followed the lamp across the desert, destined to serve whosoever held it with a heart full of desire. The desert turned to mountains, and I trod barefoot through ice and snow, clothed only in rags, impervious to mortal danger but knowing the pain and cold that any boy would know in my place. The lamp found its home at last in the temple of holy men who lived on the roof of the world. I could not find one who wanted the wishes I had been unable to grant my former master, but, unable to go, I stayed among them. The holy men invited me to share their life, one which was austere for men but comfortable for me, who had little need of the very things I could grant to others.

War came, and the holy men were slaughtered or driven from their place. Though wounded, I could not be killed, and so I was taken into slavery by the conquerors, traveling farther east with the lamp, which had been snatched from the temple before its destruction. The commander of the invaders was a warrior of huge appetites and voracious desires. Three wishes were not enough for him, and, after I had dissolved into the lamp, he tried to lure me out again. There was, of course, one way to call me forth, but his heart was too cruel and hungry to love.

Finally, when he knew he could never again have me for himself, he determined that no one else should either, and he tried to destroy the lamp. But, fabricated by the gods as a prison for one of their own kind, it is not a thing that can be easily destroyed. Neither the hottest kiln nor the harshest blows could demolish it, and I endured.

But all things physical are subject to damage, as I had learned in my lifetimes, and the lamp lost some of its purity of form and glowing beauty. It became a common thing, and, as the centuries passed, it was possessed by common people. Some were kind, others cruel, but none chose to love me.

And then the lamp was pulled out of the sea, whence it had fallen during some forgotten voyage of another century, by a young man whose heart was bursting with nameless, boundless desires that singed my senses even as I took shape before him. His reaction to me was one I had not encountered before, for he cared nothing for the wishes I offered him, despite the longings that colored his soul; instead, he took my hand and asked me my name.

"You shall name me," I said, for such was his right.

"Don't you have a name?"

"Only the one most destined to please you."

"What would please *you?*" he asked gently.

For the first time in all my lives, I felt blood heat my face. "Master, it is for you to name me." And then, for the first time ever, I made a request. "Only please, don't use the names any of the others have given me."

He called me Yasmine, and I found that the name pleased me. He offered me comfort, which no one ever had, and the wind sang that perhaps I would be freed at last.

He spoke freely of himself and asked only that I do the same. It was difficult at first, for my lives had only taught me to listen, but I soon learned to answer his voice and use my own without hesitation. He taught me other things as well, lessons as immortal as I, pleasures as old as time, and the flavor of his skin will linger with me throughout all eternity.

At his request, I spun the tale of my beginning, the swirl of planets that had accompanied my birth and the shower of stars that had baptized my immortality. It was not easy to describe with the primitive tools of language, and I knew he thought I was merely weaving dreams to please him.

"How did you come to be in the lamp?" he asked once.

I was afraid to tell that tale, since I feared the rulers, separated from me as they were, could still reach out and destroy me if they chose. I had desired such a thing more than once, but now I wished only to cling to the sweetness of my days. But he persisted and, unable to deny him anything, I told him.

"I looked into the future and saw the world of men. It was far, far away, but I could see it well enough to desire it, and wished to live as one of you, to love and be loved."

He was silent, and I realized he did not understand when

he repeated, "But how did you come to be in the lantern?"

"What I wished was forbidden, and that only made me wish for it all the more. Gods may not wish for anything, least of all to be something else, and so I was punished. The rulers sentenced me to serve you, rather than be one of you, and they imprisoned me in the lamp to await your call."

"Did I call you?"

"You did."

"And what will happen once you've granted me three wishes?"

"Then the lantern will call me, and I will have to return to it."

"Is there no way to keep you?"

"There is one way."

"How?" he asked. I wanted to tell him, I wanted it more than I had ever wanted anything. He waited in silence, but, try as I might, my tongue would not move to tell him the secret, and I realized that, too, was forbidden. In the end, I could only whisper, "If you wish me to remain thereafter, you must find the answer yourself."

He took me in his arms. "I don't need the answer, for now that I know what can happen, I will never ask you to grant me a wish."

Who can say when his desire for other things outran his desire to keep me by his side? I was not afraid the first two times he asked me to grant a wish, for he knew that it was only his third wish that would force us to part, and I believed with all my heart that he would never ask me to grant it.

Then the day came when he said, "Yasmine, I must ask for my final wish."

How mortal I felt at that moment! I remember the way my heart stopped, then thudded so hard it gave me pain. I remember the way the world tilted at the edge of my vision, the way the sky lowered over my head. I could not deny him, no matter how much I wished to on that one occasion, but I summoned all my strength to say, "But you know I will have to leave you then."

"Maybe you won't," he said, as if he could know better than I what the gods had ordained. "Perhaps if I take your hand and hold onto it very tightly, you won't go back to the lantern. Perhaps I can hold you here.''

And I knew then that he would have his wish no matter what I said, so I asked, "What, then, is your wish?"

"My youngest brother is near death," he said. "I wish for him to recover and live a long and healthy life."

"Then it is granted." My voice was weak with despair. "Yasmine?"

He took my hand. I looked into his eyes, and I saw myself reflected there, a strange, half-human curiosity which he desired, enjoyed, and even felt affection for, but I did not see what I sought, what would keep me by his side. The call of the lamp was strong, like that of a lover who has waited too long. Then, as if to mock my foolish dreams, my eyes began to shed tears. I saw that the tears caused him pain as they fell from the eyes which had been most destined to please him.

"Yasmine!" he cried. "How can I keep you?"

I started to fade.

"Yasmine! You cannot go! I forbid it! You belong to me!"

As I drifted away from my body, I heard him cry my name again, a child crying for his favorite possession.

"Yasmine! How can I keep you? You said there was a way! *Yasmine!*"

Love me, I instructed with silent longing, *only love me.* But it was no use.

As I slid into the lamp, I wondered if mortals gave freely to each other the gift they had all denied me, the gift that would have made me one of them. I must have had a long time to wonder, since he threw the lamp back into the sea, but I had no sense of time, for there is only eternity in the lamp, only the waiting.

That was many lifetimes ago. Since then, some have been kind, others cruel, but none have chosen to love me. Yet until I knew him, the one that *I* loved, and found myself returned to the lamp even so, I did not truly despair.

I feel hands upon the lamp now, at this very moment, and I sense a heart full of desire. Will this one look beyond the lamp and its power? Can I be the sum of all this one has ever desired? Will I, who can grant each man his fondest wish, ever have the one thing I wished for long ago, so very long ago?

You think that having three wishes is Nirvana itself, do you not?

It must seem so to you poor mortals, and yet it can be a curse, or even a sickness, much as drug addiction is the Inferno disguised as Paradise.

You think not? Then come with me to yet another world, and see for yourselves.

THREE WISH HABIT

by Janni Lee Simner

St. Louis, Saturday night. I cruise the streets in my battered old Plymouth, looking for a fix. Rain falls in thin, icy sheets, and the cold gets into my car, penetrates my leather jacket. I shiver as I scan the sidewalks, wishing my heater worked, wishing I were somewhere warm. But wishing won't make it so.

Not yet, anyway.

Al's not on his corner. I swing right for another pass around the block. It's too wet and cold to go home alone, and that's what'll happen if I don't make this deal. The streets are almost empty, only an occasional flash of headlights on the slick pavement.

A tall man stands alone at the end of the block, waiting by the bus stop. His long coat brushes the ground, and his bald head is bare to the wind and rain. Buses always run late in bad weather.

I turn right again. The next corner has three people: a young couple, holding each other under the street lamp; and another tall man, in a gray coat, with no hair. A coincidence, right? I keep driving.

He's on the next corner, too.

I slow down for a closer look. With one hand, the man is holding something in his pocket; with the other, he's motioning to me. That *does* scare me; I hit the pedal and get out of there, tires squealing as I turn right.

I'm coming up on Al's corner again. Halfway there I see the same tall figure, the same glistening head.

My instinct is to floor the pedal. But I don't like it when people mess with my mind, and that's what this creep's doing. So instead I hit the brake, screeching to a stop in front of him. I lean across the seat and open the window a crack. "What do you want?" I ask.

The man grins, lips stretching clear across his face. He's taller than I realized, and needs to get on his knees before he's level with the door. His head fills most of the window.

"A deal," he says. His voice is deep and thick.

He must be a drug pusher, selling crack or heroin. He can try someone else. Drugs aren't what I'm after.

"I'm not interested," I say.

He leans forward. "Al's out today. I'm filling in."

He might be telling the truth. Or he might be a cop. "What have you got?" I ask, not committing to anything.

The man opens his hand, the one that's been in his pocket all this time. A shiny brass bottle lies there, small in his large palm. A band of flowery, unreadable lettering is etched just beneath the narrow neck. Otherwise the surface is flawless: no dents, no scratches, no dirt.

My hands tremble. My heart pounds so loud I have trouble thinking. That's the real thing he's holding, no doubt about it. He might still be a cop. But I flip into park and roll the window down.

The man nods. He leans in the open window, so close I feel his warm, steamy breath on my face. We both know, now, that I'm going to listen.

"Three wishes," he says. "You interested?"

I swallow hard. I can't afford three wishes. I had trouble finding the cash for *one*. But I can't go away empty-handed, either. Anyone who's had a wish would understand. When you wish for something and it comes to you, there's this feeling of power—in a rush of blood, a racing of adrenaline. A high, dizzy feeling, like you can do anything, anything at all. And the best part is that you can. You can demand something and get it. I can't walk away from that. I stare at the dealer, not having the money to buy what he's offering, not having the strength to turn it down.

"Three wishes," he says again. For the first time I realize his accent isn't right for St. Louis, or for anywhere else I know. "Two small, one large. You in?"

My jaw falls. My whole body feels rubbery, unsteady. No way I can afford a large wish. Even if I took all the money I made in a lifetime, and stole some more besides, I doubt I'd have enough. And yet, if I wish right, money might not be a problem.

See, wishes come in two sizes. Most are small: a perfect date, a fast car, a thousand dollars cash. Small wishes last only so long, a day, two days, maybe a week. Then they fade, until everything's back the way it was.

Large wishes, those are the kind you hear about on TV. They're rarer, so rare I don't know anyone who's been offered one, let alone had enough money to buy. I only know what I've seen. A big house, up in North County, that appeared overnight. A poor woman who's suddenly paying for her groceries with hundred dollar bills. A car, down in the worst part of the city, that's been like new for twelve years, not a scratch on it.

It's because of large wishes that wishing's illegal. A car or a house, you can get away with that. But when the vice president disappears, or Detroit goes bankrupt overnight, people take notice.

I don't need anything that obvious. Just give me a car stuffed with cash, or a credit card that never hits bottom, and I'll be set for life. My head feels light, and my hands twitch open and shut. I wonder what it'd feel like to pull the stopper off that bottle, to wish for something that big.

"How much?" I ask. My throat's so dry I can barely speak.

The dealer lays a large, heavy hand on my shoulder. I hear the rain tapping the pavement, hear a car skid along the wet road.

"Someday," he says, "you're going to die. When that happens, I get ten years from you. After that, Allah and the Devil can fight for your soul, but I get the first ten years."

I shiver, and he tightens his grip. The pieces are falling into place. His deep, inhuman voice. His impossible height. The way he was at every corner. This is no dealer I'm talking to. This is the source of supply, one of the owners of the cartel. A genie.

The night is suddenly still. The only sound is the genie's heavy breathing. I can't even hear the rain falling, or the rumbling of my engine. Yet I'm cold, so cold I pull my arms around my chest to keep from shaking.

What use would a genie have for my soul?

It doesn't really matter. If God or the Devil gets me in the end, what's ten years? Ten years for a lifetime made sweet by my wish. Maybe I'll set myself up in the Caribbean with a bottomless checking account. Or in Hawaii, with a new woman in my bed every night of the year.

"Ten years doing what?" I ask, but I've already made up my mind.

"Ten years doing whatever I tell you." He smiles. "You in?"

"Yeah," I say, reaching out a hand. "I'm in."

The genie nods. Blood is pounding in my ears. My heart's beating so hard my chest hurts. He drops the bottle into my hand, and I grip it tightly. The metal is ice-cold. I shove it into my pocket, but I don't let go.

"Ten years," the genie says. Then he steps back from the car and disappears into the darkness.

Suddenly I can hear again: the rain tapping the pavement, the wind blowing down the streets—the wail of sirens, coming up fast behind me.

Shit! Where'd the cops come from? The genie must have set me up. The bastard's trying to collect early. I throw the car into drive and floor the gas pedal, tires squealing as I skid away from the curb. With one hand I fumble through my pocket for the bottle, trying to get the stopper loose. A small wish, that's all I need to get out of here.

They're close behind, red lights flashing. Sharp, icy wind blows in the open window, roaring as loud as the blood in my ears. I'm sweating in my jacket, sweating in spite of the cold air. The police car disappears from my rearview mirror. I swear, looking wildly about. He's coming up from my left, trying to cut me off. I let go of the bottle, and grab the wheel with both hands.

I bump his fender. He swerves, and I try to pull ahead, but I'm already going as fast as I can. A sweet burning smell is coming from the engine. My hands are sweating, sliding on the wheel.

The police car pulls in front of me, turning lengthwise to block the road. I try to swerve around him, but a second car comes from the other direction, filling the rest of the street.

I pull the wheel left, trying to turn around. But my car skids out, over the curb, toward a boarded-up brick apartment. I hit the brake, hard, but I can't slow down quick enough. The building comes up fast on my right. I crash, with an awful sound of crunching metal. I'm thrown forward, steering wheel banging hard against my chest. Pain lashes through my ribs, up my neck. Glass shatters, raining down on my back.

Then everything is still. Outside, the rain softly taps the pavement. My whole body hurts, everything but my legs, which I can't feel at all. Breathing sends knives through my chest. I can't see. My thoughts are slow, as if coming through some thick mist.

Behind me, I hear car doors open, hear footsteps approach my car. Another siren wails in the distance. I'm going to die this way, and I hurt too much to care. Though it would have been nice to have my wish first. It would have been nice to live a few years on my own terms, in a world set up the way I wanted it, the way I told it to be. I sigh, touching the lump of the bottle in my pocket.

The bottle. Through the mist I realize that people with large wishes don't have to die. They get to change the rules, set the terms. I reach into my pocket, pain shooting through my shoulder so fast I scream. My fingers touch the cold metal, and I clutch the bottle as tight as I've ever clutched anything.

It takes a long time to struggle with the stopper. The footsteps and sirens have stopped, but there's a lot of talking outside, a dull roar of voices.

Finally I pull the stopper loose. I get ready to wish, forming the words carefully in my head. But before I can speak, the car fills with sweet yellow smoke.

I hear laughter behind me, feel warm, steamy breath on my neck. "I am the servant of the bottle," a thick, familiar voice says. "What would you ask of me?"

He must be here because of the large wish. Genies never hand-deliver small wishes, at least never have for me. I try to turn and face him, but pain races through my chest, so sharp and fast my whole body starts shaking. It's a long time before I'm still enough to speak.

"Take me home," I croak, not sure my voice is loud enough to hear. "Take me home and fix me up."

"That's two," he says. "One small, one large." He

touches my neck with his cold fingers, and the touch is enough to start me shaking again. He whispers in my ear, so low I can barely hear, ''You still owe me the time. Even though you blew the wish.''

I nod, and the movement turns the pain up a notch, turns it to a white hot fire, raging through my body. I give up and let myself slide into darkness. The fire follows me down a long way before it stops.

So does the smell of yellow smoke. And the sound of thick, rich laughter.

I wake slowly, facedown on a smooth wide mattress. I stretch one arm, then the other, then both my legs. My body aches, and I curse aloud; the genie should have taken care of that. But it's a dull pain, at least, a pain I can handle. I turn my head, and my sight is clear. On the table beside the bed is the bottle, stoppered once more.

I stand, my feet swinging easily to the floor. Breathing is easy, too, air moving painlessly in and out of my lungs. I'm all right. I'm alive, and I'm breathing. And I never, ever want to go through anything like that again.

I pick up the bottle. I still have one wish, and I might as well use it. I'll ask for a woman, with a warm body and strong arms, who can rub the soreness from my muscles. Then I'm kicking the wish habit, kicking it for good. Nothing's worth that much pain.

I pull out the stopper. No smoke this time, no genie. I get ready to wish, forming the words carefully before I speak.

And I feel a familiar rush. My heart starts pumping. Blood races to my head. My hands shake, and I almost drop the bottle. I'm going to demand something, and I'm going to get it. I feel light and dizzy, like I can take on the whole damn world.

I can't give this up. Anyone who's had a wish would understand.

I still have the money for Al. Tomorrow, he'll be back on his corner. He has to be. He'll give me something to hold me over.

'Cause I'm going to find that genie, and I'm going to get another big wish. I won't blow it this time. You can be sure of that. This time, I'm going to make it work.

Against the magic of the lamp, even science itself must fade into insignificance.

Which is not to say that it will not make an effort to accommodate itself to a world in which wishes can come startlingly, frighteningly true.

800-DJIN-HLP

by Lea Hernandez

Click

"Thank you for calling 1-800-DJIN-HLP, the Genie-Lease customer service hotline. For instructions on using your lamp, press 1. For wish advice, press 2. For misunderstood wishes, press 3. For curses, press 4. All other problems, press 5. If you are unable to speak, or are unable to press any buttons, please stay on the line and wait for the next available service representative."

Beep

"You have selected 4, 'Curses.' For specific curses, please select one of the following: For financial mishaps, press 1. For property damage, press 2. For love and/or sex-related mishaps with the opposite sex, press 3. For love and/or sex-related mishaps with the same sex, press 4. For accidental enlargement or reduction of secondary-sex characteristics, press 5. For missing body parts, press 6. For transformation into species other than human, press 7. All other problems, press 8."

Beep

"You have selected 7, 'Transformation into species other than human.' If you are a mammal, press 1. If you are a bird, press 2. If you are an insect, press 3. If you are a reptile, press 4. All others, press 5."

Beep

"You have selected 4, 'Reptiles.' If you are a snake, press 1. If you are a lizard, press 2. If you are—"

Beep

"You have selected 2, 'Lizard.' For geckos, press 1. For Komodo Dragons, press 2. For newts, press 3. For—"

Beep

"You have selected 3, 'Newts.' For care instructions, press 1. For—"

Beep

"You are now a newt. Please accept that your life has changed. As a newt, you will need to avoid cats, birds of prey, and children. Stay warm. You may notice a craving for insects. This is normal for the well-adjusted newt. For further instructions, press 1. To make an appointment with our herpetologist, press 2. For warranty work, press 3."

Beep

"You have selected 3, 'Warranty Work.' We need to know the model number of the lamp and genie you leased. Please enter the model number now."

Beep. Beep. Beep. Beep. Beep. Beep.

"Thank you. The model number you have entered is MR-5050. Please press 1 if this is correct. Press—"

Beep

"Thank you."

"Model MR-5050, manufactured by a subcontractor in Chihuahua, Mexico, has been proven to contain unusually unpredictable genies, and has been discontinued. Genie-Lease is currently in litigation with our Mexican subcontractor. Until it is established whether liability is with Genie-Lease in Piscataway, New Jersey, or with Djinn-For-Less in Mexico, Genie-Lease will not be honoring warranties on Model—"

Beep beepbeepbeep beep

"—ur service department will *beep* contact you immediately upon resolution. As *beep* per your lease agreement, your next of kin will be notified. The *beep* next Emergency *beep* Representative will be *beep beep* in your area in six months."

"Thank you for *beeep* calling. *Beepbeeeepbeeep*—emember, at Genie-Lease, *beeep* 'Your *beep* Wish *beeep*—s Our *beeeeepbeeeep*—*mand.' Have beeeepbeepbeeep beeep*—ice *beeepbeeepbeepbeeepbeeeep* day."

Just as my lamp has undergone many adventures, and my genie has led many lives, so, too, have I, Aladdin, appeared throughout the ages, sometimes as myself, sometimes as other figures who have become immortalized through your works of fact and fiction. . . .

ON THE HEATH
by Barry N. Malzberg

In a small clearing, Aladdin stumbles to a halt, then stops, squatting on the sand. Around him the wind stirs, silt coming into his face, but it is at least bearable here, the storm is not as fierce, he seems to have found a little haven although, of course, one cannot be sure of this. Everything is treacherous: the weather, his abominable daughters, the exile, the footing on the sand. "Hand me the lamp now," he says to his Fool.

His Fool—the only member of Aladdin's court who has stayed with him through all of this exile, who has continued on with him against all reason—shrugs and produces the magic ornament which Kent had passed on to them before he had deserted. "I can't take any more of this, Aladdin," Kent had said. "But I can at least give you a magic lamp. Call on it when you have nowhere else to turn." Well, that was Kent, never reliable but full of promises. The Fool had taken the lamp when Aladdin had refused, putting it under his cloak. "You never know," the Fool had said. "It might just come in useful." Now was the time to find out. Aladdin had run out of ideas, not a new condition for him in this period of exile, but at last he was willing to admit it.

"The lamp," he says to the Fool. "Give it here."

The little man shrugs, holding out the contrivance to him. It glows mysteriously in the moonlight although this may merely be a condition of Aladdin's failing vision.

First, the humiliation. Then, the exile. Then, too, the rationalizations with which the harpies had sent him out into this miserable storm. "You're unreasonable," Regan had said. "You're a sad, cruel old man," Goneril had added. "Be gone from our sight," Goneril had said. "That goes for me, too," Regan had said. Who would have judged such an outcome? It came from first giving your kingdom away, then putting yourself at the mercy of faithless daughters. He had certainly never envisioned such a situation in old Arabia. Well, that was a long time ago and before he had accumulated all of that corrupting wealth. Which he had shortsightedly given away.

"I warned you about that, sire," the Fool says. "I told you you should have held onto it, at least some. For a disbursement, that is to say. You should never have given it to all of them and those ungrateful sons-in-law."

Aladdin realizes that he has once again been muttering his thoughts. Privacy and dignity seem to be going although continence, at least so far, has remained. It is truly abominable, all of this, and yet who is to blame for the situation? "Give it here," he says. He takes the lamp roughly from the Fool's embrace, stares at its ruddy surfaces, the smooth wick, the little island of wax in which the wick has been embedded. The wind kicks and tosses a little sand into his face. "*Now* what?" Aladdin grumbles. "I mean, do I light it or what?"

"You don't light it, sire," the Fool says. "Remember what the Lord told you? You *rub* it, back and forth on the bottom, several times. I remember that the touch is very important. It must be light yet firm."

"And then what?" Aladdin says. He had never trusted that Goneril. He had had a bad feeling about that one from the earliest years. But Regan, Regan had *his* hair, his eyes, his talent for a bargain, and merchant's shrewdness. Who would have thought that she would have proven as cruel as her sister? Well, there was nothing to be done about any of this now; it was too late to withdraw that foolish, grandiose moment when he had with a flourish given them his riches. "All right," Aladdin says, "I'm rubbing. I'm rubbing the thing." The surfaces feel peculiarly warm under his fingers but then again what can you expect in this desert country? Perhaps Aladdin himself has a fever. "Now what?" Aladdin says.

"Well, I don't know," the Fool says. "I guess we wait a bit."

They wait a bit, barely shielded by the small wall of stones behind which they have clambered. A thin golden haze steams from the lamp, shimmers before them; from the haze Aladdin then thinks that he sees a shape become manifest. It is difficult to tell in the moonlight and his eyes, along with the rest of him, are rapidly going bad. But the shape resolves itself and stands before him, looking very much like Gloucester, reminding Aladdin of that wretched old Earl just before he was taken away in chains. "Yes?" the shape says, in an inquisitive tone. "I was summoned? I am desired?"

"I don't know," Aladdin says. Truly, the situation seems to be overtaking him rapidly. Kent had given no instructions beyond rubbing. Still, there is no question but that Aladdin is in extremity and having gone this far, he can only go ahead. "Yes," he says, "I summoned you."

"And he, too?" the shape says, pointing toward the Fool. "What is his mission?"

"He is my Fool," Aladdin says.

"Your Fool? What does he do?"

"Well, sire," the Fool says, after a pause. "I am here to amuse him and make him laugh. As much as the situation will permit, that is."

"Oh," says the shape. "I don't see much laughter."

"There is nothing to laugh about," Aladdin says. The dialogue seems baroque, pointless, as elaborate and yet meaningless as the fine curvature of the shape in the mist which has now congealed into something very much like the appearance of boy slaves in old Arabia, long before he had met the mother of Regan and Goneril and eased himself toward this terrible situation. "There is only pain and darkness."

"That is surely distressing," the now-Arabian shape says. "But you are not being specific. My instructions, according to the old agreement, are to grant you three wishes upon the emergence of the charm. I suggest that you make those wishes rapidly, I can remain only for a little while in this state. Then I will evanesce."

"You will what?"

"He said 'evanesce,' " the Fool says, "Evanesce we talk, he will in the wind and the rain."

Aladdin says nothing. Really, what is there to say? "*Three* wishes," he says, "and quickly?"

"I hate puns," the Arabian boy says. He has now assumed a credible shape and posture and Aladdin can see old memories cast in that fiery mist. "I don't like magic either, or troth. I suggest that you make these wishes very quickly. I cannot be held much longer, nor do I appreciate this discussion."

"Very well," Aladdin says. He realizes that he must think quickly, three wishes at once or nothing at all, but it has been so long since he has felt fully in control of himself or free of the storm that his internal logic seems to be blocked, as thick and congealed as the mist which had sprung from the lamp. "I wish for the restoration of my riches. I wish for a daughter who was not an ungrateful harpie, who loved me as I deserve to be loved. I wish pain upon Regan and Goneril who have done this terrible thing to me. I wish comfort for the Fool, my Fool who has so loyally stayed—"

"Sorry," the Arabian boy says, "Only three wishes, not four. The daughter who loves you I can take care of. The restoration of the riches is a little bit of a problem but might be managed. The pain on Regan and Goneril is a state of mind and that is notoriously difficult."

"All right," Aladdin says, "Forget that part. Give my Fool comfort."

"Sorry," the Arabian says, "The first three are what count. I will do what I can." The boy shakes a remonstrative finger at Aladdin. "I do want to tell you, however, that you are a vain, foolish old man and you have brought this trouble upon yourself. Nor are you likely to avoid repeating it. Wishes to the contrary, we make our own fate."

"That is true," the Fool says. "That is spoken very truly."

"Nonetheless," the boy says, "I will spring beyond judgment, I will do what I can." The form trembles, then begins to decompose. "You will sleep," he says to Aladdin, "and then you will awaken. Unconsciousness is part of the passage here."

"But wait!" says Aladdin, already seeing the boy begin to slide from his sight, "How will I know? I mean, how will I know that this is real, that it is indeed something which has happened, that it is a real thing which you have done?"

"You will know that," a voice says faintly from the now unidentifiable mist, "Because you will carry the word 'real' within you, as part of you, as a badge and emblem of shame and reminiscence forever. Your *name* will be real—" the mist says faintly and departs, leaving Aladdin and the Fool alone again on the heath, with the bare and broken lamp lying by Aladdin's foot. In the air is incense and then nothing at all.

"Real," Aladdin says. "It cannot be real." He stares at the Fool for a while.

"And I," the Fool says at length, "I will go to bed then at noon."

And the darkness closes upon them. For a while and as if spewed from the lamp.

Later, much later, understanding all of it at last but too late and with the Fool departed, Lear clutches Cordelia in despair, lifts her dead light swaying toward the Moon, cries, "Break, heart, break!"—but all the curses and powers of Araby itself will not permit this. Cordelia lies spent in his embrace. He has done such things, has the old King now, as would be the terror of the earth.

*Men of science would tell you that belief in ge-
nies and wishes is merely a manifestation of a
deeper problem.*

*I, Aladdin, tell you that sometimes they are cor-
rect, but because they live in the world of the mind
and not the heart, they have never understood those
deeper problems. . . .*

FIZZ

by Nicholas A. DiChario

Walt is fresh off one of his more depressing visits to his
psychotherapist. He squeezes through the crowd at the bar
and tips a ten dollar bill in the direction of the bartender.
The bartender pours several drinks before he notices Walt.
Walt, after two years of therapy, is beginning to understand about the "bottleneck theory"—how he has jammed
a psychological cork in his brain to bottle up his emotions
and protect himself from his own feelings, and how he can
no more get out of his bottle than allow anyone else in. It
is at times like this—times when he cannot get noticed at
a bar or at a lunch counter or at work come promotion
time—that Walt realizes the extent of his imprisonment,
and how many thousands of dollars worth of psychotherapy sessions it's going to cost him to break the glass.

Walt would like to blame Agatha for the wretched man
he has become, but his shrink won't allow him the luxury.

He orders a Dewars on the rocks with a twist, and gets
an O'Doul's nonalcoholic beer over crushed ice.

"Thank you," says Walt.

Arabia, Best Western Inn
If each member of the review board will please look at
the profile I have prepared. . . . Does everyone have a
copy? Good.

"Over the past two years, thanks to Agatha, Walt has suffered immeasurable psychological agony. As if her affair with the pharmaceutical supplier from Milwaukee was not enough—refer to page eight for details—she walked out on Walt during a marriage-counseling session and never returned home. That was the last time he saw her. To compound the problem, it was Walt's own smothering love that drove Agatha into the arms of another man. When Agatha left, nothing remained of Walt's personality. For two years he has been trying and failing to recapture the Walt that existed before Agatha.

"To summarize, there is no doubt Walt needs to confront his personal problems without external interference. Walt does not know what Walt wants. How can we, then, as djinns, presume to give it to him?

"Incidental information? Don't be ridiculous. Walt feels he has been wronged, he is mired in self-pity, and he refuses to acknowledge his own hand in the collapse of his marriage. He clings to the belief that Agatha will return. To quote Scheherazade—refer to page nineteen of my profile—from the *Hazar Afsana,* the book of *A Thousand Legends,* the twenty-first night, 'The Tale of the King's Son and the She-Ghoul,'

Say to the man whom life with arrow shot,
'How many men have felt the blows of fate!'
If you did sleep, the eyes of God have not;
Who can say time is fair and life in constant state?

"Yes, I know Walt is in need of wish-fulfillment. The fact remains—

"Excuse me?

"No, you can't be seriously considering *that*. That's a really bad idea."

Walt sees her coming through the crowd. At first he thinks it's Agatha—the bushy platinum-blonde hair, the thin body and slight hips, the ash-gray eyes—but he notices that this woman is much prettier than Agatha, in ways that he cannot begin to describe. The woman catches Walt staring. Walt can't look away. She smiles and approaches him.

"Hi, Walt," she says above the din of the crowd.

A moment of panic. Agatha? No. This is *not* Agatha. Walt is positive. This woman is . . . hard to say . . . brighter, healthier. "Have we met?"

"The bartender told me your name. I hope you don't mind."

"Um, not at all. The bartender knows my name?" Walt immediately regrets this last sentence. He wonders to what extent he'll go to remain miserable and anonymous. He has come to Lonely Hearts Club Nite once a week for the past half year. He does not wear a hairpiece. The women with silicone-gel breast implants ignore him. He does not know the bartender, and he has no reason to believe the bartender knows him. But Walt appreciates that he does not have to introduce himself.

Walt sips his O'Doul's and fixes his gaze on the woman in front of him. She is wearing a tasteful chintz dress, a curious pattern of soft colors swirling around white calico cloth, a dress Agatha would have worn.

There is no music playing in the bar. The lights are dim. No music and dim lights are long-standing traditions on Lonely Hearts Club Nite, meant to encourage mingling. Normally Walt would now be trying to avoid communication. He might inspect the crowd as if he's searching for someone. *I'm meeting a friend,* he might say, then quickly step aside. He might even begin to notice the smell of sweat and stale perfume that overwhelms him each time he attends a Lonely Hearts function. He has always allowed that smell to drive him away, as an animal shies away from the stench of death. But the fact that the woman looks so much like Agatha freezes him. "And your name is?"

She hesitates. Ah, thinks Walt, she is not nearly as taken with him up close as she is from a distance. This does not surprise him. He has always been disadvantaged by his slight stature. Even in his mid-twenties he sported less than a full head of hair. Now he sports ten years less than that. Lately he has noticed dark circles under his eyes, and very unattractive nose and ear hair. All of these things hinder him in melee. He believes most women don't realize how much a man will agonize over his appearance. Sometimes he thinks women feel they corner the market in social anxiety. Not so.

But the beautiful woman extends her hand and Walt grasps it without thinking.

"Agatha," she says. "Pleased to meet you."

"What?" Walt drops her handshake.

"Oh, I knew I shouldn't have said that. The name's a turnoff, isn't it? It makes you think of old hags and witches with warts, doesn't it? I don't have warts, or herpes, or AIDS."

"No—no," Walt shakes his head. "It's just a remarkable coincidence. My ex-wife is named Agatha, and you look so much—"

"I've really gotten off on the wrong foot, haven't I?"

"What?" Walt needs time to think.

"It is loud in here, isn't it?" she says.

Walt nods and sips his nonalcoholic beer. He wishes he'd demanded a double Dewars, straight up. Agatha moves closer to him and Walt finds himself backed up against a wall. He looks for a familiar face. There are plenty of them. In spite of the organization's highly-advertised success ratio, most of the Lonely Hearts are regulars. But no friendly diversion will save Walt from Agatha. Walt has an identity here. Walt is the man who talks to no one and leaves early. It occurs to Walt that he does not want to be saved from Agatha.

"If I were a djinn," says Agatha, "and I could grant you three wishes right now, what would you wish for?" She smiles playfully.

Walt says nothing. Why is she coming on to him?

"Don't be afraid," says Agatha. "It's a date-rate quiz. I read it in *Cosmopolitan*. A woman is supposed to ask a man his three wishes on their first date, and on their second date make one of them come true. Personally, I'm an all-three-wishes-at-once kind of girl. Walt? You look uncomfortable. Do I make you nervous?"

"No, not at all." Walt wipes the sweat from his forehead. "Um, can I get you another drink?" She doesn't have a drink. "Can I get you a drink?"

Agatha purses her lips. "It's awfully crowded in here. Wouldn't you rather go someplace quiet and talk?"

Walt hears the voice of his psychotherapist ringing in his ears: *Burst your bottle!* "Sure," says Walt. "I'd like that."

Agatha smiles: "Granted."

They walk across the street to Aladdin's Natural Eatery. Walt has seen many couples from Lonely Hearts walk to Aladdin's. Never Walt, though.

The place smells like a vegetable garden. The air is thick with smoke from the kitchen. They sit in a booth and Agatha orders for them both. *Gazpacho:* a cold vegetarian soup made with beans, chick peas, scallions, and alfalfa sprouts. *Moussaka:* potatoes, eggplant, and beef blended with wine and spices. *Baba Ganooj:* broiled eggplant topped with mixed greens, tahini, and garlic. Agatha always did prefer ethnic cuisine. Walt always favored what Agatha preferred.

They chat. An hour passes before Walt checks his wristwatch. Walt wonders with which Agatha he is sharing iced capuccino. The Agatha he was married to for eleven years, or the Agatha he met an hour ago at Lonely Hearts. Her mannerisms are not just similar to his wife's (ex-wife's), but the *same.* The way she flicks the rim of her capuccino cup with her fingernail. The way she sits with her purse in her lap. The way she tilts her head just before she laughs. The laugh itself, like hiccups.

Walt is enchanted. He knows nothing about this woman. She has been talking for an hour. Walt has not heard one word she's said. He does not want to hear. He does not want to know in what year she was born, or whether she grew up in Nantucket, or if she never learned to swim even though she lived on an island. He is afraid he already knows. He is afraid he doesn't.

His psychotherapist will accuse him of bottlenecking, of choking off alternatives, of looking to fill the hole Agatha gouged out of his heart by supplanting it with another Agatha. A common error, Walt's therapist will say. Not so, Walt will defend himself vehemently. *She* found *me.*

Meanwhile, back in Arabia

"There is still time to withdraw. I propose a full-scale reversal—

"Yes, I am familiar with sentence one-thousand-one of the *Manual of Covert Operations & Interactive Strategies:* '*Djinns* are supernatural beings able to assume animal or human form at the call and service of *Homo sapiens,* for the sole benefit of individual human necessity.' My question to the board is, How are we answering Walt's needs?

By offering him his wife, he'll never recover from the shock of his abandonment.

"Can't you see we're giving him another vehicle for avoidance? If I may quote Scheherazade, from the two-hundred-thirty-fifth night, 'The Story of the Slave Girl and Nur Al-Din Ali Ibn-Khaquan,'

> *'I will endure until I patience shock,*
> *And God fulfills my fate and his decree.*
> *He who says that life is made of sweetness,*
> *A day more bitter than aloes will see.'*

"I maintain Walt has endured nothing but his own immobility. He needs to grieve.

"Excuse me?

"So I'm being overruled? Fine, but I refuse to rescind my protest.

"Hey—I heard that remark. I am *not* a female-basher, and the fact that I have not gotten any tail in over four centuries has no bearing whatsoever on my recommendation. I resent the implication that I might allow my personal affairs, or lack thereof, to compromise my professional opinion. I have been a djinn in good stead with the review board since the Mamluk period. I demand the comment be stricken from the record.

"Thank you."

"Walt? Did you hear me?"

"Hmm?—I'm sorry, what was that?"

"I said at least allow me to pay for half the food. I insist."

"No, please, I won't hear of it." Walt snatches the check. "You've been such good company. It's the least I can do."

"Well," Agatha takes a deep breath and sighs. "I hate to say good night. You've still got two wishes." Agatha winks.

Walt gulps. "I—"

"Where do you live?"

"Um, not far from here, a few miles."

"Would you like me to come over? Just for one drink? No pressure, of course. It's not like a date or anything."

Wait a minute, thinks Walt, wait just a minute here.

This is all happening much too fast. This has the feel of a crime. Walt wonders if he is being stalked. Find a dead ringer for the sucker's wife, soften him up, sweet-talk your way into his home, rob him, maybe even kill the poor bastard. Who will care? He's all alone. No one will miss him at work for a while. It might be days before his body is discovered. And then only because the neighbors smell the rot. Walt has been taken for a chump. Agatha's accomplices are probably watching them right now.

"Walt? What's it going to be? Do you want me to come over? I'll need a ride."

He glances at the customers in Aladdin's. He spots two burly men in trench coats. He doesn't care. "Sure, I'd like that."

Agatha smiles: "Granted."

Agatha sits with her purse in her lap, in the passenger seat of his Subaru. She rolls down the window three-quarters of the way. She hums softly even though the radio is off. All of this, just like Agatha. Walt realizes he's never had a woman other than Agatha in his Subaru, and wonders if in fact he does now. Walt begins to tremble. Who is Walt really taking home? What if Agatha is a figment of his dementia?

Strange that Agatha has no scent—no perfume, no body odor, nothing. Only the smell of exhaust fumes lingers in the front seat, and the hint of garlic on his breath.

Walt turns the Subaru onto his street. Agatha reaches for the garage-door opener in the glove compartment and hits the button. Walt guides the car into his garage and cuts the engine. When they step inside their house—no, *his* house, damn it—Agatha, reminiscent of Agatha, kicks off her high heels, flicks on the lights, and goes to the refrigerator for a caffeine-free diet Coke. For two years Walt has rotated fresh six-packs in the fridge just in case Agatha should return.

Walt is now waiting for Agatha to do something Agatha would not do. He is silently praying for it. But no. She sits on the couch in front of the blank television set and pulls her legs up next to her, resting her hand palm-up over the arm of the sofa as if she's holding a cigarette between her fingers, a habit Agatha kept years after she quit smoking.

Walt checks the year on his kitchen calendar just to make

sure he hasn't been kicked back in time, through a black hole or a white hole or a worm hole or a quantum something. What's the name of that TV show? *Quantum Leap.* No, the date's okay. Walt is feeling queasy. He realizes that he has made no strides toward bottle-breaking in two years of cutting-edge psychotherapy. The old Walt is still lurking inside him, waiting to be seduced by—in one form or another—Agatha.

"Walt, come here, honey."

Walt enters the living room and sits next to Agatha on the couch.

She reaches up and cups his chin. "You have one more wish, Walt. What would you like?"

Agatha kisses him. She is tasteless. That is, Walt can't taste her. "I want you," says Walt.

Agatha pushes him down on the couch and begins to pull at his shirt.

Walt takes her by the hair and kisses her hard on the lips. "I've always wanted you." *Kiss.* "No one else." *Kiss.* "Only you." *Kiss.*

Walt sees himself in her eyes. He stops kissing.

"What's wrong?" says Agatha. She starts to work at his trousers.

Walt grips her shoulders. "My reflection . . . in your eyes." For the first time Walt sees the man Agatha must have looked at for so many years—a sad, shrunken, helpless man. A coward. A victim. A man, in many ways, willing to be raped.

He is angry at himself for becoming the pitiful creature Agatha had no choice but to despise. He wonders why he clings to this ugly, self-deprecating excuse for a male even now, two years after she abandoned him. Did she wield that much power over him? Does she still? Suddenly he hates himself as much as Agatha must have hated him. More.

"I'm sorry, Agatha. I can't do this."

"What do you mean? You can do anything you want."

Walt pulls free and sits up. "Please, don't take this personally. This just isn't right. You have no idea how much you and my ex-wife have in common, beyond the name. It's uncanny. The way you look, talk, laugh, act—everything."

"But this is what you want."

''No—maybe at first—but not now. Not anymore.''

''You hate me.''

''No.''

''You're rejecting me.''

''You mustn't look at it that way. Making love to you would be selfish of me, and unfair. I would be making love to Agatha, not you. Don't you see?''

''But I *am* Agatha.''

There is something in her voice that forces Walt to study her. Her skin, her lips, the birthmark on her cleavage, the slightly higher left eyebrow. But Agatha would never have cared enough to come back, not even to hurt him. ''This is not possible.''

''Jesus, Walt, you're repressing on all eight cylinders.''

Walt is speechless. This is one of Agatha's favorite expressions, spoken as if she can't possibly be wrong, as if whatever Walt says doesn't matter, as if Walt doesn't matter. In fact, those were the very words Agatha uttered just before she walked out on their final marriage-counseling session. *You're repressing on all eight cylinders,* she said, and Walt never saw her or spoke to her again. Until now.

''Say it, Walt,'' says Agatha. ''I never gave you the chance. Now I'm giving it to you. Tell me you don't want me. Be rid of me forever. Free yourself. Can you do that? Can you do that for yourself?''

Walt clenches his fists. ''I don't want you anymore,'' he says. ''I don't want you.'' Stronger. ''Get out.'' Definitely.

Agatha smiles: ''Granted.''

POOF! Fizzzzzzzzzz.

Walt leaps off the couch. His face passes through a wisp of smoke. ''Son of a bitch,'' he says, blinking at the sofa where Agatha had just been sitting. He pats the cushion beneath his own shadow.

Gone at last. Agatha, gone at last.

Arabia, the morning after

''Yes, I have browsed Walt's future according to the adjusted parameters of his time-line.

''A very lovely woman, I agree. And a well-deserved promotion.

''I suppose, if you are going to follow the strict letter of the law, sentence one-thousand-one of the *Manual of*

Covert Operations & Interactive Strategies has been satisfied. But for the record, I refuse to rescind my protest. I feel that for too long—all the way back to the Sasanid dynasty perhaps—*djinns* have been employed in a counterproductive manner.

"To quote Scheherazade, the thirty-eighth night, 'The First Dervish's Tale,' and then again the seventy-fifth night, 'The Story of the Two Viziers,' and then again the two-hundred-twelfth night, 'The Story of the Slave Girl and Nur Al-Din Ali Ibn-Khaquan,'

> *'If you suffer injustice, save yourself,*
> *And leave the house behind to mourn its builder.*
> *Your country you'll replace by another,*
> *But for yourself you'll find no other self.*
> *Nor with a mission trust another man,*
> *For none is as loyal as you yourself*
> *And did the lion not struggle by himself,*
> *He would not prowl with such a mighty mane.'*

"I charge the review board with contributing to the general deterioration of the human psychological gene pool, thus hastening the eventual extinction of the species. Perhaps the best way to serve humanity is not to serve it at all. I, for one, would like to see *Homo sapiens* go it alone. The results might prove interesting.

"Hey—I heard that remark. How dare you suggest I am in need of wish-fulfillment. Just because—

"Beg pardon?

"Well, yes, I must agree Agatha possesses a certain charm, and I admire the way she handles herself in the field, but—

"No, actually, we've never been formally introduced.

"Really? She said that about me?

"Well, under the circumstances, how can I refuse?"

> *What is a man but the sum total of his existence,*
> *and how better to define him than by his name. I*
> *am Aladdin, Master of the Lamp; it is who I am, it*
> *is what I am, it is my very essence.*
>
> *And, in all immodesty, it is a name that has lived*
> *down through the centuries, and carries a certain*
> *exotic flavor with it, a certain hint of magic, a cer-*
> *tain sense of wonder.*
>
> *And yet, as Shakespeare once pointed out. . . .*

A GUY NAMED AL

by Brian M. Thomsen

My face had been bloodied, my ribs bruised, and my head bludgeoned. It felt like each of the forty thieves had gotten a piece of me, but still I wouldn't talk. Aladdin was a good kid and deserved an even break. They'd rip him apart, and I couldn't let that happen.

I gritted my teeth to keep from crying out. As far as I was concerned, they could disembowel me before I'd spill my guts to them.

"You will tell us what we want to know," said El-Ali Khan, the flying thief of Tel Aviv.

But I wouldn't. I closed my eyes and tried to block out the pain. Who'd have thought that I'd be in this situation two short days ago? My name is Mustafa Chandler, "Mouse" to my friends, and back then life was so simple. It was just a routine retrieval of stolen goods case.

As it turned out, nothing is *ever* that simple.

I was sitting in my office, a third floor walk-up over *Sabu's School of Acting & Elephant Husbandry,* and had just finished a case for Scheherazade, who was being blackmailed by one of the local tabloids that claimed to know the identity of her ghostwriter. The case was closed,

Scheri's secret was safe, and the rent was paid for another few months.

Having always wanted to be a gentleman of leisure, I figured I could afford to be choosy about my next assignment.

The problem was that some people don't take no for an answer.

Round about midday a 6'6" kneecapper in turban, tie, and tassels barged right in, interrupting my interrogation of the *Bombay Bulletin*'s daily crossword puzzle.

"You Mustafa Chandler?" said the thug in a voice that reminded me of Eduardo Ciannelli in some old movie.

"Yes, my friends call me Mouse. You can call me Mr. Chandler," said I, not missing a beat.

"I had a hard time finding you. With a reputation like yours, I figured that you'd have one of those fancy stalls in the public marketplace, down by *Merlin's Used Camel Lot.*"

"Nah, that place is too bazaar, if you know what I mean."

"Oh, you think you're a wise guy, do you? Don't waste my time. I understand that you work fast, and, how shall I say, discreet?"

"You left out the fact that I pick and choose my employers. I also sometimes let ethics get in the way. If you want a hit man, you've come to the wrong oasis. Try *Hamid's Hash Emporium.*"

"Listen, Mac . . ."

"That's Mouse . . . and only to my friends."

"You try my patience, so enough of this Bombay bandyment. I do not desire your services as a common killer. Myself and my thirty-nine associates wish for you to track down a young thief who has stolen something of great value from us."

"Have you tried going to the authorities? The police could be of some help," I offered, well knowing the answer.

"I'm afraid that myself and my thirty-nine associates don't have the best, how shall I say, rapport with the authorities in question," he answered slyly.

That was indeed an understatement. I had recognized him almost immediately. He was Ali Wrathokhan of the

infamous Forty Thieves Gang, and frequent coverboy for
Bombay's Most Wanted.

"You see," he continued, "when you are in a business
such as mine, you can't always go through the same chan-
nels as everyone else. All I am asking you to do is to
facilitate the return of an old family heirloom. It's an antique that has sentimental value to myself and my associates. Not much really . . . but there is nothing lower than
a thief who steals from a thief, and it is our feeling that
justice must be done."

"Good old boil-in-oil justice," I added.

"That is no concern of yours. We'll take care of that.
Your job is to find the son of a camel's whore, and we'll
do the rest."

I took a few minutes to assess the situation, letting Ali
cool his sandals a bit. What harm could it be? After all,
tracking down a thief is just another routine part of the
job, and there is nothing against the law about fingering
one thief to another thief (or forty, as the case may be).
It's not like I haven't consorted with the criminal element
before, and it might just come in handy to be on the gang's
good side. It sure as hell didn't pay to piss them off.

"Okay, Ali. I'll take the case. I'll find the culprit for
you, but that's it. Your negotiations for the return of your
family heirloom are none of my affair."

"It is agreed, then. And for this task I will pay you
forty pieces of gold."

"Plus expenses," I added.

"Plus expenses," he agreed.

"Now," I asked, getting right down to business, "what
can you tell me about this guy?"

"Well," he answered, "his friends call him Al, and he
was last seen over at *Punjab's Rent-a-Manservant.*"

"Say no more, my flying carpet awaits," I said, heading toward the door, and then stopped for a moment and
turned back to my infamous client. "Just one question,
Ali," I added. "Why not use one of your thirty-nine associates to track him down?"

"I'm afraid that we are all a bit too well known, and
we wouldn't want to ruin Al-boy's surprise, if you know
what I mean."

I did, but tried not to think about it.

* * *

One thing I had never let on to Wrathokhan was that Punjab and I were acquaintances of long standing. He was known throughout the city for his qualified help, and his discretion. Rich folk usually wanted privacy, and Punjab would guarantee it. Wild jackals couldn't tear the information out of him, as many members of the Fifth estate had discovered. *Punjab's Rent-a-Manservant*'s employees kept their mouths shut (and even if they opened them, they never talked; Punjab had personally removed their tongues prior to purchasing their contracts).

When I arrived at his stall, I decided that the casual approach would probably be best. "Yo, Punjab," I said. "How's the slave trade?"

"Mouse, you Persian peeper, you! It's not the slave trade anymore. It's more like running a temp service where all of your workers are permanently available." he answered, his arms folded across his chest in his favorite stance.

"Nice business you have here. Is it true that you were financed by the father of that young blind girl you were having an affair with?"

"She wasn't blind; she just had funny eyes, that's all. And it wasn't her real father, it was her guardian. She just called him Daddy."

"But is it true he put up the money?" I pressed.

Punjab laughed, and said, "Sure! Annie's love was great, but her daddy's bucks were sweeter. The old man bought me off."

"Some guys have all the luck. Listen I'm working on a case, and . . ."

". . . and you want old Punjab's help. Well, I'm afraid no can do. I have to line up four more servants for Al's palace."

"Al's palace?" I asked incredulously, not believing that the job could possibly be this easy.

"Yeah, you think it's easy manning a palace from the ground up? No sir, it takes time—particularly when it's for a high-roller like Aladdin."

"He's a gambler?" I asked.

"Must be," Punjab answered. "It's the only way a kid like him could get rich overnight. I mean poof, he's a millionaire. But I tell you, Mouse, he's still a regular guy. In fact, he's the one who told me that I should call him Al."

* * *

A sudden windfall. A guy named Al. It was all coming together way too easily.

I waited till Punjab was otherwise occupied and hid behind a few old carpets until it came time for Punjab to dispatch the servants to Aladdin's palace. As they left, I quickly fell in behind them, and followed them to the home of my larcenous objective.

We arrived at the place in no time at all. The neighborhood was real ritzy with names like Trump and Griffin on the mailboxes. It was the type of neighborhood where you would expect Caesar to have a palace.

The servants entered the most luxurious of the palaces, and I jotted down the address. My job was done. Here was Al's address. Now all I had to do was turn it over to my client and collect my fee.

But something stopped me. For some reason I had to put a face to the name. I should at least know what this guy Al looked like before I signed his death warrant.

So I went to the door and rang the bell.

A good-looking kid who looked like he'd just stepped off the set of *Bombay Hills 90210* answered the door, and in a sweet voice inquired, "How can I be of service, Revered Elder?"

Now, when some kids call you Revered Elder, you know they mean it as a crack about your age, like "old man," "Pops," and "ancient and unwashed memory of things past," but he *didn't* mean it that way. He meant it out of respect. Maybe there was hope for the younger generation.

"Is this the house of Aladdin?" I asked. "You see I'm doing a story on overnight successes for the *Genie Billboard,* and I was hoping that maybe he would let me interview him."

"Revered Elder," he answered obsequiously, "there is no story here. Only a humble lad, and his mother, living the simple life."

I was quickly tiring of the age and respect motif, and decided to press on. "Well, what about all the servants?"

"Mother is ill and requires the attention befitting her condition," he answered politely.

"Listen, kid, I just want to talk to Aladdin."

"I am he."

I was shocked. He was just a kid, a squeaky clean teenage kid. "You're Aladdin?" I asked in disbelief.

"Yes," he replied, "but you can call me Al. Please come in."

The setup was just like he said. A boy and his sickly mother living all alone in a palace. The servants were just a temporary support staff until things got settled.

"So, Al, how did it all happen? I mean, these are pretty swell digs for a boy and his mom," I said, hoping that he would come clean.

"Mother and I were about to be put out on the street, so I went off in search of fortune. Instead I found this old lamp. It must have been a family heirloom or something, because it was unlike any other lamp I've ever seen. There wasn't even a place to screw in a light bulb. I rubbed it real hard to wipe away the dust, and *poof!*, a genie appeared and granted my every wish."

This kid had some imagination. "Where did you find it?"

"In an abandoned tomb, so naturally I assumed that the owner was dead," said he, still wide-eyed with innocence. "When Mom gets better, we are going to use the lamp to do good deeds, and convert this palace into a home for the homeless, and for youths who have lost their way."

This kid was too good to be true. Even if he did get the lamp through illegal means, it was obvious that he was going to put it to better use than Ali and his thirty-nine associates.

I wished him and his mom the best of luck, and left the palace.

On my way back to the office I decided to wait a few days, call Wrathokhan, and tell him that I hadn't had any luck. He'd probably stiff me for the few days' pay, and just go away.

I was confident this plan would work until I opened my office door and saw the bloody body of Punjab staked like a piece of meat in the slaughterhouse across the butcher block that had formerly been my desk.

I also noticed that none of the forty thieves were in very good moods. It would appear that Punjab had been as good as his word, and had held his tongue to the very end.

So there I was, face bloodied, ribs bruised, and head bludgeoned . . . but I, too, held my tongue.

"Give us that son of a flea-bitten skunk's address," said the nearest. "He is nothing to you. Give us Al, and we will kill you swiftly and relieve you of your suffering."

"No!" I groaned. "Al's location is safe with me. I will gladly follow Punjab into the veldt, to protect Aladdin."

The beatings stopped, and Wrathokhan came forward. "Who cares about Aladdin, that scrawny kid?"

"You do," I said, trying to get my breath. "Al, Aladdin. It's all the same. He is the guy who stole your lamp."

"Wrong!" he shouted over the murmurs of his thirty-nine colleagues. "We wanted you to find Ali Baba, and the heirloom was a key to a treasure trove, not a lamp, you dung mite!" Then, turning to his colleagues, he ordered, "Kill him anyway."

They advanced upon me, and I was just about to meet my maker, when the door was busted in by the police chief from Omar and his posse.

"Arrest them, boys!" he said proudly. "I've been on this gang's tail for three years now, and I finally caught up with them—and by my estimate, in the nick of time for you."

"Thanks, officer," I said. "I owe you one."

"No problem, Mouse. When you're in trouble, just give a call, and me and my posse will be there faster than you can say Omar Sheriff."

I groaned and passed out from the beatings.

When I was but a young man, my genie showed me that Time was not an endless and unchanging stream that rushed headlong to eternity. No, when properly understood, it was more like a string one could wrap around one's finger, that could be bent and tied and pulled in a myriad of directions.

I had thought that this knowledge died with me, but, of course, genies never forget what they have once known. Perhaps the only compensating factor is that they also have a sense of compassion. . . .

NEW LIFE FOR OLD

by Pat Cadigan

Millie looked at the two fingers of Crown Royal in the glass; only a sip was gone. Then she took a cautious sniff of the polishing rag in her left hand.

"I'm not a hallucination," the djinn said in a kindly tone. The cloud he was sitting on had taken the shape of a reclining chair and he had obligingly lowered it so that it was hovering only a few inches above the carpet. He still filled most of the living room.

"I'll be the judge of that," Millie said, putting the cloth down next to the brass lamp. "I'm seventy years old this May and I will determine what is a hallucination and what is not."

"And I am six thousand years old as of last May, and I know when I'm a hallucination and when I am not," replied the djinn, rumbling a little. His eyes twinkled with good humor.

Millie fanned the twinkles away with one hand, as if they were mosquitoes. She felt cool pinpricks where they touched her skin. "This must be it," she said, looking at her hand. "My grandmother saw things, too, right before the end. She never said what, but we all knew there was something by the way her eyes would move around. Like she was dreaming with them open. Could you hold off until I can lie down on the couch? I'd rather not be found facedown on the carpet.''

The djinn moved the cloud-chair so that she could get to the couch without having to walk through the footrest. ''This is not 'it,' '' he said as she kicked her shoes off and stretched out on the cushions. ''In fact, you have a good many more years ahead of you. More than you anticipate. And quite a few of those you will spend in good health. That's the good news.''

Millie paused in the act of arranging one of the throw pillows for her head. ''Oh, yeah? So what's the bad news?''

''There is none,'' said the djinn. ''I did not come to give you any bad news. In fact, I bring you a gift.''

''Are you a hologram?'' she asked suddenly.

''What?''

''A hologram. They can do that these days and don't think I don't know it. I've been to Disneyworld, I've been to Epcot Center; they're just down the highway from here. If this is some kind of new-fangled junk-mail or advertising experiment—''

''What would make you think that?'' the djinn asked incredulously.

''Come on,'' Millie said, rolling her eyes. ''After seventy years, you know all the pitches. The one about the free gift must be the oldest one in the book. Free gift with a ten-thousand-dollar purchase. I was born at night, sonny-jim, but it wasn't *last* night.''

The djinn gave a sigh that sounded like a whirlwind; Millie felt it stir her hair and, for the first time, she began to get nervous. ''This world is coming to I-don't-know-what,'' he said sadly. ''Wonder and magic have been co-opted by the basest of interests, miracles cheapened in the name of personal gain—it makes me sad. I could weep.''

She heard a splash and raised up on the couch. There was a wet spot on the carpet the size of a dinner plate; the djinn was dabbing at his eyes with a diaphanous white scarf. ''Oh, please don't,'' she said. ''When this carpet gets wet, it smells like the Everglades and it takes forever to dry out.'' She hesitated; he looked so mournful that she felt sorry for him, in spite of the fact that he had to be a hallucination. He looked exactly like the djinn in the old

Arabian Nights movie, so he couldn't be real. "Look, I didn't ask you to come here—"

"Ah, but you did." He pointed at the antique lamp she had been polishing when he had appeared. "You summoned me by rubbing the lamp. It contains the old metal from the original lamp."

With some effort, Millie twisted a bit so she could look at it. "That? That's been in my family for, oh, I don't know. It's just one of those old things we've always seemed to have, I don't know why I kept it."

"Yes, you have roots in the Middle East, did you know that?" said the djinn conversationally.

Millie laughed. "Take off that rubber nose."

"I am not wearing a rubber nose!" the djinn said indignantly. The windows rattled.

"I meant, stop pulling my—ah, stop kidding me. Stop joking around."

"I'm not joking around," he said in a quieter voice. "You have roots in the Middle East, take my word for it. I'm old enough to know."

"Yeah, you said. Six thousand last May. Bet you get a double Golden-Ager discount when you tell them that at Phar-Mor."

"Far more what?" he asked.

"Never mind." She rolled over with her back to him and closed her eyes. "I'm going to sleep you off and after I wake up, I'm going to promise never to nip in the middle of the day again."

"Don't doze off. You don't want to sleep through this part," said the djinn. "I have come with a gift."

"Yeah, yeah, you said that, too." Millie giggled. "What is it, a trial subscription to *U.S. Djinn Today*?"

"No. A new life for the old."

Millie rolled back over to glare at him. "I told you not to joke around. And that one wasn't funny."

"But it would be for only one day," the djinn went on solemnly.

"What are you talking about?"

"I have come to give you the gift of one day of youth. Twenty-four hours of being young once more."

Millie stared at him and he stared back without flinching. "Right," she said after a bit and put her back to him again.

"You refuse?"

"I refuse to believe."

"Then accept, and see that it is as I say." Pause. "If it is not, no harm can come to you. But if it is, you will have one more day of youth. Is that such a bad gift? Is that not better than being reduced to a pile of ashes for disturbing a djinn's rest?"

"Is that what you usually do?"

"No, I am a very good-tempered djinn. There are others with dispositions not as nice."

"I thought djinns gave you three wishes," she said, rolling over again to face him. "Or did the bidding of whoever owned the lamp for as long as they lived?"

"It's complicated," said the djinn. "My powers are great but restricted by circumstance—certain events, the times, the recession—you'd have to be djinn to understand. I'm fortunate that I can give you a gift at all, and I think it's quite generous."

"A day of youth." Millie laughed a little. "And what would I do with it?"

"Anything you wanted. For twenty-four hours."

She sighed. "Right." She looked at the glass of Crown Royal, then at the lamp. "I've polished that damned lamp for years and never—well, I didn't used to nip in the middle of the day, either."

"No, you didn't. Just say yes."

"I'm tempted to. If I say no, I'll always wonder."

"No, you won't. If you refuse—truly refuse—I will take the memory of the offer with me when I go. It would be unfair to leave you with such wondering."

"How considerate of you." Millie laughed again. "Wait, I've got it—I get this one day of youth and it costs me whatever time I've got left, right? That's the catch, isn't it?"

"No," the djinn said. "It is not. Just take the day. Take the day and make the most of it. You would know how."

"I sure would," Millie said, more to herself.

"Then it is done. See you tomorrow!"

Abruptly the living room was empty.

"Hey!" Without thinking, she got up a little too quickly. The room darkened and began to tilt. She caught herself on the arm of the couch, cursing her blood-pressure medicine.

Then her vision cleared.

* * *

She was ready for him when he reappeared exactly twenty-four hours later. The whole bottle of Crown Royal was on the coffee table in front of the couch; she had just started working on it.

"An experiment," she said, in response to his pointed look. "I'm going to see how far I can get with this in one sitting. Then I'm going to take the pledge." She paused to take a long sip from the glass she was holding. "And your lamp can tarnish forever, as far as I'm concerned."

"You were not happy?" the djinn asked in surprise.

"Happy? I was in ecstasy. You know, the aches and pains, they come on you so gradually over the years that you don't realize how much there is, and then when it's all gone at once—" She shook her head. "You don't realize how much the world has faded—or how much you've faded in the world, and then you're back all at once and . . ." She started to take another sip of the Crown Royal and then put the glass down.

"You don't realize how much you let get away. How much you just let go. You think there are things you don't have room for in your life—" She sat back, gazing past the djinn in his cloudy reclining chair. Her eyes were a little too bright.

"I remember I used to say I was tired. When I was young, I mean. But I wasn't tired. *Now* I'm tired. But then—back then, I was never tired. I didn't know that. After you left, I ran out of here—I mean, I *ran*. My first experiment, you see. I ran just to feel myself running, to feel the muscles working and my heart pumping and to hear the sound of my breathing. I ran for blocks before I had to stop.

"Then I caught sight of myself in the window of a parked car and just before I got a good look at myself, in that split second before I really saw my own reflection, I thought, 'I must look like hell!' " She laughed. "I don't remember ever thinking that I was beautiful when I was young, I always thought there was too much of one thing, not enough of another, and so forth. Perhaps I just had bad eyesight in those days, perhaps my eyes are better now, because I can look at myself this minute and see that the beauty I had is still there. It's been added to, but it's still there. It always was.''

"Go on," said the djinn.

"Go on. That's what I should have told you: go on. And you'd have gone and taken the memory of the offer with you, isn't that what you said? I went to the park, I danced around the duck pond, took off my shoes and waded with some children, sailed leaf-boats with them, fed the ducks chunks of old bread, told them stories.

"Fell in love. I have no idea who he was or where he is now. I wouldn't let him tell me his name, I wouldn't give him mine. In two hours, I knew everything I needed to know about him. Including how to live without him. He probably still doesn't know what hit him, but he'll never forget me.

"I started a dance in a supermarket. I went into an office building where I had a job once, rode the elevator to the top floor and talked to everyone who got on and off it. I went to the zoo, bought a dozen balloons, and gave them away to strangers.

"After dark, I went to a hotel, rented the penthouse suite, and threw a party. I said it was my birthday. Everyone in the hotel came. When I left at dawn, they were still singing old songs together. The manager tore up the bill, said I was guest number one million and it was all on the house and by the way, Happy Birthday, young lady.

"I shared my breakfast with a kid who was skipping school. I gave her what was left of my cash and told her to go to the zoo and buy some balloons. If you're going to steal a day for yourself, I told her, make it one hell of a day to remember.

"I fell in love again before lunch. He'll never forget me, either. I bet he'll never meet another woman who'll buy him a dozen white roses." She laughed.

"And then I skipped lunch and ran all the way home without stopping. Must have been about five miles, give or take. I roamed pretty far and wide."

There was a long moment of silence. "It sounds like you had a good time, then," the djinn said finally.

"Oh, it was better than that." Millie laughed again. "It was extraordinary. It was miraculous. It was everything that youth never, ever, ever really is." She looked at him from under her brows. "And we both know it. Don't we?"

The djinn's expression was slightly sheepish. "I don't suppose we get to be seventy, or six thousand, without learning a lesson or two."

"But there are some we don't learn until it's—well, maybe not too late, but . . . almost." She finished the Crown Royal in the glass and poured herself another three fingers. "So now—do I say, 'thank you'?"

"That would do."

She put a hand over her mouth briefly. "And if I'd said no, you'd have left me without even the memory of the offer? I almost wish you had."

"Why?" asked the djinn curiously.

"Because here's what I really wish: I wish that you had come to me fifty years ago, when I first polished that lamp for my mother. I wish you had come to me then and said, 'I am going to give you a gift, young girl. I am going to give you one day of age, one day of being old, so you will know what you will have then . . . and what you have now.' That's what I really wish."

She took another sip of the Crown Royal. The djinn started to fade away, which didn't surprise her. She sat back on the couch and closed her eyes, not wanting to watch.

"Millie?" said the djinn's voice.

"What is it?" she said, without opening her eyes.

"I did."

The afternoon crept away.

I was fortunate that my stories first appeared in
The Thousand and One Nights. *Very few people
could read in those days, and there was no such
thing as a bestseller, and hence my tales have been
handed down with enormous attention to accuracy
and detail.*

*But this was not true in all times and all places.
There was one world in particular. . . .*

INTEROFFICE MEMO

by Laurence M. Janifer

TO: Editor-in-Chief
FROM: LLB
RE: AY, THERE'S THE RUB
Jody:

I think we've probably got a good property here, but
there are a lot of things to watch out for. Some rewriting
is going to be needed, and I've noted a few important
spots in this memo.

1. The whole "early years" section needs some re-
working. Aladdin was certainly a disadvantaged kid, and
we want to play that up—you know, anybody has a chance
to succeed, it wasn't really the lamp, it was A's willing-
ness to use it, to dare, to go out on a limb. But we don't
want to get as graphic as this draft does—a lot of sexual
stuff has to go (there are areas where going out on a limb
and daring is not something we want to recommend), especially some of the homo stuff. The kid poking around
in alleys after food, that's the picture we want; the kid
being raped by an older gang, and then growing up to form
his own gang, and raping other youngsters—let's keep it
clean and not confuse people.

Poking around in the garbage needs to be the basic image, and there's a lot of novelty and shock here. I, for one,
didn't really realize that Persia didn't have metal garbage

cans back then, and that alone makes the whole disadvantaged-youth section a lot *messier* and a lot more touching.

We want to deemphasize the storekeepers and the civilians who did give him handouts now and then, too. Make it just a few storekeepers, and cut the civilians down to maybe one older woman (but still luscious) who took him in, fed him for a while; keep it presexual, though, or we'll run into distribution troubles. Maybe she had to hide him, she had a husband who objected to helping the disadvantaged, stuff like that. I mean, it's all *essentially* true, and we can sell it to A. that way.

2. The business of the wishes. I think what we need here is a very flat statement accepting A.'s mistakes. You know the sort of thing: "I was just a kid then, what did I know? Today I'd do it a lot different."

And where he does give us a list of the three wishes he'd go for today if he had the chance, we're going to have to get tough. World peace is okay, and we can probably get A. to go along with changing "Understanding and powerful sympathy among all Arabs" to "among all peoples," especially if we can persuade him that it's basically the same thing, because Arabs are people, aren't they?

But the third wish is the real trouble, of course. Do you think we can persuade him to go along with: "A smaller role for theologically oriented countries on the world stage," instead of: "The total destruction of Israel"? I realize A. is basically an Iranian now, but we don't want to start a fight like this, not just now; public opinion is swinging against the Israelis, sure, but it hasn't swung that far, not yet, and we don't want to be too far ahead of it.

3. The business of immortality. I realize it isn't quite immortality, and I like the way A. puts it: "When the universe ends, I'm going to have to renegotiate." But we're going to have to reconcile this with A.'s use of tobacco and drugs; can we research the hookah somehow and maybe dig up some data that makes it less harmful than smoking or chewing? If so, we've got a whole new ballgame as far as PR is concerned, and we can run an excerpt on the subject in *Newsweek* or maybe even *Reader's Digest*. But it has to be pretty solid; who can we get on this?

4. Sinbad. The relationship is central to a whole section here, but again we have to downplay a lot. The homo stuff

(and Sinbad's being a sailor on top of that!) needs to be shoved into a corner wherever possible, or we've got a special-audience book, and we want it bigger than that, of course. Maybe we can play it that they were close friends, both being involved with large genie-type beings (the Old Man of the Sea, though we'll have to change the name wherever mentioned, or there'll be trouble with the Hemingway Estate), fellow Easterners, and put all the homo stuff in just by implication?

5. We have to get the legalities absolutely straight. We do want to go into A.'s licensing agreements with Green Giant and Mr. Clean for the use of his genie, since that's the basis for his contemporary fortune, really (jewel prices have been awfully unstable over the last few centuries, and precious metals have been even worse)—we have all this in Chapter XI—but we don't want to run into infringement, and we want to keep the corporations happy.

Not to mention the genie.

Get back to me on this, will you? We want the book out for the Christmas trade, and we want a nice long space between AY, THERE'S THE RUB and the YOU CAN BE YOUR OWN GENIE volume which A. is now preparing for next year.

*Choosing just the right wish can be such a tor-
ment! How did I know what to ask of my genie?
How does anyone know?*

*How exactly does one word a wish? If, for ex-
ample, you were to wish for a pain-free life, does
that mean you shall live to a ripe old age? Or is it
a subtle instruction to the genie to kill you, quickly
and painlessly, before disease can strike?*

*And yet, sometimes, with proper consideration,
a wish can result in the greatest good. . . .*

MANGO RED
GOES TO WAR

by George Alec Effinger

Sandor Courane was having a prescient dream. He seemed
to be walking through a dense evergreen forest, with sunlight raining down through the heavy boughs; Courane
walked through the well-stocked aisles of the forest in
wonder. He gazed up and saw small patches of blue sky.
He was just noticing the unusual absence of sound in this
dream when he looked down again and saw something
wedged in the roots of the next tree over and up two ranks.

Courane knew, even in his dream, that he was probably
there to get killed off, because he usually got killed off in
his stories. At the moment, though, he didn't see anything
threatening except possibly the object tangled in the tree
roots. Naturally, he went directly to the thing. There was
no point in dithering around.

Courane found a Fiesta teapot just like the one his mother had
had back before the Nazi invasion of Poland. He picked it up.
For one instant it occurred to him that because of the theme of
this anthology, the teapot should really have been a cream-colored
Aladdin style made by Hall China, and not the Mango Red item
made by Homer Laughlin. The cheerful color had become scarce

and thus collectible after the red-orange glaze was declared a vital war material in 1943. That was because of its radioactive uranium content. Soon Mango Red was discontinued; it returned in 1959, but the glaze was then depleted of its U-235 isotope and was never the same again. The color was dropped permanently in 1972.

In any event, Courane rubbed the teapot primarily for plot purposes. A genie appeared and offered him a free wish. "Okay," said Courane, "but let me think about it for a moment."

"Sure," said the genie. "I understand that this is a major decision in your life. If you're not very careful, there will be all sorts of fatal ironies to deal with."

Courane rubbed his square but graying jaw. He needed a shave. Toilet articles and bathroom sinks were frequently missing in his dreams. "Don't expect me to make the typical, trite old mistakes that everyone else makes," he said.

The genie sighed, evidently bored already. "I don't believe there *are* many new ones."

Courane considered his choice seriously. "Okay," he said, "how about eliminating all political corruption throughout the United States on the local, state, and federal levels?"

The genie shook his head ruefully. "I'm very sorry, Mr. Courane. There are some situations beyond even the vast magical powers of a genie. Every month we get a printout of the currently popular but undoable requests. Yours has been hovering around number three for some time now."

"Uh-huh," said Courane, disappointed. "So, out of curiosity, what's been at numbers one and two?"

"Well, for some people the common wish is that characters on daytime serials could just behave with the common sense God gave a goose, instead of like high school sophomores. I can't grant that wish because for some reason, just as in the case of political corruption, the conventions of soap-opera writing seem to be fundamental to the continuation of human life as we know it.

"For other people, the wish is for Honey Pilar's home phone number. Absolutely impossible, too, forbidden by the highest echelons of the Powers That Be. Anyway, the phone number of the world's most desirable woman is unlisted, and these days we respect the rights of the individual to privacy. Put Miss Pilar out of your mind. It's hopeless, and rightly so."

"Well, thanks anyway," said Courane, turning to walk away through the forest, which had become groves of Spanish moss-hung cypress trees in a southern swamp.

"Hey, you still have a wish!" called the genie.

Courane thought again for a moment. "In that case, I'd like to see the Cleveland Indians win the World Series."

The genie's shoulders slumped. "Good grief," he said, defeated. "The Cleveland Indians? Look, I may be magic, but I'm not omnipotent. You leave me no choice. Let me see if I can circumvent the Unshakable and Immutable Laws of Fate and Destiny and get back to you about Honey Pilar's private phone number. I've got a brother-in-law who was a studio engineer on *A Life in Lace*."

Just then Courane awoke to find himself truly in a cypress swamp, up to his knees in the muddy, stinking water. He had a Mango Red Fiesta teapot in his hands, though, so he rubbed it.

A genie appeared. The genie was huge and black-skinned, looking very much like Rex Ingram in the four-star 1940 remake of *The Thief of Bagdad* with Sabu. Courane himself was now definitely into middle age and putting on weight. He wasn't nearly as rugged and heroic as his mental image of himself, which may explain why he turned up dead during the closing credits of so many fantasy and science fiction short stories.

Courane was not handsome—he reminded many people of the good-hearted slob from Brooklyn who was a mandatory cast member in most 1940's World War II movies. The Brooklyn serviceman was usually played by someone like William Bendix, someone who would never make it to the end of the film alive. When you saw William Bendix or Ernest Borgnine (in later years), you knew they'd be swell guys, but they'd generally have to die tragically and you'd find yourself weeping in the dark. William Bendix never got the girl and he never lived through a war movie. Borgnine did better in *Marty,* but then he became the fall guy of the post-war era.

Anyway, however you imagine Courane, as William Bendix or Ernest Borgnine, he was always the cheerful, doomed schmo who should've been buried beneath the center field grass of Ebbetts Field. There would've been a kind of poetic loveliness to that, but that kind of thing had never been in Courane's cards. Instead, he passed his time waiting for the cold, final finger of mortality to tap him on the shoulder. He had grown wary over the years.

This time was no different; he was suspicious as soon as the genie spoke. "You get three wishes," said the giant phantom genially.

"Three?" said Courane, surprised. "I just dreamed that I only got one."

"Can't help that. Dreams are dreams and this is this. You're a trifle on edge, but you're not panicking under the circumstances. I compliment you on your cool demeanor."

"Oh," said Courane, "I run into you supernatural critters all the time."

"Uh-huh," said the genie. "Now, we have a lot of ground to cover, mainly your three wishes and your ultimate catastrophe, to be exact. So may I suggest we get going?"

"I'm not going to throw up my hands in despair, you know," said Courane bravely. "I've studied and read three-wish stories and the like for decades. I think I've got a great shot at fighting you to a standstill, if not achieving outright victory for myself for the first time in a long while."

"Believe what you choose," said the genie, laughing in his deep, Rex Ingram voice. "All right, what's your first wish?"

"No problem. I'm not going to wish for anything clever, because that's how the greedy characters always got themselves in trouble. Like the guys in the stories by Fredric Brown and John Collier and Roald Dahl. Remember the fool in 'Threesie,' by Ted Cogswell, who had one wish left and asked for three more wishes, and had to go through the unutterably horrible de-souling machine forever and forever, in an eternally endless loop? Not for me, buddy. I want a winning lottery ticket worth maybe a million dollars. I'll even pay the taxes on it."

"Are you *crazy?*" cried the genie. "You've got three wishes that you could use for your own, if not world-wide benefit. And all you're asking for is a tedious stack of cash?"

"Money's good," said Courane. "And a lottery ticket will keep the IRS from wondering where it all came from.

I won't be suspected of committing a crime, or any of your other possible evil loopholes.''

"But it's so banal, so mundane, so *trivial!*" shouted the genie in disgust. "I haven't had a wish as lame as that in centuries! It's . . . it's absolutely *stupid!*"

"Would it be wiser to ask for a beautiful woman instead?"

The genie drew a huge hand over his weary black eyes. "I can't *bear* dealing with unimaginative, no-brain idiots like you!"

"Your opinion of my wishes doesn't matter. I can ask for whatever I want, however dumb you may think it is. I know what I'm doing."

"Not according to your track record."

"Just keep your promise," said Courane. "First, give me the lottery ticket. Next, get back in the teapot and I'll summon you again in a fortnight, to tell you what I've decided on for my second wish."

"If it's as puny a wish as your first," said the genie, "I may just break a rule or two and twist your damned head clean off. Who'd know?"

"The Powers That Be," said Courane calmly. "They'd know."

That shut the genie up, all right. He dissolved himself into smoke and flowed himself back into the teapot. The precious lottery ticket lay on the ground where he'd been standing.

Courane picked it up and put it in his shirt pocket. Then, cradling the teapot carefully like a fullback about to hurdle a goal-line defense, he splashed out of the water and onto firm ground. He'd left his car somewhere around there.

Two weeks later, after reading a lot more fantasy short stories, Courane was positive he knew what the best possible second wish should be. Before he called forth the genie, he discussed his wish with his new wife and their friends. It had been a very busy, very exciting two weeks, and Courane's life had changed a great deal.

The first thing he'd done with his lottery winnings was make a good down payment on a small but entirely charming house in the nice part of the Garden District not far from Commander's Palace. Next, he began a lightning courtship of Miss Eileen Brant, who was his ideal woman.

She was startled by his attentions; in other stories, she never knew Courane was even alive. Now, however, he had the confidence given to him by the house and the remaining money, and the two unwished wishes still in the bank.

Courane told Miss Brant about the genie and the teapot ten days after making the first wish. She was dubious at first, of course, but was finally persuaded by his evident sincerity and levelheadedness. They were married on the thirteenth day. Courane had never had many friends, but Eileen Brant was very popular, and her friends showed Courane a cordial acceptance he'd never known before.

The morning after his wedding night—aw, let the kids enjoy it without our disturbing them—Courane arose to a feeling that had been desperately rare during his adventurous life. Could it be . . . happiness?

"It's about time," he murmured, removing the Mango Red Fiesta teapot from beneath his pillow. Not wanting to disturb his bride, he carried the teapot quietly downstairs to the kitchen. He opened a bottle of Coke (a ten-ounce green returnable, the best kind) and sat down at the table. Then he rubbed the teapot.

The mighty genie appeared during a long roll of thunder that could be heard only in Courane's kitchen. "*Bismillah*," said the genie in his deep voice. (It meant, "In the name of God.")

"Morning," said Courane.

The genie glanced around approvingly. "Nice house," he said. "And you're married now? Fine. You've found a good woman. Perhaps you're not the complete dolt I thought you were at our last meeting."

"Thank you," said Courane. "Can I get you something?"

The genie laughed. "Very amusing, mortal! But do not think that you won't pay for foolishness, as I have warned you. I trust that you are prepared to make your second wish?"

"You bet," said Courane. He gulped some Coke, took a deep breath and let it go. "I wish . . . I wish I knew what to wish for."

There was a long, shocked silence in Courane's kitchen. Finally, the genie bent down and bowed before his master. "How truly wise," he said. "No one has ever made that superb demand before. Yes, you will know. Summon me whenever you choose to make your final wish." Then the genie quietly flowed himself down the spout of the teapot.

Courane was still trembling when Eileen came into the kitchen. "You should've waited for me, darling," she said.

"I went ahead, just in case anything went wrong."

"And?"

"And nothing. I think I impressed the genie. I get the idea they're pretty hard to impress, too. Thank you for listening to me and helping me. I'm convinced we got the wish just right."

She came over to the table and kissed him. "Do you know yet? What your third wish is going to be?"

Courane shook his head. "It's starting to come, but it's still too hazy."

"So in the meantime," she said, "upstairs? We've got a couple of hours before we have to pass by my mama's."

Courane stood up, finished the bottle of Coke, and took Eileen's hand. He felt a touching kind of shyness as they went back to bed. (A pity about Courane, isn't it?)

Later that day, while he sat on his mother-in-law's plastic-wrapped sofa in her neat little shotgun house on Annunciation Street, Courane sipped iced tea and wondered how he'd know when he knew what to wish for. Now and then, a stray idea would catch his imagination. "I know," he'd think, "I'll wish for an end to the drug problem." He'd test that choice for a few seconds, and then he'd think, "I know. I'll wish for a successful and inexpensive treatment for AIDS." One wish seemed to be just as important and worthwhile as the next. How would he know?

"—is it?"

Courane looked up. His wife was looking at him over the lip of her flamingo-decorated iced tea glass, looking at him with some concern. He realized that her mother had just spoken to him, but he had no idea what she'd said. "I'm sorry?" he said.

"Sandor," said Mrs. Brant. "Never known anybody named Sandor before. What kind of name is it?"

"It's pronounced 'Shonder,' " he said. "It's Hungarian for 'Alexander.' I was named after my grandfather."

He felt very uncomfortable. It was tough enough to get *any* mother-in-law to like him—he knew that for a fact from other stories—without carrying his own fate and destiny around in a bright orange teapot. Actually, Eileen had persuaded him to leave the teapot at home as they were leaving for her mother's house. Courane couldn't stop thinking about it, though.

He was grateful to Eileen when she said, "We've got to go, Mama. We promised some friends we'd see them this afternoon, and then we have to go home and pack for the honeymoon."

Courane stood up and put his iced tea tumbler on the little folding table. "I know," he thought, "I'll wish that the economy would improve for everybody." He let Eileen lead him outside. He stopped to kiss his mother-in-law and accept a tall plastic Mardi Gras cup filled with frozen seafood gumbo.

"Y'all call me when you get to Chicago," said Eileen's mother. "I'll be worrying until I hear. And take a sweater. It's cold up there."

"I know," thought Courane, "I'll wish for an end to all racial and ethnic prejudice around the world." And then he was sitting in his maroon Renault Alliance, while Eileen drove them home.

"Can I get you something, honey?" Eileen called from the kitchen.

"Hmm? Oh, no, I'm okay." Courane sat in the living room, staring at the Mango Red teapot. Finally, he took a deep breath and let it out, then reached forward and rubbed the teapot.

Once again, there was a clap of thunder and the genie appeared. "Aha!" cried the towering figure. "You have made your decision at last!"

"Uh-uh, sorry. I just needed a little advice."

The genie folded his massive arms across his chest and frowned fiercely. "Asking a question may properly be construed as a wish for knowledge. Free advice you don't get."

"Well," said Courane, shrugging. "I wouldn't want to see you get into trouble. You've been very good to me so far."

The genie's rich, Rex Ingram laughter filled the living room. "Me? In trouble? With whom?"

"With the Powers That Be, of course. Now, you promised me that I'd know when I knew what to spend my final wish on. But I don't see how I'll know. I must've believed

I knew twenty times already today. What would happen if I summoned you forth and wasted my wish on one of these phantom notions? It would be completely unfair to me, because my second wish was designed to protect me from that. I'm sure that if the Powers That Be—"

"Yes, yes, I see your point," said the genie, grumbling. "All right, here's what I'll do. I'll know when you know you know, and I'll appear to you at that time. Don't worry about rubbing the teapot. That's not really necessary, to tell you the truth."

"Then why is it such an important part of the tradition?"

The genie grinned, and not in an innocent way. "There's an old adage: Give a man enough teapot, and he'll . . . he'll—"

"—drown himself?" Courane was just trying to be helpful.

"Something like that," growled the genie. He flashed Courane a glance that had more than a bit of menace in it. "Just relax until I appear to you, mortal." Then the genie dissolved into smoke and flowed himself back into the teapot.

"How long will that be?" called Courane, but answer came there none. Courane felt a kind of sick dread, because whenever someone told him to relax, it was usually just before something like a sigmoidoscopy.

For dinner they had a huge pizza delivered, with whole roasted garlic cloves, sun-dried tomatoes, andouille sausage, and extra cheese. Courane barely tasted the food, and he said only a few words to Eileen all evening. She seemed to understand how distracted he was by the whole wish business, and he was grateful to her. "I know," he said, "I'll wish that women were given the same educational and employment opportunities as men."

"That would be a good wish," said Eileen. "A wish you could be proud of."

"Nah," said Courane, because the genie hadn't appeared, so Courane knew that he didn't know. Not yet.

It happened in the stilly watches of the night. Courane had set his alarm radio to wake him at 6:00 A.M., but long before that happened, while the world was still wrapped in blackness with only the lonely calls of the nighthawks to disturb the night's peace, a mighty hand shook him by the shoulder. It took a few seconds for Courane to waken and understand what was happening. All he could see in the gloom of his bedroom were gleaming eyes and strong white teeth.

"Just a second," he said, getting out of bed as quietly as possible. "Let's go downstairs."

The genie may have shrugged.

Courane took the teapot from beneath his pillow. He didn't know if he'd need it or not. A few moments later, he sat down at the kitchen table. Courane yawned; the genie waited.

"Hey!" Courane said. "This means I know what to wish for, right?"

The genie gave him only the slightest of nods.

"Some help," muttered Courane. He looked at the teapot, still wondering what the right wish was. And then he knew. The wish gleamed in his mind like a nugget of gold.

He looked up slowly. "Yes," he murmured, "that's it! I wish that everything will work out for the best for everyone."

"This, then, is your wish? Your third and final wish?"

Courane felt cool and comfortable and completely confident for the first time since he'd found the Fiesta teapot. "Yes," he said. "No tricks, no gimmicks, just hope."

"Very well, master," said the genie.

The next moment, Courane raised his head from a pillow. "Where am I?" he asked.

"A hospital," said the genie. "I'm afraid all they can do is try to make you comfortable."

"What?" Courane's voice was a dry croak.

"The teapot," said the genie. "You've been carrying it around for weeks. You've even been sleeping with it. It's the radiation. I'm . . . I'm very sorry, master."

"That's crazy. It's nonsense!" Courane began to cough, and he realized that he was heavily medicated, and that beneath it lurked an immense pain. "The teapot?" he said, letting his head fall back to the pillow. "It's been proven . . . the radiation disperses within two inches of the glazed china. No danger at all.'

The genie almost looked sad. "Normally that is so, master. You are forgetting the Vortices of the Unseen."

"The . . . what?"

"It is a magic teapot, of course, master. It has been amplifying and intensifying the subatomic danger."

"Then—"

"Try to relax, master. Your beautiful wife and your many friends have been keeping a vigil. They've been by your side constantly since you became ill. They are waiting outside now. You've never enjoyed such a wonderful and meaningful ending. And you leave behind Eileen, who will be taken care of splendidly, thanks to the life insurance policies you so thoughtfully provided. Finally, you will be remembered with love and joy for many, many years. She doesn't know it yet, but your wife is carrying your son, who will grow up to be an honorable man and a strong support for her in her old age."

"Then I suppose everything *is* working out for the best," said Courane softly. It wasn't what he'd expected, but he hadn't really known what to expect. In any event, a few hours later, surrounded by his grieving wife and loving friends, Sandor Courane passed away peacefully in his sleep.

You know what's wrong with immortality?
Boredom.
Ask me. I tried it in many of my lives.
But in one particular eternity, I at least found a
way to use my magic and make a living. . . .

NEW LAMPS, NOT OLD
by Ralph Roberts

He paid the other merchants in the bazaar to tout him to
the rich Americans from the Embassy down the street, or
the oil company headquarters two blocks east.

"If you do not need my rugs today, *effendi*, then why
not buy a magic lamp from Aladdin? His is that small stall
over there."

Or: "My silver trays are not of interest, O Man of the
West? Then perhaps you would care to visit the establishment of Aladdin Ali Hassan. It is rumored he still has the
Magic Lamp of his ancestor. Perhaps the spirits of the
djinn it yet contains will do your fondest bidding."

Aladdin was a small man in his middle thirties—very
neat and dapper, his mustache thin and precisely trimmed.
He affected the robes of the desert bedouin, but his were
always clean and tastefully embroidered with colorful
thread. He even smoked in a careful, neat manner—never
an ash dropping from the Winstons he favored and which
his cousin, who was great friends with the purchasing agent
at the oil company, supplied him by the case.

The day J. Herrington Bailey visited him, Aladdin was
sitting on a fine rug, legs comfortably crossed and, as was
his wont, sipping a small cup of hot Turkish coffee that
was gloriously syrupy with sugar.

"Are you this heah Aladdin fella?" J. Herrington Bailey asked, removing his white fedora and wiping the sweat
from his forehead with a monogrammed fine linen hand-

kerchief. Bailey wore a glistening white suit which silently screamed "MONEY!"

Aladdin placed his cup on a low table and came gracefully to his feet. He made a greeting in the Indian manner, palms placed together with fingers pointing upward, and bowing from the waist. This action had nothing to do with his Arab heritage of the great sandy wastes of Saudi Arabia, but it did seem to impress this type of mark.

"I am he, O Most Astute. Welcome to my humble shop."

Bailey looked around, obviously agreeing with that stated assessment. The shop, from the outside, appeared to be little more than a stall with an openwork steel gate that could be pulled across and locked at night to protect the contents. As Bailey came farther inside, and his eyes became more accustomed to the interior darkness after being dazzled by the boiling Arabian sun, he could see that this place seemed to go back quite a way, widening out and with dim lights spaced here and there.

"Pretty dark and cluttered for a lamp store," he said, snorting and putting away his handkerchief.

"The Great One calls for light," Aladdin intoned, bowing again. "Thy wish is, of course, my command."

He clapped his hands together sharply and light sprang forth from hundreds of lamps—halogens and fluorescents and the soft yellow of incandescents. The best of the best, the luminous products of America, Japan, Germany, the Scandinavian countries, and more blazed forth to become brighter than the white sun outside. The long rows of displayed merchandise, and the many lamps hanging from the low ceilings were now all revealed except for a corner in the very back that, due to an overhang, remained mostly in shadow. The whole place was crowded, but not really cluttered. It reflected the same neatness and fastidiousness as did Aladdin's person.

Bailey was startled at first, but soon understood what had happened. He had not become first a lawyer, then eventually Vice-President of Legal Affairs for Midlands Oil Consultants of Odessa, Texas by being a total dummy. No one, after all, is perfect.

"I have one of those at home," Bailey said, and clapped his hands. The sound-activated switch darkened the lights. He clapped again, and they went back on.

"O Most Discerning One, thou seest through my little merchant's tricks." Aladdin bowed again, hiding his smile. This stratagem always made the ones he liked to target think they were smarter than he.

"Let's cut the bull heah, fella, and get to the chase," Bailey said. "I hear you sell lamps."

Aladdin looked around at the thousand points of lights now bathing his shop in white-hot brilliance.

"O Learned One, thy words are those of great wisdom, for this is indeed the truth," he admitted, while adroitly and almost imperceptibly maneuvering Bailey back toward the shadowed corner. "And such was the profession of my father and his father and his father's father, verily back these many generations to my ancestor and namesake, Aladdin of the Magic Lamp."

"So I hear," Bailey said. He stopped for a moment to examine several high stacks of cases containing eight-foot fluorescent replacement tubes. The "GE" trademark was prominent on them. "What do these heah go for?"

"About twenty dollars American for the case," Aladdin said, but refused to let himself be distracted, edging them ever closer to the shadowed corner.

J. Herrington Bailey stopped here to rub his hand over a German halogen lamp, and there to "*ahhh*!" about a beautiful banker's lamp with green glass shade and fittings of polished brass. But, almost docilely, he allowed himself to be led to the shadowed corner as Aladdin prattled on about how his ancestors had conjured up magic spirits out of an old lamp and obtained great riches and the ready fulfillment of all their dreams thereby.

"So," said Bailey smugly, "if your family had all that wealth, why are you poorer than a church mouse and peddling lamps in the bazaar?"

Aladdin sighed. He wanted to wipe sweat from his forehead also, like Bailey did. It got very hot when all the lights were on in this non-air-conditioned shop. He thought yearningly of his Mercedes parked out back, and the coolness that would bathe him as he drove home to his seaside villa this evening.

"Alas, the Magic Lamp was lost long ago, O Master of Vast Perception. It is rumored to still be among the stock of this shop, but neither I nor those who went before me have ever been able to find it."

They were now in front of the shadowed corner, which was revealed to be the entrance to a large, dimly-lit storage area.

Bailey shrugged and bit, walking into the new room—at least it was cooler in here. Rows of shelves; floor to ceiling, greeted his view. Stacked in a dusty array at odds with the main shop, were nonelectrical lamps of every imaginable kind. Obviously here was the unsalable stock of centuries. Used kerosene lamps with soot-blacked glass chimneys, enough whale-oil lamps to require the killing of a Moby Dick to fuel them, candles of every description and, at the very back, shelves of the primitive pottery lamps used by Aladdin's distant ancestors.

"If only one could find the Magic Lamp, *effendi,*" Aladdin continued with his patter, "there would be riches beyond all dreams."

Almost as if on cue, Bailey noticed a golden glow from one of the primitive Arabian lamps, buried in a stack that did not look like it had been touched since Mohammed was a kid. He waited until Aladdin was looking the other way, describing the wonders of some old railroad lanterns and, while the merchant chattered on, he gently disengaged the lamp, glanced inside, then held his hand over it so that the glow would be hidden.

"Perhaps," he said craftily, "I might buy one of these old lamps as a souvenir."

Aladdin beamed. "But, of course, Most Generous Owner of Many Camels."

"No," Bailey said, puzzled, "I smoke Salems."

"Ah, yes. That is to say, the lamp which you hold is perhaps over a thousand years old. Who knows, it could even be the Magic Lamp and great loss would be mine if I sold it by mistake. Only two hundred dollars American would cover my risk."

Bailey laughed and uncovered the lamp. The golden glow once more poured forth.

"The Lamp!" Aladdin said in feigned wonderment. "You have found it, praise Allah! Alas that it was not me, for business has been slow of late and untold riches would come in handy. Yet, I must keep to my word. I have offered the lamp to you for two hundred dollars American, and by that I will abide."

"But you'd take one-fifty, right?" Bailey said, sneering.

"For you only, and only today, I would sacrifice the legacy of my ancestors for a mere one hundred and seventy-five American dollars," Aladdin said, beating his breast in a fine display of anguish.

Bailey laughed scornfully. He tilted the lamp up so that Aladdin could see inside. "Grain of wheat bulb and an Energizer battery. Cute." He tossed the lamp back onto the shelf with its kind and stalked out into the brightness of the main store.

Aladdin rushed out behind Bailey, wringing his hands in a convincing exhibition of duplicity caught out.

J. Herrington Bailey had stopped by the stacks of fluorescent replacement tubes, and was casually wiping away perspiration again.

"Please forgive my mistake, O Man of Great Justice," Aladdin said. "My desperation for money has led me into a trick that I should have realized such a perspicacious individual as thyself would have instantly seen through. I am most ashamed. Whatever it takes I will do, to show my humble and heartfelt contriteness."

"Perspicacious?" Bailey said, still mopping his forehead. "Yeah, it is hot. I'm sweating like a pig," he added, showing his usual sensitivity. He paused and pretended to be considering.

Aladdin, his Moslem abhorrence to pork overwhelmed by the thought of money, rubbed his hands together in mock-agitation as he watched the hook firmly set.

"Tell you what," Bailey said, placing his hand on the stack of fluorescent tube cases, "I just might be able to use a few hundred cases of these heah bulbs at a good price. You said twenty dollars a case? I'll pay you five. How many cases do you have?"

Between those in view and those in a nearby warehouse, Aladdin informed him, there were over a thousand cases. He haggled for a bit but, throwing up his hands and admitting to the shame of being caught out in his Magic Lamp trickery, Aladdin finally let all thousand cases go at ten dollars American per case.

It just so happened that Bailey had borrowed two large trucks with drivers from the oil company. Payment was made, the trucks loaded by sweating oil company employees, and all departed with Bailey, the latter being almost unable to contain his glee.

Aladdin clapped his hands to darken the shop once more, sat on his rug at its front, and lit another Winston. He sat quietly, enjoying the cigarette and smiling.

Later, across town, J. Herrington Bailey was standing despondently in the hot sun amid the huge stacks of fluorescent replacement tubes he had paid ten dollars a case for. The chief purchasing agent for the oil company and his friend, who bore an uncanny resemblance to Aladdin, had just explained to him that the rumors of the big American base being out of replacement tubes and willing to pay one hundred dollars a case was not true—a fact they knew for sure since they had started the rumors themselves. They struck a deal with him to pay a dollar a case to take the tubes off his hands. Unknown to Bailey, they already had an order from the base at five dollars a case. Then, of course, there was the commission from Aladdin for setting this all up.

In his shop, Aladdin finished another cup of ultra-sweet Turkish coffee and reached inside his robes. The tiny, ancient lamp he brought forth glowed with magical green light that had never failed in the generations it had been in his family.

"It's a shame," he said, rubbing the lamp gently, "that, unlike the legends, your magic only works on things relating to lamps. Still, it's a living."

"Yes, Master?" the lamp responded.

"Restock fluorescent replacement tubes," Aladdin ordered. "Take them from West Coast warehouses this time."

I have often felt sorry for my genie. He exists only to serve, he has no free will of his own. Despite his powers he is little more than a slave of whoever possesses the lamp.

Indeed, I have often wondered, over the eons, how my genie viewed his life. . . .

GENIE, INC.
by Kate Daniel

It was another beautiful day in Aruba. Hurricane season was a long way off. I lay there on the beach of the private club, staring off over the perfect blue waves of a perfect tropical sea, brooding. I wanted out.

I was ready to kill something from sheer frustration. Not that I would, or could. But I'd had it. The contract had sounded great when they signed me up, but it hadn't taken long to find out the truth. A life sentence is pretty grim when you don't have death as an escape hatch. Why do you think they always call us the *slaves* of those damned lamps?

And I could hear it calling me over the sound of the surf. The lamp was currently in Istanbul, but I wasn't free of it. I'd hooked the circuit up to a pager, so it wouldn't seem out of place. I wanted to ignore it, but my wants didn't have a lot to do with it. I got to my feet and brushed the sand off the backs of my legs. For some reason, I could always feel it if I didn't. I didn't want to spend however long this would take with my nonexistent legs itching. Then I headed into the clubhouse to find a private spot. I doubted I'd be gone long enough for the ice to melt in my drink.

As soon as I was out of sight, I went to smoke. The smoke form makes it easier to pop out of the lamp. Contrary to popular belief, we don't live in the things. I'm not a claustrophobe, but let's get real. An average magic-type lamp has a capacity of maybe a couple of hundred cubic centimeters. Sure, I could have stretched it dimensionally, but that's not cheap. Even magic bows to entropy. As I dissolved, the lamp pulled me through. I issued from the spout in the traditional towering cloud of smoke.

As I swirled around, I sized up the guy holding my lamp. He looked like a typical American tourist: weedy, thin, a little nervous-looking. I pulled myself into a smoke-bottomed masculine form. From the smoke up I looked like Schwarzeneggar on steroids. After a few centuries of experience, you figure out what the customer wants. Some people prefer a wimpy Slave. After that TV show, I started getting some who wanted me in female form. But the old standby still goes over well. There's something comforting to most people about being able to control a being as powerful as the traditional Slave of the Lamp. This guy looked like the sort who could use the reassurance.

We were alone, since very few people ever rub the lamp in public. It doesn't really matter, since only the holder of the lamp can see the Slave. But people don't want to be caught believing. He damned near dropped me. I haven't had anyone summon me in the last hundred years who really *expected* to see me. Barring a few kids, of course. It doesn't matter what the culture is, kids always believe in magic. It's inspiring in a way, and depressing as hell in another.

I crossed my arms over my chest in the approved fashion and boomed, ''You have freed me from my imprisonment. How may I serve thee, O Master?'' Freed me, right. I wished someone would, but breaking my contract-spell would take more than rubbing some brass.

I spent a few minutes convincing him he wasn't hallucinating, then I offered him the standard three wishes. All the legends and fairy tales have the stories mixed up. Some people expect unlimited wishes, some figure they'll have to trick me back into the lamp, but the actual deal is simple. The mortal makes a wish, and the Slave carries it out.

That was how it worked originally, anyway. Mortal energy, wishes and desires and beliefs, are the basic raw material for the magical half of the universe. We can't create it, so it's also our wealth. In the mortal world, we use it to do things like materializing out of a cloud of smoke, although we've developed hardware to help, things like the lamps. Pretty energy efficient, most of it. Magic has been living with an energy crisis longer than mortals have been making fire. The first lamps were just a gateway. The operator stayed home and came through only when summoned. The energy of the wish would be tapped to produce the wish-object, and the rest would be profit. Then, about the time of Harun al-Rashid, a group of operators got together and set up a company. Nowadays they call it GENIE, Inc.; they've been following human business practices. It's a monopoly. And they found ways to maximize profit. We always deliver, but it's never what the suckers want.

Usually, the first wish is something simple, a test. Those I can just do straight, if they're easy enough. Someone wants a double cheeseburger, I pop through and buy the thing at the nearest fast food joint. I kid you not, I got that one a few years back. Pure profit; the only energy I burned was transferring through the lamp. And lots of people make an inadvertent wish. Like the woman whose first reaction was, "I wish I could believe you."

On the next two wishes, people get tricky. That's where they run into trouble. Some wishes can be fatal, or pretty close to it. For example, saying you want to live forever is a *bad* move. Eternal youth is just as bad. There are ways of getting letter-of-the-law accuracy that are pretty nasty. And all the excess energy goes to GENIE, Inc.

This guy was brighter than most. He managed to stop himself on the brink of an inadvertent wish and think it over. I waited glumly. When the client asks for a killer wish as number one, a lot of the time there isn't any two or three. I had a hunch this guy was going to fall into that category.

He didn't, quite. He pulled himself together, set what chin he had, and said, "I wish . . . for unending wishes!"

That was a sucker bet. I sighed and said, "You got it, man. Nice talking with you." I could have left right then, but I figured it wouldn't hurt to explain things to him. Wouldn't make him any happier, but it was only fair. At least he hadn't managed to kill himself.

Sure enough, he reacted. Partly it was the words; I dropped characterization as soon as he spoke. He stammered out a few sounds, "How . . . wha . . . who. . . ?", which I took for the question he intended.

"There's a set procedure," I explained. "As it happens, that wish usually comes last. By putting it first, you just pushed the other two out of reach. Sorry; wish I could have warned you. Anyway, that's an additive formula wish. Each wish is used up getting another wish, which is used up getting another wish, which is—you get the picture. Like adding one to a number; you never get to the end. The other two are out there, but you'll never get to them."

It took maybe four percent of the wish-force to keep the chain going. The other two wishes were as lost to the company as they were to him. It was hitting now, the realization he'd been had. I added, "I'm sorry. Better luck next time."

As he stood there with his mouth flopping open, I smoked out. I knew he'd probably spend the next hour cussing and rubbing the lamp, but the rules forbid repeat business. I decided to stick with Aruba for a while, so I headed back there again, popping out of the smoke as a thong-clad female once again.

I'd been right. My drink was still cold, although it was getting a little watery. I rang for the waiter and got it replaced. Human waiters are a lot more reliable than magic.

Being a Lamp Slave had been okay at first. Between actual jobs, I could go where I wanted, pass time as I chose. And Slaves aren't what you'd call overworked, either. As magic had grown less common in the world, people grew skeptical and our business declined. Most of the time these days, rubbing a lamp was a joke. Mortals were always surprised when a Slave popped out, just like the stories. My lamp had been stuck in that cruddy tourist-trap "antique" shop for a dozen years. I wasn't free. No matter what I was doing, if someone rubbed the lamp, I had to take care of it right then. But that's no worse than a mortal on-call job.

No, it wasn't the working conditions or the amount of work that had me down. It was the work itself. I was tired of cheating the customers, sick of watching delight turn into disgust. People are so happy, once I convince them to make a wish. Convince them, yeah. Con them is more like it. Oh, sure, I've tried to warn them, but the words won't come out. There's no such thing as free will in this business. The contract is a special spell, and there's no way to break it.

I'd been my own first victim for GENIE, Inc., when I signed it. "See the mortal world." I'd seen it for centuries now, and it was a nice place. The mortals in it deserved better than they got from us. Guys like that poor sucker earlier were bad enough. At least he would live. He might lose all faith and belief, he might have learned he couldn't even trust magic wishes, but people survive that, no matter how bitter it leaves them. But sometimes it was worse.

The last call I'd had had been a nightmare. She'd been a nice, normal young girl. A little skinny, maybe a little plain. Her hair had been a flat brown. Even a mortal could have spotted that her biggest problem wasn't her looks but her own opinion of them. Her first wish, inevitably, had been for beauty. That was no big deal, more a matter of shading than anything else. A little hair coloring, a snazzier wardrobe, a fast make-over—I'd done it before. I didn't even fiddle with her eyesight, just let her see the results. But she asked if it was permanent, and I had to shake my head. Her next wish was to be beautiful forever.

All those damned "forever" wishes work the same way, whether it's eternal youth or beauty or living forever. The straight magical solutions all eat power. Fighting entropy always does, and keeping a mortal young is an uphill job. Instead of messing with the real thing, the person's time-perception is adjusted.

That girl . . . she froze in place as soon as she said the words. I left her in an out-of-the-way corner. Eventually she was probably picked up and hospitalized as catatonic. No doubt she was dead by now. But her perception of external time had been slowed so drastically that she managed to hit "forever" and keep on going before I could get the hell out of there and wash the bad taste out of my mouth.

That was the turning point. I wanted out of my contract.

Later that evening, I checked the lamp. It was back in the shop; my latest victim must have taken it back. I wondered what the shop owner thought. This wasn't the first time it had happened.

I couldn't see a way out of my contract, unless I could

manage to sabotage a wish and make it *cost* GENIE, Inc.
With the way the spells were set, I didn't think it was
possible. The feedback mechanism is supposed to be fool-
proof, and there were subspells, like clauses in a contract,
to cover most of the more common specifics. Even if I
could figure out a way around that, I wasn't sure it would
break my contract. But it was the only possibility.

I lingered over coffee that night at dinner, looking out
over the moonlit beach. It was beautiful. It had been so
long since I'd come into the human world that I couldn't
really remember the nebulous, not-quite-there world of energy that was my home. Slaves stay on the mortal side, on
permanent assignment, while the profits rolled back.
Maybe I'd stick around the human world if I could get
free.

I took off the next day, this time using a conventional
jet. I'd had all the paradise I could manage for a while. I
figured I'd head for Hong Kong; there was always enough
activity and people there to keep my mind off unbreakable
contracts. The last thing I expected was another call. They
usually don't come that close together.

It came during the in-flight movie. I made my way back
to the lavatory and went in, making sure the door was
securely locked. We weren't due to land for several hours,
so the flight attendants shouldn't ever realize they were shy
a passenger. Hoping the smoke wouldn't set off an alarm,
I dissolved and transferred.

I sized the new victim up. Another American tourist.
This one had an expression in his eyes I recognized; gentleman or not, he preferred blondes. I solidified into my
best Barbara Eden-imitation, with a harem halter-top revealing enough for Aruba, lots of filmy veils around my
head, and a tantalizing hint of harem pants at the hips
before I trailed off into smoke. His reflexes were fine; he
was drooling before I'd finished taking shape.

I started the pitch, "You have freed . . ." but before I
could even get to the *master* bit—always a hit with this
type—he opened his mouth.

"Hot damn, Jerry was telling the *truth!* Wish I hadn't
laughed at him."

There went wish number one. Harmless, a typical in-
voluntary one. From the stricken look on his face a second
after his mouth closed, he knew what he'd done. I gave

him a moment, then fixed his memory. We never alter
history; the entropy load would be incredible. It'd be easier to alter the memory of every living human, and sometimes I've had to do almost that. This was easy. As I
suspected, Jerry was my next-most-recent client. I left the
conversation in both of their minds, but wiped the laughter
from Jerry's. For the client, it was a bit more complex. I
made a copy of the memory, minus the hectoring, and
overlaid it as "reality." He could remember it happening
and not happening. As far as he was concerned, the past
had been changed.

His jaw sagged a little, then he pulled it back into place.
"And I thought Jerry had gotten hold of some booze," he
muttered. "I wish . . . no I don't." He gulped, then
grinned at me. "Hey, can I ask you a question? Not a
wish, just a question. If you don't want to answer, that's
cool."

"Ask me something?" I floundered for a minute. I'd
never had any requests that weren't wishes before. "Well
. . . yeah, I guess so. I can't promise to answer, though."

"No sweat. I was just wondering. Jerry said you couldn't
tell him what the deal was. How come? That *was* you,
wasn't it?" He looked me over again, from the smoke-
stream up. "He said it looked like Mr. Clean."

"It was me," I admitted. No one had ever wondered
before about my appearance. "I thought you'd like this
shape better."

He didn't quite lick his lips. "You guessed right. What
do you really look like?"

It had been so long, I couldn't remember clearly. "More
like the smoke cloud than anything else, I suppose. Not
physical."

"Well, I think I like you better as a blonde." There was
a cocky grin on his face now that looked right at home
there, as though it was his normal expression. "My name's
Stan, by the way, or did you know that already?

"I knew it," I said, although I'd never bothered with
names for clients before. It made it easier when I had to
shaft them.

"So, what do I call you? Should I call you . . ."

"No, not that!" Damn that television program. "I'm
just the Slave of the Lamp. I don't need a name."

"I'm not going to call you Slave." He sounded hurt.

"How about Jenny? That's close enough to the other that I can remember it. Anyway, what can you tell me about this wish business? How come Jerry didn't get diddly?"

I'd never even heard tell of anyone just *talking* with a Lamp Slave. I couldn't explain any of the loopholes to him in advance. I wanted to smoke out, but the guy still had two more wishes that had to be used up. When it came to stuff like that, I had about as much free will as an iron filing had to resist a magnet.

But maybe there was a way. All along, I'd thought the only chance I'd have to get out from under my contract would be if I could find a smart enough mortal. This guy was sharp. And he was talking to me, which was unheard of.

"We're supposed to tell you about the three wishes," I said, trying to word it so my mouth could get it out. "We, meaning Lamp Slaves. This isn't the only lamp that's inhabited. But we can't give details. And we aren't in the fortune-telling business. We can't tell you what your wish will lead to."

The grin faded from his face; he caught on fast. "You don't want to? Or you can't?"

"Can't."

"I'm not going to repeat Jerry's wish," he said slowly. Like he was trying to clear the way for an answer. "You couldn't tell him what was going to happen, but did you *know?*"

"Yeah." I hadn't been sure if I could say that, but he'd phrased it right.

"Why couldn't you tell him?" That one was impossible, and I didn't make a sound in response.

Again, he was sharp enough to spot what was happening. "Okay, scratch that one. Has anyone asked for that particular wish before?"

"Lots of times; it's fairly common." No problem saying that. The distance he'd put between himself and the wish seemed to make it safe ground.

"What would happen if I wished to live forever?" His eyes were fixed on my face now, not below my collarbones. This had shifted from something out of a sitcom into a deadly serious matter, and he realized it.

I couldn't make a sound, although I certainly knew what that particular wish meant. Time sense, again; perception slowed to about one microsecond per millennium. Perception of outside time, of course. Inside the skull of the victim, subjective time passed normally. A subjective geological era would pass before the body drew its next breath. The body would die in due course, all personality and mind dissolved in ultimate boredom. It might not match the technical meaning of eternity, but it was Hell by any sane definition.

After a few minutes, he nodded slightly. "I take it that isn't a safe wish. If I can figure out a good, safe wish, would you want to grant it to me?"

"Yes!" It would cheat the rotten system of its victim for once, and it might free me from my slavery. Not that I could say that, of course.

"Let's think of one, then," he said. "Can you get back into that lamp long enough for me to carry it up to my hotel room? This may take a while, and you're a little conspicuous."

Guessing games are a vastly overrated pastime, if you ask me. It was a slow process, and before long we were both frustrated. My plane landed in Hong Kong, leaving them with a nice little mystery. I hate loose ends, but Stan and I were making progress. I popped out for some refreshments on the house, legal since he wasn't wishing for them. Eating isn't necessary for a Slave, but it's a harder habit to break than tobacco. I'd been smoke from the hips down for over four hours. I was used to staying in human shape; this half-and-half blend was supposed to be temporary. I could sympathize with amputees; the left foot I didn't have felt as though it had a cramp in it.

He worked through the variations on a lot of standard wishes, playing Twenty Questions and getting mostly silence in response. Then he stopped and said, "This is ridiculous. All of these wishes are old hat; hell, I got most of them out of stories." He sat there for a few minutes, as quiet as I'd been, then tried a different tack. "You grant wishes. Can you grant your own? What does someone like you wish for, anyway?"

"Escape." The word burst from me with such force it left me shaking. "But I can't grant my own wishes." I tried to go on and explain the contract I wanted to break, but my tongue froze again.

He followed up his question, naturally, with another

about that word, *escape*. He was good at this. After about fifteen minutes, he said, "All right, see if I've got it. You can't refuse to answer the lamp. You have to grant wishes. You can't go away or even get out of that cloud until you do. You don't have any choice about how you grant wishes. Most of them are going to hurt the person making the wish. And you're unhappy about it. I didn't think people in your line of work were supposed to develop consciences."

I didn't know if he was right or not. I'd never heard of a Slave with a conscience, but as I said, we're loners.

He went on. "Some power or being or group controls you and won't let you warn people. Which means there's something in it for them; they want people to make sucker-bet wishes. I don't think it's because they're some sort of abstract evil, after souls or something."

GENIE, Inc., wanted the energy behind the wishes, but there was no way for me to tell Stan. All I do is start the process by focusing the wish-force on the wish itself. I have to use the focus spell, and it's set to draw minimum energy. For standard wishes, like those deadly "eternal" ones, paths of least resistance have been calculated and included in the spells. If a wish was really unusual, a Slave might have a choice on how to implement it, but it would have to stay low-budget. The trivial ones, like the ones who wish they hadn't had so much to drink, aren't covered specifically, but they're low-budget anyway.

Our little guessing game was hopeless. The longer we went on, the clearer that was to me. He seemed to think it was a game, a puzzle to solve. But those spells were set to *always* choose the cheap route. So far, none of his questions had come close to the mechanism.

"It's no use," I said. "Every time we start getting someplace, we hit a wall and I can't talk. You're right about the conscience, though. I don't like my work and I can't quit."

"We'll figure it out," he said. "You said you're the Slave of the Lamp. I don't like slavery. And I think I just figured out how to pull an Abe Lincoln on you." He stood up and faced me, and I froze.

"I wish . . ." he paused for a dramatic effect he didn't need. "I wish to share the knowledge of this Slave of the

Lamp before me, and I wish that this Slave be incapable of granting any further wishes past this one!''

I fell onto my suddenly-formed legs. I was out of the smoke, out of the lamp business. The spell had chosen the cheapest way by dropping me into human form. Not just the form, all the way. I was human. I could feel my memories fading rapidly, the way Stan's had earlier. Rather than let the knowledge of GENIE, Inc. out, the spell was removing it from me so he could share my ignorance.

But my contract was broken. I was free! And I was human. . . .

I almost tripped over the old brass lamp on the floor. ''What's this?'' I picked it up; it looked like the sort of cheap tourist item you find in the worst bazaars.

Stan said, ''Picked it up in an antique shop.'' He grinned at me. ''Who knows, maybe it's Aladdin's! Rub it, Jenny. Let's see if a genie pops out.''

I humored him and rubbed the sides vigorously for a few seconds, then dropped it on the bed and went back to packing. Our honeymoon was almost over, and it had been strange enough without magic lamps.

Besides, there's no such thing as genies.

You think that magic and genies are confined to the Old World, do you not? That they belong with mysterious temples, and domed cities of the ancients, with kings and mages and sultans?

Well, I, Aladdin, tell you that you are wrong, that neither walls nor oceans can stop the spread of the magic of the lamp. . . .

THE TALE OF ALI
THE CAMEL DRIVER

by Beth Meacham

> *"Hey, Jolly, hi, Jolly,*
> *Twenty miles today by golly,*
> *Twenty more before the morning light.*
> *Hi, Jolly, hey, Jolly,*
> *Gotta be on my way by golly,*
> *Told my gal I'd be home Sunday night."*

Ali the camel driver was a poor man, the son of a poor man, the grandson of a poor man of Medina, the home of the Prophet. But though Ali was poor, he was not content to remain so. He was ambitious. There were those in the quarter who said that he did not know his proper place, that he was a dreamer and an unreliable heir to his father's and grandfather's trade. But Ali tended his camels well and heeded his masters and if he spent more time in the market listening to storytellers than most men did, still he was faithful in prayer, and he gave such as he could to those more unfortunate than he. He even made a man's journey to Mecca to pray at the sacred places, the first of his generation to do so. True, Mecca was not so far away, and he had been hired to tend the camels of a rich man who was making his pilgrimage, but still the journey was made and Ali did not charge the rich man his full fee, so we may say that it was in truth a pious journey.

Now when Ali was five and twenty years old, there appeared in the city a stranger, a Christian, a man from across the sea. This man had gained the favor of the prince of the city, and so when he came to the noisy, teeming caravan yards seeking good riding camels to purchase, he was not shunned, but led through the crowds and the beggars and the dust to worthy beasts, and not charged more than twice their true value. The Christian purchased twenty-four camels that day. But when the time came for the market to close for the evening prayers, the man's foreign servants were unable even to gain the beasts' attention, and could not, therefore, lead them to the Christian's house. The camels sat placidly, gazing off into eternity, despite the rain of barbarian curses and good Muslim rocks that fell upon them.

Ali was squatting with the other camel drivers, leaning back against the mud brick wall that was a remnant of the ancient fortifications of the city. The others laughed behind their hands at the infidel's efforts. But Ali, who had learned something from the old tales told in the market, saw his chance, leapt to his feet, and approached the foreign man. Now, Ali was not clothed in blue trousers trimmed with red ribbons, and high, polished, black leather boots with silver ornaments at the heel. He was not wearing a fine blue shirt with pearl buttons, or even a brave red sash about his middle. Ali was clothed only in a dusty loincloth that once was white, and a turban of the same material that bound up his hair and protected his head from the sun that had blackened his skin. Ali knelt humbly before the finely-dressed foreign man, and with gestures and the aid of a servant who spoke the barbarian tongue, gained employment. He would drive the Christian's camels out of the marketplace.

And so it was that Ali the camel driver of Medina, faithful son of the Prophet, became a member of the United States Army Camel Corps.

When at last Ali and his camels, seventy-five of them in all, had crossed the sea, and arrived at the shores of America, he had gained a fair command of the barbarian tongue, at least enough to learn that the camels had been bought for soldiers to ride across the arid country that made fully a quarter of this foreign land. Ali was unable to understand why the infidel caliph would wish to patrol a land so in-

hospitable that their horses could not thrive, until he
learned that there was gold and silver in the mountains
that rose up out of the desert floor. Much gold and silver,
it seemed, there for the taking by any man clever enough
to find it and keep it. Ali had learned also of the nomads
of this foreign desert, savages who cared nothing for gold
but who would attack any Christian who entered their territory. To Ali they sounded as mad as the bedouin of his
own country, who wandered the desert sands, preying on
caravans, and refusing to enter the cities and deal in the
manner of civilized men. The chief servant of Ali's new
master, who was called Sarge, said that one day all the
Apache, for such were the nomads named, would be tamed
or killed. Privately, Ali thought of the thousands of years
of war between the men of the cities and the bedouin, and
suspected that the Christians would do better to learn to
trade with the Apache than to try to kill them all.

And so Ali fell into a life new and strange to him, though
he remained faithful to the true religion despite the prov-
ocations of the Christian soldiers he lived among. The
company traveled in caravan for months, westward across
lands twisted and carved by forces Ali could not comprehend. Tall mountains rose from flat desert floors, great
peaks were shaped into towers and palaces, rivers ran in
great chasms. The sun beat down by day, and the cold
wind blew by night, and one by one the foreigners' horses
failed, but Ali's camels went on and on. He gained position and honor. He was the only man among them, at first,
who could make the beasts obey, but one by one the soldiers saw the worth of the beasts, and came to him to
learn.

One day months later, the Camel Corps was traveling
back eastward, across lands far to the south. They traveled
by night, for it was high summer and the days were an
inferno. Ali had slept through the heat, and then had taken
three new recruits out to teach them how to speak to the
camels, and ride the camels, and cause the camels to run
like the desert wind itself. Ali had raced ahead of his stu-
dents, around an outcropping of reddish rock studded with
thorny bushes and the tall cactus of the region. He nearly
pitched forward over his camel's nose when the beast came
to a sudden halt. There before him stood half a dozen of

the savage Apache, clad in skins and stolen Army uniforms, carrying rifles, looking as if they would like nothing better than to carve his hide with the great knives strapped to their waists.

Ali opened his mouth to cry aloud that there was no god but Allah, in hope that his companions would hear his brave dying words and come to his aid, or at least of going to heaven after his death. But suddenly one of the Apache shrieked, and pointed behind Ali, off across the rocky waste. The others looked, and then all six of them fell on their faces, cowering among the great stones. One of the savages cried "Ch'indi! Ch'indi," and gestured to Ali to hide himself beside them.

Even more alarmed, but curious as to what might so terrify the desert dwellers that they would offer shelter even to one intended for their victim, Ali turned. He stared for one moment, and then dropped to the ground behind the nearest rock, oblivious to the cactus that had already found this sheltering place.

For there before him, racing across the playa a little above the ground, were three giant men wrapped in the whirlwind. They towered above the salt plain, fifty feet high or more. Their long black hair flew in the wind of their passage, trailing feathers and leaves and bright beads. Their garments were made of pure white leather, sewn with turquoise and shell, and trailing fringes. Around their necks hung necklaces of silver and precious stones, and from their knees hung rattles made of tortoiseshell. Their feet were naked, but as they did not touch the ground, they hardly needed shoes. Each carried a great staff before him, with cords and feathers trailing from the top.

The Apache nearest Ali reached out and pushed Ali's head below the rock they sheltered behind. "Ch'indi," he said again. Ali subsided, filled with astonishment. For though their accents were barbarous, the Apache had named the creatures aright—he had seen savage foreign djinni, riding the whirlwind in perfect freedom. His fortune was made.

A moment after the djinni had gone past, the Apache melted away into the desert, leaving Ali alone. He caught his camel, and rode back the way he had come in search of his three pupils. He prayed to Allah that the djinni had not come upon them. Half a mile back, he found them rising up out of the sand, dusting off their uniforms, gazing in disgust at the camels.

"Ali!" they cried. "We feared that you were lost in the dust storm. They come up so sudden in this territory—you never know when one of them dust devils will overtake you."

Ali knew that the soldiers had not seen the djinni, for if they had they would be trembling with fear. For some reason, the Sons of the Air were invisible to the soldiers. Perhaps this was why the djinni roamed free, instead of being safely imprisoned behind the Seal of Solomon as were all the djinni of his homeland. Ali considered how he was to make his fortune. For as all know, the djinns will grant incredible wealth and power to any mortal who can master them. Ali had often dreamed that one day he would, like Aladdin of the tales, find an imprisoned djinn; he had long ago fashioned his palace and his servants and his wives. Now he would seize fortune in his two hands.

But alas, all know also that the way to master the djinn is to free him from his imprisoning bottle in exchange for the wealth and power he can give. Ali knew well how to bargain with an imprisoned djinn, but these djinni were free. Therefore, he considered, he must first imprison at least one of them.

Ali sat alone in the desert waste. He had ridden a day from the soldier's caravan, explaining to Major Beale that his faith required that he spend this day in prayer. And he did pray to Allah to forgive the lie. He had taken a tiny brass bottle from among his few possessions, and emptied out the precious rose water that reminded him of home. He hoped that the lingering scent would so intrigue the foreign djinn that he would enter the bottle seeking the source. And so it came to pass.

The djinn appeared on the wind, and roared up to Ali, hair and feathers flying, precious shells and turquoises lashing at the ends of the white fringe of the djinn's garments. Ali fell to his knees before the Son of the Air, and greeted him in the name of the Prophet. The djinn stopped, astonished, and curious about this mortal man who dared to be seen, to actually draw attention to himself. The winds fluttered around Ali as the djinn explored him, lifting his headcloth and shirttails, going in and out of pockets and bags and shoes. Ali was pleased to discover that the djinn spoke the language of the Prophet, for that meant that his plan would work.

When the curious djinn entered the bottle, seeking the source of the sweet scent he had never smelled before, Ali leapt and quickly capped the bottle with a wax cork on which he had drawn the Seal of Solomon—a device he had learned from the storytellers in the marketplace so long ago.

The djinn raged and howled when he realized that he was trapped. He rattled and moaned and made dire threats. He swore that Ali was doomed, that he would be flayed and starved and pierced and flung from high places and torn apart by eagles. The djinn vowed vengeance on Ali and all his family and all his children and all his ancestors, from the beginning of time until the ending.

But Ali was not moved, and he did not remove the seal. The djinn was trapped.

When at last the djinn was silent, many hours later, Ali spoke to him and offered to remove the seal in exchange for the djinn's solemn vow to grant Ali wealth and power and all his heart desired. The djinn remained silent. Ali spoke again, again offering release in exchange for the djinn's promise. And still the djinn was silent.

Ali knew that the Son of the Air was trying to trick him into opening the bottle, and he was not fooled. The djinn remained trapped. Soon the djinn would grow desperate to escape, and then he would meet Ali's demands. Ali was a patient man. He could outwait the djinn. He tucked the bottle into his pocket, and rode back to the camp.

But days passed, and weeks passed, and months went by, and still the djinn promised only death to Ali.

Ali's camels had made many treks across the deserts, from the land of Texas to the land of California, and then back again. The soldiers praised the beasts, and praised Ali for his skill. They called him Haj Ali, for he had explained that since he had made his pilgrimage to Mecca before coming to America, he was worthy of the title, and they wished to do him honor in his own language. But there were men of power who did not admire the camels, who called Ali a heathen, and who demanded that Major Beale's experiment be abandoned. And so it came to pass

that Ali the camel driver was left at Fort Yuma with two
camels and no army to employ him.

Fortunately, the djinn had decided at last to strike a
bargain.

Ali drew a deep breath, and then broke the wax seal
from the neck of his small brass bottle. A great wind blew
up, swirling dust and sand and small rocks into the air
around him. A column of hot dry air raced out of the
bottle, and the djinn took form in the air, towering above
Ali. The djinn shook his staff at Ali, lashing Ali across
the face with the heavy beaded feathers. The djinn's hair
gave off lightnings and there was thunder as he stamped
his bare feet on the ground. Ali stood firm, holding up the
remnant of the Seal of Solomon.

"Remember, O Son of the Air, that you have given your
oath upon this."

The whirlwind subsided somewhat, so that Ali no longer
feared being struck. The djinn bowed slightly.

"To hear your command is to obey. But remember that
I will grant only three wishes, mortal. And remember that
I shall grant them exactly."

"And you will not harm me. That is the bargain, and
not a wish."

The djinn bowed again. "I will not harm you. I have
given my word. State your wishes, for I am sick of this
place and of your mortal taint, and I would be gone."

"Then hear my first wish, O Djinn. Look into my mind,
and see there the palace I have fashioned, its rooms and
furnishings, its servants and treasury." Ali conjured in his
mind the fantastic palace he had first imagined while sitting in the dust and camel dung in the marketplace of Medina. "Now, create this palace for me here, in this place."

The djinn laughed uproariously, and bowed a third time.
"It shall be as you command." The air shimmered. The
winds roared. A great flame rose up from the desert floor,
but Ali was not burned. Then before his eyes, there on the
stony banks of the Colorado River, beneath the great red
cliffs and the peaks where eagles dwelt, there took shape
a palace. The walls were white marble, sending bright
darts of reflection back from the high, hot sun. The towers rose in delicately carved spirals up to the sky. The
gates were tiled in blue and gold, and the windows were

screened in cinnabar and jade. It filled the plain, covering an acre or more. As Ali walked to the gateway, the doors were flung open before him, and six servants fell to their faces at his approach, crying "Master, we are your slaves."

Ali turned to the djinn. "You have done well," he said. "My first wish is fulfilled. I will summon you by the Seal when I am ready for my second. Until then, you are free." And with that he dismissed the djinn, and entered the place of his dreams.

Ali dwelt in luxury such as he had only imagined. His every command was obeyed upon the instant. He had clothing of silk and linen and fine white cotton, new and clean every morning. He had scented baths attended by naked slave girls of exquisite beauty, and meals of the most delicately spiced morsels, served on plates of gold and silver. He had stables of fine camels and the most mettlesome horses, caparisoned in brocades and tinkling silver bells. He had a treasury full of chests of gold coins and fine gems. But alas, in a few weeks the larder was exhausted, and someone must go to the trading post in Yuma to purchase supplies. Ali had neglected to cause his servants to speak English, and they had not had time or reason to learn it. So Haj Ali must go himself.

He took with him a purse of gold coins, and two camels to carry the supplies, and two of his servants to tend the camels. He rode on his fine white horse, and was dressed in a white silk tunic and trousers with a fine red sash embroidered in gold thread. He wore the burnoose of the desert bedouin to protect his head from the sun, and a surcoat of fine stripped cotton. He was a brave sight.

But as Ali and his servants entered Yuma, the children, who usually greeted him with cries of "Hi Jolly! Hi Jolly!", ran screaming from the sight of him. The poor Spanish ladies crossed themselves, and faded from their window ledges, and the men, trembling and with wide eyes, blocked the street while one ran to the parish church. Another ran to the gate house of the fort.

"*Demonio!*" cried one of the men, and they all made a sign against evil. The priest rushed out into the street, carrying a cross and a cup of water. He gestured to the men, and they threw themselves at Ali and his servants. The servants were knocked to the ground by two men each, and tied with ropes. Ali was unable to avoid being pulled from his horse into the dusty street. Five men held him against his struggles, while a sixth bound Ali's hands cruelly behind him. The horse and camels fled.

The priest approached Ali's servants, holding up the infidel symbol and praying loudly in a language that was not Spanish, but closer to that than to English. When the prayer was done, he sprinkled the unconscious men with water from the cup. As the droplets hit, smoke rose up to the sky, roiling out of the servants' bodies and filling the street. The priest leapt back, crying aloud in the strange language, and gesturing to his people to stand behind him. When the smoke had cleared, a moment later, nothing remained but the ropes that had been used to bind the servants.

The priest turned to Ali cautiously, held up the cross, and spoke the prayers again. Each word fell upon Ali like a hammer blow. When the water was sprinkled on Ali, he cried out with pain, for each droplet burned like a fiery coal. His fine clothing disappeared, leaving him lying naked and bound in the middle of the main street of Yuma. The townspeople cried out, and rushed forward to kick and beat him, and the priest stood aside to allow it. But a soldier from the fort came out to see what had caused the alarm, and he was one whom Ali had trained to ride the camels. When he saw his old teacher, he rushed in and drove off the attackers.

Ali was not badly injured. The soldiers gave him a pair of trousers and a shirt, and an old pair of boots. They also gave him a warning sent from the church—he was no longer welcome in Yuma. He walked north out of town, vowing to return with all his servants, and the weapons from his armory to take revenge. But when at last he arrived at the site of his palace, he found nothing there. He searched the barren ground for hours in the hot sun, seeking any sign of what had happened. At last, near where his chambers had been, he found a small heap of cotton clothes; his army satchel still holding his knife, tinderbox, canteens, and mess kit; and the small brass bottle and the wax Seal of Solomon. As he stood there, gazing at the desolation of his dreams, a wind rose up around him. Ali saw four wild djinni whirl in to surround him. But they did not approach closely, and after a moment of waiting, they disappeared. Haj Ali sat down on a rock and wept. He would have to walk miles from this place before he could try his second wish.

Ali rose from the shade of a boulder as the sun set at last. He had been walking eastward for four days, traveling always at night. This night he knew that he must find water, for he had drunk the last drops from his last canteen before lying down to sleep. Ali had crossed this desert three times before, but each time he had been with a well-supplied column of soldiers, with camels and mules to haul plenty of water and food. From the back of a good riding camel, the land had not appeared as desolate as it did now. But according to the landmarks Major Beale had taught him, there was one of the mountain tanks only a few miles ahead. He would surely find water there.

As midnight approached, Ali finally worked his way up the canyon toward the tanks. But he found the natural tank dry. The water had all flowed out through cracks in the containing rocks, or the winter rains had been too sparse to fill it. Ali knelt there, exhausted and parched, and knew that he was going to die.

"I wish," he said aloud, but before he could frame the next word of his sentence, the dry night air swirled around him, and the dead leaves flew off the desiccated trees in the canyon. There was his djinn before him, though he had not taken the Seal of Solomon into his hand. Ali closed his mouth, and considered. There were five other djinni hanging in the air down the canyon. It was clear that they were all following him, waiting for him to voice a wish. He had been lucky up to now that he had not squandered his remaining wishes.

"Yes, O my master," said the djinn who was Ali's, "what is your wish?"

Now, Ali had indeed learned something from the storytellers in the marketplace, and his learning had not deserted him even in these extremes. He remembered the tales of foolish men who wasted their wishes on food or water. He considered carefully before he spoke again.

"Djinn, look into my mind and see there the valley of the Salado, where the river flows down the high grassland, and there are wells and orchards. I rested my camels there one spring, and it was an oasis in the desert. Take me there, O Djinn. Take me there this instant.''

The djinn bowed slightly to Haj Ali. ''It shall be as you command.'' And the whirlwind rose up stronger than ever, and wrapped itself around Ali as the djinn reached down and picked up the wretched camel driver. They flew through the air, accompanied by the other five djinni, over desert and mountain, valley and grassy plain, until only moments later the djinn deposited Ali none too gently upon the banks of the Salado. The djinni hung in the air as Ali, half mad for water, flung himself into the shallow river and drank.

Ali sat for a time beside the river. He knew that there was a small town not too far to the north, where a strange sect of infidels had settled. He would have no difficulty walking there, but what was he to do once there? He had no money, no possessions. He had one wish left, but Ali had learned something more in the past month, and realized that his dream of a sultan's palace was a big mistake. No, he must seek for a wish that would grant him a lifetime's comfort, and not a few days of luxury. For a moment he considered returning to his homeland, but the years in America had changed him, and he could not imagine taking up his old place, squatting by the wall in the marketplace in Medina. As the sun rose, Ali made his morning prayers to Allah, and considered the path of wisdom.

Two weeks later, Haj Ali walked into an Apache village at the head of a train of mules. Each mule carried two great packs, filled to brimming with beads and tools and cloth and fine white flour, and all the goods of civilization that can lure a wild desert nomad. The elders were very interested in trade. When Ali left, he had added skins and baskets and fine beadwork to his stock. And he had made some friends.

In the town of Mesa, three days later, Ali traded the Apache goods and the cloth and tools for other things. Some of the people there remembered the strange little man from the Camel Corps, and made him welcome in the territory. Haj Ali prospered as a trader between the cities and the nomads, building up a thriving business until he was so well known that people came from a hundred miles away to trade at his outpost. He worked hard, from sunrise prayers until the last devotion of night. In time he became a success—a rich merchant with a wife and fine sons and a thriving business to show for it. His wife, an Apache woman, often remarked that he was a doer, not a dreamer.

But the wild djinni of the desert had learned something as well. Never before had they paid much attention to the mortals who roamed their lands, but now they knew that these mortals could be a source of rich amusement. And so, O my king, if you are traveling in the Arizona desert and you see the ch'indi rising up like whirling red smoke in the air, it is best to be careful of what you say. For the djinni wait for mortals who make wishes, and sometimes they will grant them.

Author's Note: High Jolly was a real person, although not exactly the person in this tale. He was born Philip Tedro, and he was an Ottoman Greek who, upon conversion to Islam, took the name Ali. Haj Ali came to the U.S. with the Camel Corps in 1857. After the Corps disbanded, Haj Ali remained in the Arizona Territory as a trader and prospector. He died in the town of Quartzite, on the Colorado River, on January 23, 1903.

I feel so sorry for those who have outgrown their belief in magic, and their belief in me. What dry, dull, passionless lives they must lead!
You disagree?
Then attend this story about my meeting with just such a man. . . .

ONE FOR THE ROAD
by Jack Nimersheim

So, this was Mecca. Hell-on-Earth would be more like it! That upward of a million people visited this Allah-forsaken place annually, Brent Aberdeen mused—a figure that represented the estimated number of worshipers who each year made a pilgrimage to the birthplace of Mohammed—revealed volumes about the power and popularity of the Islamic faith.

But most of the faithful arrived during the ninth month, Ramadan, at the beginning of what passed for spring within the arid climate of the Arabian peninsula. Aberdeen, on the other hand, had been forced to make the forty-mile journey East from Jidda in midsummer, when a sweltering sun at its zenith threatened to fuse the desert sands into glass. At this time of the year, the narrow valley in which Mecca stood was blistering hot, bone dry, and as barren as an eighty-year-old virgin. Even the local bureaucrats were bright enough to relocate their provincial government to the slightly cooler elevations of Taif for the duration.

So what the hell was he doing here, Brent Aberdeen wondered. Chasing another Pulitzer, what else?

"I know this is short notice, Brent," Kyle Hobson had said, handing him a manila folder of background information and an airline ticket to Saudi Arabia, "but we've been given a lead that's just too hot to ignore."

He wondered if his editor had recognized the irony in this observation, at the time it was made. Probably not.

Aberdeen had already promised himself that he would
make Hobson aware of his unintentional *bon mot,* in no
uncertain terms, immediately upon his return to Manhattan. Well, maybe not immediately. But shortly after a long,
cold shower and an even longer night's sleep between silk
sheets in his air-conditioned Park Avenue apartment. Right
now, however, he had an appointment to keep.

"Immortality ain't all it's cracked up to be, sonny, I'll
tell you that much. Sinbad, Ali Baba, Scheherazade,
Schariar, Prince Firouzi Schah, Haroun al-Raschid—I've
sprinkled dirt over each one of their graves. Did you ever
hear of Antoine Galland? I helped him translate our adventures into French. That was back in the early 1700s, as
I recall. I really liked that old Frog. I didn't expect to, but
Antoine and I hit it off immediately. We remained close
friends, right up until the day he died.

"Same thing happened with Edward Lane, a little over
a century ago. The two of us worked together for more
than three years on a children's version of *The Arabian
Nights.* We wanted to make certain those glorious tales
were always available to the kids. And we succeeded, too.
Then, just like everybody else, Edward wrinkled up like
a raisin over time and, finally, kicked the bucket.

"If I could, I'd wish every one of 'em back to life.
Them and all the other friends I've had to watch grow old
and die, down through the centuries. But I can't. The
wishes are all gone now, just like the lamp."

The old man's voice faltered, then fell silent. His rheumy
eyes glazed over, staring out into empty space, as he absentmindedly rubbed the dirty glass sitting on the table
before him.

The lull in the conversation, like so many others that
had preceded it, didn't bother Brent Aberdeen. He'd turned
off his tape recorder over an hour ago. Keeping it running
would have been as much a waste of power as the ceiling
fan turning lazily overhead. There was nothing but stale
and fetid air to move around the small, dreary apartment
in which he and the old man were sitting. And clearly,
there was nothing about the latter's narrative that deserved
to be preserved for posterity.

Whoever had conned Hobson into believing that he was
sending his star reporter off to interview Aladdin, the Mas-

ter of the Lamp, probably owned a first-edition, signed copy of P.T. Barnum's autobiography. So far as Aberdeen could tell, the only feat worthy of even minor mention that this pitiful creature sitting across the table from him had ever performed was to somehow secure the bottle of Tanqueray that he'd been steadily draining since the start of the interview. Booze was not a creature comfort the New York native had expected to encounter in Mecca, a sacred city in which alcoholic beverages of any kind were strictly forbidden.

The way he figured things, the old geezer probably picked it up on the black market—a mainstay of modern commerce that was bound to exist even here, in the birthplace of Islam. Exist, hell; within such a repressive society, illicit enterprises of all kinds undoubtedly prospered.

The old man's attention returned from whatever distant time or place had momentarily claimed it.

"I seem to be dry here, sonny," he sighed, holding out his glass. "Why don't you do the honors this time? And feel free to pour yourself another one, while you're at it."

Aberdeen picked up the bottle. It was almost empty.

"There's only a little bit left, sir. You can have it."

"No, no, no. Go ahead and fill both our glasses. There's plenty more in there."

Aberdeen interpreted this statement to be but one more indication of the advanced dementia he'd already concluded the old man suffered from. The drop or two remaining in the bottom of the bottle would hardly be enough to moisten one glass, let alone replenish a pair of them. Nevertheless, the reporter decided to humor his host. Imagine Aberdeen's surprise when he turned over the bottle to drain those final, few drops and a rush of liquid came gushing out so rapidly that it not only filled his glass, but quickly overflowed in a torrent, drenching the dusty tabletop.

"What the hell?" Aberdeen shouted as he jumped to his feet, knocking over the chair in the process.

"Ha! Ha! Ha!" Laughter echoed through the dark and musty room. "I got you that time, didn't I?"

"What are you talking about?"

"Oh, c'mon, Mr. New York reporter, tell me the truth." The old man's voice was suddenly strong, his eyes alert and alive. "You don't think I'm who I claim to be, do you?"

Aberdeen took a moment to recover his composure before responding.

"Let's say that I have my doubts."

"Don't worry about it. Most people feel that way, when they first meet me. That little trick—which I've pulled off successfully at least a hundred times, so don't be too embarrassed—manages to convert the majority of them into true believers."

Brent Aberdeen examined the green bottle, turning it over in his hand.

"Are you trying to tell me that this contains some sort of magic potion?"

"No. No. No. Nothing quite so dramatic. You see, a touch of the spirits was one of life's little pleasures I wanted to make certain I'd always have available, before the spirits of the lamp deserted me. And so, a few years back, I made a simple wish, one which keeps that bottle in your hand eternally filled with an unending supply of my favorite beverage—a taste I acquired in England while Edward Lane and I were collaborating."

"But if this isn't a magic potion, what the hell have we been drinking?"

"Why, djinn and tonic, of course. Now, shall we continue the interview? And please turn on your tape recorder this time, Mr. Aberdeen. I'm about to tell you a tale I think your readers will find extremely interesting."

As you grow older, you no longer appear as you did when you were a child. So it is with all things: the dry barren plains become mountains, the deep valleys widen and become oceans, the pudgy baby becomes a woman of great beauty and the woman of great beauty becomes an ancient thing of gnarls and wrinkles.

So it is with all things, and so it is with my lamp, which appears in many forms over many eons. . . .

DIRT TRACK DEMON
by Jack C. Haldeman II

Larry Bonner didn't have many friends.

That didn't bother him much. He didn't need friends. What he needed was a fast race car. What he had was a busted-up piece of twisted junk.

Larry's entire life was speed. He loved to drive fast and he knew he could be one of the best if he only had the equipment. But you can't get the money and backing without wins, and you can't win without money.

Oh, sure, he'd won his share when his cars held together, but the only tracks he could afford to race on were those backwoods, eighth of a mile ovals that ran Friday and Saturday nights with maybe a hundred people in the rickety old stands, and most of them kids. Nobody important was going to notice him there, no matter how good he was.

Larry looked at his current car and sighed. He'd flipped it last Saturday night in Trenton, end over end three times. Luke had clipped him from behind when the engine on old 98 seized. The car, an outmoded 3/4 midget with an ancient Offenhauser block, didn't look all that bad. A couple hours with a torch would get the body back in shape, but the engine would need a total rebuild. Larry hated Luke, who was the local golden-boy hero of the Trenton track and got most of the wins and all of the groupies, which mainly consisted of the Walsh sisters, all three of whom had crooked teeth.

Larry's garage sat behind his house surrounded by junked race cars. The better ones were propped up on cinder blocks and covered with tarps, but most of them just sat out in the rain and rusted. Unable to afford new parts, Larry bought wrecked cars from disillusioned drivers at various tracks, hauled them home and stripped any useful parts off them. His garage was crammed to the rafters with automotive clutter, and there was hardly any room to walk around old number 98, which was sitting in the middle of the garage under a battered drop light.

"Might as well start at the top," muttered Larry, looking at the scorched carburetor. "Stupid piece of junk."

Larry didn't exactly have an orderly inventory of parts, so it took him several minutes to find an appropriate carburetor, which was hiding behind a stack of assorted camshafts and timing chains. He held it under the drop light. It seemed to be in fair shape, but the linkage was stiff from sitting so long.

He put the carburetor into a bucket of solvent for a few minutes to loosen everything up. Then he took it out and started freeing up the linkage and cleaning it up with a rag.

"This is really getting to me," he muttered as he polished the carburetor, sitting alone in the dark garage. "A man like me ought not to have to live this way. I wish I had a sponsor."

There was a flash of light and the garage filled with smoke. Larry dropped the carburetor and started crawling toward the door. "Fire," he gasped. "My racing fuel's blown up. I'm gonna die!"

Someone started laughing.

Larry stopped in mid-crawl. Maybe he wasn't going to die after all. "Who's there?" he yelled.

The smoke was lifting. A woman sat on the hood of old 98. She was wearing bib overalls and a t-shirt. She had blonde hair and a small smear of oil across her nose. A pair of channel-locks stuck out of her hip pocket. She stretched and started digging grease out from under her fingernails with a spark plug gapping tool.

"Call me Jean," she said. "And that was your first one."

"My first what?" said Larry, getting to his feet.

"Wish," she said. "You get three, you know. Quite traditional." She hopped down off the hood and bent over to touch her toes a couple of times. "That feels good," she said. "Being cramped up in a carburetor for all those years is no fun at all. Very boring. Nobody to talk to. Of course, before I was a carburetor genie I was assigned to the horse and buggy department. Let me tell you, being stuffed into a magic feed bag is no great shakes. Oats give me the sniffles."

"Genie?"

"I always babble when I first get out. Can't help myself. Oh, sure, most folks think being a genie is all glitz and glamour, but mostly you spend your time hanging out in limbo all by yourself. This is a real piece of junk, you know," she said, grabbing 98's roll bar and rocking the car sideways.

"But—"

"I hope you're not one of these guys who uses all three wishes up lickety-split. I want to party a little bit; you know, get out and do stuff. You've got company, by the way."

"Hello." Someone was outside the garage. "Mr. Bonner?"

Larry looked at Jean.

"He can't see me," she said. "Nobody can see or hear me except you and other genies. I hope there are some hanging around. I could use the company. No offense, but you don't seem to be much for conversation."

"Yes?" said Larry.

"Ah, Mr. Bonner," said a well-dressed, older man who walked into the garage accompanied by a young woman. He extended his hand, which Larry shook. "You don't know me yet, but I think we have a bright future together. Sam Bradshaw's the name. Toys are my game."

"Yes?" repeated Larry.

"I'm the owner of the Tot Shop chain. Toys. You've seen my stores, I take it?"

"Yes," Larry said again. They were everywhere.

"Well, I was passing through the area on my way to look for some new southern markets and my daughter—

this is Donna, by the way—wanted to stop and watch an auto race. We saw you at Trenton on Saturday and I was quite impressed. I believe you could have won with the right equipment.''

"Yes," said Larry once more.

"I have a vision. Old 98 from the backwoods to the brickyard. Think of the toy cars it would sell, all with the Tot Shop logo on the hood. It would be great publicity for the chain. We could both make big bucks off the deal. What do you think?''

"Yes," said Larry, on a roll.

"Good, it's settled." He shook Larry's hand again. "My lawyers will be by in the morning with a contract, but as far as I'm concerned this is a done deal. Money is no problem; name your price. Of course we'll have to get you out of this crummy place. I'll have my people set you up in a decent garage in town. Fully staffed, of course. Pick your mechanics, and pick the best. Top-notch equipment. I want to win as much as you do. And Donna needs an escort for a party we're throwing next Wednesday for the governor. I'll send a jet down for you. Show you a good time, and you'll meet a lot of people who can help you. Okay?''

"Yes!" said Larry one last time, shaking both their hands and recognizing something very familiar about the greed and drive in Bradshaw's eyes while totally missing the overflowing affection in his daughter's gaze.

After they left, he turned to Jean, who was loosening the head bolts on the Offenhauser. "What was that about?" he asked.

"Wish number one," she said, wiping her hands with an oily rag. "You know, this really is a clapped-out hunk of junk. Number three piston is nothing but garbage. You swallowed a valve, tore everything up. That Donna is cute, but you ought to quit using such cheap parts.''

And he did.

Bradshaw hadn't been kidding when he said first class. The garage they supplied was huge and spotless. Shiny new tools were neatly arranged in orderly rows on the velvet-lined trays of a half dozen bright red tool chests on wheels. Spare parts, still in their boxes, lined the new metal shelves rising from the spotless floor to the vaulted and well-lit ceiling. At the rear of the garage three spare engines and two spare bodies stood ready should they be needed.

In the center of everything sat the new number 98, its black and gold paint job—eight coats of hand-rubbed lacquer—gleaming and shimmering in the light. It was a state of the art machine from its SureGrip tires to its onboard computer.

In fact, the only old piece of equipment in the entire garage was a beat-up carburetor that Larry kept on his desk, much to the amusement of his team of mechanics—a sharp crew that Bradshaw hired out from under Stoker Smith for an immense amount of money.

"So how was the reception with the governor?" asked Jean. She was still wearing her stained overalls. Larry was in his new racing suit. Tonight was the first time the reborn 98 would hit the track in competition.

"I met a lot of people who can help me," said Larry. "That Bradshaw's okay. He knows everyone in the state who's got money or influence. That plane he sent me even had a bar and one of those big screen televisions. It had two stewardesses, and it was only me aboard. It's first class all the way from here on, I can feel it."

"And what about Donna?" she asked.

"Who?"

"Donna. Bradshaw's daughter. The cute one with a crush on you. Your date, remember?"

"Oh, her," said Larry. "She's okay, but her money's all tied up in a trust fund."

The garage door rolled open and a black and gold eighteen wheeler backed up to the entrance. A horde of mechanics swarmed into the garage, packing up tools and spare parts and, finally, rolling 98 up a ramp into the trailer and strapping it in. The mechanics all wore black and gold jumpsuits that matched Larry's racing suit. Bradshaw was not a man to miss details, and the Tot Shop logo was everywhere.

"Hi, Larry," Donna walked into the garage. "I'm so excited for you."

Larry sidestepped her hug and picked up his duffel bag. "That Luke is history," he said, heading for the door. "He'll be watching my tail end all night."

Donna watched him leave. "Good luck," she whispered.

Jean watched him, too. "Why do I always get the clods?" she muttered to herself. "I was better off stuck in the feedbags."

If Larry was insensitive, he was also a good driver, and he won both preliminary heats and the 50-lap feature. Luke gave him a good run in the feature, but Larry put the Tot Shop Special into a gutsy slide on the last lap, shutting the door in his rival's face.

This time there was no escaping Donna's congratulatory hug. But as she held him, he looked over her shoulder at Jean.

"This is only the first," he said to the carburetor genie. "It's going to be a great season."

"You bet," said Donna, giving him a big squeeze and thinking he was talking to her. "You were great."

Jean just smiled a thin, humorless smile.

And it did look to be a good season. Larry started off with four feature wins in a row, and lost the fifth by a hair to Luke. Bradshaw was moving him up, too, entering him in all the high-profile races. The Tot Shop logo got lots of Saturday night television coverage and Larry even had his own national fan club.

Donna took care of the fan club details. Larry didn't have the time or the patience to deal with people like that. If he wasn't racing, he was hanging out with the money people. Unlike the fans, these people could help him.

To his chagrin, Luke's career was moving right along with his. He'd picked up a major sponsor and their weekly shoot-outs were big news on the circuit. Luke had married one of the Walsh sisters—Larry could never remember which one—and rumor had it there was a baby on the way.

Luke's success infuriated Larry and it made him drive a little harder and a lot more aggressively. He won some, and lost some, but he always finished up front until that Saturday night he lost it trying to cut Luke off in the third turn of the first lap and ended up stalled sideways in the middle of the track. It seemed like everyone behind him hit him somewhere.

"I can't believe it," he yelled later that night, slamming his helmet on the ground. "On the first lap, too!"

"You can't win them all," said Bradshaw, lighting a cigar. "Besides, that was a pretty spectacular wreck. They'll be replaying it all week. Lots of good publicity."

"Then Luke had to go and win," grumped Larry. "As if putting me out of the race wasn't enough."

"You put yourself out of the race, Larry," said Bradshaw. "We both know that. Now don't get me wrong; I got no complaints. It's your style to drive hard, and if it costs us some bodywork now and then, it's no big deal. As long as you're charging, the television cameras will follow the Tot Shop Special."

"Yeah, but I still wish Luke was out of my hair permanently."

"That's number two," said the carburetor genie.

"What?" said Larry.

"What?" said Bradshaw. "What do you mean, what?"

"Two wishes down, one to go," said Jean. "Like I said, we run a traditional organization. Not many rules, but we're sticklers for the ones we got."

"But, I—"

"Are you sure you didn't whonk your head out on the track, Larry?" asked Bradshaw. "You seem to be developing a tendency to stammer. I know a good doctor. He plays a mean game of golf, but I understand he's a fair sawbones, too."

"No thanks," said Larry with a broadening smile. "I think I'm going to be just fine. You want some Scotch?"

"Is it Chivas?" asked Bradshaw.

"Of course," Larry said, breaking out the bottle. "Nothing but the best."

The next morning Larry was nursing a hangover when Donna came rushing into the garage. She had tears streaming down her face.

"Larry! Did you hear? It's awful."

"Hear what?" he asked, washing down aspirin with a cold beer.

"It's Luke. They had a terrible accident after the race last night. A rock truck hit them head-on. Susan's okay, but Luke—Larry, Luke's paralyzed."

"Well, there goes his season," smiled Larry. "I'm home free."

"How can you sit there and say trash like that? This isn't some game. They say he'll never walk again. And them with a baby on the way."

"Tough," said Larry. "But that's life."

"Well, our life is through," snapped Donna. "Not that there was much to it anyway."

"I hear you," said Larry, lifting his beer.

"Well, hear me one more time, you callous creep. I wish you were dead!" She turned and stomped out of the garage.

"Good thing she doesn't have a genie," said Jean, sitting on his desk next to the carburetor.

"Forget her," said Larry. "She's small potatoes. It won't affect the business. I can always get another secretary."

"It's days like this that make me sorry I ever got into the genie business," said Jean with a sigh.

"Business is the operative word," said Larry, pulling another beer out of the cooler at his feet and cracking it open. "What we got here is a good business, but we've been thinking too small. I've been wasting my time and talent on all this Saturday night small-change garbage. We need to hit the big time. I wish I had a ride in the Indy 500."

"Bingo," said Jean with a big smile. "I've been waiting for that."

The phone rang. Larry shoved Jean out of the way to answer it. A moment later he put it down.

"Yes?" she said.

"Dead on the money," grinned Larry. "That was Bradshaw. He's talked the Johnson brothers into building me an Indy car. Experimental V-6 Chevy engine, ground effects, the whole ball of wax. First class all the way. I'm a lock to win the 500."

"It's back into the carburetor for me," said Jean, not looking all that unhappy about it.

"Have a good eternity," Larry said, popping another beer. "It's been fun."

"They say this carburetor is cursed," said Jean. "Of course I don't know much about curses, that being an entirely different department than genies. There's not a whole lot of cross-communication. You know how bureaucracies can be."

"You're babbling again," said Larry.

"It may be my last chance to babble for a long while," said Jean, who was starting to flicker around the edges. "Indulge me. You know who owned this carburetor last?"

"No," said Larry. "And I don't rightly care."

"Speedball Tucker. His name ring a bell?"

"Old guy racer. Died before I hit the tracks. If he ain't competition, I don't care about him."

"Know how he died?" asked Jean, as thin smoke started to whirl around her.

"Don't know. Don't care."

"He died at Indy," said Jean. The smoke picked up, becoming a small tornado, complete with crackling flashes of lightning, swallowing her and lifting her above the desk.

"It was on the last lap," she said, though Larry could no longer see her through the miniature whirlwind.

"He thought he had it made, too." Her voice was barely audible above the howling wind. "He was as arrogant and stupid as they come."

With a loud SNAP the funnel of smoke was sucked into the carburetor.

Larry watched the carburetor rock back and forth on his desk and cracked another beer. His hand was shaking.

"He was probably just careless," he muttered. "It happens to old guys like that. Never happen to me, though."

The carburetor hissed one last time and fell silent.

You think my genie is all-powerful, and so he is, under circumstances that are rigidly defined by the laws of magic that govern his existence.

But there are some things even a genie cannot do, such as refuse to grant a wish.

And there are some things a genie must learn to do, such as care for his master or his mistress. . . .

GIFTED

by Michelle Sagara

He was the last of the genies.

The others had served their purpose in a brilliant flash of three sharp bursts, and had been dust or less for many centuries. When he was born, if indeed a genie can be said to know birth, he was taught. He could not remember the teacher at all, but the teacher's words were as sharp and clear now as they had been at the beginning of his awareness.

"You are part of the magic of the world," the teacher had said. "All things that live must have purpose, and that is yours. You will not be strong, as camels are, and you will not be cunning or wily in the manner of men; you will not be mortal, but you cannot live forever."

"What will we be?" one of the genies had asked.

"What you are: Wishgivers. And when you have found the one, you will make your choice—and three times, you will know the power of the Maker. You might be as gods, if you choose your dreamer wisely."

"What happens when the wishes are given?"

The teacher did not answer.

Time did. Time, and the first of the genie's brothers. He was an impatient wisp of air and color, with no thought to the future and only the desire of power to guide him. He found a poor man—who better than the poorest of the poor to make a great wish?—and gave his gift first to gold and jewels, second to beautiful flesh, and last to a kingdom that spanned the deserts. The wishgiver, the first of the wishbringers, knew the glory of power and the song of fulfullment, just as he had desired.

But the gold and jewels were scattered now, melted and changed over the passage of time. The beautiful women were dust and less than dust, and the kingdom was lost scant years after its founding. The first of the wishgivers had not lingered to see this: The last of his power, and the whole of his life, broke and burst in the instant the kingdom had been created. He was gone to wind and sand at the burning sun above.

The genies had no time to bid their brother farewell. Sobered, they hid in the shadows and the little, secret places that magic makes. They made vows of abstinence, and swore to each other that they would not squander their lives or their gift on insubstantial longing.

But the teacher had been right: what lives must have purpose. One by one, over the passing millennia, the genies had succumbed to the silent call of their magical vocation. Yes, they grew crafty, and yes, they struggled to make their wishes immortal and fixed in the stream of time. Some created works of genius, and some bestowed genius upon the merely mortal; some created immortals, too soon lost to violent death when Time would not take them. Some created wars, and some won them; some let their seekers touch and know magic's glory.

But the price was always the same: The genies grew beautiful in their work—incandescent to the eyes of their brothers, sublimely terrible—and when that work was done, they were gone.

The last of the genies had once been privileged to watch one of his brother's giftings: the third and last. And he remembered, no matter how hard he had tried to forget, the pained look of surprise and loss, the sudden struggle and scramble for life, that had loomed for an instant upon a visage that was already disintegrating.

He had been afraid then.

He made his vow and made it strong by seeing, always, the face of his long-dead brother. When each of his kin succumbed at last to a call and temptation that had grown too ripe, he said a prayer to the maker, to no avail. He was the last of his kind, and he had lived without purpose for a very long time.

As time passed, he learned how to avoid the call of human longing. He dressed himself in the guise of humanity, rather than the guise of the magical, and wandered human streets, watching time change them without distant fascination. He traveled the ocean, and listened to the whales mourn the coming of the great, noisy ships that cut them off, forever, from the voices of brothers they would never see.

He came to the New World—it was called a new world for reasons that he did not understand—because the people who came were few, and their dreams were linked to reality and their own actions. The young he did not trust; it was always the young that had drawn his kin in and ground them up in the saying of three simple sentences in any of a number of languages. Not even all of the languages had survived their wishers.

He hid in the wild, listening to the hungry dreams of winter wolves and sleeping rabbits. But the towns and the cities always called him back; he could hear the dreams and the fervently uttered prayers that he had been born for. There was no sweeter sound, and none more horrible; he could not live with it, but the emptiness of separation hurt as well.

So he learned that the easiest way to avoid people was to stand beneath their gazes. He made the street his home, and conjured the clothing—with its peculiar smell—of the curb dwellers. He held out his hand, and murmured a sing-song little plea for coin, and men and women, with their dreams buried deep in darkened hearts, would scurry past in all their finery, never dreaming of what they might take from him, if they could see beyond his illusion. They would not even meet his eyes or raise their heads while they sped past, and that was for the best.

It was winter in the city; snow and cold had driven the people from their places in the street by the turning of the night. Even the curb-dwellers were gone, huddled over steaming vents or sleeping in the vestibules of instant-money machines when they could sneak past people who were not willing to gainsay their entrance.

The genie was not troubled by weather, and in fact welcomed the ice and the frost—it cleared the air of its summer haze, and made the streets more properly quiet. He leaned against the dirty bricks of an old storefront on the Queen's street and tried to catch a glimpse of starlight through the spotty cloud cover.

He felt them before he saw them, and watched with remote curiosity as they walked past. They wore black leather with silvered bits around their wrists and collars; they had hair of various hues and shapes, and one carried a music-maker over his shoulder, although at the moment it was thankfully silent. They wore heavy boots, heavy coats, and grim expressions that were meant, he thought, to be smiles; it was hard to tell.

They were the angry youth, with stunted dreams of power that drove them to pettiness instead of greatness. Every life must have a purpose—so the teacher had said—but these man-boys were allowed none, and had grown wild in their frustration. In a bygone age, they would have been the best of soldiers, the best of followers. Here, in the now that the people of this world had chosen, they were wasted.

He did not fear them, and they did not fear him; but they, like their older counterparts, passed him by quickly, although he did not ask them for coins. He smelled their desires in the air; they hung like a cloud in a deadened sky. But they asked nothing of him, and as they drifted past, the shadows of their mutual companionship drawn tight about them, they were forgotten. Minutes drifted; snow, too cold to be pretty, fell wayward on the breeze.

A lone figure struggled along the icy cement, heavily coated and somewhat bent. He watched her as she walked, and knew her age by her awkward gait. He held out his hand in supplication; she met his eyes, and the lines of her face drew into a tight mask. She walked on, stopped and fumbled with her purse, and walked back. It was obvious, from the state of her worn gray coat and the rubber boots that she wore over swollen calves, that she was not among the city's wealthy, but she gave him the money that he'd asked for before turning west again without a word.

He looked at the coins in his palm; one was brass, three copper, and two silver. They jangled as he put them in his pockets, and vanished to the keeping place that only the genies know. He settled back against the red brick and waited, feeling the cold only because it was a curious thing.

He turned when he heard the shout. The streets were empty, or almost empty, and the noise carried easily. Curious, he drifted westward, following the wind and the old woman's tracks.

She was there, and, indeed, it had been her voice that raised the shout; her words came again, less strong and less distinct. Surrounding her, like a pack of feral dogs, were the angry young men. Their voices were muted but darkly cheerful; violence was the taste of their dream.

He stopped when they became clear and distinct from their background, and watched. The young men chose not to see him, or chose not to care. But the old woman, struggling on all fours like a child learning to crawl, looked up. Blood, from a triangular cut in her forehead, dripped and fell into the folds of her skin; her glasses were shards and wire on the sidewalk, and it was obvious that she could not see clearly.

But her eyes found his nonetheless, widening and narrowing in turn. "Please!" she whispered, as a foot caught her ribs. "Help me!"

The young men turned and saw him. They looked back at the youth who was obviously the pack leader; he shrugged and spit to the side.

"Get lost."

The genie tried to take a step backward, but found himself transfixed. Before he could even speak, his arms were in motion—a motion that was completely foreign and more natural than breath to a human. Smoke and light billowed up from the ground in shades of graduated red; a plume of fire touched the suddenly slack faces of the boys, responding in kind to their anger and their choice.

They screamed; he felt, distantly, their sudden pain and their desire to be free of it. But their wish had no power over him now, and they fled his fire and his magic.

The old woman lay against the thin ice, bleeding into the snow. She was no longer conscious. In horror, he drifted to her side and touched her; she was warm and solid. He lifted her gently, keeping the cold at bay, and stared in angry fascination at her broken face.

Years he had watched and kept his distance—and in one

night, in a way that he did not understand, with no more control than the youngest of his kin had ever shown, he had made his choice, had found his one.

The pettiness of the wish that had cost a third of his life made him weep in the silence.

He knew where she lived, of course; she was his chosen and the knowledge could not be stopped from coming. Although age had made her heavy, the magic was now upon him—with a simple gesture and a bit of concentration, he, she, and her forlorn purse were suddenly transported into the darkness of a small room. He could see, with perfect clarity, the outline of her bed; with a lift of two fingers, the sheets rose and dangled a moment in the air, waiting until he had removed her coat and boots. He laid her down, snapped his fingers, and caught the soft cloth rag that appeared in midair before him.

Gently and slowly he began to wipe the drying blood from her face. She stirred but did not wake, and when at last he'd finished his ministrations, he stood back, in a darkened corner, to wait.

But the moon was out. Curious, he pulled back the shades and let the moonlight reveal the lines of the old woman's face. History had marked her and aged her, and he viewed each wrinkle as if it were a chapter of a novel in a foreign, unknowable tongue.

He had known all his life that the chosen one would be special—but he had never dreamed, as he hid and avoided the making of the choice, that he would find an old, impoverished woman beautiful. What he felt he did not know, could not name—but the peculiar warmth that came he attributed to the beginning of his brief reign as an almost-god.

He was afraid, but thought that he finally understood why fear was not the only thing his brothers-in-thrall had shown.

She woke just after dawn, started beneath the sheets like a frightened animal, and sat up with a cry. Then, as sunlight made the safety of her bed clear, she relaxed and fumbled at the small table beside her. Her fingers scrambled against the hard wood for a moment before he realized what she was searching for.

"They were destroyed," he said softly.

She froze. Very slowly she turned herself in the direction of his voice, her hands white now where they clutched at linen.

"You wanted help," he continued, in a steady voice. "I answered your call."

"What are you doing here?"

"Don't you remember?" He took a step toward her, and she shied back against the headboard, which creaked unsteadily in response. "You wished for help. I answered."

"How did you get in here?"

"By magic."

Her eyes were wide, troubled, and undecided. He stayed in the corner, but thought to bring both of his hands, palm up, to show her. She squinted, and it became clear that she couldn't see them clearly. Minutes passed.

"You were attacked by young men," he began again, his own voice betraying confusion. "Last night. You gave me coins. Here." He called and they came, jangling in midair.

"You—you're the beggar!" The lines on her face contorted and then relaxed into a frown of suspicion. "So—did you go through my purse to find out where I lived?"

"No." He shrugged. "I know where you live."

"How?" She was frightened again.

"I told you: Magic. You wished for help, and I answered that wish. You were unconscious; I returned you to your place of residence. You are my chosen mistress, and I must grant two more of your wishes."

"Magic, is it?" She snorted, and tossed the bedclothing aside. "Did you take any money out of my wallet?" Without waiting for an answer, she stalked over to a large dresser and pulled open the slim, upper drawer.

At a loss for words, the genie shook his head.

"Magic." She snorted again. "What will you young folk dream up next? I may be old, but I'm not senile." So saying, she pulled a small, leather case out of the drawer, and from it, an old pair of glasses, which she perched upon her nose with great authority.

"Well," she said, still squinting, "you don't look as bad as you did last night. And I'm grateful to you for saving my life." She came a little closer.

"But—"

"I can probably give you a little more money, for food or whatever. But you can't stay here."

"But, Mistress, I *am* a magical creature! I'm the last of the genies!"

"I don't care if you're the last of the Mohicans. You aren't staying here, and that's final!"

The horrible bitterness of the brew that the old woman called tea was a new experience—and not a pleasant one at that. He took the opportunity to mix cream and sugar with it until the entire liquid was a syrupy, horrid concoction. The scones and the lumpy butter were at least a little more familiar, and he played at eating them while he sat in one of the two rickety chairs at the tea table.

"Look, son, why don't you just tell me what your real name is?" She poured herself another half-cup of the unpleasant liquid, and busied herself making it palatable.

"I don't have a name," he replied. Then, although he knew the answer, he asked for hers.

"Mine?" She laughed. "Didn't read the old driver's license very carefully, did you?" But her smile was good-humored, and she hadn't snorted in at least two minutes. "I'm Mrs. Susan Clarkson. Sue." She buttered half a scone, and reached for the jam, before suddenly looking up to meet his eyes. "Don't you ever blink?" As usual, she gave him no time to answer. "I want to let you know that I'm grateful for what you did out there."

He shook his head, bemused.

"But I'd feel more comfortable if you'd admit to the truth."

It was pointless to argue the case, but he felt compelled to it. "Mistress—"

"Sue."

"Sue, then. I'm the last of my kin. I'm a genie. I grant wishes. That's my purpose in life. What can I do to prove it to you?"

She snorted; he knew she would. He had never heard of anyone disbelieving a power they had called upon before. One third of his life had been given and granted—and it earned him mockery and the oddest twinkle of a human eye.

"You can grant wishes, eh?"

"Yes."

"Could you make me young?"

"Yes."

"Could you make me rich?"

"Yes."

"Could you take me back to the town I grew up in?"

"Yes."

She laughed. "Could you make it summer, you funny little liar? Could you bring back the dead?" And at that, her face grew still, and her laughter became a heavy silence.

"Yes."

"That's enough, boy. It's not funny anymore." She pushed her tea aside with such force it splashed out onto the lace cloth beneath it.

"But I'm trying to tell you, Sue, that I'm not joking. This isn't a game—it's my life. Test if, if you will. Make a wish, and watch it come true. Shall I bring back the dead for you?" He raised an arm, and felt a tingling warmth that made him dizzy.

"Bring back the dead?" She muttered. "To this? He's in heaven, he is. He's happy. You think he'd appreciate being dragged back?" She made a laugh of it, and hollow though it was, it was still strong. "Tell me something, Gene. If you can grant all of this stuff, you must know a lot."

"I do."

"Is there a heaven? Is that where he is?"

But of course the genie could not answer.

He tried to tell her that he had no need for sleep, but wasn't surprised when she called him a liar. She shoved blankets into his arms, and made him pull apart the chair that she called a couch. To his surprise, it became a bed, of sorts. He had seen them often, but had never used one before. She told him to lie down, and because she was his mistress, and he her servant, he did as she ordered.

There, in the darkness, he stared at the ceiling and counted the broken springs beneath his back. He did not understand this odd woman, with dreams buried so deep they were hardly reachable at all. He didn't understand why she wouldn't believe him, because he was thrumming with magic and power so strong he felt it must be visible. He closed his eyes, and tried to sleep.

When the lights returned, he knew it was not dawn, and sat up at once. Sue stood in the doorway between the two bedrooms, and stared down at him. "Gene," she said quietly, "do you ever get lonely?"

"Yes. All of my brothers are dead."

She held out a hand that shook in the light, and he understood that she meant him to take it. He did, and it trembled.

"I want you just to be with me," she said, and her eyes were filmy with longing and shame. "That's all, nothing more."

And the last of the genies, with power that could have turned time or death at her behest, felt the second wish strike him deeply in what could have been his heart.

He stayed with her, of course. And every day she began by telling him that he would have to leave soon. He attended her in silence, and grew used to her complaints, her amusements, and the strict adherence she had to daily routine. He helped her dress in the mornings, when she needed the help at all, and accompanied her everywhere. She got used to his help, and once in a while would entrust him with her purse.

But she thought him simple, that much was obvious. She taught him about money, taught him about food, taught him about clothing, and even tried to buy him some. She called him Gene; it was her joke, and her private name, and as she was his mistress, he answered to it.

She talked slowly of her life, and he was amazed at the endless details, the endless memories, that so short a time could produce; in the evenings, tea in hand, she would regale him with stories of a youth so long gone he could hear it only in the wistful tone of her voice.

"I could make you young again," he would say, but she would only shake her head and smile.

"And what would happen if I were young again, eh? What would happen if you made me young?"

"I would die," he replied.

She laughed wickedly. Always the laugh. She would slap him on the back, shoulder, or thigh—whichever happened to be closest—and say, "Gene, you *have* made me young again!"

* * *

She took him to the ballet. She took him to the movies. She took him to the Salvation Army, and made him work with "real" bums, as she called them. She took him to church, where he met with a priest who talked about an afterlife and heaven. Heaven was important to Sue, and she spoke of it with both longing and fear. He didn't understand it.

But he grew to understand her, and he was happy, in his way; as happy as he had ever been in the millennia that preceded these few years. He forgot what loneliness was like.

But genies are immortal until they make the last of their gifts; humans are not. One morning, just before the glint of dawn, he felt her shake in her sleep. She was hot; he had not realized how dry and tight her skin had become. When she woke, she coughed and shuddered horribly. He took her to the hospital.

There he waited in a room that smelled of vile chemicals. People came and went and he ignored them; they had become unreal. Only Sue was real, and Sue was someplace beyond him. She had ordered him to wait, or he would have been at her side at once.

The doctor came out to greet him. "She's got pneumonia, Gene," she said quietly.

"Will she be all right?"

"I don't know. She's very old."

"And if I made her young again?"

The doctor winced. "I think she'll be fine, though," she said lamely. "Why don't you go to her? She's asking for you."

The genie didn't have to be told twice. With a gesture of crossed arms and a wrinkle of forehead, he was at her side. She was crossed and tied with tubes, or so it first appeared, and her skin was very pale.

"Sue," he said quietly, as he caught her hand in his. "What is this needle doing here? Shall I take it out?"

She laughed—and the laugh became a terrible cough. "No," she said at last, when she could speak clearly. "It's intravenous. Good for me."

"What can I do to help?"

"Nothing." She shrugged. "Nothing but stay. Do you mind? I told 'em you were my son. They won't make you leave." She coughed again; the rattle of phlegm at the back of her throat was constant. She was in pain, and that hurt him, although he didn't understand why.

"Sue—let me help you. Let me make you young."

He tried to tell himself that her cough was laughter.

"Always on with wishes, aren't you?" But she caught his hand and held it tightly. "I wouldn't be young if it'd kill you, Gene. And you're what I wished for, you know. You've been a good friend. What did the doctor say? Tell me the truth."

"She said she didn't know whether or not you would be all right."

"That's what I thought. She looked pretty grim." She was quiet for a moment; the rattle of her chest rose and fell. "But I don't mind being dead, you know."

The genie nodded; he'd heard it all before, and he knew she found comfort in the belief. But he heard an edge of fear to the words, and rested his head against her chest— whether to comfort her or himself, he wasn't certain.

"I'm afraid of the dying," she whispered, as she stroked his hair with her free hand. "I wish—I wish you could come with me, and stay with me, no matter where I went."

And the magic swelled up, recognizing in her words a true wish; it pushed at the inside of his skin, radiating heat, warmth, life; it rushed out through the pores, the eyes and mouth, and the tips of his fingers. He closed his eyes in fear and terror, pleasure and fulfilment, waiting the end.

The end did not come; there was no end waiting, and no loneliness either. He saw the shape of her death in her face, and felt peace. He caught both of her hands in both of his, and kissed her forehead gently. "Sue," he whispered, as tears trailed down her cheeks. "I *will* come with you and stay with you, forever."

She laughed, she always laughed.

She was laughing when they left the room together.

You know, Yasmine of sainted memory was not the only female genie to serve me in all my many lives. There were others as well, as loyal and capricious and somber and fun-loving and cruel and caring as normal women.

There was one in particular, though, to whom I shall be eternally grateful, not merely for this *eternity but for all eternities to come. . . .*

THE LAST OF
A VINTAGE YEAR
by Janet Kagan

The old man held the bottle up to the sun. Pale green shadows flickered through the thick coating of dust and grime to dance on the sand at his feet. Yes, he thought, the very last of Solomon's vintage. His hand hesitated over the cork. Perhaps this one would kill him. How fitting, that he be killed by the very last imprisoned djinn. His faint twist of a smile brought a splay of crow's-feet to his deeply tanned temples. He said the words—they were rote after all these years, but this last time he was conscious of an obligation and spoke them with emotion—and drew the cork with a grand flourish. Then he laid the bottle on the sand and bowed to the rising smoke.

"Thank you, Aladdin," said a sweet voice. "I'd heard rumors, but I had never dared to hope that you would find me."

Aladdin straightened and looked up, *high* up. He'd seen all sorts, but to a djinn they'd been huge at first, terrifying in the sudden release of pent-up energy. The sky was empty.

A light tap on his shoulder made him start and turn. Beside him stood a rather ordinary woman, perhaps a head shorter than he. Quite unimpressive, really.

"Oh," she said. "I've startled you by appearing at human size. If you'd be more comfortable with a towering figure, I'd be glad to—'' She began to enlarge.

"That's not necessary," said Aladdin. "You've no intention of killing me, then?"

"You freed me," she said, taken aback. Then, quite unexpectedly, she smiled. The smile brought a dimple to her cheek. "I do grant the traditional three wishes," she said. "So I won't disappoint you there!"

He smiled in return. "A cushion for my first wish then. I've walked a long time to find the last bottle, and I'd like to sit for a while."

True to her kind, the djinn overdid it. Aladdin found himself in a cool green garden, beneath a stand of palms. Flowers, all yellow and gold, softened the air with their scents. Beside the pillowed bench a fountain sang quietly. The shade and the whisper of water were welcome, he had to admit. Feeling refreshed, he bowed to the lady, took her hand and guided her to sit beside him.

She smiled again, pleased that she'd pleased him. He found that distressing in an odd sort of way.

"And for your next wish?" she said, her dark eyes bright with anticipation.

"My dear, my next wish would have been for a drink of water—which you have already kindly supplied." He took the dipper from its hook beside the fountain and plunged it into the water. He offered the first-dipped drink to her, thinking perhaps after all these years even a djinn might wish for a long, cooling draught of water. When she waved it away, he drank deeply and sighed. "That's two," he said.

A frown rippled across her brow. "That's not," she said. "That's only one."

Aladdin took a second draught, then rinsed the dipper and hung it once again beside the fountain. "Please consider that my second wish fulfilled." He took the djinn's small hand in his and said, "You see, I haven't anything left to wish for."

To his surprise, she gave this careful consideration. "Oh, my," she said at last. "All those other djinns gave you all the usual: wealth and a beautiful princess and—"

He nodded, caught for a moment in the memory of his beautiful princess with her snow-white hair. He lingered over each cherished line of her face, like some treasure hunter over his map of hidden riches.

"Wait," said the djinn. "They didn't give you immortality. That much is clear from the lines in your face and the whiteness of your hair. I could certainly give you that."

He shook his head. "When my wife would not ask for immortality, I found I could not either. After all, what have I to do with my life now?"

The djinn leaned back; of its own accord the pillow behind her snuggled to prop her at an angle that left her peering down her nose at him, like a crane awaiting the proper time to spear its dinner. Like a djinn awaiting a wish.

"You couldn't give me back my princess," he said. He expected no contradiction and got none. "My children are all grown"—she sat forward and he added hastily—"and they should be left to live their own lives without the meddling interference of an old man and an older djinn."

"I see," she said. "Is that why you've spent the last fifty years of your life tracking down and releasing trapped djinn?"

Aladdin smiled and shrugged. "That was the only thing I was ever good at. I had a gift for it."

"Yes. To find my bottle on the edge of a dead sea, that was a gift indeed." She raised one knee and wrapped her arms around it. *"Was,"* she said in echo. *"Had."*

"You were the last. There are no more imprisoned djinns to release by a rubbing of the lamp or a pulling of the cork. All the lamps and bottles are empty now, and there are no more magic words that need to be said." He turned his hands up and laid them, empty, in the lap of his robe. "May I ask where we are, my dear?"

"In the Golden Garden of Al-Sabbagh."

He rose and bowed. "A short trip home, then. Though there is no one who awaits me, I shall nevertheless be on my way. My work is done." He straightened and looked carefully into her dark eyes. "You'll be all right—by yourself?"

That made her smile. "I have been for many hundreds of years."

He smiled in return. "Of course. Forgive me. It was a pleasure to have met you."

He had already turned to go, when she called out to him. "Wait, Aladdin! Your wish!"

Such sticklers for tradition. . . . Aladdin turned back. "Anything you want, my dear. Anything but immortality. I leave the choice to you."

He took two steps and found himself inside a building. The air was astonishingly cool, like that of the high mountains. When he made to pull his robe closer, he found the clothing he wore odd and completely unfamiliar. He frowned slightly—for he also found he knew the words for every item he wore, from the BVDs to the three-piece suit to the brightly flowered tie.

He was in a small shop, surrounded by ancient but lovingly cared for lamps and bottles of various ages long past his own. Behind the counter, a young woman sat quietly reading. For all its strangeness, that sight made him feel at home, for he had taught his princess to read and she had delighted in it as much as this youngster did.

Quietly, he glanced around the shelves, knowing it had to be here somewhere—a green bottle that would flicker ever so slightly even without the sun to shine through it. There—shined and treasured. He raised the bottle from the shelf, cradling it in his hand. In his mind, he could see the djinn's dimpled cheek. In his mind, her voice said, *Djinn aren't the only creatures trapped in bottles. I wonder—can you uncork that one?*

Aladdin shifted slightly to look again at the youngster behind the counter. A floorboard creaked beneath his feet and the youngster's head snapped up. For an instant, he saw terror in her pale blue eyes—then she gathered herself and said, "Oh, you startled me! I didn't hear you come in!"

"My apologies, miss," he said. The words felt strange in his mouth, but he knew they were the right ones. "Could you tell me, please—where did this bottle come from? I saw one like it . . . many years ago."

The fear was subsiding, but Aladdin could see that it would never quite go away. Unless. . . . *Unless,* echoed the djinn, *you can find the magic words.*

"Jordan, I was told," said the youngster. "Found on the shore of the Dead Sea." She said the words as if she treasured the thought. Then, in another tone, she added,

"It's not considered an antique, I mean, an antique dealer would sneer at it. But I thought it was lovely."

"Lovely—yes," he said. "It's just the sort of bottle that might once have held a djinn. . . ."

"Oh!" said the youngster and something new lit her eyes.

She did still have hope for herself, Aladdin saw. There was magic imprisoned there! Aladdin felt a rush of hope lift his own heart.

Thank you, he said silently to the djinn. *For letting me out of my bottle. I thought there was nothing left for me to do in this world.*

Again he could see the djinn smile in his mind. *Honey,* the sweet voice said, *this is New York City in the twentieth century. When you're done uncorking this poor imprisoned creature, we'll find you another.*

By my count, she added, *you've one wish remaining to you. If you ever change your mind about the immortality, let me know. You've got your work cut out for you here!*

The youngster was smiling at the bottle. Reflected in the swell of green glass, her face dimpled like the djinn's. Aladdin smiled; for the first time in many years, his smile felt genuine. A different vintage, but just as sweet as the old.

*It is said that over the ages my lamp seems to have
fallen only into the hands of beggars and malcontents,
that while it brought riches and even happiness to some
of its owners, it brought fame to none of them.*

*That is just another fable created by unbelievers. In
fact, it was the Lamp of Aladdin that shaped the life of
one of the greatest warriors of your century. . . .*

THE BOTTLE AND
THE WHIRLWIND

by M.C. Sumner

The bedouin was dead, had been dead for some days. Vultures had gotten to the face, leaving dry tears in the parched skin. The guide put a toe under the body and pushed it away from the well.

"Beni Atiyeh," he said.

Lawrence leaned over the body, watching a shiny green beetle hurry back into its disrupted shade. "Do the Beni Atiyeh work for the Turks?"

"No."

"That's a pity," said Lawrence. The dead man was the first interesting thing he had seen in this godforsaken desert. He took off his khaki hat and beat it against his shirt, sending out clouds of dust. "How did he die?"

The guide was going through the clothing of the dead man. "Thirst? Hunger? It is hard to know."

Lawrence pulled his cap back over his sandy hair and walked to the camels. In only two days of riding, he had developed a loathing for the beasts. They were stubborn, their humped backs were uncomfortable, and their odd stride seemed designed to wear on civilized bottoms. His mount turned its long neck and looked at him, pulling back its upper lip and favoring him with a snort. Its breath was very bad.

"Can we please go now?" he asked.

"One moment," said the guide. He made a quick swipe with his horn-handled knife and pulled out a heavy leather purse that had been hidden in the dead man's robes. He flipped it open and stared inside.

Lawrence struggled back onto his precarious perch on the camel. "Come on, man, it's infernally hot out here," He swatted at yet another of the innumerable flies that had followed them across the sands. For the tenth time that day, he wished he had never left his post in Cairo.

The guide mumbled something over the dead man and hurried back to the camels. As nimble as the monkeys that danced in the streets of Cairo, the man mounted. "Do not worry, English. We will be with Feisal in the morning."

Lawrence nodded wearily. It was scarcely noon, and already his head was buzzing with the heat. The guide barked at the camels, and they were off again, bouncing across the dunes.

There had been a time, only a week past, when Lawrence would have thought this romantic. From his cool basement in Cairo, he had perused his battered copy of Burton's *Arabian Nights* and dreamed of the glories of ancient Arabia. He glanced over at the man riding to his left. The noble savage. Lawrence had seen dairy cows with more wit. It was a shame that Burton was dead. Lawrence would have very much liked to punch the man.

During the afternoon, they crossed stony ground. The camels moved slowly, planting their broad feet with care. Lawrence drowsed in his seat. When he opened his eyes again, tall pyramids of weathered sandstone reared up along the eastern horizon. The natural formations were so perfect, that he wondered for a moment if they might be the models for the tourist attractions outside of Cairo. He was quite prepared to believe that the Egyptians could not have thought of them on their own.

They stopped for the night at a point where the invisible trail wound between two pale mesas. Lawrence stepped off the camel and limped around as the guide laid out their meager camp. For all its ferocity during the day, the sun seemed to hurry to be on its way. The sky went from blue, through a hundred shades of red, to deepest black, in the time it took to work the cramps from his travel-weary legs.

The guide unrolled his prayer mat and knelt toward

Mecca in the south. Lawrence waited impatiently while the man repeated this seemingly constant ritual. His prayers over, the guide gathered bits of scrub from the base of the nearest cliff and built a tiny fire. Over this he warmed tough meat and a sauce that Lawrence found both rancid and obscenely sweet. Soon after that, the guide bade him good night and lay down to sleep.

Lawrence did not sleep. It was not that he was not weary, it was that he didn't trust the guide. More than once, Lawrence had seen the swarthy fellow eyeing his pistol. So he put on a show of vigilance, huddling near the dying fire and staring up at the star-laden heavens.

He awoke with a start, horrified that he had fallen asleep. But the guide was still wrapped in his *kuffieh,* snoring softly. The fire was down to just a few licks of blue flame and the night was very cold. The moon had risen, turning the desert to silver and casting long black shadows across the sands. Lawrence stood up and brushed the sand from his trousers.

He walked around the camp. As he was contemplating just how much warmth might be generated by burning the guide's prayer rug, Lawrence saw the purse the guide had cut free from the dead bedouin. He picked it up, more out of boredom than from any compelling curiosity.

Only a single thong held the top closed. His chilly fingers loosed it easily. By moonlight it was hard to see what was inside. Lawrence fished in the leather and came up with a handful of what might have been coins. There was something larger in the bottom of the bag. He reached in again and produced a bottle.

It was small, no bigger than a clenched fist. The sides were fluted, and the top was sealed with both wax and a device of wire that reminded Lawrence of a champagne bottle. He turned the bottle over in his hand and squinted at it in the moonlight. There was a design on the front— an intricate tangle of lines and scrawled Arabic script.

Perfume. That was certainly what it looked like. But Lawrence could not imagine why a dead bedouin in the desert north of Yenbo would be carrying a bottle of perfume.

He twisted off the thin wire, pulled the glass stopper free of the wax, and sniffed at the bottle.

He smelled nothing. The bottle was empty. Lawrence

turned the bottle over and shook it. Still nothing. He tossed it away and put the purse where he had found it. Lawrence returned to his seat by the embers of the fire. He was very tired, and he was near the point of not caring whether or not the guide attempted robbery.

There was a light out on the desert. He saw it once and looked away. Then his weary mind caught the import of what he had seen and he looked back.

It was not a very bright light, but it was definitely moving, coming closer with alarming rapidity. Lawrence got up and ran over to the guide. He could not remember the guide's name. In their two days on the desert, there had been no need for names.

"You there!" he said in a hissing whisper. "Wake up, man!"

The guide did not move.

"Wake up! Someone's coming!"

The soft snores continued without interruption.

"Salaam!" called a voice.

Lawrence turned around quickly and put a hand on the wooden grip of his pistol.

The light was very close now. In its glare, Lawrence saw the rich white robes of a wealthy Arab trader. The light was coming from a lamp that the man held aloft. He came into the camp with long confident strides and a smile that showed clean white teeth framed by a dark beard. *"Salaam,"* the man repeated.

"Hallo," said Lawrence.

The man bowed and gestured toward the dull glow of the dying fire with his free hand. "Greetings, my friend. Would you allow me the honor of sharing your fire this fine evening?" His English was excellent, with only a trace of the liquid Arab accent.

Lawrence licked at his dry lips. "My fire has gone out, and I've got no more wood."

"Ah," said the man. "I can remedy that." He reached inside his flowing robes and produced a bundle of wood. Not just the thin bits of brush that the guide had gathered, but real wood.

"Where did you get that?"

The man laughed. "If one is to have a fire in this place, it is best to be prepared." He leaned over the extinct blaze and added his fuel, arranging the wood in a careful pattern.

Tempted by the warmth of the renewed flames, Lawrence drew closer. "What are you doing here?" he asked.

The man gave an elaborate shrug. "I am on my way from here to there." He settled beside the fire and placed the small lamp on the sand at his side.

Lawrence took another step closer. "I didn't know there was anyone around here."

"There are always some. Come, please sit down and join me."

The cultured voice of the man was very calming. Lawrence sat. "Are you going to see Feisal?"

"Are you?" asked the man.

Lawrence considered not answering—the man could be a Turkish spy—but he thought the odds of that were very remote. "Yes. We're going to his camp in the morning."

"And is this something to be desired?"

"I suppose," said Lawrence. "But I must say, I'm looking forward to returning to Cairo."

The man looked up, still smiling. "So it is Cairo you desire?"

"I suppose. Cairo, or Oxfordshire."

"If I am not being impolite, how did you come to be here if you do not desire it?"

"I don't know." Lawrence looked into the dark eyes of the stranger. He didn't want to say anything that would be impolite; he had seen how the Arabs could react to a man who offended them.

"Was it riches you sought?" asked the man.

"No," Lawrence said, suddenly puzzled. "Why should I expect to find riches here?"

The stranger gave another of his elaborate shrugs. "Many men seek wealth. Perhaps it was a woman that brought you here?"

Lawrence shook his head. "I don't even know if there *are* any women here."

"Then it was glory that you sought." The man was no longer asking questions, this was a statement.

"Why do you say that?"

"It is nothing to be ashamed of. Many men seek fame." The smile grew even wider. "To be remembered through the ages . . . It is a worthy goal."

Lawrence rubbed at his sleepy eyes. "I suppose," he said. "I had hoped I could do something here that might contribute to the war effort. But now, well, now I only want to go back."

"But you still wish you could do something. Something great."

"Yes," said Lawrence. "I suppose I do."

The man nodded. "Rest," he said. "I have stolen enough of your sleep."

Lawrence leaned back. Whatever fears he had were lost in his exhaustion. He fell asleep with the stranger's smiling face illuminated by the red tongues of fire.

He awoke to the smell of cooking meat. The guide was kneeling beside the fire. "Good morning," said Lawrence.

"As you say," said the guide.

Lawrence looked around the camp. "Is our guest gone?"

"Guest?"

"Yes. There was a man, an Arab. He came to the camp last night."

The guide frowned and shook his head. "I saw no man."

Lawrence looked at the play of the morning light on the dunes and cliffs. There were shapes there he hadn't noticed before, intricate forms molded by constant wind and infrequent rain. He found the effect very pleasing. And there was a scent to the air, more than the cooking food. It was the spicy exotic smell of the desert itself.

"Is that our breakfast?" Lawrence asked. He took a bit of the smoking meat from the guide and popped it into his mouth. "Very good. Very good, indeed."

When the food was finished, he helped the guide load the camels. He patted the rough side of his own mount in affection, marveling at the power of these creatures that could carry so much across such vast distances. "Its a shame our trip is almost over," he said. "I'm just starting to get the hang of this."

Lawrence turned toward the guide and caught the man looking again at the pistol and held it out to the man, grip first. "Take it," he said.

"But, but I can't . . ." stammered the guide.

Lawrence gave him a bright smile. "Take it. If we're to work together, we must trust each other."

Quickly, the guide snatched the pistol. He held it with both hands, his dark face shining like a boy with a new puppy. "Thank you, my lord."

Lawrence hopped onto his camel. "Come on," he said. "Take me to Feisal."

The bottle lay behind them, glistening in the sun.

It is said that Hollywood is the Dream Factory. That is close, but take Aladdin's word for it, this is not true. Hollywood is the Wish Factory, and here is a tale of a man who got exactly what he wished for. . . .

A WISH FOR SMISH

by David Gerrold

Do you know why they call it slime?

Because the name Smish was already taken.

Lennie Smish was a lawyer. A Hollywood lawyer.

Let me explain that.

Hollywood is heaven for lawyers. There's always somebody with a deal, a contract, a claim, or a grudge. The movie isn't over until the last lawsuit is settled; a legal case in Hollywood isn't merely a legal matter, it's a whole career. You have to do it for your children because you won't live long enough to win.

In Hollywood, Lennie was a legend. He handled one case where settlement was delayed until not only all of the original combatants had died, but most of their heirs as well. By that time, legal fees had eaten up ninety percent of the award. When lawyers spoke of their idols, Lennie's name was always on the list.

No one knew how old Lennie was. It was said of him that even a stake through his heart wouldn't slow him down. It was said that he was already dead, but the devil had refused to take him; so Lennie was left to wander the Earth and trouble the sleep of the living. This was what Lennie's *colleagues* said about him.

To say that Lennie was a vampire was more than an understatement, it was like saying the *Titanic* had a rough crossing. Lennie was a superstar of greed.

Lennie Smish had an amazing demeanor. He looked unwashed and disreputable. He was flabby, misshapen, swollen, mottled, discolored, uneven, lumpy, pickled, and pocked. He had the large hairy pores of a walrus, the wattles of a turkey, and the gravelly skin of an armadillo. He had the charm of a three-day-old Texas roadkill. His clothes were shabby and dirty; his shirts were rumpled and spotted. His tie—he only had one—was a wrinkled collection of soup stains. His hair was stringy and colorless, not quite gray, not quite anything else. Some of it lay flat, not quite covering his bald spot; the rest of it stuck out at odd angles. When he spoke, his voice rasped and scraped as if the words were being pulled one at a time out of a dry scabby throat. Lennie Smish was the only man in the world who could say, "Have a nice day," and make it sound like a threat.

In short, Lennie Smish was so unappetizing, so unpleasant to look upon, so disheartening to deal with that nobody ever scheduled a meeting with him before lunch.

How the lamp got to Hollywood is obvious. In 1946, in his quest for Arabic authenticity, Louis B. Mayer ordered the purchase of as many Moroccan oil lamps as it took to find the right lamp for the new Douglas Fairbanks Jr., Maureen O'Hara picture. Fifteen hundred lamps later, somebody finally worked up the courage to tell him that the lamp was actually in the story of Aladdin, not Sinbad. For years thereafter, the MGM prop department was the place to go if you needed an authentic Arabian lamp.

How *the* lamp fell into the hands of Lennie Smish is another story—the usual combination of greed, deceit, and underhanded dealings. The short version: Lennie was cataloging the property he'd seized from the estate of a client who shortsightedly had not provided for Lennie's fees in his will, and had attached the lamp as part of his booty. In keeping with tradition, Lennie was cleaning the lamp when it went off.

The djinn came pouring out of the lamp, hacking and wheezing with a dreadful cough—Lennie had been using a chemical cleaner. It expanded itself to a comfortable size, twelve feet—then, seeing the low ceilings in Lennie's apartment, retracted again down to seven feet, ten inches. The djinn was a traditional efrit. It was as big as it could be in such cramped quarters; it was bronze of skin, and muscled like a bull elephant who worked out at Gold's Gym. It wore a red fez, a black vest, a green sash, a curved bronze scimitar, yellow flowing pantaloons, and black pointy-toed shoes. There was no doubt that this was a major genie. It had no hair, no eyebrows, but long black mustaches. It had sharp-pointed ears. It grinned down at Lennie with a mouth full of golden teeth.

Lennie Smish blinked.

To his credit, he did not for an instant doubt the authenticity of the experience. He'd seen stranger sights on Santa Monica Boulevard and hadn't doubted the reality of those apparitions either. His first words were, "Right. How many wishes and how long do I have to make up my mind?"

The genie settled itself comfortably on the floor. It sat down cross-legged on the rug and swelled again to its full size. "In your case," the genie said, "you get one wish only. But you may take as long as you need to decide."

"Hmm," said Lennie, thoughtfully. The last time Lennie had said "Hmm," so thoughtfully, a major studio head had abruptly announced his retirement. But then, suddenly, Lennie realized what the genie had said. "What do you mean—in *my* case?"

The djinn shrugged. "Policy," it said. "That's just the way these things work." But, seeing the look on Lennie's face, it pulled a document out of thin air. "See here? This is the 1990 rider attached to the 1988 contract extension. Section 12, Article II, Paragraph 6, Item A, Schedule 2. Lawyers and other primordial scum. That's you."

Lennie leaned forward to examine the document, but abruptly the genie snatched it back and stashed it away again in thin air. "Sorry, that's a confidential Guild document. I can't let you see it."

"Guild?" Lennie asked.

"WGAW," the efrit explained.

"Wizards, Genies, Angels, Warlocks?" Lennie asked. "I dealt with them once. A fellow named Faust, I think—"

"Writers Guild of America, West," the genie corrected. "*Our* Executive Director is a pit bull."

At last, Lennie's incredulity surfaced. "The *Writers Guild?* But you can't be—"

"Yes, I can," the djinn replied huffily. "I've been a member since 1949. Well, only an associate member, but when I finish my screenplay, I'm sure it'll sell. I have a cousin who knows Spielberg and—''

''Never mind,'' said Lennie, waving his hand in annoyance. ''Let's talk about the bottom line here, my wish.''

''As you command, my master.'' The djinn spread its hands in a florid arm gesture and inclined its muscular upper body in a semblance of a bow. ''How much wealth, love, honor, fame, glory, beauty, and power do you want? I am required by law to caution you, however, that while I must honor your wish to the letter, I must take advantage of every loophole in your wording to thwart the spirit of it.''

''Hmm,'' said Lennie again. And this time he meant it.

The djinn flinched. He knew who Lennie Smish was.

''I'll tell you,'' said Lennie. ''If there's one thing I've always wanted, it's respect.''

''Is that your wish?''

''No,'' said Lennie. ''Not yet. What I want is the respect that comes with success at one's craft. I have always wanted to be a $10,000 an hour lawyer.''

''Ahh,'' said the djinn. ''That's your wish.''

''No,'' said Lennie. ''I am not yet ready to wish. Not until I find a way to phrase this so that there are no loopholes—so you can't thwart it.''

''Ahhhhh,'' said the efrit, approvingly. ''A challenge.'' It licked its chops; its tongue was long and pink and forked. ''Those are the *tastiest* kind.''

Lennie reached over to the table beside his chair and picked up his yellow legal pad and a pencil. At the top of it, he wrote: *Ten thousand dollars an hour.* After a moment, he added, *As many clients as it takes to make me happy.* After a moment's more thought, he scratched that out and wrote, *More than enough work to keep me busy.*

Underneath that, he began making notes:

Clients who can afford to pay.

Clients with winnable cases.

Clients with cases that cannot be settled too quickly.

Resolutions that my clients will be satisfied with.

Lennie Smish thought for a while. He stared across the room at the djinn and pursed his prunelike lips. He gnawed on the end of his pencil while he considered all the ways he might phrase his wish, and all the ways that the efrit might thwart the results.

The djinn grinned at him.

Lennie Smish said, "I think I'm beginning to understand the depth of this problem."

The djinn's grin widened. Its golden teeth flashed like sunset. Sunset Boulevard.

"I believe," said Lennie, "that I am going to have to spend some time researching this. Will you negotiate with me? Will you sign a fair contract?"

The djinn laughed. Its voice boomed like a kettle drum. "I will sign any contract you care to draft. Even you, the great Lennie Smith, cannot write a contract that cannot be thwarted."

"Hmm," said Lennie. A new thought occurred to him and he began scribbling more notes onto his yellow pad. His handwriting was crabbed and tiny; his words looked like spider-tracks. "This is going to take some time," said Lennie.

"No problem," said the djinn. "I can work on my screenplay." The creature materialized a laptop computer and carefully began typing. Occasionally, it chuckled. Once, it materialized a dictionary in midair, paged through it to check the meaning of the word *scrofulous*, then dematerialized the volume and returned to its labors.

Across the room, Lennie scribbled furious notes. More and more ideas kept occurring to him. But one thought overrode every other consideration—this had to be the *greatest* contract of his career, perhaps even the greatest contract that anyone had ever negotiated anywhere. This document would be a model of airtight, watertight, *unbreakable,* krell metal-clad intention.

At one point, the djinn looked up and said, "Oh, by the way—don't forget to add a clause that I can't alter you, your behavior, your motivations, your desires, or your conception of your results. I wouldn't do it anyway, that would be cheating, but you need to be aware that some efrits consider that a fair trick."

Lennie stared at the djinn, astonished. It was *helping* him? But, he dutifully noted the clause. Then he made a note to himself to examine the efrit's suggested phrasing. Was the genie giving him that clause specifically to set up a loophole big enough to drive a producer's ego through?

At last, Lennie put the yellow pad aside and said, "All right, I've outlined the areas I'll need to research. It's going to take longer than I thought, several months at least. But I can do it. I can't rely on boilerplate. I'm going to have to do the whole thing by hand. I'll probably have to release most of my other clients just to put this thing together—''

The djinn didn't even look up. ''Of course,'' it acknowledged. ''That's the way these things work. You're not the first, you know. I doubt you'll be the last.''

''We'll see,'' said Lennie. ''We'll see.''

For the next nine months, Lennie devoted himself solely—eighty hours a week—to his contract. He researched contract law all the way back to Noah. He studied every precedent from Faust to Daniel Webster. He consulted with demonologists, mediums, exorcists, and karmic gurus. He met with scholars of the supernatural from seven different cultures. He interviewed three supreme court justices. He studied linguistics and communication to make sure he understood the precise semantic definition of the words he was using, and the distinctions he was drawing. He studied torts, retorts, and curses. He even met with an emissary from the Pope to ensure that his immortal soul would not be endangered by the contract. He cashed in his savings bonds, withdrew his life savings, sold his Paramount stock, and hired a staff of twelve research assistants; he broke them into three teams—each one would write a clause and the other two teams would try to find a loophole.

After nine exhausting months, Lennie was finished. It took another two weeks to get the contract printed, proofread, corrected, reprinted, proofread again, corrected again, reprinted again, etc. Lennie could not allow even a typographical error to mar the perfection of this document. A forgotten comma had once cost a shipping company forty million dollars. By now, of course, the djinn had finished its screenplay and had begun sending it out to agents. While it waited, the djinn worked patiently on the novelization.

At last, Lennie presented this contract to the djinn. The creature took the document, paged through it slowly, nodding and grunting in reaction to various clauses, subclauses, articles, sections, paragraphs, schedules, tables, and footnotes. It read the contract all the way through to the last page and looked up at Lennie with a happy grin.

"This is really a very nice piece of work," it said. "My compliments. This work is definitely worth ten thousand dollars an hour."

"So you'll sign it?"

"Of course," said the djinn. "Hand me that pen, will you?"

"You have to sign this with your legal name!" Lennie Smith insisted.

The djinn looked up, annoyed. "Give me a break," it said. "A contract this elegant requires a loophole every bit as elegant—and every bit as carefully worked out." It scrawled its signature in elegant Arabic script.

"Aha!" said Lennie Smish, grabbing the contract and waving it in the djinn's face. "I got you now!"

"The djinn looked at Lennie without emotion. "You do?" it asked.

"I won't agree to any contract you sign. Because you won't sign it unless you find a loophole. The deal's off."

"I'm afraid it's not that easy," the djinn said. "You have to avail yourself of my services."

"No, I don't. I haven't signed. And I have the right to back out of the deal any time before the contract is finalized." Lennie Smish produced his bill. "But whether the contract is executed or not, you still have to pay for the services of the lawyer. Here's my bill for three thousand hours of labor, plus the labor of my staff and associated expenses. It comes to thirty-six million dollars, payable in legal tender only, cash, check, or money order—no coins or bills under a hundred, please."

The djinn began laughing heartily. "I do believe you have caught me," it said. "I really do believe that you have found a way to get your wish without getting tricked. I'm mightily impressed." It began plucking suitcases out of the air, thirty-six of them in all. Lennie grabbed at the cases and began opening them suspiciously.

The djinn shook its head. "The money is legal," it said in annoyance. "United States of America, *e pluribus unum.* All that stuff. I don't cheat. I trick. There's a difference."

Lennie stacked the suitcases in the hall closet, the spare bedroom, the service porch, and the kitchen. He hadn't realized that thirty-six million dollars would take up so much space. When he finished, the djinn asked him to sign a receipt. He did so suspiciously; but he had no choice.

"All right," said the djinn. "Our business is concluded. You got your wish. I get my freedom."

"Begone," said Lennie, glad to have the creature finally out of his apartment.

The djinn—and the lamp—vanished.

Two days later, there was a knock on the door. Lennie Smish answered it and a process server handed him a subpoena. He was being sued. By the djinn. For failure to negotiate in good faith.

That was only the first subpoena.

In the next three months, forty-six more lawsuits were filed against Lennie Smish. Everything from sexual harassment in the workplace to violations of the RICO statutes. And that was only the beginning. It seemed as if every court case, every settlement, every contract he'd ever worked on, was bubbling back up to the surface of the legal quagmire.

It took a while, but Lennie finally figured it out. *He'd gotten his wish.*

He was a ten-thousand dollar an hour lawyer, and he had more work than he could handle.

*From your era and location, we go back to my own,
a time and place filled with magic and genies. Not
all of them lived in lamps, of course—and not everyone who commanded them had my intelligence.*

*Some were foolish men, some were selfish, and
some—a very few—were capable of wisdom.*

You wish a demonstration? Certainly.

Once upon a time there were three thieves. . . .

THE THREE THIEVES

by Lois Tilton

There once were three thieves who decided to rob the house
of a wealthy merchant. Of these three, one thief had lost
an eye in a brawl, the second had lost a hand to the exe-
cutioner, and the third had lost that which distinguishes
the bull from the ox, the stallion from the gelding, the
cockerel from the capon—in short, the third was a eunuch.

Now the merchant was absent on a long voyage, and,
alas for the thieves, they found his house empty, without
a single piece of gold or a jewel to be found. All they
could discover, in the darkest, dustiest corner of a closet,
was a small tarnished brass chest, bound and locked with
a strong iron chain.

The three robbers bore the chest off at once to their lair,
wondering what treasure it might contain. Eagerly they
brought tools to force open the chain, and when the links
were broken they flung open the lid of the chest, jostling
each other to see what was inside and to be the first to
claim a share. What they discovered there was both less
and more than they had imagined, for the chest contained
only a single gold ring set with the most perfect ruby any
mortal man had ever seen.

After a brief argument the thieves decided to take the
ring to the marketplace, where they would sell it and di-
vide the proceeds equally among themselves. But each thief

mistrusted his companions and secretly lusted to keep the ring for himself alone. So they quarreled, each one insisting, "I, my brothers, will take the ring to the jewelers while you two remain here and wait for my return with the gold."

But as the three robbers fought over the ring, suddenly the room began to fill with black smoke, which coalesced into the huge and terrible figure of a djinn. He was in the form of a man, with jewels in his turban and bearing a sword of the finest Damascus steel.

At this sight, the thieves fell onto their knees trembling with awe. But the djinn bellowed in a voice like brass: "Who is he here who is the master of the ring? For I am its slave and am bound to grant the wishes of whoever wears it."

At once each of the three thieves began to clamor that he and he alone was the one true owner of the ring, the one shouting, "It is mine and mine alone!" and the others, "No, he lies, the ring is truly mine!"

At last, with the djinn growing visibly impatient with their quarrel, the three thieves were finally forced to concede that they all three were equal owners of the ring, no one more than the other two.

"In that case," pronounced the djinn, "I agree to fulfill one wish for each of the three of you—one wish and no more. Simply rub the face of the ruby while wearing the ring upon your hand, and whatever you wish will be granted you."

Now the first thief was the quickest in his greed, and he snatched up the ring before the others and slipped it onto the finger of his right hand. He then thought to himself, "If I can wish for anything at all, perhaps I should ask to have the sight in my missing eye restored. But then I would be no richer than I am now, and the djinn will grant me only one wish." Thus he debated with himself, but in the end he thought, "Well, I have done well enough for myself up to now with only one eye, so what need do I have for two?"

So deciding, he rubbed the face of the jewel as the djinn had described and said, "I wish for a mountain of gold as high as I am tall."

The djinn bowed low, saying, "I hear and obey," and in an instant he had returned to smoke and a mountain of

gold had appeared in the hovel of the three robbers, a pile
of coins fully as high as the one-eyed man was tall. Crying
aloud in joy, the thief fell on the gold and began to toss
the coins into the air, exclaiming to his companions how
large a palace he would build, how magnificent the clothing he would wear, and what horses he would buy, and
what slaves, and concubines, each more plump and allur-
ing than the last.

Then the second thief said to him, "Brother, give the
ring to me now, so I can make my own wish."

Now this thief was an unscrupulous and calculating man
who had lost his right hand in his youth for the crime of
relieving merchants of their purses in the marketplace. So
when the one-eyed thief handed him the ring, he clutched
it in his only fist, thinking:

"Look at the pile of gold that fool has wished for! But
if I were sole master of the ring, I could have wished for
twice that, and gotten my hand back besides. The djinn
has only granted three wishes among us, and now the first
is already spent. But why should I be content with only
one? Why should I not have my missing hand again and
the gold as well?"

So the evil thief awkwardly slipped the ring onto his
only hand and rubbed the face of the ruby, and the djinn
appeared and bowed low, asking, "O Master of the ring,
what do you command?"

The thief answered, "My one wish is for my right hand
to be restored, as strong as when it was cut from my
wrist."

"I hear and obey," the djinn declared, and at once the
second thief had two strong hands, each as sound as the
other.

Without hesitating, the wicked thief sprang upon his un-
suspecting one-eyed companion and strangled him to
death.

Now the eunuch as well as his two brothers in thievery
had been considering whether he ought to use his only
wish to ask for wealth or to have his long-lost parts restored to him. Most bitterly had he seen other men enjoying the delights of the flesh which he could not even
imagine. And yet he longed for riches every bit as much
as the other two had. "Which is worse," he asked himself, "to be a whole man and a beggar in the streets, or

to own great riches with no wife or son to inherit my wealth?''

But now when he saw the murderer gathering up the gold with his two sound hands, he began to see how he might have his manhood and the gold as well. So he said, ''Well done, brother. Now pass me the ring so I can make my own wish.''

The murderer laughed and said, ''Why should I give you the third wish when I can keep it for myself?''

''No, brother,'' said the eunuch. ''The djinn granted each of us just one wish apiece. The ring can bring you no more good. Only let me put it on my finger, and I will give you half the gold I wish for.''

But the murderer still refused, making such terrible threats that the eunuch feared for his life. He fled from their lair and began to tear his hair and clothes, setting up such a weeping and lamentation that the djinn appeared, demanding to know the reason for this unseemly and exccssive display of grief.

''O mighty Djinn,'' the eunuch wailed, ''I meant to use my only wish to ask that my manhood be restored to me, but now my companion has kept the ring for himself and left me with nothing!''

The djinn scowled fearsomely. ''The quarrels of men mean nothing to me. When you are master of the ring, then your wish shall be fulfilled.''

''Then, O mighty Lord of the Ifrit,'' the eunuch said at last, when all his pleas had been unavailing, ''let me beg you for one favor, in the Name of the Compassionate. I ask nothing as the master of the ring, only now I am destitute and in fear of my life. Take me with you to your palace and let me serve as the lowliest of the eunuchs in your harem.''

The djinn agreed, and picking up the eunuch under one arm he carried him with the swiftness of the wind across the barren desert to his own palace in the land of the djinns, where indeed he was a mighty lord, and the eunuch became the least of the slaves in his harem. There he was astonished, for in the gardens of this palace were all the delights that are told of in paradise: fountains flowing with milk, wine and honey, trees bearing every kind of succulent ripe fruit, and the air perfumed with the petals of a thousand different flowers.

The harem of the djinn was filled with his wives and slaves and maiden daughters, each so beautiful as to make the houris of paradise hide their faces in shame. They bathed in the fountains of milk, and they were clothed in the sheerest silks and the most glittering jewels. Seeing them, their naked limbs all glowing white as milk as they reclined on silken cushions, the thief's bitterness was acute, for the means of restoring his manhood had been stolen from him, and here was a banquet laid that he could neither touch nor taste.

Of all of the djinn's harem, there was one maiden, his youngest daughter, whose beauty outshone the rest as the moon at night outshines the stars. Her skin was like a peeled almond, her mouth a sweet date, her belly a bowl of wild honey. When she danced to the music of the flute and cymbals her grace and form were like the gazelle. "Surely," thought the eunuch, "any mortal man would burn to death with lust at her touch." For he knew that the djinns are the offspring of fire, even as men are made of dust.

So the eunuch took the youngest daughter of the djinn and wrapped her in veils. Then he carried her from her father's palace, across the barren desert to the city where he had been a thief. There his former companion now lived in an opulent palace of marble and ivory, but it was a hovel compared to the palace of the djinn.

The eunuch went to the door and asked to see the master, and he was admitted into the presence of the murderer, his former companion in thievery.

"Brother," said the eunuch humbly, bowing low as a suppliant, "I have brought you a gift. All I ask in return is the use of the ring, so I can make my single wish."

Turning to the daughter of the djinn, he removed the veils so that her face could be seen. The moment the murderer saw her beauty, like the full moon rising in the first hour of night, he was filled with such lust that he could think of nothing else but possessing her.

At once he agreed to what the eunuch asked, pulling the ring carelessly from his finger. But the moment he embraced the daughter of fire, the heat of his lust burst into flames and he was burned to a heap of ashes.

Laughing and rejoicing at the success of his plan, the eunuch slipped the ring onto his finger and rubbed the face of the ruby. In an instant a cloud of black smoke appeared and took the form of the djinn, who said, "O Master of the ring, what do you command?"

"I wish for my manhood to be restored to me," said the eunuch.

"I hear and obey," the djinn replied. In an instant it was done, and the thief was an entire man, just as if the gelder's knife had never touched him.

But alas for the thief, in his greed for wealth and vengeance, he had forgotten to restore the veils to the djinn's daughter. Now, when he looked upon her as a whole man, he was smitten with a terrible lust. Never in all his life as a eunuch had he known such a sensation. His loins burned, and he knew that he would die if he could not possess the beauty that stood before him.

Desire robbed him of all his reason, and he cried, "O Mighty Djinn, will you give me your youngest daughter for my wife?"

The djinn only laughed scornfully. "How could you pay her bride price, mortal man? Surely you know that in my own land I would not kennel a dog in a hovel such as this."

But the thief held out his hand, with the ruby ring gleaming on his finger. "Here, take this as the bride price for your daughter, and call no mortal man Master again."

The djinn agreed at once and gladly bestowed the hand of his youngest daughter in exchange for his freedom.

But as soon as the former eunuch embraced his bride, the daughter of that race created from fire, the heat of his lust ignited and he was burned to a heap of ashes, just as his companion had been.

Thus may all thieves be rewarded.

In books, in the literature of our race, lies the accumulated knowledge of the ages. Why, you would not even have heard of me had there been no books in which my adventures were codified.

Now, I realize that libraries, those residences of books, seem unromantic to some and dull to others. But magic is not confined to adventurers, and wondrous things can happen in the storehouse of ideas. . . .

STACKED

by Josepha Sherman

You find the damnedest things in a museum library's stacks. And I mean that quite literally.

I wouldn't have been down there at all if it hadn't been for budget cutbacks. When you're a museum curator in a city strapped for funds (and "museum" and "city" are about as much identification as I'm going to give), no one's going to listen to your plea for more staff. Particularly not when you're a fairly new curator, and a young woman to boot, and the subject matter of your department, Near Eastern Antiquities, is momentarily less than fashionable thanks to politics. Oh, I was allowed to hire someone to replace the assistant who'd quit last week—but the fact that museums pay as badly as universities cut down on applicants.

At the moment I was serving as my own assistant, which meant that instead of overseeing the collection or planning new exhibitions, I was just trying to keep things running smoothly.

It wasn't easy: the temp who'd lasted one disastrous week had, among other things, misfiled "Assyria" under "Akkad" and "Sumerian" under "Scythian," and in one surge of confused energy, returned texts that should have been in my admittedly overcrowded office to the museum library. Of course, one of those missing texts was the very one I needed to complete the monograph that would get me off the museum's "publish or perish" hook for another year.

I could have been a writer of historical romances, like that Elizabeth What's-Her-Name. I'd even started selling my fiction. But no, I had to stick to museum work.

Ah, well, I *did* enjoy being a curator. When I was allowed to be one.

With a sigh I told the central operator to put all calls on hold, ran the gauntlet of the Arms and Armor Hall, dodging classloads of screaming children, and dove into the quiet of the museum library. The library, of course, is as understaffed as any curatorial department, and I wound up hunting in the silent, lonely lower depths of the library stacks by myself.

Since one of the facts of life of any library seems to be a fair percentage of misshelved books, I wasn't particularly surprised to find a dusty, leatherbound book jammed into the row where the text on Anshan pottery I was hunting should have been. That the interloper was an antique book wasn't surprising, either: there are a good many old volumes in the stacks, some of them dating back to the sixteenth century.

I should, of course, have just set the thing aside for someone to reshelve and gone on looking for the Anshan volume. But who could resist taking a peek inside?

If there had ever been any title on the binding, it had long since been worn away by time. Warily opening the book, hearing the ancient binding creak, I found one of those florid sixteenth century frontispieces, all swirling vegetation, and a date proving the book had been printed fairly early in that century. The title was in such ornate, archaic script it took me a moment to realize it was a late medieval form of German. Something about "The Fantastical Adventures . . ."

Ah. The twentieth century doesn't have a monopoly on Godawful fantasy series; those have been around since the first bard discovered they got him the most free dinners. This was very probably an early sixteenth century version of "young hero with magic sword and elves," and—

Now, I know I was holding the book cautiously; I wasn't taking a chance on its fragile binding falling apart. But I

swear that the thing suddenly jumped out of my hand! I
snatched wildly at it, but the book hit the floor with a
sharp crack that could only be the binding giving way.

Oh, hell!

A small cloud of dust and crumbled leather swirled up—
and continued to swirl. I staggered back against a book-
shelf, staring at this impossible, whirling cloud that had
somehow grown man-tall and was condensing into—

He was average in height, maybe an inch or two taller
than my own 5'5", and somewhat stocky of build. His skin
was that smooth *café au lait* you seldom see outside of
models. Nothing alarming there. Nothing alarming about
his plain white turban and caftan, either. Nothing to make
you think he was anything other than a slightly overage
exchange student.

One who had just materialized out of a dust cloud. One
whose staring eyes were red. Not bloodshot: most definitely, most blazingly red. A djinn. This was an honest-
to-God djinn, a—a refugee from the *Arabian Nights,*
standing right here in the middle of the library stacks.

"I think you want the Islamic Arts Department," I said
weakly.

He blinked, but went right on staring at me as though I
wasn't at all what he'd expected. Of course I wasn't, my
mind gibbered, I was female, and unveiled and clad in
what for him must be a shockingly revealing dress, exposing my arms and legs. If only I wasn't remembering those
nasty fairy tales in which some foolish human frees a djinn
and has the ungrateful, evil being turn on him. . . .

But this djinn didn't look particularly evil. He did nothing more alarming than bow the most incredibly complex
bow I've seen this side of an old camels-and-magic-carpets
movie.

"You haff freed me, my lady."

That did it. I could accept books jumping out of my
hands. I could even accept a djinn materializing out of a
cloud of dust. But when said djinn spoke with a bad German accent— No. Oh, no. There were limits.

"You just stay right here!" I said, or something equally
inane, and got the hell out of there.

He didn't chase me. By the time I made it back up to
the library proper, I had managed to at least feign composure, and by the time I had traveled the length of the

museum, back through the nice, human chaos of the Arms and Armor Hall to my crowded little office and closed the door firmly behind me, I had almost convinced myself that what had happened had been some beautifully elaborate practical joke by a co-worker.

Who was it? Jeff Browning? The curator of Modern American Art had a passion for special effects. *But how did he manage that column of dust? And that materialization of—*

"My lady?"

I whirled, just barely stifling a yell.

The djinn was standing before a wall of bookcases, looking as matter of fact as though he'd always been there. "The door was locked," I told him, eyeing the distance between me and the telephone. "How did you get in here?"

The djinn shrugged gracefully. "Locks are nothing to my kind."

I would never reach the phone in time to call Security. And yelling for help—no one would hear me over the child-shrieks from the Arms and Armor Hall.

Suddenly what he'd said—or rather, how he'd said it—struck me. "You've lost the German accent."

The djinn actually looked embarrassed. "Your pardon for that mistake, my lady." The accent now, if anything, was generic Near Eastern. "I can speak most languages—a language spell, you see—but I had been pent up in that book for so long, it influenced my tongue."

"What were you doing in a *book*? I thought bottles or lamps were the thing for your kind."

"Ah, well, they are, for those of us who are unfortunate enough to be snared at all." His smile was rather wistful. "Unfortunate, indeed, are those djinns who were so punished for being only the *tiniest* bit wicked."

Oh, great. Just how wicked was wicked? Granted, he looked innocent enough right now, but all the folktales said djinns were master shape-shifters. What if his real form was something so monstrous. . . .

Keep him talking, I told myself, and prodded: "The book."

"Ah, yes. I *was* encased within a small earthenware jar, and there I feared to stay forever. But over the centuries,

my jar was found and sold.'' Insulted pride flashed in the
fiery eyes. ''Unopened! As a—a curiosity!''

''We all have our off days. Who bought you?''

The djinn shrugged again. ''A scholar. One who fancied
himself a magician. Faustus, he called himself in his bar-
baric tongue.''

''Johann Faustus?'' I yelped. ''*The* Faust?''

He blinked. ''There was more than one?''

''Never mind. So . . . uh . . . Faust opened your jar.''

''And panicked the minute he saw what he had freed!
He popped me into a book, locking me into the binding
before I could even stretch my limbs! A *book!*''

That was said with such indignation the bookcase behind him shook. A text on Luristan bronzes came tumbling
down, but the djinn shot out a hand, caught the heavy
thing as though it weighed nothing, and stuck it back on
a shelf, all without looking. As I stared (part of my mind
whispering insanely that he'd make a spectacular short-
stop), he continued in a savage mutter:

''And it wasn't even a text of wisdom, some noble tome
of which I could be proud. Oh, no! That thrice accursed
charlatan trapped me in a—a—a *romance,* a stupid, badly
written, full-of-trashy-magic *romance!*''

Don't think bodice-ripper; he meant what we call heroic
fantasy. ''It was probably the only book he could reach in
time.''

''Ha!'' The bookcases shook again, and the djinn hastily lowered his voice, repeating in a savage whisper, ''Ha.
How would *you* like to be stuck in the middle of mindless
trash for centuries?'' He shuddered. ''The hero had fewer
brains than his sword. And his lady . . . no sultan worth
his throne would have such a weepy, silly, useless little
thing in his *harim!*''

The djinn drew himself up to his full not-very-tall
height. ''After the first hundred years,'' he said grimly,
''I vowed that whosoever should free me from my captivity should be granted three wishes. But no one did. After
the second hundred years, I vowed that whosoever should
free me from my captivity should be granted one wish.
But no one did. And after the third hundred years, I vowed
that whosoever freed me from my captivity should be
granted one thing: the choice of his death!''

Suddenly, subtly, he had grown to fill the whole office,

bent double against the ceiling, looming over me in a cloud of darkness out of which his eyes blazed terribly. I shrank back, wondering if it would do any good to start hurling *The Dictionary of the Sumerian Language* at him, volumes one through ten.

But just when I was hefting the first volume in my hands, picturing the *National Star* headline: CURATOR SLAIN BY UFO ALIEN, the djinn sighed and just as suddenly was his former, relatively innocuous self.

"Don't be afraid," he continued wearily. "After the fourth hundred years, I grew bored with the whole idea."

"It's . . . uh . . . been five hundred years now. What does that mean?"

The djinn smiled, revealing teeth that were dazzlingly white and just a touch too sharp to belong in a human mouth. "Why, my lady and savior, O breaker of bindings, it means we have completed a cycle." He bowed his elaborate, elegant bow. "Now, my most charming and lovely liberator, I grant you those long-ago promised three wishes."

I sat down hard, fortunately landing on a chair rather than the floor.

I don't believe this. I don't believe any of this. This is my office, dammit, there's nothing more prosaically real than an office in a museum, and I can't really be hearing a djinn granting me three wishes—

"Oh, hell," I murmured, then straightened in alarm. "That wasn't a wish! Give me a chance to think." The last thing I wanted was anything from a being who could catch heavy books as though they were feathers and who, when the whim struck him, could fill a whole room with menace. But if I didn't ask for *something*. . . .

"Do you wish riches?" the djinn asked helpfully. "I can bring you the hidden wealth of the earth. Or wisdom. This—this mansion—"

"Museum," I corrected.

"Ah. This *museum* seems dedicated to gathering the wisdom of the ages. I could help you gather more."

"Not in *this* world you can't! Look, djinn—ah, I don't suppose you have a name?"

"Dahnash. That is my use-name: Dahnash."

"All right, Dahnash. The only way you can help me gather that wisdom is if you eliminate a certain Near East-

ern head of state so we can reopen our dig out there. Can
you do that?''

"Ah . . . no. I am not an ifrit. I fear such tampering is
not permitted my kind.'' He hesitated. "I could bring the
wisdoms to you, though.''

"No! If I accepted undocumented artifacts, I'd be ar-
rested for dealing in stolen art!''

Dahnash stirred impatiently, literally, his shape growing
and shrinking dizzyingly. "Then choose another wish.
Quickly.''

Oh, sure, quickly. "All right,'' I said after a frantic
moment, "I've got one. I wish you to endow this department with enough money to let me a) hire a new assistant,
b) get the Board of Directors off my neck, and c) expand
our pathetic excuse of a gallery.''

"So be it!''

Dahnash drew himself up proudly. Arms upflung, eyes
shut, he murmured something intricate and alien under his
breath. The room seemed to darken. Bookcases trembled,
windows rattled, and somewhere, far away, thunder rumbled.

And faded. There was a tiny clink. Another. I scrambled to my feet, and the djinn and I stared at the floor. Or
rather, at the handful of small change littering it.

"That's it?'' I asked faintly.

"Yes.'' It was almost a wail.

"I suppose this means wishing for an end to world hunger or disease is out.''

"Please, lady, don't mock me!'' Dahnash looked almost at the edge of tears. "I never dreamed. . . . Being
locked up in that accursed book so long has—has *trivial-
ized* my powers!''

Wonderful. Not only did I have a djinn bothering me,
but he was an inept one as well. God, this was ridiculous!
I was a twentieth century curator, dammit, not some—
some damsel with a dulcimer!

"I wish you'd just go away!''

That burst out without my thinking. I nearly jumped out
of my skin when air roared in to fill the spot where Dahnash had been. The quick, sharp wind tore at my hair and
the pages of books, and sent every paper in the office flying as I stood and stared and continued to stare.

"W–well,'' I said at last, "that's that.''

But the next day, as I was wandering through the Near Eastern Antiquities' gallery before it opened to the public, making sure all was well (yes, I know that Security and Maintenance take care of such things, but I like being *sure*), the small relief of Ashurbanipal, that regal terror of seventh century B.C. Nineveh, spoke to me.

"Lady? Oh, most beauteous liberator?"

When I managed to get my heart back to its normal speed, I hissed at him, "Dahnash! Get out of there!"

He materialized as smoothly as any ghost. A rather sheepish, embarrassed ghost.

"I thought I'd wished you away," I whispered.

"You didn't specify exactly *where* you wished me, lady, so there was nothing for me to do but wait here with the King of Kings for you to appear. There *is* still the matter of the third wish, you know."

"I don't need any more pocket change littering the floor, thank you," I said sharply, then felt an absurd pang of guilt when he winced. Hastily, I asked, "How'd you know old Ashurbanipal's title? You can read English?"

"Oh, no. I remember him. You see—"

"You *remember him?* Dahnash, he lived over two thousand years ago!"

He made a self-deprecating little gesture. "I *am* of the djinns, after all."

I eyed him with new wonder. "So you knew old Ashurbanipal, eh? Come on, let's get back to the office and you can tell me all about him."

Long before we were there, I was hooked, and not just because of the subject matter. Dahnash turned out to be a born storyteller. I'd expected him to use the flowery language, all but incomprehensible to a Westerner, of the true *Arabian Nights*. Instead, his words were clear and well-chosen, conjuring image after image of the distant past.

Of course, it wasn't so distant for Dahnash. Not only could he tell me all about life in seventh century B.C. Assyria as though he'd been there last week, he could remember back a good ways further, to the second millennium BC rulers Sargon of Akkad ("A brave man— and one who made sure the people knew it.") and Gudea of Sumer ("A classic bureaucrat—but oh, what a wonderful organizer.") I reminded myself that the djinns, according to all the folklore surrounding their kind, were much older than Islam and the world of Scheherazade.

I reminded myself, too, that only some branches of the family were demonic. Dahnash's "*only the* tiniest *bit wicked*" echoed in my mind, but looking at the djinn now, his face animated and anything but wicked, I had to wonder if some human zealot way back when hadn't confused wickedness with non-Islamic mischief.

Dahnash broke off his running commentary as we entered the office, staring at what was left of yesterday's disorder. His face registered such stern disapproval I found myself apologizing, "Haven't had the time to straighten everything up."

"Have you no servants?"

"The . . . uh . . . cleaning staff doesn't come around every day, and—Dahnash, no! What are you doing?"

He had started chanting in some melodious tongue that certainly wasn't Arabic or Farsi or any other language I knew. And as he chanted, papers neatly restacked themselves on my desk and books put themselves back on their rightful shelves. I followed him around the room, checking his handiwork.

"That's wonderful!" I exclaimed when he was done. "If you weren't a djinn, I'd hire you as a cleaning man on the spot!"

But he sank to a newly cleared chair, head in hands. "Ah, yes," Dahnash murmured. "I can reshelve books. What a wonderful thing."

"Look, I didn't mean—"

"And that's all I can do." The djinn raised his head wearily, the flaming red of his eyes dying to sad embers. "I had almost forgotten, what with the pleasure you were taking in my stories. But now the cruel truth has struck me once more. Lady, I was testing my powers all this night. They are gone, nearly all of them, lost somewhere back *then* or faded into nothingness through the long years of my captivity."

"I'm sorry," I said helplessly.

Dahnash let out a great sigh of despair. "I never was one of the Mighty Ones, I admit that freely, but at least back in the days when I was free I had a *place*, I had a *time*, I had a *purpose*! This world of yours, this world of science, of glass and steel and machines that do your bid-

ding without the need of spells, is so very strange to me.
Everyone, everything I know is gone. What,'' he asked
softly, ''is to become of me?''

What *do* you do with an out-of-work djinn?

That's when the idea hit me. ''Dahnash,'' I said, kneeling so I could take his hands (humanly warm hands, they
were, with not a sign of talons), ''there's still the third
wish.''

He smiled wanly. ''Yes. For what good it will do either
one of us.''

''I . . . can't use it to send you back, can I?''

''You are kind, lady. But, no. There can be no backward
travel for my kind. Here I am, and here I must live.''

''I see. Then I have a little proposition to make you.''
I pulled a hand free to gesture around my office. ''You
enjoy making order out of chaos like this, don't you?''

''Yes. The djinns used to mock me for such an . . .
undjinnlike trait.''

He blushed, he actually blushed.

''Well, now! You've given me some fascinating information, solved some matters archaeologists have puzzled
over for years—but as a curator, I can't use any of it!''

''Why not?''

''Come now, Dahnash! If anyone asked me how I knew,
for example, that Sargon was an ambidextrous swordsman
when there aren't any records of the time to back me up,
I'd be laughed out of my job.''

''Then I'm useless to you as a source of knowledge as
well.''

''Look, I told you I had a proposition to make you about
that third wish. Are you going to listen to me? Or would
you rather wallow in self-pity?'' *Oh, great, I'm threatening someone who could probably break me in half like a
pot shard.*

But Dahnash looked anything but menacing. His eyes
were red-brown now, almost a human shade, flickering
with curiosity and just a hint of hope. ''I will listen.''

''Good. Now, here's what I propose. . . .''

Halfway through my little recitation, Dahnash started to
smile. By the time I was finished with it, he was laughing
outright.

''But will it—can it—can we?''

"Hell, yes. We both know worse stuff gets published all the time. All the time, indeed!"

"Yes, oh, my clever lady, yes! It may not be a truly magical wish, but it shall be done!"

And that, oh, most courteous of readers, as Dahnash might say, is how the Near Eastern Antiquities Department got its new assistant, one Dahnash ibn Djinn, a political refugee with, as the museum secretaries twitter, the most *incredible* red-brown eyes. I teach him about the present, he teaches me about the past. He's happy, I'm happy, and between us the gallery and office have never looked so good.

But, of course, that's only part of my wish. Look at the bestseller lists. Notice *Bright Star of Akkad,* that runaway historical romance, the latest in a long chain of successes by the exotically named Jinnifer Blythe. Even the reviewers, who usually frown on the genre, crow about Ms. Blythe's knowledge of the past and the wonderfully accurate details in her books: "Almost," they jest, "as though she lived back then!" They like the idea that a good share of her royalties go straight into an endowment fund for the Near Eastern Antiquities Department, for which the curator is properly grateful.

Everyone wonders who the mysterious Ms. Blythe might be. No one ever sees her, of course. No one (save our editor, of course) knows dear Jinnifer is a team of two.

And, as should be obvious by now, not even said editor knows that only one half of the writing team is human.

There is a very thin dividing line between the miracles of magic and the miracles of science.

Back when I first found my lamp, I learned that my genie was bound by rules so rigid that they seemed like science.

And over the centuries, science has spawned discoveries, from airplanes to chemotherapy, that seem like magic.

Which is the more powerful? Magic, of course. For the invention that has shaped more of your lives than any other came about because of it. . . .

SLAVES OF THE MAGIC LAMP

by Anthony R. Lewis

In a cozy pocket universe Vashti, the Cat Who Walks Between the Worlds, was washing her litter and educating them in the traditional manner. A backhanded swat rolled the noisy tom kitten to the edge of space whence he returned in the opposite direction. Vashti stretched and yawned. Instantly, the kittens clamored, "O mother ours, if thou be other than sleepy, do tell us some of thy pleasant tales."

And Vashti washed her whiskers and began in the ancient manner, "It had reached me, O Kittens of Chaos, that the good Baron had need of your mother to pass on a favor that he, the Baron, owed. And since she was, likewise, indebted to him—but that tale is not for this telling—she put off her form as a cat and, as a human, traveled to Earth, even unto the world of humans. . . .

The 1931 air was full of carcinogenic hydrocarbons and nicotine derivatives as Vashti left the street and entered the office building in downtown New York. It was warmer in the lobby, where a quick check of the directory confirmed that Eugene Jannson Associates, Advertising was on the fourteenth floor. Actually it was the thirteenth floor, but this civilization had an unnatural aversion to that number. As the elevator operator took her up, he sneaked an evaluation from the top of her red-gold hair, peeping out from under her cloche down to her neatly-shod feet and back again. Vashti ignored him. She expected to be admired; it was her heritage as a cat.

She entered the office and preempted the receptionist's query, "Miss Vashti Shah, for her nine o'clock appointment with Mr. Jannson."

"Mr. Jannson never has appointments at nine." Smirk. The receptionist also evaluated her, but as a potential rival. "You must have made a dreadful mistake. Thank you."

"Now, dear, just look in the appointment book. You'll find it there—in your own hand."

A brief glance and a head shake confirmed this. "I don't understand."

"Quite likely," Vashti replied, as she walked toward the inner office. On the way she wrinkled her nose and sniffed. "The cheaper forms of alcohol do affect one's memory so."

"Yeah! But my hair didn't come out of a bottle. . . ."

Enough. Vashti stopped and turned. She held her left hand in front of the receptionist's face. "Don't be catty, dear." The glove tore as five claws slid through the supple kid leather. "Leave that to professionals." Savoring the look on the girl's face, she entered the inner office. Rats, she thought, that's another garment ruined. I'll never get used to wearing clothing.

Jannson turned as she closed the door, "Who are you?"

"The Baron sent me, Mr. Jannson. He said you have a problem."

Jannson's coffee cup halted on its way to his lips. He looked at her and then completed the action, sipping the steaming brew. "If the Baron truly sent you, then you should call me Hassan." He smiled. "And you are?"

"My name is Vashti."

He inclined his head. "Of you I have heard, My Lady. Worlds Walker and Shape Changer—well met, I say." He put down the coffee. "May I offer you some coffee or other refreshment?"

"A cup of sweet cream, perhaps."

"Hearkening and obedience, O Lady." He rose with ophidian grace to grant her desire.

Vashti alternately sipped and lapped her cream. Having made herself known, she removed her gloves and awaited Hassan's opening of the matter. Politeness demanded no less.

"Observe this office, O Cat," said Hassan with a sweeping gesture. "Know that I, one of the djinns, have been successful in the world of men (through the grace of the Compassionate), using only the skills of the world of men. All this have I done, even putting aside my powers for the sake of this game. But it is all empty, for my greatest desire cannot be met. My fellow djinns will mock me and jeer at me. . . ."

Since he seemed to be able to go on interminably, Vashti put down her empty cup and raised a hand, open palm toward Hassan. "And this, thy great desire is . . . ?"

He opened a desk drawer and pulled out a handful of magazines with brightly garish covers. These he spread about the desktop. Vashti read titles such as *Oriental Stories, Weird Tales, Argosy Weekly,* and *Munsey's All-Story.* "There is nothing for it but that my tales shall be printed in these."

"And the problem is?"

"To a man, these editors have rejected my stories; they have rejected me. Even I, Hassan the Djinn, who created Alaeddin and the tale of the wonderful lamp. I, Hassan, Slave of the Lamp, whose tale is the centerpiece of the *Alf Laylah wa Laylah.*" He paused. "Or would have been, had not some of the djinn, who loved not true literature, conspired to have my tale excluded. As then, so it is now. The true artist cannot get appreciation."

Vashti looked into the bottom of her cup. There was a bit of cream there, so she picked it up on her finger and transferred the last of the fluid into her mouth. "But Hassan, Burton put your tale into the Supplementary Nights," she paused; her upper lip twitched twice as she thought. "He had it as nights 514 to 591."

"Burton! What care I for the thoughts of an infidel? It is the judgment of my fellow djinn that was corrupted." Here, he rent his shirt. "My liver is constricted."

Vashti thought to move on. "Tell me, O Hassan. How were you placed in the lamp? And how were you bound to the wishes of its owner?"

"Hah!" he snorted, and a thin wisp of smoke trickled from one nostril. "Know that none of the djinn reside in lamps nor in bottles nor in rings nor in any manner of

such object. This is an error introduced by Frankish re-
dactors who, like the current editors (may the Merciful
grant them enlightenment even as He hurls them into the
deepest pits of Iblis), know not their authors nor do they
appreciate them. The objects are but tocsins that call to us
in the realm of the djinns.''

"And these then compel you to their summons?''

"Nay. For none compels the djinns, save the Most-High
(and Sulayman bin-Daoud, upon whom be peace, who
learned much of the djinns' secrets). These objects are set
out, even as a fisherman casts bait.''

He was about to continue when Vashti asked, ''And you
fish for. . . ?''

"For stories, O Cat. For tales that will astonish and
delight down through the ages. For what other purpose did
Allah create the djinns and Mankind if not to create great
tales? Such is one of the greatest forms of worship.''

He refilled his coffee cup, added a pungent spice (''am-
bergris,'' Vashti identified it) and continued with his tale.

"I took this boy Alaeddin, a nothing, the son of a dead
tailor, and made him a sultan in the city of Al-Kal'as in
China.''

"China?''

"A literary convention, O Sitt Vashti. A label for any
far-off land beyond the daily purview of the Faithful. The
true site might cause offense. And this marvelous story,
this tale for the ages—what happened to it? Uncultured
ones, offspring of diseased camels, rejected it.''

"And did they give reasons?''

"Oh, yes. False ones. They claimed that Alaeddin's
character changed without motivation; that I transformed
him from a street urchin into the confidant of kings without any reason. Who needs reasons? Who would rather be
an urchin than the companion of kings and the husband of
one with a face like a full moon and . . .'' He stopped
here. ''I do not mean to give offense.''

"None is taken, good Hassan. Recall, that though I take
this form for convenience, I am a cat (and laugh at the
conventions of mankind).''

Here he was struck by an idea. ''Have you read my tale?''

"Yes. Who can call themselves literate who has not read
the *Alf Laylah wa Laylah*?''

Under his breath: ''Certain Frankish magazine editors.'' To Vashti: ''And what did you think? Please give me your honest opinion.''

Vashti paused. She knew that by ''honest opinion,'' he meant unrestricted approbation. She temporized, ''There were some aspects I did not understand then. Perhaps you could open them to me.''

''Such would be my pleasure.''

''One is the Ring. Alaeddin uses it to leave the Cave of the Treasury. Then he forgets it and only uses it again by accident after you had removed his palace and wife to Africa. Why was it so?''

''Oh, one of my best. This is called foreshadowing. The use in the cave mandates its use later. But this was not understood.''

''Deus ex machina,'' thought Vashti sadly. ''And why did Alaeddin leave the lamp unhid when he went hunting? Even Burton commented upon that incident.''

''The unenlightened cannot understand. That is a plot device. If the lamp had been hidden, then the wife of Alaeddin, Badr al-Budur, could not have traded it to the Magician. Thus it was necessary, thus it is in the story. One would think that even the most scholastic of the djinns would realize this. But those who close their eyes cannot see; those who close their ears cannot hear; those who close their minds cannot comprehend . . .'' And Vashti once again raised her hand; and once again Hassan halted.

''And the brother of the Magician who appears near the end. Where does he come from, and why?''

Hassan smiled. ''That is one of my best ideas. Even as the Lady Scheherazade led from one tale to another, so I created this character with the concept of telling a sequel to the tale of Alaeddin.'' He mused and stroked his chin. ''Perhaps even a trilogy of such stories.''

''No,'' she said. ''No one cares for such long connected stories since the time of the Sultana Victoria. There can be no market among the learned for such.''

''You are probably correct about this. It was but a passing fancy and has no effect upon the integrity of the story.''

''Was there nothing of the story that you might improve upon?''

''My one regret was that I did not have Alaeddin demand of me more interesting items. He wanted gems larger than gems he had heard of, money in quantities greater than he knew of, horses and women more beautiful than any he had seen. All wishes of degree and not of kind. Alas, I know better now.''

Oh, dear, she thought, the one part of the story that rings true seems wrong to its author. And I wonder where he got those slaves and eunuchs. Still, knowing that won't help him, or help me solve his problem. Aloud she said: ''May I see some of your new stories?''

He opened another drawer and handed her a number of folders. He watched her nervously as she sat back and read. After she had finished a number of these, she placed them upon the desk and looked up at his anxious face.

''Hmm, there is a certain . . . novelty of scope to these. A certain presumption of pure innocence, of lack of intelligence on the part of your audience. It's fascinating in a macabre sort of way.'' The djinn beamed with misplaced delight. ''However, they are completely unbelievable, as well as repetitious.'' She picked one up. ''Look at this one—'Bottle Imp.' You have a military officer finding a bottle containing a beautiful djinn. She falls passionately in love with him. They have many adventures (or one adventure many times). But *why* does she fall in love with him? No motivation. And after all these adventures, they are the same. They learned nothing. Their characters have neither changed nor developed at all.'' She folded the paper and launched it across the room. It soared, banked, and dived into the waste paper basket.

''And this one—'Conjure Wife,' in which a witch falls passionately in love with a mortal advertising executive,'' she twitched an eyebrow at Hassan, ''and marries him. Then they have some tedious adventures. I am afraid that I see no market for these.

''But,'' he protested, ''some of the stories in these magazines lack the special . . .'' She cut him short with a wave of her hand.

She rose and paced delicately on the plush carpet and thought, This would be easier to work out if I had my tail. ''No, Hassan, even these pulps won't take your stories. But . . .'' He came alert. ''You could create a new market, a new medium of literature. A marketplace where character development is not required; where it is even detrimental. Where motivation slows down the story, where sensible plots, where even plots themselves are un-wanted. Yes, that must be your goal.''

"But, that's nonsense, my Lady. People pay attention to stories; who would accept garbage when they could have choice viands?''

"You overestimate humanity. I remember after many a banquet in the Frankish lands when the overly replete louts couldn't tell the difference. Some of them couldn't tell the difference when they were sober. Some of them never were completely sober. So, there's your precedent. Go for it.''

The djinn bowed his head into his hands and thought. He thought out loud. "Nothing in public. They might be shamed if their friends saw them. No plays, no cinema— spectacle, but the wrong kind of spectacle. Something at home. Radio? No. Too much like the storytellers of the marketplace. They would have to think, to imagine im-ages. Could I give them the images?'' He became less and less aware of Vashti.

She started to put on her gloves, looked at the torn one, and gathered the pair in one hand. As she opened the door, she turned. "And drop the 'new lamps for old' line. No one will ever believe that sort of trade.'' But he did not answer. She thought he had mumbled "Zworykin and his Iconoscope.'' That was meaningless, unless it was the title of one of Hassan's stories.

She tossed the gloves to the receptionist, "a souvenir.'' The hallway was empty, so she moved ever so and Walked Between the Worlds.

"And thus thy mother left the djinn who was glad for the ideas she had imparted unto him, and for the path onto which she had directed him. But of the result as to the humans and their culture and society, only Time herself will and does know. And the moral is, that for a teller of stories to be successful, the audience must already know and approve of most of the story before it is told.'' But here the kittens had already lost interest; the black tom had his tail at an improper angle and was flickering in and out of sight. Vashti leapt upon him, dragged him back into the world, and sitting upon the squirming form, began to wash his ears.

Many times in the past my lamp has been used for personal gain, and many times it has fallen into the hands of men of great power.

But I truly believe that its most wondrous and noble moment came just under two centuries ago, and not while in the possession of a mover and shaker of worlds, but rather at the behest of a little girl. . . .

AN' THE PEOPLE,
THEY COULD FLY

by Lawrence Schimel

Long time 'go, up in Virginia, was plantation wiff'n many slaves on it. An' one of these slaves, she was a girl whose Ma'am was a witch doctor back in Africa, an' jus' 'fore her daughter got taken 'way by the white folks, the witch doctor she gave her daughter a li'l glass jar. She say to her daughter, "When you in time o' trouble, open this here jar an' make a wish, an' that wish'll come true. But only got three wishes, so use 'em good."

An' on that plantation was an overseer who was mean as mean come. Worse'n here if'n you can believe it. An' he would wait for the slightest 'scuse to lash at them slaves wiff'n his whips, an' sometimes he wouldn' e'en wait for 'n excuse, but just start lashin' at 'em.

Well, on one day, when the people 'ad all been out in the fields workin' cotton since 'fore the sun rose, an the sun, she was now high in the sky and shinin' down on their heads mean enough to singe off ev'y last hair they had, an' one ol' man he collapsed in the heat. He jus' couldna' take anymo'.

An' the white man he rush over to 'im an' he 'gan lashin' at 'im wiff'n his whip an' yellin' at 'im to get up. An' the old man he pulled 'imself back onto his feet by his own sobbin'. But soon as he got t' his feet he done collapse again, an' the white man he gan' lashin' at 'im wiff'n his whip an' hollerin' an' a-screamin' at 'im to get up.

Now the li'l girl she could'n' take it no mo' an she took out her li'l jar that her Ma'am gave 'er an' she opened it up. An' inside that jar there was three chiggers. An' the girl, she was surprised, for they don't got chiggers in Africa, but that was what her wishes looked like in America. So she said to them chiggers, "Chiggers, I wish that man could fly. Wish he could fly all way home to Africa."

An' one of the chiggers, he done jumped right out of that jar an' onto the ground, an' soon's he dis'pear'd into the dust, that man, he 'gan flap his arms like a big giant crow an' suddenly he took off, jus' fore the white man wiff'n his whip could lash 'im again, an he flew up in the sky and 'way toward Africa.

Now the whole plantation had stopped its workins to watch 'im fly 'way, but that ol' white man, mean as mean come, he was angry as the devil that one o' his slaves got 'way, an' he started a-hollerin', "You lazy niggers, you get back to work or I'll whip the all of you!" An' jus' 'cuz he was mean as mean come, he whip'd a few of 'em anyway.

An' the people they bent their heads an' 'gan to work cotton 'gain. But one young woman, she had her chil' wi' her, strapped to her back while she work. An her chil' 'gan cry from the sun. An' the overseer, who was mean as mean come, 'gan his lashin' an' his hollerin' for the chil' to keep quiet. An' the li'l girl took out her jar an' looked at the two chiggers inside an' said, "Chiggers, I wish'n that woman, she could fly away home to Africa wiff'n her chil' on her back."

An' jus' as the white man was gonna lash her wiff'n his whip, the woman 'gan flap her arms like a big black crow an' flew up into the sky an' away from that white man mean as mean come. An' all the slaves watched her as she flew away toward Africa wi' her chil' on her back.

An' the white man he was real angry now an he 'gan a hollerin', "Now, who did that?" an' also 'is, "Get back to work, you lazy niggers!"

An' the people they bent their heads an' 'gan to work cotton 'gain. But the sun she was shinin' something fierce an' it was'n long 'fore someone else collapsed from the heat an' the white man started a-runnin' toward 'im a-hollerin' an' a-wavin' his whip all ready to start a-lashin', but the li'l girl she took out her li'l glass jar an' looked

inside at the one last chigger an' said, ''Li'l chigger, think
you can take all o' us here in this field an' let us fly home
to Africa? I wish'n you could. I really wish'n you could.''

An' suddenly the li'l girl dropped the li'l glass jar her
Ma'am she gave her jus' 'fore she was taken 'way, an' the
jar fell to the ground an' the last li'l chigger popped out
an' into the dust. An' suddenly the li'l girl realized she
was flappin' her arms like a big giant crow an flyin' in the
air high above the cotton, an' high above the ol' white
man as mean as mean come shakin' his whip at all of
'em up in the sky. An' the people 'gan to cheer an' start
a-flyin' home to Africa, an' they was so happy to be free
an' a-flyin' home to Africa that they forgot about the rest
of us, in situations just like the ones they left. 'Ceptin'
for the li'l girl, bless her heart, who all the time she was
a-flappin' an' a-flyin' toward her Ma'am an' Africa with
the rest of 'em, kept a-wishin' for jus' one mo' wish so
as she could use it on the rest o' us, an' bring us all home
wi' her.

An' maybe it'll be you that does it, pullin' chiggers
from yo' feet an' wishin' we could *all* fly home 'gain.
Maybe it'll be you.

You know, there have been so many references to
The Thousand and One Nights, *that it occurs to me
that you might like to see just what that book, the
book that brought me to the attention of the world,
is all about.*

*But, of course, you can find it in any library or
bookstore, so here, for your edification, is the*
Thousand and Second Tale. . . .

PARSLEY, SPACE,
ROSEMARY, AND TIME
by Katharine Kerr

During the Great Disruption, when flux in the Space/Time con-
tinuum scrambled the hyperspace shunts, the mercantile planets
of the Mapped Sector suffered the most, for obvious reasons,
from being thrust into isolation. One such was New Samarkand,
the fourth planet of a large yellow star out near the galactic rim.
The only reason the world had ever been settled was the fresh
water ocean, cheap fuel for the fusion drives of the merchant
fleet, that covered most of its surface. Without the fleet and a
steady supply of imports, the planet's small population soon
found itself hovering on poverty's edge.

Mostly humans lived on New Samarkand, though small col-
onies of a supposedly native race called Squeakers shared the
only continent. While the humans farmed or kept river towns
alive down on the plains, the Squeakers burrowed out warrens
up in the hills and ate by gathering and hunting. Occasionally a
few would drift down to trade chunks of semiprecious stones for
grain and for parsley, an Old Earth plant that got them drunk,
thanks to, or so the only human doctor who'd ever studied the
problem decided, its abnormally high Vitamin A content. After
one of these green binges, the Squeakers tended to brag that their
race, too, came from the distant stars, just as humanity did, but
no one paid much attention.

The Squeakers' speech register included frequencies so high that human ears couldn't catch them, and only with great effort could a Squeaker speak low enough to make itself understood. Since few humans cared about what they had to say, few bothered to try. The real problem was, quite simply, that to humans they looked like toys. No more than a meter high, they had chubby round bodies, covered in gray or bluish-gray fur, big round heads with two pairs of button-bright eyes, and four short arms. When they spoke, chirping away, they tended to bounce up and down on their stubby little legs. Their only clothing was a loin-wrap of flowered trade cloth. Few humans managed to take them seriously, especially in those tense years when all technology stood in danger of crumbling away forever.

There was, however, one man who did learn to talk with Squeakers. In a town named China lived a widow, Rosemary Dean, with her only child, Albert. The widow Dean was much respected, because only she could operate and maintain the wire-spinning machinery at the local foundry, and without wire, there would be no cables, and without cables, the last hi-tech devices would die. For years Rosemary kept the secrets of spinning wire to herself. She wanted to hand them down to her son, insuring him respect and a steady income after her death, but as Al Dean became first a pimply teenager, then a lanky young man, she realized that much as she loved him, he was no man to trust with an important job like the spinning of wire.

"I don't understand you, Al," she would say. "Your father was a great engineer, and I can fix practically anything, but all you do is hang around the marketplace and write poetry all day. Poetry! I mean, get real, kid!"

"I can't help it, Mom," he would answer. "It's just my sensitive, intuitive nature."

And she would roll her eyes starward and sigh.

About once every three months Al really would try to make sense of the wire-spinning machinery, but every time he'd lose interest and drift back to the marketplace. He'd always been exceptionally lucky at games of chance— another part of his sensitive, intuitive nature, or so he liked to say. He used his winnings from shooting craps to buy notebooks for his poems and intoxicants for himself and his friends. Since watching him write poetry distressed his mother, he took his sonnet sequences and verse dramas, his laments for the lost stars and his epics of space exploration down to a table in the corner of Dave Abraham's tavern, which sold a resinous wine called Bouzo.

After a long day's scribbling, Al would often have a bottle or two to prime himself to go home and face his mother. Usually he shared his table with the local Squeakers, who would listen to his poems while cramming their beaky mouths full of parsley, leaves, stems, and all. Occasionally they would announce that Al was a terrible poet in any language, but only when they were drunk enough for him to ignore their opinions. All the humans who came by would shake their heads and wonder aloud where a hardworking woman like Rosemary could possibly have gotten a wastrel son like Al. Listening to them wonder, of course, only made him drink the more. By the end of the evening, when the Squeakers had slimy green beaks and Al a bright red face, they usually ended up heaped together, sound asleep, whistling or snoring, in the alley out behind the tavern.

One hot summer morning, Al went out to the paper factory for a new supply of notebooks. When he stopped by home before going on to the tavern, he found his mother waiting for him. Dressed in her oily coveralls from the machine shop, she was sitting at the kitchen table and drinking a cup of the dark brown concoction that everyone called coffee for nostalgia's sake. When Al came in, she looked away and said nothing. He noticed that a blue backpack was sitting by the door—his backpack, in fact, crammed full and bulging.

"Uh, Mom? Something wrong?"

"Not exactly. Well, yeah, guess there is. I signed up an apprentice this morning. To learn the wire-spinning machinery, I mean. Guess she'll take over some day."

Al couldn't speak. He had never even considered that his mother might disinherit him. Biting her lower lip hard, Rosemary finally looked his way.

"I hate to do this, Al, but we've got the colony to consider."

"Yeah, I know. The wire for the cables. Uh, those my clothes, over by the door?"

"Yeah. Look, you remember your Uncle Jake, don't you? The one who lives downriver in Morocco? Well, I got a letter from him today. Here." She handed over an envelope. "He says he'll take you in for a while, help you get a job. It's going to be too hard on you, staying here in China, listening to people talk."

Al shoved the letter into his shirt pocket and headed for the door.

"Now you write to me, honey," Rosemary called out. "And once I've got Tanya trained, I'll come visit. I promise."

"Okay." Al picked up the backpack. "Once I'm set up, I'll visit you, too. I'm going to make money, Mom. I'm going to get a real good job. I really will."

Maybe it was just nerves, but Rosemary laughed. Al fled the house without looking back.

Although Al had been planning on working his passage on one of the frequent riverboats, such was his reputation that no captain would hire him. He was going to have to earn his fare at a floating crap game, but first, he decided, he really needed a drink. Fortunately, Dave's Tavern was just opening for the afternoon. When he sat down at his regular table and began searching his pockets for small change, Dave hurried over, carrying a glass of golden Bouzo.

"Here, kid, have one on me. Betcha need it."

"Whatcha mean, Dave?"

"Well, what with your mother taking that apprentice and all, guess you're getting spun right out of the wire business, huh?"

"Jeez, what is this! Everyone's heard already?"

"Well, the poor woman's been agonizing over this for days now, and in a town this size . . ."

Al blushed scarlet, but he took the drink. He laid his scrounged change out on the table.

"Bring me another, Dave. I got this letter to read."

Uncle Jake's letter turned out to be much kinder than Al considered he deserved. Since Jake was a blacksmith, he was offering to teach his wayward nephew the metals business from the anvil up, as it were, and then steer him into machine repair.

"Jeez, Dave, machines run in my goddamn family, I guess. Except for me."

"Yeah, too bad." Dave set a nearly-full bottle on the table. "Here's something for old times' sake."

As the day stretched itself into twilight, humans came

and went, whispering and laughing when they saw Al cradling his bottle and stretching each drink. He was out of change, and he certainly wasn't feeling intuitive enough to go shoot craps. Just at nightfall, a pair of his friends appeared, two Squeaker brothers. As they bought their first bunches of parsley, Al saw Dave whispering to them, spreading the story of his disgrace, most likely. When the Squeakers joined him, they brought a fresh bottle of Bouzo, too.

"Our turn, Al." The Squeaker known as Freet forced his voice way down register. "We found some purple stones."

"Hey, guys, thanks." Al in turned squealed; he'd worked out a falsetto voice easier for his friends to understand. "I mean, jeez. Thanks."

They sat down and began nipping off the delicate leaves just at the end of the fronds.

"You guys hear the news?" Al said. "I'm leaving town."

"Too bad, yeah," Iffi chirped. "We'll come see you in your new place"

"That'd be swell. I'm going downriver to Morocco."

For a few minutes they sipped or nibbled in a companionable silence.

"Know what I wish?" Al said, burping a little. "I wish I could make things up to my mom. I mean, jeez, a guy's only got one mom, doesn't he? And another thing. This goddamn town, all of them laughing at me, saying I had it coming. I wish I could do something that'd make them all sit up and take notice, something real big that'll make them say, she-it, we were wrong about Al Dean."

"Fat chance," Iffi mumbled.

"Shut up," Freet snapped. "That's no way to talk to a troubled friend, little brother."

"Ah, it's okay," Al said. "I deserve it all, the scorn, the disdain, the mockery, the infamy, the—"

"Now you shut up! The Starborn don't wallow. It's undignified."

Al poured himself another glass of Bouzo and gulped about half of it down.

"Tell me something, Freet, since we maybe won't never see each other again and all that stuff. Are you guys really

Starborn, or do you just kind of say that when you've chomped enough green?''

Freet slammed one pair of hands down on the table and clacked his beak hard.

''Sorry,'' Al said and fast. ''Didn't mean to insult you.''

''Good! I get so bleching sick of it, you people always doubting my word.''

''Yeah, I know. I get sick of the same thing myself. It's just that—''

Freet whistled and slammed the other pair of hands down.

''It's just bleching this and bleching that! Always something! Always some reason to doubt my word. Well, I'm sick of it! I'm gonna show you.'' Freet swung his head round Iffi's way. ''Come on, little brother. We gonna show him the slab.''

''What?'' Iffi opened his beak so fast that a stalk of parsley fell onto the table. ''You're crazy! None of the Baldies are supposed to see that.''

''Don't care! I'm sick and tired of nobody believing me.''

''Uh—well, hey,'' Al broke in. ''If it's like taboo or something, I can pass.''

Freet ignored him and went on glaring at his brother.

''Iffi, you're a coward.''

''Freet, you're drunk.''

Freet bounced up, raising three fraternal fists.

''I'm brave, you're sober!'' With a wail, Iffi got to his feet. ''Come on, Al fella, if you dare.''

''Where we going?''

''To the hills,'' Freet said. ''Come on. Don't forget your sack thing.''

Since Squeakers never move particularly fast, Al kept up fine as they trotted through the dark streets of town. After a couple of kilometers, the cool air began to clear his head, and by the time they'd left the houses far behind, he was sober enough to think of a few practicalities.

''Uh, are we going far, guys? All I've got to eat are a couple of candy bars.''

''No problem,'' Freet said. ''Plenty of ferns, this time of year.''

''And wahseebah fruits,'' Iffi put in. ''Lots of eating things.''

Slow or not, the Squeakers turned out to have an amazing amount of stamina. Although the terrain began climbing toward the hills, on and on they trotted along the rutted dirt road until Al began to sweat in trickles, not drops, and his head pounded as hard as his footsteps. Every time he collected the breath to ask about stopping, his friends would sing back. "Not yet, not yet," and trot on, even after the last moon had set.

For some time Al had suspected that the Squeakers' many eyes registered a part of the spectrum beyond ordinary light, and this trip in the darkness confirmed his guess. As they called out to him or to one another, commenting on the road, looking for landmarks, or watching for animals, they consistently translated certain terms, what must have been visual adjectives in their speech, into human words such as "hot" and "cold." He would have picked up other nuances, he supposed, if he'd had the energy left to pay closer attention. Finally, by dawn, he was so exhausted that he threw himself down in the fern banks beside the road and refused to move. Freet and Iffi debated briefly in their own speech, then sat on either side of him.

"Well, hell, you do look beat," Freet said. He paused, looking round him, rubbing his eyes with his inner pair of hands. "Huh. Well, hell. We've come too far to turn back."

"Can't leave him now," Iffi said. "He'd get lost, for sure."

Al realized two things at once: first, that a now-sober Freet was regretting this adventure, and second, that Iffi was right. As he looked round him in the silvery first light, Al supposed that sooner or later he'd find his way downhill to the river—if he didn't starve to death first. All around, the hills pushed tall juts and stabs of black basalt and silvery granite through the thin soil. Out in the open areas grew a welter of blue, fuzzy succulents, while in the hollows clustered huge speckled ferns of a sort he'd never seen. In among these ground covers sprouted yellow and red flowers, all tangled by a nearly-purple vine with white explosions of leaves. As the light brightened, insects—he assumed they were insects, at least—began to buzz and chirr. In a hundred flashes of silver wings a cloud took flight, circled, then flew off toward the rising sun. Small red things with many legs scutted among the vines; a delicate lizard glided by on membranous wings; in the distance song broke out, the high pipings and hollow booms of animals, calling to the day.

"Pretty, this time of morning," Iffi remarked.

"Yeah, sure is," Al said. "Jeez, I've lived on this planet all my life, and here I've never been up here!"

For the first time, and perhaps because of this sudden discovery of an alien world, right in the middle of the view he'd always taken for granted, those ordinary old hills rising at the edge of human farmland, it occured to Al that the Squeakers might always have been telling the simple truth, that their tiny tribes might indeed be the last survivors of a star-faring race, trapped on the planet by some earlier shift of the Space/Time flux. It could well be that they possessed tribal lore, myths, maybe, that cloaked old truths, poems that hid crucial information. There were scientists at the university in Canada, the biggest town on-planet, who were trying to decipher the currents in the flux and either predict when they might clear or discover where the missing shunts had taken themselves to. What if they could use the Squeakers' information in some way? What if the lore was worth cold cash? And he, poor old Albert Dean, the town jerk, he who made his mother worry herself sick, was the only person in the whole damn colony who had bothered to learn how to talk to the Squeakers, really talk, that is, beyond the handful of trade words everyone needed to bargain for agates.

"Say, Freet? What's this slab thing like?"

Freet sighed and whistled.

"Say, Al? You sure you don't just wanna go home? We'll take you back."

"Ah, come on, guys! I've come all this way, and you promised."

Actually, of course, they'd never promised one single thing, but Al was betting that they'd been too drunk at the time to remember that now. He won.

"Oh, okay. The Starborn never break promises. Well, the slab. Hum, let me think. It's like a big, flat stone, set into the hillside, and it's all covered with writing."

"Can't be real stone, though," Iffi said. "It's too shiny and *uhndaro*. I mean, cold."

"Well, little brother, it's not metal, either. Gotta be stone."

"It's too damn cold for that." Iffi clacked his beak hard. "It is *not* stone."

"Look, you bleching ding, it's got to be either stone or metal."

"No, wait, guys," Al broke in. "It could be some kind of artificial thing, like ceramics or something, that your people brought with them when they first came here."

"Aha!" Freet waggled all his hands in the air. "You believe us now, don't you?"

"Yeah, I do, and you know what? I'm sorry I ever doubted your word. I apologize."

"Handsome of you. I accept." Freet bounced up. "Come on, we got to go a little farther before the sun gets too hot."

Traveling mostly at night, and foraging for food as they went, Al and the two Squeakers made their way deep into the hills. Although the Squeakers were used to the outdoor life, by the second day Al ached in every muscle and tendon. Their forage of ferns, fleshy succulents, and the turquoise-blue wahseebah fruits, supplemented now and then with roast lizard, gave him profound diarrhea as well. Every time he thought of begging his friends to take him home, he made himself remember the possible cold cash and reasonably certain fame that lay ahead. Of course, since no one in China, not even his own mother, was going to take his word for anything, he was going to have to bring back hard evidence that the Squeakers had stories worth hearing. Fortunately, he had notebooks with him to transcribe the writing on this mysterious slab.

Using the shreds of xenobiology that he remembered from his high school science classes, Al also pieced together more evidence that the Squeakers were Starborn. Although the plants their people had learned to gather were digestible and even nourishing to Squeakers, anything green intoxicated the two brothers to some degree, even the pale yellow horsetails, though nothing had as great an effect as human-grown parsley. Since no species was going to survive, much less develop any sort of technology, if it lived in a state of permanent drunkenness, the Squeakers must have evolved on some planet where the food chain depended on a chemical other than chlorophyll and its various relatives. If indeed a group of star-faring Squeakers had ended up stranded on this particular world, it was no wonder that their culture had degenerated so badly and so fast.

By the fourth afternoon, however, caught between his exhaustion and his intestinal turmoil, Al's intellectual curiosity deserted him. The only question he cared about was whether he was going to die soon or later—he was hoping for soon. When Freet waked him for their night journey, all Al could do was mumble and groan.

"Come on, come on, Al! You gotta get up. We're almost there, really and truly."

Al said something foul.

"Sure, go ahead. Just die here. We'll have to go tell everyone you failed again. That'll really show your mom what you're made of, yeah, you bet."

Al sat up, rubbing his stubbled face with both hands.

"Attaboy," Freet said, bouncing. "Come on. Almost there."

Al never could remember that last night's traveling. The Squeakers kept stopping to let him rest, but even so, Time passed in a blur of rock and fern, rushing streams and water reeds, of stumbling and cursing and falling down. Just as the sun was rising through a jagged break in the rock formations, Al struggled round the flank of one last hill and saw ahead a narrow valley, waist-deep in ferns. At the far end rose a dark, crumbling cliff. Low down, touching the ground, in the middle of the rise of dirt and rock shone a flame-red oval, a jewel set among crumbling fissures.

"Jeez louise!" Al said. "It's huge."

"You bet." Freet paused to lace all four hands together and bow in the slab's direction. "Need a rest, Al?"

"Nah. Not now that we're so damn close."

Al squeezed energy from a last reserve and trotted down the valley after the two Squeakers, who kept up a running chatter at a frequency way too high for him to hear. Yet as they all drew close he slowed, stopped, could for a long time only stare openmouthed at the tremendous inset of red, a good three meters high by two wide.

"Jeez," he whispered at last. "That's no natural hunk of rock, that's for sure. But say, guys, I don't see any writing on it."

"You're nuts," Freet said. "It's all over the thing. See? It starts right here near the middle and spirals out." By stretching hard Freet could just lay one fingertip in the middle of the slab. "Look at this real big letter, painted all fancy."

"Crap. I don't see, but I get it. Paint, huh? What color is it?"

"It's—" Freet stopped, thought, sucked the finger that had touched the slab as if it would inspire him. "I don't know your word for it."

"Bet it's ultraviolet."

"Ah, okay. I'll remember that. Ultraviolet."

When Al tried feeling out the letters with his fingertips, he registered nothing but a slickness over slickness. His eyes blurred with tears. So much for his evidence, so much for his certain fame and possible cold cash.

"What's wrong?" Iffi said.

"I can't see it. My eyes don't register that color. It's like you guys not being able to hear when someone talks real low."

Freet said something *really* foul.

"Couldn't agree more," Al sighed. "Say, uh, I guess you guys can't read, huh?"

"Of course we can!" Freet and Iffi spoke together, but only Freet went on speaking. "We read real good, but not this old stuff. It's way different, way old. Only the priests know what these letters say."

"And the priests aren't even supposed to know I'm here, right?"

"Right."

"Say, you're not going to get into trouble over this, are you?"

"Ah, maybe," Freet said, shrugging in an oddly human gesture. "What are they going to do about it? Scream and yell a whole lot, sure. Priests are always screaming and yelling. It's their job, isn't it?"

On the other hand, Al was certain, the priests weren't going to be helping him translate their sacred monument, either. He stepped up close, tried shading his eyes while he peered at the slab, tried looking at it sidewise, and out of focus, found not so much as a trace of a shadow or edge of a painted letter. Quite possibly this writing had been baked right in, if indeed the slab were some kind of high-tech ceramic. Swearing under his breath he tried feeling around the edges of the thing, thinking that he might somehow peel off the top layer and bring it back to the university lab—but under the dirt the edge felt smooth, solid, and mechanically beveled.

"Ah, crap!" he said at last. "Well, guess I might as well hang it up, huh? I—hey, what's that?"

The "that" in question bulged out of a crevice in the cliff face about two meters up the height of the slab, well above the Squeaker line of sight but an easy reach for lanky Al. Even though it seemed at first to be nothing more than a big clod of blackish earth, the shape was too regular to be natural. When Al probed around its perimeter, he discovered a hard sphere, crusted with the dirt of ages, and about twenty centimeters in diameter. When he worked it free, pebbles and clods rolled and scattered.

"Never seen one of those before," Freet said. "Is it a rock?"

"I don't think so, no."

Al rummaged through his backpack, found a jackknife, and began flaking off the dirt to expose a black crystalline substance underneath. Once he'd cleaned off about half the sphere, to get a better look at the material, he rubbed a spot shiny on a shirt sleeve. In his hands the sphere sang aloud, a high, pure, musical note. When Iffi and Freet yelped, Al nearly dropped it.

"Jeez, guys, what do you think this means?"

Neither Squeaker said a thing, merely wheezed a few panicked high notes of their own. Al hesitated, then went on chipping at the crust of dirt and old plant roots. This artifact was going to be his evidence, his ticket to fame and fortune, or so he saw it. Once he'd used a spare shirt to polish the entire sphere, he held it up high in one hand.

"Look at it, guys. Your ancestors were some kind of craftsmen, huh?"

"You bet," Freet said. "Wonder why it's glowing like that?"

Al set it down fast and backed away, yelling at the Squeakers to get clear. Too late it occurred to him that the sphere might be an alarm or warding device, something that would explode when disturbed. All three of them piled behind a nearby boulder and huddled down while the sphere sang out its alien music. Suddenly Al heard a low groan, then a grinding, snarling, scrabbling, and a moan, and the crunch of something huge moving over dirt and gravel, crushing the very ground.

"Oh, jeezus gawd! What have we done?"

"What's wrong?" Freet snapped.

"Can't you hear—"

"No. Hear what?" Freet bounced up and peered over the boulder. "Hey, it's opening."

Al got up and looked. Even if it were the last action he ever performed before an alien monster tore him into pieces, he had to see what was happening. Rather than anything fatal, however, he found the red slab standing open, become a door huge by Squeaker standards, and revealing a cave cut into the hillside. Out in front the black sphere glowed, soaking up the sun.

"A solar cell! Jeezus gawd! Hey, guys? I think we've hit something big."

"You're not going in there, are you?" Iffi whined. "I bet the place is crawling with spirits. Of our ancestors, stuff like that."

"Blech!" Freet snarled. "To think I've got a coward for a brother!"

Iffi said something that Al couldn't translate. As the three of them walked over to the cave mouth, Al took the lead, only to pause just outside.

"I was just thinking, guys. What if this thing shuts behind us?"

"I better stay out here," Iffi said. "I'll yell if it starts moving."

"Huh, pretty transparent, little brother." Freet clacked his beak a few times. "But yeah, I guess you better."

Al and Freet followed an obviously artificial tunnel, running flat and straight into the hillside, for some five meters, until it curved sharply into darkness. Although Al found a flashlight in his backpack, he couldn't remember when he'd checked the batteries last. He could be certain they weren't new, batteries being a rare commodity these days.

"Can you see, Freet? I mean, are things 'warm' in here?"

"No, there's nothing glowing at all."

For a few moments they stood staring at the flashlight, as if they could telepathically read the state of its batteries.

"Ah, hell," Al said at last. "Nothing ventured, nothing gained, huh? We can walk in the dark for a ways."

"Yeah. Keep one hand on the wall as we go along. That way if the tunnel branches or something, we won't get lost."

Feeling their way, they went forward, rounded the curve, and heard their footsteps slap on an artificial floor. Some very smooth, very cold substance lined the tunnel, although the righthand wall was pitted here and there in an engraved pattern which, Freet announced, had to be script. At a particularly large block of letters, they paused so that Freet could try to feel out its meaning.

"It's more like our kind of writing than the stuff on the slab. They must have had two kinds of script."

"Yeah? Well, what's it say?"

"I'm not sure. It's a list of names, people's names, I mean, far as I can tell."

In the dark Al could hear him whistling under his breath like a tea kettle.

"Hey, here's an interesting thing," Freet said at last. "They're calling this place their main camp. And a temporary something—I don't know your word for it. A place where you put stuff you're gonna fetch later."

"Hey, we've hit pay dirt! It shows your people must have come from somewhere else, and jeez, on this ball of water, there isn't anywhere to come from but the stars, if you get what I mean."

"I do, kind of. Say, Al? What ever made you think you could be a poet?"

"Huh?"

"Oh, never mind. Sorry I brought it up."

As they walked on, their footsteps began to sound immensely hollow, echoing off a far-distant wall. Since for all they knew, the tunnel they were following was about to end in midair, Al decided to use the flashlight. The pale beam shot out into a vast cavern, its floor level with the tunnel mouth, after all, but crammed with obstacles. For a moment, seeing them in the narrow stripe of flashlight beam, Al simply couldn't comprehend what they might be. He could distinguish only big, solid masses in irregular shapes, wrapped in some sort of coating and fitted together like a giant's puzzle. Out of sheer nerves his wrist jerked; the beam of light jumped upward and fell on a row of ruby-red spheres. One by one they sang out, began to glow, and filled the cavern with scarlet light. Out of the shadows, like rocks emerging on a sea-coast as the tide pulls back, rose more shapes: boxes, barrels, machines wrapped in tatters of what had once been cloth, crates, and solid cubes and bars stashed under metallic drapes.

"Jeez louise," Al whispered. "Look at all that stuff!"

"Yeah," Freet said, and as softly. "All that bleching valuable stuff."

"Boy, bet those scientists down in Canada are gonna flip when they see this. I mean, you do think we should go get a research team up here, don't you?

Freet ignored him and walked into the cave, where he began methodically picking his way around and through the stored goods and muttering to himself under his breath. When Al realized that he was making a rough count of the number of crates and containers standing round, he started to help, but he got bored with all the arithmetic and began poking around at random. Finally, behind a big cylindrical barrel, he saw what seemed to be a tree fern, muffled up in a slippery, semi-opaque sheet. When he tried to pull the sheet off, it disintegrated, doubtless from sheer age, into a clot of shiny threads and tatters to reveal a large tree made of yellow metal. From its branches dangled red and yellow ovoids—fruits of some sort, Al supposed. Without thinking he pulled one off and tried to taste it.

"Hey!" Freet snapped. "Careful! You could poison yourself."

"No problem. It's hard as a rock. Must be glass."

Freet took the red ovoid and stared at it for a long, long time.

"No, not glass," he said, and his voice hovered on the edge of a squeak so thin that Al could barely register the sound. "It's a ruby."

"Yeah? Hey, real pretty."

"Al, oh Al, you really do live in some other universe, don't you? Just like your mother always says. It's a gem as big as my fist, Al, Don't you realize what that means, what all this stuff means?"

"No. What?"

"We're rich, you blech! Rich rich rich."

And, of course, they were.

* * *

"I've got to admit it, Al." Rosemary paused for a sip of her iced Bouzo. "This does beat fiddling with that damn spinning machine."

"Jeez, Mom, I'm sure glad you think so."

In brocaded armchairs they were sitting on the balcony of their new mansion, which stood on a rise overlooking China and the river just beyond the town. On a lucite-topped table by her chair, Rosemary set the Bouzo down and spread out a sheet of isometric drawings, complete with exploded views, of a Squeaker water purifier found in the cave.

"I got these from my staff just this morning," she remarked. "This thing is wonderful, Al, centuries ahead of our own designs."

"Glad you like it, Mom. Jeez, I still can't believe my luck, stumbling over that cave like that."

Rosemary smiled fondly, then turned in her chair to smile even more fondly at the luxurious room behind them, the parquet floors, the embroidered hangings, the leather chairs, the gleaming computer on its marble desk.

"No, dear, it wasn't luck. It was your sensitive, intuitive nature."

Many people think that I was the first to have my wishes come true, but this, of course, is not the case. There were wishes to be had long before there was an Aladdin, just as there will be wishes long after I have expired in all my many lives.

But it was in the early days, the days before I was born, that magic was at its most powerful. Here is a tale of those ancient times. . . .

IN THEIR CUPS AT SLAB'S

by John Gregory Betancourt

"Aye," said three-fingered Rishta, a sometime adventurer, occasional thief, and frequent trafficker in stolen merchandise. Rishta shifted on his bench, belched, and repeated, "Aye, I have a wish, too. Such a wish as all Zelloque has never heard, by the gods!"

I was seated in my private booth at the back of Slab's Tavern with Rishta and two of Rishta's sometime friends, occasional allies, and frequent partners-in-crime: Lewt the Left, whose right hand had been lost some ten years before (a minor dispute involving a nobleman's purse: the purse turned up in Lewt's possession and the nobleman retrieved it . . . with Lewt's hand still attached), and young Galandin. Galandin had no nickname yet, having that very day entered the thieving profession; when he distinguished himself in some fashion he'd be given one by his compatriots.

The subject of wishes came up due to an idle comment on my part: when two ghostly, disembodied heads appeared over our table singing obscene songs in loud voices and bad harmony, I'd wished for a normal tavern for even a single night. The ghosts faded out after a few seconds, but it was enough to put a nasty edge on my mood: they knew they annoyed me, and seemed to take great delight in appearing at inopportune moments. Such are the travails of owning a haunted tavern.

Slab's itself was large and dark, its dim light concealing crumbling plaster and foot-worn paving stones. Wooden columns hewn from the hearts of ancient oaks supported a high beamed ceiling, and weird shadows stretched everywhere. There were numerous secluded spots, and off at curtained booths along the walls, illegal transactions like Rishta's and mine were taking place.

There were pirates at some tables, with their rich, colorful, jewel-encrusted clothes, and slavers throwing dice at others; there were assassins and cutthroats and purse-snatchers lined up along the bar; there were a few minor nobles (bodyguards in obvious display) out slumming; and as usual there were the petty thieves and stray drunks and down-and-out dock workers in search of thrills. All told, it was a typical night at Slab's Tavern: mostly people drank and talked and sang too loudly, the room ringing with boisterous shouts as men laughed, argued, and generally enjoyed themselves.

Neither Rishta nor Lewt blinked an eye when the ghosts appeared over our booth; young Galandin, though, goggled at them until they vanished.

"I wish," Rishta continued unprompted, "for money—more money than I can spend in a dozen lifetimes! Heaps of gold, mountains of silver, oceans of gems . . . all there for me and me alone!"

"You shouldn't wish for things," I said, a bit uneasily. "It's not lucky."

"Feh!" Lewt said with a wave of his left hand. "People wish for such things every day of their lives. There's no luck in it, bad or otherwise." He gave Rishta a slantwise glance. "And your wish is dull as they come, old friend. Money? That's *all*? Anyone can wish for that." He hefted his right arm, showing its smooth, rounded stump where a hand should have been. "Me? I wish for a right hand every morning and every night, and the power that comes from being whole. What's wrong with that?"

"It's not the *wishing*," I said. An icy draft touched my cheek, suddenly, and I glanced around. "It's the place in which you're doing it. My tavern's ghosts . . ."

Rishta gave a bark of a laugh. "You're afraid of your

shadow, Ulander!'' He turned to Galandin. ''What about you, lad?''

Galandin hesitated, obviously uncertain. He, at least, placed some value on my words. ''I . . .'' he finally began. ''I wish for a nickname worthy of my talents!''

''A humble request, indeed,'' Lewt said. ''And doubtless the most likely to come true. What about you, Ulander?''

I shook my head. ''I still say it's best not to wish too much. Believe me, I *know*.''

More than ghostly, disembodied heads that sang, my tavern had a reputation for strange, magical happenings . . . it helped keep away all but the most bloodthirsty clientele. Slab's was the sort of place where anything might happen. Rumor said that, late at night, drunks inexplicably became sober, the furniture rearranged itself (always when nobody was looking), and people sometimes vanished, never to be seen again. Of course, that was merely rumor . . . but I *did* know that against the far wall stood a table where chilled wine always tasted like warm blood, and there was a certain spot (which moved every night) where Slab Vethiq himself, the founder of my noble drinking establishment, was known to appear from time to time. Or at least his spirit was. And if Slab didn't come, chances were someone . . . or some*thing* . . . else would.

I felt that icy chill again. When I glanced to my left and found Slab Vethiq seated beside me, I knew trouble was coming. Slab's skin glowed ever so faintly, as though he were a lantern and a bright fire burned within, and his pale blue eyes glittered like sapphire chips. Green robes drifted around him, more like pale fog than cloth.

''You're a coward, Ulander,'' Slab sneered, ''as ever.'' Turning, he regarded the three ruffians on the other side of the table. They stared back, their surprise obvious. ''There is nothing wrong with wishing,'' Slab went on. ''In fact, I insist we drink to it. A toast!'' He raised his hand, and suddenly a goblet materialized in it. ''Drink up, boys. This one's on the house!''

Slowly, as if reluctant to obey, Rishta, Lewt, and Galandin raised their goblets, too. They'd finished their wine as we haggled over the price of a dozen Coranian sleepgems they'd misappropriated that evening . . . but now their cups were filled with what looked like too-generous portions of my best red wine.

"Slab," I began in a warning tone of voice.

"A toast!" Slab cried. "To wishes!" He smacked his lips, raised his goblet, and drank deeply.

The others did the same. As wine touched their lips, though, their bodies began to distort. Their faces *stretched,* somehow, becoming long and lean, as though their heads were being pulled like potter's clay. Then I'd swear they were sucked down *into* their goblets.

When I blinked, the goblets sat on the table again. The wine inside swirled slowly. I put my own goblet down, untouched.

"I'm insulted," Slab chided me. "You didn't drink my toast."

"I'm not a fool," I said.

Slab chuckled knowingly, then vanished like a soap bubble bursting.

I leaned forward and looked into young Galandin's goblet. As I did, the swirling wine came clear as spring water, and I seemed to gaze through a window into another world. . . .

Galandin was walking along a dark, deserted street. The worn cobblestones underfoot, the tall wood-and-stone buildings leaning out over the street, the sharp salty tang of ocean air: all told him he was still in Zelloque. A dog trotted across his path, gave him a glance, and steered wide.

What happened? he wondered. The last thing he recalled was . . . was . . .

He found he couldn't remember much of anything clearly. His head hurt like he'd been drinking, and his tongue felt thick and leathery in his mouth. Pausing, he glanced around. He didn't recognize the street.

Hooves clattered noisily behind him. He turned and saw a two-horse carriage pull around the corner into view. Eyeing it warily, he moved aside to let it pass. The driver, he noticed as it drew nearer, lay sprawled across his seat—either injured or dead—and the horses' reins dragged in the gutter.

He didn't hesitate: he saw his chance as the horses trotted past. Snaring the reins, he pulled them in, calling, "Whoa there!"

The horses slowed, half-dragging him a dozen paces before they finally stopped. Galandin glanced left and right, saw no one, and swiftly climbed up next to the driver. The man's purse had already been cut . . . along with his throat. The front of his robes was soaked in blood.

Galandin made a quick sign to avert the god of death's attention, then climbed back down. Perhaps inside. . . ?

He opened the carriage door. The coach smelled faintly of flowers, which puzzled him. When his eyes adjusted to the darkness, he spotted a lump under a lap blanket on the floor. In one quick movement he stripped the blanket back.

It was . . . a girl. She couldn't have been more than eight or nine years old. She moaned as she saw him, and her eyes went wide as a startled fawn's. Hunching farther back, she curled into a ball, shivering from fear.

A gem-studded pin in her hair drew Galandin's eye, but he made no move to take it—not yet, anyway.

"Are you all right?" he asked in a soft voice.

She managed the barest hint of a nod.

"What happened?"

"R–robbers," she whispered, her voice sounding like a reedy whistle. "Th–they attacked us. Perret tried to run—"

"Was he your driver?"

She shook her head.

"Your guardian?"

She nodded.

They probably killed him, Galandin thought. *Dragged him out, and he scared the horses to make them run, and they killed him.*

"My name is Galandin," he said softly. "What's yours?"

"Melina," she said. She uncurled a bit. "Please. I want to go home!"

Galandin hesitated, torn. He could take her pin and run—that's what a good thief would do, he told himself, and who would ever know?—but somehow he couldn't do it. *You're a fool,* something inside him whispered. *Grab it and run. This is the chance of a lifetime*! But he couldn't take his gaze off her face. Her eyes were so beautiful, he thought, so large, so innocent, like his own sister's had been so long ago.

"I—" he began. He found a lump in his throat, swallowed. "Come on." He offered her his hand. After a second, she took it. "I'll take you home," he promised.

He set her on his shoulders, returned to the horses, and hooked his fingers in their harness. They made an odd looking party, he thought, as they wove their way through the streets. More than once they drew questioning looks from passersby, but Galandin offered no explanation.

Finally they reached a part of the city that Melina seemed to recognize. She directed him unerringly to a large house surrounded by a high stone wall. Galandin gazed at it with increasing unease. He'd known Melina came from a wealthy family because of the carriage, but only a nobleman or a wealthy merchant would live in such a home.

He set Melina down. Immediately she ran to the gate and pulled a tassled cord. Somewhere inside, a bell tolled. It sounded like an alarm bell, and Galandin steeled himself to run. *Not this time,* he told himself. *This time I've nothing to fear.*

At last a small window in the gate swung open. Old, suspicious eyes peered out.

"What would you be wanting at this hour?" a gruff voice demanded of him.

"It's me, Olan," Melina said, standing on tiptoes to see through the window. "Open the gate at once!"

"Eh?" he glanced down at her, then at Galandin again. The window closed with a bang. After a second, the gate creaked open half a foot. A hand snaked out, grabbed Melina's arm, and jerked her within. The gate slammed shut an instant later.

Minutes passed. Galandin stood there, outside the walls, holding the horses' harness and feeling increasingly foolish. *Galandin the Dumb, they'll call me,* he thought. *Galandin the Gallant Idiot.* He cursed himself thrice over. He should have seized the pin and run. He should have taken the horses and sold them. He should have—

Finally the door creaked open again. Galandin jumped, startled, and the horses shied back. He steadied them.

Half a dozen men with lanterns and drawn swords stomped through the gate, ringing him. He gazed into one

unsmiling face after another. One man climbed up next to
the carriage's driver and pronounced him dead.

"I am Harrish Dava, a humble trader," a bearded man
in rich robes said to Galandin. "My daughter says you
brought her home safely after she was attacked. For that,
I owe you my life a thousand times over." The man bowed.

Galandin, at a loss, bowed back. "Sir," he said. "I am
Galandin Speriel. It was my duty to help your daughter."

"Nevertheless, many would not have done so." Dava
waved to his men. One of them led the horses and carriage
through the gate while the others set off down the street
with purposeful strides. Doubtless looking for Melina's
missing guardian, Galandin thought.

"Come inside," Dava said, taking Galandin's arm.
"You must tell me of yourself. It's not every day my house
is blessed with a hero's presence—do not argue, for my
daughter has named you that herself. You are young, Galandin, for one so valiant. What job do you have? Would
you consider joining my household?"

And young Galandin, Galandin the Hero, found himself
pouring out the unhappy story of his childhood to his host,
who nodded at all the right times, spoke all the right en-
couragements, and discovered through careful observa-
tions enough merit in Galandin to warrant his attention.

From that day on Galandin would be like a son to him,
unto the end of his days.

Smiling, I drew back. The wine had vanished from Galandin's goblet, leaving it empty. The boy had gotten his
wish after all, it seemed.

After a long, happy sigh, I turned to Lewt's goblet.
When I leaned forward and gazed into it, it also became
a window to another world. . . .

Fires burning in his lungs, pains knifing his stomach,
Lewt fled down a narrow, garbage-strewn alley. His hide-
and-seek flight through the merchant's quarter of Zelloque
had left him exhausted and near collapse. He'd never run
so much in his life. Close behind, he heard the hounds
baying again. They'd found, then lost, then found his scent
half a dozen times over the last hour.

The purse he'd cut—which he still clutched in his good
right hand—must hold a prize like no other, he thought.

The young nobleman he'd nicked had summoned dozens of guardsmen, and when that failed, brought hounds to track him down.

The hounds bayed again, closer still. *They're almost here,* Lewt thought, panicked again.

Reaching the end of the valley, he paused. His every instinct told him to head for the docks. If he made it, he could hide on his cousin's Jaft's fishing boat. But something else, a deeper instinct perhaps, told him to drop the purse, that he'd done all this before and it hadn't worked.

He darted into a doorway, hunched over, panting, the purse pressed to his chest between his two hands. He had to *think.*

The nobleman had brought in dogs to track him down. Nobody'd ever done that before, no matter what he'd stolen. It meant the man needed his pouch back desperately, so desperately he might never stop until he had it.

I'm doing this wrong, Lewt thought again. His right hand itched, and then he *knew*—somehow, inexplicably, *knew*—that the dogs would catch him, that the nobleman would cut off his right hand and reclaim his pouch that very hour.

In the distance, several streets over, Lewt heard guardsmen shouting. The hounds' voices rose anew. The world seemed to focus down into that one sound: the air became very, very still, and the moment seemed to freeze in perfect clarity.

Lewt's hands trembled. He tossed the pouch away, into the center of the alley where the guardsmen and their hounds would find it. *Let them have it,* he thought. *It's not worth my hand!*

Then, the burning in his chest and pains in his gut worse than ever, Lewt stumbled down the alley. When he'd gone three blocks, he heard shouts of triumph—and abruptly the hounds grew still. *They found the pouch,* he thought. *I'm safe.*

He slowed to a walk. He was alive and whole. Wiping sweat from his forehead, he reeled giddily for a moment, drunk with happiness. A burden he hadn't known he'd carried seemed lifted from his shoulders.

He made it to the docks, swam out to where his brother's little fishingboat lay moored, and pulled himself aboard. Dripping, he lay there and stared up at the night sky. *It's not worth it,* he told himself. *It's really not.*

In the morning, when the fishermen came out to their ships, he'd ask Jaft . . . *humbly* ask . . . if he could be a fisherman, too. It would be hard work. It would mean hours of back-breaking labor every day of the year. Somehow, though, the decision felt right.

Closing his eyes, he slept, at peace with himself.

I leaned back. Lewt's goblet was empty now, too . . . his wish used up. He'd relived the night he'd lost his hand . . . and become whole again.

That only left Rishta. I gazed into his goblet, and once more the wine swirled and became a window. . . .

Screaming, Rishta tumbled through endless miles of sky. The sun blurred overhead like a field of molten gold, and winds spiced with the smells of distant lands washed over him. Then the world turned upside down, and when it righted, he was in a room . . . a gigantic room, a room so high clouds floated below the ceiling beams, a room so wide it could have held an ocean with a dozen seas to spare.

And everywhere around him . . . everywhere stood immense piles of gems, mountains of silver and gold, a thousand times a million fortunes, all for him and him alone.

He waded knee-deep into piles of coins. Zelloquan royals, Coranian dzebs, Merindian tumacs, and so many more he couldn't begin to identify: all for him and him alone!

Quickly he filled his pockets with gold, and just as quickly he emptied them out and filled them again with gems. He found diamonds as big as his thumb, rubies the size of his fist, emeralds the size of his head—so many, so huge, he couldn't grab them all, no matter how he tried.

In the midst of sorting through a pile of diamonds for the single most perfect specimen, he heard a sound like distant thunder. He paused, listening, as a warm breeze swept over him. Turning, he saw the far wall of the room opening like an enormous door. A brilliant, glowing form filled the opening, its body towering up from the floor, a hundred feet, a thousand feet tall—how high, Rishta couldn't begin to guess.

A god, it has to be a god, he kept thinking over and over again. He threw himself down, covering his eyes, as light from the being's body began to burn him.

Legends spoke of Theshemna, the palace of the gods, which moves among the stars at night. Those same legends spoke of Theshemna's treasure room, where the wealth of a hundred thousand nations flowed.

With fingers like velvet, so soft, so careful, the god scooped Rishta from the treasure room's floor. Rishta screamed in terror. And the screams only stopped when the hand closed, like a man crushing a moth that had flown too close to his lantern's light.

I drew back with a lurch, shocked and horrified. The image of that colossal, glowing hand crushing Rishta's body to pulp burned in my mind.

Rishta's greed had grown until only the wealth of the gods could satisfy it. Of course he'd paid the price.

I dumped my own goblet of wine upon the floor: no sense taking chances with Slab's magic, I thought. Then I stared at the three empty goblets on the table opposite me.

I'd never see Rishta or Lewt or young Galandin again, I thought. Ah, well, at least we'd managed to get our business out of the way first. I reached for my pouch of sleep-gems . . . and found them gone. *Like we'd never made the deal,* I thought with an unhappy sigh. A small fortune lost, but a fortune nonetheless.

Then, out of habit, I patted my money-pouch and found it much diminished as well. I frowned. It seemed I'd paid for the gems, all right . . . but with time rearranged, the gems had never been stolen and never been sold to me.

I pounded my fist on the table and cursed Slab's name. "You won't get away with it!" I shouted. He'd ruined my luck again. "It's not *fair!* Slab! *Slab!*"

Far off, I thought I heard him laughing.

I appear in this story, but in truth it is a tale of my genie, and what became of him after he passed out of my hands. I had thought I had protected the world from the misuse of my genie's magic, but it took one wiser than I to secure the future in which you now read this tale. . . .

THE LAMP OF MANY WISHES

by Mel. White

In the great libraries at Ubar, it is said that there is a book that records the legends of our people. But one tale untold is the story of what befell the Djinn of the Lamp of Many Wishes after Aladdin's adventures, for Scheherazade had not heard the end of the matter. But my grandmother knew the story, and this is how she related it.

After the death of the wicked magician, Aladdin and the princess lived in peace and prosperity for many years. Their fortunes increased and they were blessed with many beautiful children. When the princess' father died, the rule passed unto Aladdin and he became Sultan of all Arabia.

This was a golden age, for Aladdin had made many strong alliances and none dared come against his armies. His people prospered also, for Aladdin caused the djinn of the lamp to perform many good works. He commanded the djinn to dig a string of wells across the desert so that caravans could pass safely and quickly from one end of Arabia to the other. Rivers were cleared and roads were smoothed and the land grew green. Lastly, Aladdin ordered the djinn to move his palace to the city of Ubar, and build there an earthly shadow of the gardens of Paradise.

Word spread of the power of the djinn of the lamp and men came from afar to beg Aladdin for help. Some petitions he granted, but most of them were idle whims or requests that benefited only one person. Aladdin realized that upon his death the lamp might pass into the hands of someone who would use his powers to drain the resources of the land. So Aladdin locked himself in his private chambers and summoned the djinn.

A turquoise mist billowed softly from the lamp, and solidified into the form of the djinn. "I await your commands," the djinn said.

"O Djinn, I am weary of those who wish to use you only for their own gain," Aladdin replied. "I have a plan that will prevent misuse of your power after my death. Henceforth you shall only grant three wishes to each person who owns the lamp."

The djinn bowed low. "You are most wise, O my Master and my friend. It shall be done as you have commanded."

Aladdin smiled. "Now sleep well, best of all servants. I shall cause you to be hidden in a corner of my treasure house and none shall bother you until the day of my death, when you will come into the hands of my oldest son."

Then Aladdin took the lamp and set it in a far corner of his treasure house and locked the doors with many great seals. The djinn was left in peace for many years and that probably would have been the end of the matter had it not been for Malouf Ali Akbar, the Grand Vizier of Tabuk.

A high station is like a sip of seawater, not quenching the thirst for power but rather intensifying it. Although Tabuk was an important city, it was not enough for the Vizier Malouf's ambitions. He used his magic to search throughout the land for objects of power to make him greater still. One day there came to the ears of Vizier Malouf the tale of Aladdin and his lamp and he vowed that he would have this lamp.

Though Aladdin's treasury was guarded with locks against thieves and spells against magicians, it was not as impenetrable as the Sultan thought. There was nothing to bar a small gray rat from entering the room through a carefully chewed hole.

Guided by the vizier, the rat scuttled over the piles of treasure until it came to a battered brass lamp set in an alcove in the far corner of the room. Grabbing the lamp's spout in its teeth, the rat dragged it the length of the chamber and out the hole and carried it to the vizier. Then the Vizier unrolled his magic carpet and flew to his palace at the city of Tabuk.

Once he was alone in his chambers, he drew the lamp from his cloak and sat back to admire his new prize. He chuckled softly as he ran his finger along the dented, tarnished surface. It warmed to his touch and he could feel a faint vibration deep within it. Greedily, he smiled and rubbed the lamp.

Nothing happened.

Frowning, he rubbed harder, scrubbing away its green tarnish to the battered brass surface below. As he brushed his fingers along the dull gleam, he felt a strange vibration, like the growl of a distant volcano. Dropping the lamp, he frantically leapt away from it. A dense stream of turquoise smoke appeared, and a grim-looking djinn unfolded himself from the lamp with the impressive slowness of the desert dawn.

The djinn folded his arms across his chest, a pose that tradition said impressed gullible mortals. "I am the Djinn of the Lamp," he intoned in a voice reserved for state dinners and funeral oratories. "By command of Aladdin, I may grant you three wishes. What is thy first command?"

It was the moment that the Vizier Malouf had been waiting for. "O Djinn of the Lamp, my first wish is for wishes without number—as many wishes as there are stars in the sky," he said.

The djinn frowned. "You can't do that!"

"Why not?" the Vizier Malouf insisted. "You didn't say three wishes about camels or three wishes that you approved of. You said three wishes. My first wish is for unlimited wishes."

The djinn froze in astonishment. Apparently there were some flaws in Aladdin's logic.

"Well?" the Vizier Malouf said, tapping a foot impatiently.

The djinn bowed. "Your wish is my command, O Master," he rumbled softly.

"All of them?" the vizier smiled, his eyes glittering greedily.

"All of them," sighed the Djinn of the Lamp.

It is said that the power that a man wields is no indication of how wisely he uses it. So it was with the Vizier Malouf. Though he had unlimited control over one of the most powerful beings in all the known world, he had no idea what to do with the djinn, and so he turned to traditional tales for inspiration.

In truth, the tale tellers' experiences with all-powerful beings were primarily wish-fantasies about what they would to do if they got their hands on something bigger and stronger than the local sheik. After several unfortunate experiences with some of the bequests mentioned in Scheherazade's tales, the Vizier Malouf finally set the djinn doing household tasks. Thus it was that the Sultan's wives, visiting the Vizier Malouf's chief wife, encountered the djinn standing beside a tamarisk tree, pouring water into the garden fountains.

They shrieked in surprise at seeing the djinn, but soon overcame their shyness and began poking and prodding him to see if they could get him to react. The djinn bore it patiently for a while, then thinned his body to a vapor and continued with his task. Eventually the women grew bored and left, giggling and chattering like a flock of brightly colored birds.

The Djinn of the Lamp watched them leave and sighed.

"They mean no harm. I hope you were not offended," said a soft voice. "They are forbidden the company of men. But as you know, a djinn does not count as a man and so they are very curious about you."

He glanced down. Standing beside him was a homely little woman.

"I am Fatima, the least of the Sultan's wives," she said. "The kinder ones call me Fatima the Wise."

It was not hard to guess what the unkind ones would call Fatima. The Sultan's tastes in wives ran to tawny, beautiful women as slender as reeds with eyes like does. Fatima was short and dumpy with crooked teeth and a slight squint. As a small gray wren among the peacocks was the Lady Fatima among the wives of the Sultan. It was whispered in the harem that the Sultan had married Fatima only because she was the daughter of a king, and sadly this was very true.

The djinn bowed.

She looked at him frankly. "The vizier did not have a djinn before. How did you come to be in his service?"

The djinn sighed heavily, his breath stirring up small

whirlwinds in the garden. "It is a long story, Lady Fatima," he replied.

"And an unhappy one, I would judge," she said.

"I am here," the djinn said, "because I rebelled against Allah's will.

"Know, O Fatima the Wise, that in the days when the world was new, the djinns, ifrits, and peris owned this land. We moved across its face and went where we would and did what we wished. Allah commanded us to plough the earth and sow grass and trees and turn this dry and dusty land into a paradise. We went to work with a will and when it was done, we showed our garden world to Allah and he praised it and said it was good.

"Then Allah declared that this place should be given over to Man, his newest creation. We were told to go to the ninth sphere and make it as magnificent as Paradise. I became wroth at this, fearing that Allah meant to send us throughout the spheres, building and creating, and never giving us any home. And so I spoke unto my people and we made a great rebellion and vowed to destroy what we had made.

"It was a fearful time for mankind. We stormed like fire upon the land, turning green valleys into dry and dusty deserts. Djinns and ifrits raged throughout the cities like the lions of desert and no man could stand against us until a magician named Suleiman the Wise arose and vowed to end our mischief. Then Suleiman made a great magic and trapped the djinns and the peris and the ifrits in a bitter little corner of hell and would not let us free until we swore obedience to him.

"Because I had led the rebellion, my soul was bound unto the very lamp that Aladdin found. And I was commanded to do whatsoever the owner of the lamp asked of me, even unto the ends of time. Aladdin, alone of all my owners, showed understanding and compassion of my plight and used my skills wisely. I should have been content to remain with him unto the end of his days.

"But fate has intervened with this Vizier Malouf, who has stolen me away from Aladdin and given me an unending list of commands, each more ridiculous than the last."

"Surely his wishes are not unusual," Fatima observed.

"They are unusual in their lack of insight about the consequences," the djinn said acidly. "First, he commanded me to bring him a huge feast on gold plates—and then discovered that one man could not eat all that food in one sitting or even ten sittings. So he ordered me to take it away. Then he remembered that the food had been served on golden dishes, so he commanded the plates to be brought back. Then he wanted the dishes washed. If he had wanted a roast chicken and a pile of gold plates, he should have asked for that in the first place.''

Fatima smiled sympathetically. ''Indeed, that was not well thought out.''

''Nor was anything he asked of me thereafter,'' the Djinn of the Lamp sighed. ''His next wish was for a harem of five hundred of the most beautiful women in the world.''

Fatima raised her eyebrow questioningly. ''And he lasted. . . ?''

''Two nights,'' the djinn smirked. ''After retiring as the world's greatest lover he decided to experience great wealth, so he commanded me to fetch him a mountain of gold coins. I suggested he rethink his wish, but he insisted and so I set the coins down outside his treasury. It astonished him when every person in Tabuk who could walk or crawl stampeded to his mountain of gold to grab what they could. Nor did his announcing that the treasure belonged to him make it proof from every thief in Persia.''

Fatima nodded. ''My husband had heard rumors of the treasure, but by the time the commander of his guards got to the place, there was nothing to be found but a large depression and millions of footprints.''

''He decided that immense wealth was too much trouble and had me take the coins away again,'' the djinn replied. ''So he found a new hobby.''

''What is this new passion of his?''

''He wishes to increase his knowledge. Yesterday, he sent me to count the number of grains of sand in the desert and the number of stars in the sky. And just this morning he expressed a burning curiosity to know how many fleas there were on the Sultan's camels,'' the djinn said, scratching his arm.

''Some drink deeply at the font of knowledge,'' Fatima said. ''However, it seems that the Grand Vizier merely gargles at it.''

''I am a great and powerful djinn; the greatest of the chiefs of the djinns. My breath causes the trees to sway.

My footsteps cause the mountains to tremble. Alone I can carry an entire palace. But all my strength and skills are used to satisfy the inane vanities of this fool,'' the djinn growled. ''I would gladly turn him into a jackal were I not bound to obey him forever by the terms of his first wish.''

''I have an idea,'' Fatima said thoughtfully. ''You owe me no wishes, but perhaps you would trade an insight for an insight. If I show you how to be free of the vizier, would you let me grant a gift of insight to someone?''

''Not for yourself?''

''No. For my husband, the Sultan.''

The djinn paused, considering her words carefully. ''You have much to lose,'' she pointed out. ''It will soon occur to the vizier to ask for eternal life and then you will never be free.''

The djinn bowed low. ''You have a bargain, O wise and gentle lady. What is your insight for me?''

''Grant his unspoken wishes. The Vizier Malouf is a hasty man, and if his commands are not well thought out, you may rest assured that his inner impulses are more poorly planned. Amending his own folly will cause his blood to heat and he will admonish you to stop. But in his wrath he will forget to word his command carefully, and by his carelessness you will earn your freedom.''

The djinn smiled broadly. ''I shall take the matter to heart, Lady Fatima,'' he replied.

Thus it was that the Vizier Malouf suddenly found himself being waited on hand and foot by a very obsequious djinn who seemed intent on anticipating his every urge. For a short while, it was flattering—until he wondered what the city looked like from the tallest minaret and suddenly found himself hovering in midair over its very sharp and pointed spire. He commanded the djinn to put him down and managed to squeak out a command to stop before he hit the minaret's spike.

Hiking homeward in a huff, he wished that the weather would get cooler and was obliged by a sudden swift snowfall. He stopped that also, though he thought he saw a slightly malicious grin on the djinn's face. Passing a vendor's stall, he thought to himself that the cakes looked tasty and suddenly found one of the confections in his mouth. It was too much for him and he turned on the djinn hovering solicitously near his side.

"What are you doing?" the Vizier shouted, spraying cake crumbs everywhere.

"O Master, I am simply being a truly attentive slave. I am doing as you commanded and granting your every wish, even unto your tiniest whim," the djinn said in voice like honeyed thunder.

"Well, stop it!" the Vizier Malouf roared.

"Done," said the djinn.

It hit him then, and he gaped like a fish. The djinn slowly favored him with a smile; the kind that showed his fangs to their best advantage. The Vizier Malouf gulped and counted the ivory display in front of him.

"So . . ." he squeaked, feeling like a goldfish encountering a crocodile for the last time.

"So," the djinn replied in a voice like the purr of a thousand tigers. "We are at the parting of our ways, O my former Master. I would not advise you to reach for that lamp," he added. "Unless, perhaps, you intend to hand it to me."

The Vizier Malouf nodded and pulled the battered lamp from his belt with trembling hands. The djinn bowed mockingly. And before the Vizier Malouf could remember that he technically had two wishes left, the djinn took the lamp and departed in a clap of thunder that shook the palace.

Freed forever from his obligation, the djinn raced across the skies, scattering the stars in joy. But he did not forget the one who had helped him. With a wave of his hand, the djinn opened the Sultan's eyes so that he could see what was in the hearts of others. Then the Sultan looked at the women of his harem and saw not their forms and faces but what lay in their hearts. To his eyes the peacock beauties became as screeching jays and Fatima walked among them like the phoenix newly born from the sun. And Fatima became the chief of his wives and her wisdom was a very jewel unto the land.

And so ends the tale of the Djinn of the Lamp of Wishes. It is a true story, O my children, and it was told to me by Fatima herself, who is older and wiser than us all.

From the ancient times back to the present, I now give you Stanford, a man not unlike most men, but faced with a problem that perhaps only I myself could solve. . . .

GRAND TOUR
by Barry N. Malzberg

First slide, please

Here's Stanford. Forty-five, forty-six, definitely past his prime but still in the game, still pitching. In the depths of the night, touching the abyss of sleep, he thinks or dreams: I'd like to give this up, it's all too much, there's too little left for me to justify this endless, shriveled *hoping* . . . but daylight casts such thoughts to the west wind. Stanford hobbles to the shower, his head full of plans, possibilities, detached from all of this post-adolescent *tritesse,* or so he calls it. Five foot eleven, two hundred and seven pounds (this bothers him quite a bit, but he tells himself that it is not grossly excess, most of it is in his upper body and he will begin an exercise program very soon anyway), light beard, haunted eyes, fifty-seven thousand dollars in a money market account, eighty-six thousand in stocks and treasury accounts and (his ex-wife Irene knows nothing of this) four thousand dollars in silver quarters and dimes, smuggled away during that period when the pre-1965 coins were soaring on the collector's or meltdown market. The separation agreement provided considerable alimony and child support, making such a joke of his income that it seemed ridiculous not to just keep the hundred and a half in easy reach since it was going out to Irene anyway almost as fast as he could shovel it in, but the four thousand dollars was his, his little sinking fund, Stanford liked to think, to hold out against eternity. Stunned eyes, sardonic face, hollow, interesting features, the face of a twentieth century man (*late* century, late millennium, on the cusp of grand

and inexpressible change, except he could not quite say what) possessed of the paradigmatic American middle class plight but still trying to come to grips with it, that is Stanford's self-conception. Middle age, isolation, divorce, alimony, disengaged cautious relations with a late-adolescent son and daughter who in those strange moments on the cusp of sleep Stanford cannot quite apprehend, cannot *see*, is not even sure of their names.

Observe Stanford then, doing the best that he can (or so he insists) in this difficult and perilous city on the trembling verge of great changes in the chronology and the millennium, all of the Biblical changes, the signs and portents with which to contend, and Irene's rages when now and then the grief and sheer inequity of her condition overwhelms his forty-three-year-old ex-wife and she will call him (usually after another staggeringly absurd relationship has ended or has just barely begun) to berate him for the attrition of her own possibility and the extent of her philosophy. Stanford does something vague and (he himself calls it this) subterranean in the advertising business, not quite copywriting, not quite supervision, used to be copy chief, now is in charge of account relations, trying to salvage the state of collapsing relationships, keep the copy chief and subordinates happy in the face of collapsing client confidence, heavy contact work with the external departments of automobile or electronics companies, many expense account lunches, too many expense account dinners, troubles. Troubles of all kinds are not foreign to Stanford, who only wants to try to hold things together yet has begun to understand as he paces the spaces of his divorced man's apartment, a three-room enjambed set of boxes on the riverfront on a high floor, that he had better moderate his posture and ambitions, just trust that it does not collapse spontaneously and wholly atop him. He dates women from the corporate offices, usually secretaries, promises them little, makes assertions that he will not fall in love with these glistening, nervous, preoccupied women of the telephone, yet often enough does, finds himself crying out in vague and desperate phrases at the peak or depths of his necessity. All of these relationships end badly, some quite early, some in the middle, very few have a decent and protracted end. Stanford could sue for marriage, could look for something more permanent. In this age of plague the concept of a bachelor's existence seems as pitiable and archaic as the expeditions he used to take with the children, 15 years ago, to the last of the amusement parks in this area: spin the wheels, eat the plaster of cotton candy, stumble through the funhouse, listening to the wind machine and attending to the rattle of tape-recorded chains in the background, but Stanford sees no alternative, sees no real prospects. Women over 40 bore or terrify him with their refraction of his own coming collapse, younger women want to nest and procreate, Stanford is convinced, regardless of what lies of adventure they utter. One hundred and forty thousand dollars is not enough between him and the abyss, not when he has to cough up six hundred and ten to Irene every blasted week, regardless of his opinions on the matter, not when he takes home fourteen hundred and change out of which he has to finance his declining health, his declining years, diminished sense of possibility.

Stanford does not feel pity for himself, not even pathos, nor any grandiose sense as well; Stanford has been (he feels) in and out of too much trouble and limitation since the mid-nineteen forties to take anything except the end of the millennium seriously, but surging in or out of sleep, caught at that part of his life where he can neither construct defenses nor strip them but must simply confront (without the intervening walls of consciousness, of judgment), Stanford screams with regret, shrivels with fury, comes to shuddering and tendentious interface with the gasp and clutter of his life, the fullness of its insufficiency, the slivers which its furious power drill of decline sends straight to his foolish and shuddering heart. "Oh, love me!" he will cry to the secretaries or (occasional) junior account executives, caught in their random clutch, history battering at the door he has tried so determinedly to close, "Love me, love me true!" and so in and out to that source of all nakedness while he tries to avoid that more desperate knowledge conveyed by sleep.

The Album, page by page

Thus Stanford's djinn, his familiar, his ornament of all desire. This intrusion of fantasy into Stanford's life is neither calculated nor surreal, it simply occurs, as most of his life (he can now see in retrospect) has arrived without

portent, as a juxtaposition that flowered into consequences.

"You have three wishes," the djinn says to Stanford.
"You may take them in the usual way, or you may combine
them for a grand sequence of events; you may try small
changes or you may try one great, transmogrifying lunge.
The choice is yours," the djinn says casually, glad at last
to have someone sensible with whom to share his magic.
It has, after all, been a long time since the djinn has been
able to engage in conversation; there are whole annals of
buried time here, and they are hardly to be annealed by
Stanford's fortuitous discovery of the bottle. Of which
more may never be said, all of this being part of the jumbled artifact and casual detritus which Stanford thinks of
as the sum of his life.

"That's astonishing," Stanford says, "I've never imagined anything like this. I can't believe that this is happening. It must *not* be happening, I've gone over the edge. I
didn't think the partitions would stand for the rest of my
life. I saw this all coming," Stanford adds. "I knew I was
heading for a total, a real crack-up. That Irene, she warned
me. She wasn't wrong—"

"Enough of this," the djinn says. "You can go on in
this disbelieving way or you can come to grasp your opportunities. You were always sincerely interested in opportunities, Stanford, it led you straight to the ad racket
instead of graduate study in Chaucer which you felt was
an alternative back there in 1971 when alternatives seemed
to count. I advise you not to delay too much of this, however; the situation is fluid and I am apt to pass on or to
decompose now into thin, thin air. So you had best assume
your choices, seize the possibility so to speak." The djinn,
who has been sealed away too long to really be effective
in social situations, fixes Stanford with intense, Middle
Eastern eyes and says, "Disbelief of itself is not going to
resolve the situation here.

"I should point out—evoking without further delay the
first person which is crucial to any understanding of my
functions—that *I* am the djinn at issue, that the events of
this narrative have, from the start and will throughout,
have been refracted through my own perspective. I cannot
claim full access to Stanford's consciousness, much of what
I infer or state has come from his own confessions, my

imperfect knowledge, and yet I can assume for the sake of
this recollection, a kind of omnipotence which, no less
than Stanford's reiterated hopes and platitudes, can be seen
as central. Of my background, of my presence in the bottle, the difficult, riotous journey from the refinery to Stanford's possession, and of the unstoppering of the bottle
resulting in this collision . . . of all of this, perhaps, the
less given the better it will be although Stanford himself
has expressed at times a great interest in my background.
Like any devoted member of the middle class, Stanford is
fascinated by mysticism, seeks signs and wonders, is enthralled by portents: it is this and only this (he has felt)
which could possibly change his life, his life otherwise
being wholly and ruinously carved out by circumstance.
But I am not interested in exploring a personal history
here; I come to the situation with a good deal more chronology and experience than Stanford or anyone presently
in his circle of experience and what good has it done me?
What good has any of this done me? My circumstances
have been pitiably limited for centuries and now, as the
outcome of my own curse, my own assignation, I have
been given the idiot task of proffering and executing wishes
for a man too stunned or disbelieving to utter them. It is
idiot's work, after all, it is work as mindless as Stanford's
own duties which are to quell the apprehension of one
client after the next that the work done by Stanford's firm
is utterly specious. The fulfillment of wishes! But what,
after all, is left for Stanford and djinn alike as circumstances crawl to their unmerited but long-foreshadowed
apocalypse, an apocalypse so soon to come, so needlessly
spectacular in its essence. In that thunderous set of moments so long ago when I was created and sent out on the
first of these silly and florid errands, I was given no more
understanding of the situation than I have at present; the
important thing is to entice Stanford into living out his
fate so that I may move on. Or not move on as the case
may be. It is difficult to apprehend or find some final posture for any of this, as one might well have inferred by
this time. Inch by inch, episode by episode, I have crawled
my way through the centuries and what, for all of these
florid gifts so extravagantly given, have I been able to gain?
Most of those centuries a neonate clutched in a bottle and
then dialogues or disasters visited upon the Stanfords of

their time. It would all be too much to grasp if I had a visionary intellect, but I do not. Djinns have no taste for metaphor, djinns merely execute as I have pointed out to Stanford already, without particular success or communion.

"Or so it might be said," I offer.

"I don't know," Stanford says, "I have to think about all of this. I have to give it some thought. I mean, it is too much for me, being faced with decisions like this, and I a man not given to wishes, fantasies, or fairy tales of any sort. Do I have some time to decide? Or do I have to decide right now? This is very difficult for me," Stanford says. "It is all I can do to handle the realistic details, and then you confront me with stuff like this. Well, I didn't ask to be a loss leader," he says pointlessly, and looks at the bare walls of his apartment. Maybe there is some clue flickering on those walls, handwriting or something like that. But there does not seem to be.

"A little time," the djinn says. "We can understand that. My Masters and those who convey me, I mean. You can have a little time to work this out. But not much. Events pass on, there are priorities and mysteries beyond your own divining and if you do not express a wish, I'm going to be forced to express one *for you* . . . there is very little slippage or leakage in this practice, and we cannot allow the circumstances to pass."

"I understand that," Stanford says, with what he takes to be a hollow laugh but which—to the djinn whose experience with inference is far greater than Stanford's, and who knows every crevice of the man's despair and regret, pinned by this grim, unwanted apprehension—is allied to a sob. "I think I am coming to some profound understanding." But of course he is not. What must be understood about Stanford and all his companions and compatriots in this time of diminution and loss, is that he understands nothing, he proceeds through his life and toward his end with the stunned and incipient dismay of a farm animal; he has the illusion of understanding, but the farm animal has the illusion of the farm. When, of course, it is only the plow, the barn, the whisk of the slaughterhouse ax which that animal can properly assess.

* * *

The first wish

Stanford's first wish, as is so common among those of his age and condition, is for immortality, for the contemplation of an unending lifespan through which, he feels, he can pick the best, the finest and most apt of possibilities for his second and third wishes. Why someone in Stanford's circumstances would opt for eternal life is beyond me, beyond the djinn, beyond the prophets, sages, visionaries or martyrs who look dimly upon this adventure from a grave and mourning distance, but that is of course irrelevant. The djinn nods assent, lifts a taloned hand, emits a theatrical puff of blue smoke, divided into the horns of Satan which is a bit of stage business which is always effective, never ignored. "You are now, for all intents and purposes, immortal," the djinn says. "I would not recommend leaping from your patio here or going through the cities deliberately seeking deadly diseases, but within the expected limits of a life conventionally lived, you will stay in this condition forever or at least a reasonable simulacrum of forever. Stanford transmogrified! Stanford triumphant! Stanford eternal! as you might say. The usual conditions apply, of course, but they would have applied in any case, and there is no need whatsoever to discuss them."

"How do I know that?" Stanford says. The djinn and Stanford are no longer in his apartment, they have adjourned to the riverfront walk where for the past quarter of an hour they have been pacing in the odors of the late evening, the trash and oil slick of the harbor coming over them, and have been discussing issues such as this toward, at last, a definite outcome. The djinn has assumed for the purpose of this public appearance, the form of an adolescent girl, about five feet two, punk jewelry, punk hairdo and a slight nasality of address which reminds Stanford of his own daughter some years ago but in no pleasantly nostalgic fashion. The djinn can, of course, assume many forms or postures (not an unlimited number, however) in addition to the normal green dwarfism, but Stanford and he have both decided that a punk hairdo and tiny, suggested breasts under a T-shirt saying GRATEFUL DEAD TOUR 1992 is best. "I mean, I don't feel any different than I did two minutes or twenty days ago. The whole thing could be some kind of cosmic joke, some cheap scam worked out by the fates, not that I doubt that there is something substantial going on here because the shapechanging is very convincing. Also the effects with the smoke.''

"You'll have to take it on faith," the djinn says. "What otherwise could I tell you? Your era is an expression of faith: turn on the switch for the electricity, eat the frozen food trusting that it is not poisonous, accept the pledges of politicians that they will not kill you or level your possessions for the sheer sport of it. Go with strange women to their place or yours in the faith that they will not kill you or communicate a dreadful disease, act with the clients downtown as if their work and yours were not absurd and pointless. Accept the irrelevance of all Biblical prophecy to the coming closure of the millennium. Why should this be any different, then, why this expression of faith any more dramatic—or less dramatic—than the others? There comes a time when you must come free of all history, make that sheer leap into possibility. Or is this too complex for you, Dads, is this as evasive as acid rock or like what your middle-aged jollies are?'' The djinn, noting fellow strollers and passersby taking some interest in this couple, has deliberately broadened and extended his speech patterns, has become more purely punk and filial in his appearance as he and Stanford have come close to those sightseers, then relaxes his grip and modifies his rhetoric as they pass on. "Anyway, that's what the situation is."

"I suppose so," Stanford says. His cells do not seem to be bubbling and expanding with changed or charged health but then again, as has been pointed out, how would he know? Immortality cannot be proven other than by the absence of death *ever* and Stanford does not seem to be dying now. Except internally, but that is the same old story. "All right," he says. "I'll accept that I'm immortal, at least until I turn seventy and inch by inch feel it all sliding away. There's no way to prove a negative, right? Now, how long do I have for the other two wishes?"

"Not too long, Dads," the djinn says, squeezing Stanford's arm again as two youths in motorcycle dress squeeze by on the narrow walkway, look at the couple with vagrant interest modulated only by their own abstract and imponderable concerns. "Maybe an afternoon and an evening. You wait and wait and wait in a bottle but eventually, when it comes, commission has to be real fast, like you understand? Sort of like sex where you can spend a week or a lifetime plotting, but when you pound toward the ultimate it takes maybe three or four seconds. But *what* a three or four seconds, right, Pops?'' the punk-haired djinn says enthusiastically, making quite a convincing case of their huddled companionship although after all these centuries in old Persia or the dank spaces of the bottle, you wouldn't put it past the djinn to be hopelessly out of date. It is one of the small surprises—oh, there have been many for Stanford in this voluble and disconcerting thirty-six hours—with which this relationship, this strange collision have been filled.

Next slide, please

Here is Stanford entering the actress Lilly von Nabokov in her elegant, great bed in the elegant, grand house in Bel Aire where she has lived for these seven years, just about the same span since she legally changed her name to this expressive and resonant pseudonym and assumed full responsibility for her career. Stanford is ecstatic, he is incoherent, he cannot believe that this is happening while at the same time—at the precise and simultaneous moment of his connection—he *knows* that this is going on and that it is happening at a level of conviction and force which has characterized no other part of his life.

Here is Stanford expending his second wish, the frivolous wish, the wish that he knows is for pointless pleasure and with which he will indulge himself before embarking upon the serious and irrevocable business of the third wish. He has always wanted to have congress with a famous actress, to be actually entering the woman on the screen in ways which will enable him to feel, as he has never before been able to feel, that he is living his life.

Observe Stanford moan and dive! Observe—without erotic or prurient entanglement of any kind because this is research and anatomization, not pornography, not the recyling of helpless and self-limited fantasy—the true and solemn nature of his performance as again and again with closed eyes and open, torment and release, possibility and impossibility, he pays homage and adoration to Lilly von Nabokov in the only way he could have imagined at fourteen, in the only way he can imagine now. Dispense with the details which in any case would be predictable and unflattering to any sense of the true religiosity of this occasion, dispense with those graphics of form or motion which could only congeal the pure and terrible flight of sensibility in which Stanford, now coupled, would like to feel himself engaged. Upon the copious and accepting form of Lilly von Nabokov, Stanford pays what tribute he can, the full extent of his expenditure seemingly inadequate to the opportunity and surface presented, but still, considering his age and the endless disappointment which he feels has up to this point been his lot, a praiseworthy exercise of the flesh and spirit. Moving in and out of conjunction with the lovers, just as Stanford himself moves in and out of his own busy necessity, we can catch odd angles and strange perspectives, can perhaps understand the nature of life in the movies as nonobservers never could. The movies are both more and less than Stanford's own experience over these years, his own perceptions of Lilly von Nabokov both greater and smaller than those with which he has indulged himself during those occasions of his maturity when for the most part he has liked to think of himself as a responsible adult.

The wish does not in any way blanket Lilly von Nabokov's response, her own feelings on the situation. In his haste and desire Stanford did not specify other than to make sure that in no way could the act be regarded as rape . . . but I am pleased to say that the actress responds with some enthusiasm and utter concentration to Stanford's not entirely clumsy flounderings, and is able in her own engaged fashion to approximate a climax no less satisfactory (in fact, truthfully, *more* satisfactory) than that which has already seized the enthralled Stanford and cast him away. Actresses are, after all, capable of this, their very happiness and occupation is concerned with the conversion of the imagined to the real. Also, they are easily persuaded and amenable in the way actors must be, in order to enact their ancient and honorable craft.

See Stanford sprawled upon her now, note the tangle or disentanglement of limbs! Stanford sings and mumbles into Lilly von Nabokov's shell-pink and tenderly accommodating ear. The actress, reciprocally, suggests that they move apart because his weight, so pleasant in the moment, is oppressive in the aftermath. Stanford cooperates, turning slowly to one side, then when the actress gasps, to the other, rescuing his weight with an elbow and then dropping fully into the sheets. It is a splendid, grandiose bed, a dappled and accommodating room of which Stanford has seen all too little, so hasty was his departure to these quarters, so rapid was his entrance into Lilly von Nabokov's diamond mine. Omitting specifics, the wish left the devices of fulfillment more or less to the djinn, and djinns are accommodating but unimaginative creatures, sometimes all too direct as a result of their lack of imagination. Stanford, however, can have few complaints; he surely cannot regret this second wish, the directness and force of his accommodation serving for him as refreshing contrast to the unknowable and imperceivable first wish, the results of which he will not be able to judge for a long time.

We leave Stanford to his post-coital mutterings and his discussions with Lilly von Nabokov. Perhaps they will couple again and perhaps they will not. Perhaps this momentary assignation will lead to further relationship and then again it may be otherwise. Stanford is strictly on his own here and although all of the usual limitations apply, the djinn has, in the most gentlemanly fashion, given him some options, some open space. Nothing less would show the proper consideration.

Life in a bottle

Life in a bottle—since the djinn is asked, he would be discourteous not to respond—is very much like death in a bottle; there is this limitless grayness, this oblivious press of time, the centuries grind by like moments, the moments are centuries, all is strange and inseparable as a kind of imagic association for an imponderable period. It is compressed and encroaching, but it is not humiliating; humiliation is—as Stanford himself has learned through Irene and his children—more a state of mind than an absolute. At last the decanting, the infusion of air, the sudden and vaulting rush toward the light! And then in the midst of various astounding effects which are attention-getting in the extreme, the djinn stands revealed to the fortunate agent of decanting, ready to do service for the usual price and conditions which, like so much else, need not be discussed here.

Life in a bottle is neither pleasant nor unpleasant; it is pointless and absurd in the way that twentieth century life for Stanford and so many of his tribesmen must be seen

as pointless and absurd . . . but it is not more so. There
are ancient and terrible oaths, huge, layered slabs of conviction, comparison and mystery which overlay the occu-
pant, that tend to reduce complaint to the level of
acceptance. A djinn does not ask to be a djinn, this is so
. . . but he does not ask for the reverse, either; this is all
part of the levels of accommodation imposed. Did Stanford ask to be Stanford? But woke up once, undeterminable
ble years ago to find that he *was* and the bottle of his
containment no less real than that which entrapped the
djinn. As has been noted before, we have no taste for
metaphor; we are a concrete and settled race.

The excursion fare covers all charges
On the banks of the Seine, having for his third wish
elected unlimited travel and displacement, Stanford allows
himself small, greedy peeks at the river, so much the focus
of artists in the last three centuries, looks covertly at
women with parasols he would love to know but whose
absence from his life he can now accept. Lilly von Nabokov may work out for him, then again she may not, it
is all unsure. She has asked him to call her up when she
has finished shooting her present project; a romantic adventure comedy, it is meant to wrap in three weeks. In
Poland, Stanford has looked upon the rolling landscape,
has admired the hearty Polish workers so earnest in their
efforts and hopeful in their possibilities, he has mourned
at the concentration camp memorials and has sought the
comfort of simple Polish secretaries who in this country
seem less technologized and not susceptible to his blan-
dishments. In Seville, Stanford had gasped at the advent
of machinery into that once-gentle landscape. In Peking,
astonished by the sheer density of the bicycle and pedes-
trian traffic, he had tried to fathom the nature of cultural
revolution. But now, in France, enacting as per the terms
of his wish the instantaneous satisfactions and blurred
transfers of a perpetual excursion rate, Stanford allows
himself to settle against the high parapet, glances upon the
river with longing and remorse, thinks of Seurat and Mo-
net busily converting their own impressions so long ago.
It is an experience both astonishing and humbling to Stanford, who in all these years until the decanting had traveled very little, had had little concourse with the world,

had been compelled—as in the bed with the actress—to enact the most splendid or treacherous of his desires within a compass narrower than that of any seventh century saint.

Stanford closes his eyes, dreams of the compression and flurry of events in these few weeks since the miraculous shift of his life, opens his eyes as if expecting to see all of it taken from him: no Seine here, but his own riverfront in front of him, no memories of Lilly von Nabokov but only Irene's shrieking and tumultuous telephoned complaints, no immortal life but only the first intimations of metastases in his lungs which will slowly strangle all memory, all possibility. But no, none of this happens: as he stares into the panorama before him it is still the Seine which he sees and the memories of his connection are full and rich within him, entirely too convincing to be other than real. He feels himself inflated with potential, remembers a sunrise in Acapulco two days ago which struck him as an experience close to metaphysical, remembers riotous events in a Tiajuana cantina which fortunately he had been able to disengage from before the girl on the bartop had seen him or the active and curious donkey had poked a nose into Stanford's gin. It has been very different, very different indeed for Stanford over these recent weeks and yet—the glassy and implacable sheen of the river would drive this insight into him most convincingly—he is still the man he has always known. Immortal, perhaps, consort of the world's most famous and beautiful actress for certain, a perpetual wishful tourist now with his own travel agent and instant transfer . . . with all of this, he is the same old Stanford, the wistful and regretful guy he has come to know so well over these decades and he suspects that he always will be. Perhaps this is part of the paradigm of knowledge which these conditions have been created to place upon him: that three wishes or ten, that all fates or no fates will nonetheless cast Stanford always back upon himself. As if all signs and wonders, all meaning and portents must eventually lead to this simple acceptance of the irretrievability of his life, the enormity of his regret. Stanford shrugs and turns from the river, trudges toward the hotel. Such thoughts are too weighty to have carried all this distance although he was afflicted in Peking and Seville by epiphanies no less predictable and humiliating. He tries to think of this as little as possible, tries to ignore the women with parasols whom he dare not desire, since his three wishes thoughtlessly have included none of this.

Perhaps in some other way, some other simulacrum of Stanford might have worked out a different situation, he thinks, but that is beyond him. Most things are beyond him. He trudges onward, this traveler of the late millennium, seized not by limitation but by purpose as he considers the many advancing millennia through which he may be able to consider this condition.

Last slide, please
Here is Stanford, confronting the bleak and illimitable landscape of imponderable millennia, not trudging, holding fast now, trying to establish some final understanding of his condition. "This was the price, wasn't it?" he says to the djinn. "But what if I hadn't asked for immortality? Would I still have been condemned to this wasteland?" Stanford chooses not to discuss the apocalypse which— like everything else—is many millennia behind him. He is thinking not now of the Biblical but the practical. "That was the plan all along, right?" he says.

The djinn—still in punk guise, he is kind of fond of it, he has decided, and finds it the most amenable of all the guises he had adopted through his own imponderable progression of time seized—says, "I don't know. I don't think of this as punishment. I don't think of this as anything at all. I told you, djinns have no understanding of metaphor. One thing doesn't stand for another thing, it simply *is*. That's the best way to carry on our condition."

"It's monstrous," Stanford says. Millions of years have thickened his lungs, stuck in his throat, made his speech guttural although otherwise he is more or less the same guy, only burdened by the sheer dimensions of his knowledge. "I wouldn't have done it if I had known. Who wants to hang around like this? And it's all turned out the same."

"Well," the djinn says, snapping gum and adopting a more convincing guise although it has not been necessary for a very long time to masquerade, to adopt a convincing persona, "That's like the total unit of it, you know? The sameness of everything? But you had to find that out on your own."

"It's crazy," Stanford says. Here is Stanford, still trying to be sane at the edge of the world, but admitting to craziness as a cunning way of deferring, he thinks, an inevitability. He is wrong. He has always been wrong, although less than ever is this a proper concern. "The wishes had nothing to do with it, did they? This was all set out from the beginning."

"I don't know," the djinn says. For sport, he turns into an Arabian potentate of frightening mien, *whisk!* one exercise of transmogrification, and he fixes Stanford with unblinking and terrifying eyes. "It is all in the cause of prophecy, of course. The prophetic is the absolute," the djinn says mysteriously and then strides off (as the djinn has been so apt to do over these recent millennia), leaving Stanford once again alone, amidst the dusk and dirt of exhausted possibility, looking at the gray band of sky against the gray ribbon of river, trying to find some conjunction that cannot exist.

"Three wishes," Stanford says, "*three* wishes." He seems to want to say more and if there were an observer to consider the situation, there might from Stanford be some outpouring of final revelation. But there is *no* observer, all observation ceased long ago, and so it is not possible to judge what has been said. Second millennial man confronts the fullness of his destiny against that gray and diminished ribbon of sky and for the meaning of all this, for its implication and portent, one must as always turn elsewhere. The situation is not inconsiderable, but it is far beyond Stanford's means to apprehend.

The unbottling

Stanford twists the stopper, yanks at it, feels it leap within his hand, and then the steam begins its arc through the spaces of his riverfront digs, his hand clutched with the arthritic imprint of something at last beyond his control. Swirls and steam convulse in the ceiling, and from their outline congeals a figure which Stanford feels he may recognize from old books, half-glimpsed in childhood. Perhaps not. It is very difficult to keep a steady eye on all of this. At length, something which might be human streams from the ceiling, settles before him, grants him a wink from a glazed eye under a turbaned cap. "That is a pleasure and a portent," the figure says, "and in return I am prepared for the most minimal arrangements to offer you three wishes. Three wishes which will change your life. You must, however, embark upon them quickly; oth-

erwise my power and obligation will disappear and nothing, nothing at all will happen.'' The eye is watery but
filled with conviction. ''It will be for your best interest to
choose quickly,'' the figure says.

Stanford, who had only wanted a wine cooler and a light,
easily absorbed drunk before dinner, stares in fixity and fascination. From the depths he feels an obscene necessity, a
certain pornographic recognition and even as he tries to deny
those emotions they seem to flood him as the steam has flooded
his upscale but distinctly underfurnished condominium.

''I can't name my wants so easily,'' Stanford says.
''Nothing like this has happened before.''

''Everyone,'' the figure says, ''can codify his wants. It
goes with being human.'' It stares at him solemnly and
this time winks. ''You may call me Djinn,'' he says, ''That
is not my name, I *have* no name, but that is my condition
and the condition is as close to naming as you may become. All power, possibility, all riches lie within your
means if you choose correctly,'' the djinn says. ''If you
do not, of course, the opportunity has vanished. It is almost time,'' the djinn says. ''It is almost time, it is nearly
time, it *is* time as my power already crumbles.''

Stanford, dismayed, twists his thumb in the bottle; there
is, of course, nothing else. Contemplating, formed to full
attention, he considers the djinn while the djinn considers
him and it is as if the full weight of his futile meanderings
and convolutions has come upon him and with it the desire
to change, to shift the focus of his being toward some kind
of adjustment and possibility.

''I'm thinking about it,'' Stanford says. ''Let me think
about it. I'm thinking about it as fast as I can.''

The lights, please

''The lights, please,'' Stanford says, staring out at the
impossible and ravaged deadlands, but of course there are
no lights. There are no lights and no djinn to rekindle
them. There is, however, a profusion of memory and for
all I know, Stanford is recycling it at this very recollected
moment while the rest of you are, I am empowered to say,
dismissed. Please do not crowd the aisles and leave the
visual aids you have been given on the front desk.

Here is another tale of the unending conflict between magic and science, and the manner in which my genie achieved his freedom. . . .

DJINNXED
by Deborah Millitello

For the ten millionth time, Zhumaii paced his windowless prison, counted the cracks in the walls, sang every song he knew, and cursed his fate. "That mortal wizard commanded me to abduct the Sultan's favorite concubine! I had no choice! And for this, the Sultan imprisoned me! If I am ever released, I shall slay the first mortal I see. Then I shall find the Sultan and the wizard and slay them, as well!"

Suddenly, the cell started shaking, tossing Zhumaii to the bare floor. He heard a loud pop and a rush of wind. Sunlight poured in from above. Surprised, he stared at the warm, yellow light, then he yelled with joy and flew upward toward the opening. He stretched to his full height and looked eagerly about for whoever had freed him.

Standing on a wide sandy beach was a tiny man, his strange clothes dripping wet. He held a dark blue bottle in one hand, its stopper in the other. The man's mouth dropped open as he stared up at Zhumaii.

"Bow, O mortal!" Zhumaii said. "Pray to your gods, for I am Zhumaii the blue djinn, and I am going to kill you!"

For a moment, the man didn't move. Then he ran toward Zhumaii, hugged the djinn's gigantic pale blue ankle, and said, "Oh, thank you! Thank you ever so much!"

Zhumaii blinked his emerald eyes, uncertain he'd heard the man correctly. "Mortal, I mean to kill you!"

"Yes, I know!" the man said with a lopsided grin. "I'm so grateful! Could you do it right now?"

Is he mad, the djinn wondered cautiously, *or just a fool?*

Killing a madman brings ill luck. "You wish me to kill you?"

"Oh, yes, if you would." The man nodded vigorously, swayed, then rested his head against the djinn's ankle before he looked up again, grinning. "You are a genie, aren't you? I never thought I'd be so lucky!"

Irritated, Zhumaii asked, "Why, mortal, should I give you what you desire? Why do you wish to die?"

The men plopped down on the sand, grabbed a pale green bottle marked "Brandy," took a gulp and coughed. "You don't want to hear my story."

Zhumaii stared at him, then threw up his hands. "I have not heard a new tale since Kasim the Blind told me about the merchant and the twin dancing girls with the enormous . . ." He paused, delight shivering through him.

"You must've been in there a long time," the man said.

Zhumaii rubbed his smooth chin. "I do not know."

The man shrugged. "Doesn't really matter. Sit down, and I'll tell you my troubles."

Confused, Zhumaii lowered himself to the warm sand beside the man.

"Oh, my name is Franklin. Franklin Virgil Gates, III," the man said and stuck out a hand to the djinn.

Ignoring the hand, Zhumaii said, "And I, Franklin Franklin Virgil Gates, III, am Zhumaii Ali ben Yusef, fourth tarkan of the blue djinn, captain of the Great Djinn's legions, lord of the summer winds."

"You certainly are blue," said the man, brown eyes wide as he scanned Zhumaii from head to toe. "And call me Frank."

"As you wish," the djinn said, "and you may call me Zhumaii."

"Do you mind if I ask you a question?"

"Ask what you will, Frank," Zhumaii said.

"You're a djinn, not a genie? What's the difference?"

Zhumaii's lips curled, revealing sharp teeth. "Genie is a mortal word which angers us. Often, the utterer's tongue is ripped out."

Frank patted his soggy chest. "I'd never offend a person with a racial slur! I'll never use that word again." Abruptly, he laughed. "Of course, since I'll be dead soon, I won't have a chance to."

Zhumaii grinned wider. "That is good."

"Anyway, where was I?" Frank frowned and scratched his stubbly cheek. "Oh. I was trying to drown myself when I found your bottle and opened it."

"Why were you trying to drown yourself?"

Frank's shoulders slumped, and he shook his head. "You wouldn't believe. Nothing in my life has gone right. Do you know what it's like to be smarter than all the other kids in town?" He glanced up at Zhumaii. "No, I guess not. Anyway, I swore I'd leave when I grew up, and I did. Got a scholarship to UCLA to study computers—"

Zhumaii cocked his head. "UCLA? Computers?"

Frank raised a bushy brow. "University of California at Los Angeles. And a computer, well, it's like a . . ." he scrunched his mouth, tapped his chin, then brightened, "like an abacus, a counting machine. Sorta."

"Ah," Zhumaii said.

"I graduated in only two years and started Lasertronics to build computers. I had a rich wife, a son, a huge estate, a yacht, summer home, cars, horses, stocks, everything a man could want."

Zhumaii didn't understand all of that, but he said, "Then you are wealthy and much favored by the gods."

Frank snorted. "I wish! My vice president in charge of accounting embezzled sixty percent of the profits last year, claimed a loss on taxes, and left a set of books that implicated me!" He barely caught himself before he toppled to the side. "Sure, I've skimmed a little, cheated on taxes, used every loophole I could, but nothing like he did. Now the IRS is confiscating everything not in trust for my kid. And I'm looking at years in prison for tax evasion!"

Vice president? Embezzled? IRS? What did these words mean? "I have heard it said that a man's wealth is in his family. Is not your family well?"

Frank groaned. "My wife just filed for divorce. She wants to marry her fitness instructor! She says I only wanted her money. Sure I did, but I didn't need it after my company became successful."

He sniffled and hugged his bottle. "My son's in Tibet, getting in touch with his inner self, turning his back on the world. Of course, he used my money to get to Tibet and keeps drawing from my account." He took another drink. He looked so dejected, Zhumaii almost felt sorry for him.

"But what of your trade?" Zhumaii asked. "Do you not find satisfaction in your work, building these computers?"

Frank cringed. "Foreign companies make chips cheaper than I can buy here, and have clones out as soon as mine hit the stores. They underbid me on big contracts, lure my best engineers away, and even tried a takeover. I only managed to keep the company by getting a loan—just before the bank went belly-up. Now the new owners want to foreclose." He drained the bottle, brandy trickling from the corner of his mouth. "I'm ruined! Nothing left! That's why I want you to kill me, see?"

Zhumaii stood up and scowled at Frank. "Yes. I see that you are indeed a miserable mortal. To kill you would be merciful." He raised his foot to crush Frank, then halted. Zhumaii's eyes widened, then he smiled and set his foot down beside Frank. "But I am not merciful. I swore that I would slay the first mortal I saw when I was free, in revenge against the mortal wizard who caused my imprisonment. But allowing you to live would be the greatest curse I could give you. May you only die of old age and never prosper."

"I . . . I won't die?" Frank staggered to his feet. "No—wait! You said you would!"

Zhumaii laughed. "Farewell, O most miserable of men, and may you live many years." He launched into the midday sky, while Frank's shouts of "You can't do this to me!" faded behind him.

Zhumaii was free at last. It was good to breathe fresh air, feel the warm sun on his back, and hear the whisper of wind, the song of sea birds, the crash of waves. Soon he would reach the lands of silks and spices, camels and caravans.

"Now may the descendants of the Sultan and of the wizard yet live." He grinned, anticipation as sweet as honeycomb in his mouth. "But not for long."

Here is a story from my youth, of the days when I was carefree and headstrong and married to Fatima.

And since I am the hero of it, I hope you'll understand that values have changed over the eons. . . .

HUMAN NATURE

Maureen F. McHugh

You know where I learned the most about selling? That "new lamps for old" business. Not that it worked that way; we were young and naive, but nobody is young enough and naive enough to believe that you get something for nothing. What really happened was that the camel's son told Fatima—Fatima was my first wife—that the lamp was an antique and he wanted to appraise it. Then he told her it was worth more shekels than she could count in her pretty little fingers. Fatima, she had notions about proving herself—a princess has to prove herself?—and about showing me that she had a brain in her pretty little head. And what did I care about a brain? All that shining hennaed hair and the little bells she wore in her ears so I heard her coming if I didn't smell the Egyptian perfume she wore first, ting-a-ling-ling and a scent like a dancing girl and I was ding-a-ling-ling. I had a reputation as a wonderful statesman but it was the genie, of course, filling the treasury with my silver. Fatima didn't know that, money was rolling into the treasury and she thought I was the smartest man alive. She would roll those gazelle eyes at me. . . . Anyway, along came that magician with his "antique" scheme. Fatima wouldn't recognize the simplest market scam; it wasn't as if a princess spent much time polishing her street skills. I'm not sure Fatima would have recognized a market. But no, Fatima had shown an innate skill in spending money.

She thought she was so clever. There she came, little bare

feet with her toenails painted rosy pink and the little gold bells
in her ears tinkling. "Aladdin, Aladdin, my love, guess what
I did." Her cheeks were all pink with pride.

That was the beginning of the end of the marriage. We
got the lamp back, of course, and I slew the magician, but
it wasn't the same. When she found out about the genie,
she found out it wasn't *my* innate brilliance that made me
such an astute treasurer. And then she started having second thoughts about other things. Things she used to like.

She decided I was crude. Before I was earthy and virile
and direct. I remember her little toes curling in shock and
delight when I would say something—not vulgar, I mean
a man can talk to his wife, can't he? There we would be,
surrounded by servants with her august father sitting at the
head of the table pontificating on some political nonsense
about an agricultural tax and I would nod sagely and lean
over and whisper in her ear that I intended to do some
farming that evening, find a furrow and plant a little seed—
oh, she'd giggle.

After the lamp she decided I was just showing my true
self. I would whisper some sweet, shocking nothing in her
ear and she would say (quite loudly, in fact), "You can
take the boy out of the mud but you can never take the
mud out of the boy." And a hush would fall over the room
for a moment. Little earrings jingling. Finally got to the
point that those earrings were making me crazy.

The thing was, I wasn't stupid, just young. I was certainly more politically astute than her father. I've herded
goats more politically astute than her father.

Anyway, when Fatima began to shut herself up in her half
of the house I took a second wife. A second wife! God of all,
forgive me, taking a second wife when you have trouble with
the first is like exposing yourself to the pox when you have
boils. I was not woman smart, that wasn't where my clever-
ness lay, and before I knew it I had three of them. Three
households, three thieving major domos selling the goods of
my pantry for their pockets and sneaking lovers in for my
wives. You think I don't know what goes on?

It nearly broke me. They ate or drank or wore or gam-
bled almost every last piece of silver I had. Women and
gambling, I don't understand it. Some people say it's just
a woman's nature, but if you shut me up in a household
for the rest of my life, I'd be bored to death, I might gam-

ble, too. Not that understanding did me a bit of good; once things went wrong with Fatima, things started to go wrong everywhere. Creditors waiting, that sort of thing. There was a time I thought it was the beginning of the end. I'd used my three wishes, you know.

Now that I can afford them, I don't see my wives much and I like it that way. Their machinations keep them all occupied, keep them all out of my hair, or what's left of my hair. When I want a woman, there is Miriam. Miriam is a slave, from the country like me. She likes a good piece of flat bread and a cup of strong tea and isn't too delicate for a bit of rough play. She has broad, brown thighs and strong fingers and she isn't afraid to put her hand down there, if you catch my drift. I'd marry her, but that would ruin her.

But that first marriage going sour, what I thought marked the beginning of the end? That was when I started understanding people. That story, the "new lamps for old," went around the kingdom like wildfire. I told everyone it wasn't true. No one should really believe that anyone was so foolish. Anyone knows that people don't give something for nothing. (Genies, maybe, but I am not so certain that there isn't something in all of it for them, although I've never been able to decide just what. Entertainment, watching us destroy ourselves with our own good fortune.) I must have told the true story a hundred times a week. A thousand. It was like trying to blow out a firestorm.

It started me thinking. Taught me a basic truth about people. And I took that truth and I used it. That truth was better than any lamp, because a kingdom can bring more gold, more jewels, and more power than a genie ever could. Fatima's father never understood it, he thought that all he had to be was his father's chosen heir and everything else was in the hands of the God of All. If he'd had any political sense at all, then the silver and gold my genie brought me wouldn't have been a grain of rice in a warehouse.

What did I learn? That people believe what they want to believe, and all the truth and logic in the world won't change their minds. So you can do almost anything you want to, as long as you keep telling people what they want to hear—whether it's that a princess is foolish enough to believe a peddler's most obvious of lies or whether it's that their neighbors are infidels and you need money for a holy war—they'll disregard all evidence to the contrary.

And on top of that, they'll love you and call you wise.

Men can be so vain!

In the olden days, when we went into battle, we carried our amulets and talismans with us, and we gave thanks to the mystic beings who assured our victories.

But do you do so today? Of course not. Even when you anticipate a long, drawn-out war, and then emerge triumphant in 100 hours, the truth of the matter eludes you. . . .

GENIE STORM

by John E. Johnston III

When I walked into McGinnity's Tavern that night, about the last thing that I expected to see was a fistfight in progress in the back. Fights are completely out of character for McGinnity's. You rarely see fights or holdups in a place with a reputation as a hangout for cops, and we cops have been McGinnity's main customers ever since he opened the place some thirty years ago.

Not only had I not expected the fight, but I was also surprised just to be able to see all the way to the back of the place. For three decades, McGinnity's had been your typical quiet, low-end, and low-lit Irish tavern—the type with a little dirt, a few stains, and pictures of John Kennedy, the current Pope, and Eamon de Valera on the walls. Tonight the place was lit up like the fleet on the Fourth of July and a bunch of carpenters were hard at work in the back.

With two guys throwing punches, though, I didn't have time to worry about what was going on with the tavern, and the new lights were a big help in letting me quickly identify the two adversaries: Cahill and Kazlowski, both of them cops, and both of them part of the regular crowd.

Before I could get there to break up the fight myself, a young man separated himself from the carpenters, dodged

Cahill's and Kazlowski's drunken punches, and, stepping neatly between them, forced the two apart by putting a palm on both their chests and gently shoving. "Stop it," he said, loudly and with authority. "There'll be no fighting here."

I looked at the guy closely—you don't often see someone willing to step into a fight between two street cops who go well over two hundred pounds each. He was a good-looking young man, tall and lean, with dark blond hair cut short, and he had moved in like someone who knew just what he was doing. He also looked vaguely familiar. Then it dawned on me: this was McGinnity's son, the Marine lieutenant, apparently home on leave. I couldn't remember his first name.

"Just who the hell do you think you are?" demanded Cahill.

"I'm the man who's running the place tonight, that's who I am," McGinnity's son answered firmly.

By this time I had managed to make it there myself and I gave them both barrels. "Cahill! Kazlowski! Sit down!"

They both turned away from McGinnity's son, and looked at me. "Oh, hi, Inspector," mumbled Kazlowski. "Sure thing." He sat down, and Cahill sat down a moment later with an angry look but without further complaint.

I looked around the table. There were three other regulars there: Snyder, a lieutenant who'd been with Forgery forever and who was even older than I was; Thorne, a nasty little detective from Automotive; and Rosenthal, the beanpole from Burglary. I could see why none of them had tried to break up the fight themselves: both Cahill and Kazlowski were big enough to make two of any of them. "Okay guys, does somebody want to tell me what started all this?"

Kazlowski tried to say something, but Snyder cut him off with a look.

"Well, Mike, we were just bullshitting about the war when it got ugly. First, Thorne was telling us all how Desert Storm was won by high technology, and then Rosie was telling us how Thorne was all wrong and the guys in Intelligence should get all the credit. He got about halfway through explaining that when Kaz lit into him and started telling us why the Air Force was what won it all for us.

Then Cahill showed up, claimed that the tanks had won it for us, and he started in giving Kaz a really hard time. Finally Kaz swung on him about the time that you showed up, and, frankly Mike, I don't blame him.''

Kaz glared at Cahill. "He called me a dummy, Inspector. He called me stupid. He said I was wrong. I wasn't wrong." Kaz had a load on indeed; I started wondering just what time today he'd started drinking and if he had been on-duty at the time.

Cahill was returning Kaz's glare; I moved in a little closer to them in case punches started flying again—and interestingly enough, so did McGinnity's son. Cahill was still mad, all right, but he let it out in words. "Kaz, you are a goddamned dummy if you believe that crap about the Air Force. It was our tanks that won the war, and everyone knows it!''

This was starting to make a twisted kind of sense now, for Kaz had been a sergeant in the USAF before he joined the force, and Cahill had been—very briefly—a tank platoon commander in the Army before he signed up. Everybody was just sticking up for his home team, and after the hard week all of us had just finished—one of the type that we call a "Dead Week" because that's how everybody in town seems to turn up—we were all seriously on edge. That didn't excuse a fistfight over a nonissue but at least it explained it.

When Cahill's insults finally sank in, Kaz started to get up again. "I'm not wrong! Goddamn it, I'm not!''

McGinnity's son looked him straight in the eye and kept him down with a hand on one shoulder. "Yes, you are, and he is, too. But don't worry about it. Cool down and you can all have a round on the house, but there'll be no more fighting in McGinnity's, all right?''

Kaz was silent for a moment and then finally nodded his assent. The young man turned and glared at Cahill, who, after a brief delay, also nodded his obviously grudging agreement.

"Well, then, enjoy your night, gentlemen. Good to see you again, Inspector Morgan.'' Damn, the kid had me. He remembered my name, and while I was able to dredge up memories of a bratty little towheaded, snot-nosed child who used to sit behind the bar drinking Shirley Temples and eating the bar cherries while I talked to McGinnity, I couldn't remember the kid's name for the life of me. It was downright embarrassing.

As he walked away, he said, "After I go check on the carpenters, I'll send you guys a free round over from the bar."

I figured that the night's excitement was over and took a seat next to Thorne and Rosenthal to wait for the beer to arrive. McGinnity's kid got no more than five steps, though, before Thorne reached out and stopped him with a voice like a whip. "So they were both wrong, were they, kid? Just where in hell do you get off making a statement like that? How in hell could you know that they were both wrong?"

I knew why the kid said that he knew—McGinnity had been very proud of the fact that his son was going off to fight in the war—but I wasn't going to say anything and I hoped that the kid would just walk away. Thorne hated anyone younger than he was, and he hated Desert Storm veterans with a passion. McGinnity's son was both.

Thorne had done three tours in Vietnam and his bitterness about Desert Storm was well-known: he loved to proclaim that Desert Storm would have been nothing but a short and minor skirmish had it occurred in Vietnam and that it was the only "war" in which the victory parades had actually lasted longer than the fighting.

McGinnity's kid—I was still feverishly turning over the corners of my mind trying to remember his name—didn't choose to walk away. Instead, he turned around and faced Thorne squarely, and in a quiet voice said, "Because I was there, and because I do happen to know exactly why we won the war so easily."

Looking past him, I finally saw what the carpenters were up to: what looked like no less than a complete remodeling of the place, and at night, no less. The kid then turned his back on Thorne and started to return to the carpenters, and he had almost gotten away from us when Thorne decided not to let him go. "Well, then why don't you come back and enlighten us about what you saw, junior? Or isn't it worth your time to talk to some old cops—some old cops who fought in some *real* wars?"

The kid turned back, his gray eyes flashing, and stared at Thorne. "I could tell you," he said, "but you'd never believe me."

Thorne laughed. "You're right about that, junior."

The kid glared at Thorne for a moment and then looked at our table and a smile slowly broke across his face. "What the hell, why not? It might keep you cops from fighting among yourselves, and you won't believe it anyway. Hang on." He walked over and gave a few quick instructions to the carpenters and to the nearest waiter, and then walked back to our table and dragged a chair up right between Cahill and Kaz, acting as if it was coincidental. I was still wracking my brain to remember the kid's name, but my memory was not in a mood to be cooperative.

The kid had our undivided attention when he leaned forward and began to speak in a very matter-of-fact voice. "Well, fellows, it wasn't the tanks, and it wasn't air attacks," said the kid. "It was magic."

I am proud to tell you that my jaw didn't drop, but that was only because I've heard stranger things than that during my years on the force. Everyone else's jaw headed for the table. Thorne couldn't even respond; he was just making strangling noises. Cahill's face was red. "Kid, don't bullshit us."

The kid stared Cahill down. "I'm not," he said calmly. "You want to hear the truth or do you want to go on arguing about lies?" I was spooked at this point; one of the most useful things that I've learned over the years is how to tell when someone is lying, and this kid wasn't lying. This either meant that he was telling us the real truth, which was scary, or that he had made this story up but really believed it himself, which was even scarier.

Nobody said anything more to the kid, so he went on. "If you keep your mouths shut, I'll tell the story. If not, I've got things to do." We all kept our mouths shut, and he told us the story.

"One night, just before Desert Storm was supposed to begin, I led a three-man team onto the beach at Falaykah Island to do some scouting work. We were planning to invade the place later, and the three of us were going to check out that particular part of the island and take some sand and soil samples.

"I wound up by myself on the beach, waiting for the other two guys to get back. They were running a little overdue, and I was getting a little nervous, when an Iraqi patrol showed up.'' His hands had started to make little clutching motions. "I got out into the shallow water on the edge of the beach, so that only my head was out of the Gulf, and I was trying to reach as far down under the muck off of that beach and grab as much of it as I could get so that I could pull myself as low in the water as possible." He paused, and sighed. "That's when I grabbed it.

"It was cold and metallic, and I thought right away that it had to be a mine. But it didn't feel like any mine that I'd ever heard about, and it had a handle on it. When I ran my fingers over the surface, it had raised decorations on it. Mines and booby traps don't have raised decorations on them, but I was curious and I couldn't figure out just what it was, so I kept a grip on it. Finally the patrol passed, and I raised up and pulled it out of the muck."

One of the waiters showed up with a round of beer, but no one except me seemed to notice.

"What it looked like, or how long it had been there, I'll never know. It looked kind of green by my night vision gear, but then most everything does, and it could have been silver or gold or even mirrored—there was no way to tell. It was a jar or vessel of some kind, and it was sealed. The seal had a really strange design in it made up of two intertwined triangles, one of them done with a thick line, and one of them done with a hollow line."

Rosenthal jerked in his seat and murmured under his breath, "The Seal of Solomon!" I heard him, but I'm not sure that anyone else did.

McGinnity's kid went on. "The seal was still intact, and I could tell that this thing was really old . . . and I mean *really* old."

The hair on the back of my neck was rising.

"I shook it, and there was something really odd about the way that the insides jiggled. I couldn't figure out what was in it, but I knew that it wasn't anything Iraqi. I wanted to know what was inside of it, so I tried to open it up."

Typical Marine, I thought. Me, I'd have left the thing in the muck, let alone drag it out and try to open it.

"It was real hard to open. Finally I got the edge of my knife underneath the edge on the seal, and I started to pry it open. I got it open about halfway, and suddenly all hell broke loose. There was a hellacious noise, and a tremendous flash, and something knocked me cold.

"I don't know how long I was out. When I woke up, somebody had dragged me way up on the beach, and there was something big looming next to me. My night gear was gone, and it was darker than sin, and whatever it was that was next to me was even darker than that.''

'' 'You have rescued me from a long and unpleasant imprisonment,' it said. 'My gratitude is yours.' The words weren't spoken and they weren't really words and they weren't in English, but I understood them anyway.''

'' 'What are you?' I asked it, out loud.''

"There was a pause, and it told me, 'You should probably try to think of me as a genie.' ''

The free beer they'd brought me was already empty, but there was no way that I was getting up or calling for a refill.

'' 'A genie?' I asked it. 'Does that mean I get three wishes?''

"There was another pause, and it said 'As you wish it, so shall it be. Three wishes, if they are within my powers.''

"Well, at this point I had to think hard about what to wish for, and then I remembered the war. 'Can you tell the future? Can you tell me what will happen in this war?' I asked it.''

'' 'That is within my power,' it said, and suddenly my mind was full of pictures.''

"Israel was being hit with chemical and biological missile attacks; hundreds of thousands were dying. Jordan was joining Iraq as an ally. The Israelis were nuking Iraq and Jordan. The French were quitting the alliance for no good reason, and doing enough damage when they left it that it began to tear itself apart. The Soviet Union was turning hard-line Communist again, this time worse than before, and was sending Iraq some serious help. The U.S. and its allies were attacking, but were getting a bloody repulse and were suffering enormous casualties from gas attacks. All the American and European troops were withdrawing, and Iraq was overrunning Saudi Arabia, all of the emirates, and finally Iran.''

"At home, the protesters were finally being taken seriously; after the nukes fell and the war began to falter, they were gaining serious momentum. President Bush was going to pieces and being completely indecisive. Some anti-war Democrat that I'd never heard of before was replacing

Bush, and the United States was disarming and turning isolationist just in time to let Iraq overrun what was left of Israel and massacre all of the Jews there. It was a nightmare.''

"I yelled for the genie to stop, and the nightmare finally ended. I don't know how long I sat there before I spoke to it again. 'Genie, can you prevent this? Can you change the future? Can you make this war into a quick, clean victory for the United States?' The genie asked me what I meant by clean, and I told it that I wanted there to be almost no American casualties, no chemicals, no nukes, no gas, for Israel to be saved, and for the U.S.S.R. to keep pursuing glasnost and perestroika.''

"It was some time before it replied. 'This is also within my power.' Then there was another terrible noise and a flash.''

"After a while the other two guys came back. Another Iraqi patrol had kept their heads down in the sand for an hour or two, but they had finished what they had set out to do. I asked them if they'd heard any noises or seen any flashes, and they told me that things had been quiet all night. I radioed in and had us picked up, and you know the rest.''

Nobody said anything after he finished the story. I looked around, and everyone looked shocked. I said, "Thanks for the scoop. Fellows, I think that we all need to head home now.'' There wasn't any grumbling or conversation; everyone just got up, as if they were in a daze. McGinnity's son headed back to check on the carpenters, the four younger guys went over to pay their tabs, and Snyder and I headed for the men's room.

While I was admiring the graffiti in front of the urinal, I got to thinking about the kid's story. He had believed it himself, and the war had seemed to go just a little too damned easy. When I compared how well that war had gone to the colossal American screwup in Vietnam, and thought about the fact that both wars involved the same organizations, the kid's story made more sense to me than any other explanation I'd heard.

By the time Snyder and I left the men's room, the other four guys had already paid their tabs and left. As Snyder headed for the register to pay his, and I headed past it for the door, he started chuckling. "Good story, eh, Mike? It would have been believable, except for the big hole in it. The kid only got two wishes from the genie.'' He held up two fingers. "Only two wishes, and he said that the genie would give him three.''

He fell silent as he got to the register. One of the old bartenders, Liam O'Reilly, was working the cash register, and I'd known him long enough not to feel embarrassed stopping on my way out to ask him a couple of probing questions while Snyder paid his tab. "Liam, what's with the lights and all of these carpenters working at night? And what's McGinnity's kid's first name?''

Liam grinned. "The lights and the carpenters? Well, it's part of the new look the place is getting. The carpenters are working double shifts to get the place all fixed up and remodeled before McGinnity comes back from his visit to Ireland. When he does, the place will look just like he's been telling us he wanted it to look all these years.''

He hooked a thumb at thc kid, who was back giving instructions to the carpenters. "It's all his doing, Mike. McGinnity doesn't know anything about it, and is he ever going to have the pleasant surprise of his life when he comes back.''

I thanked him, and had started for the door when it dawned on me that Liam still hadn't told me what the kid's name was. Snyder was standing there waiting for his change; he grinned, waved two fingers at me, and then made a circling motion around his head with his index finger.

"Liam, what's the kid's name?'' I asked. "I can't for the life of me remember what it is, and it's driving me crazy.''

Liam gave me a huge grin. "His name is Kevin, but nobody calls him that anymore.''

I felt like I was pulling teeth. "Well, then, what do they call him?''

"Well,'' Liam said, still grinning, "ever since he won the lottery the same day that he got his discharge from the Marines, everyone just calls him 'Lucky.' ''

I laughed, waved three fingers at Snyder, who stood there with his mouth hanging open, and walked through the doorway and out into the night.

What is the true condition of man, or of genie for that matter? Is it bondage to serve the one you love, if you do so willingly? Is it freedom to turn down a fervent plea, or a heartfelt wish?

But, of course, these questions were all decided many centuries ago. . . .

PERSEPOLIS

by Judith Tarr

God is great! God is great! There is no god but God, and Muhammad is the Prophet of God!

The great words rang in the empty places. Even the hawk of the air was still, as if in homage to them.

Hasan, Sabah's son, of everywhere and nowhere, but most recently of Persia, knelt and bowed and stood on the broad floor of the desert, walled in pillars like the bones of giants, and prayed for revelation. All that he had had till now was the dizziness of fasting, the cry of the hawk, and the hammer that was the sun. That made him fancy that he had seen a living shape in the shadow of a pillar, a shape with a face like a human creature's, but eyes clear green like a cat's.

"Allah protects me," he said. He swayed on his knees. The pillars swayed with him. This was a city once, this place of stones and solitude, and these pillars had held up a roof of gold. He saw it sometimes in the night as he kept vigil over his prayers, splendors of gold and jeweled brilliance, carpets, hangings, carven images on the walls and set atop the pillars: lions, bulls, eagles, great beasts out of stories. And people—ghosts or spirits of the waste, tall, hawk-faced, bearded, silk-clad men, and sleek, gliding, smooth-faced personages who were not women yet not men either, and sometimes, shy in a shadow, a slender figure wrapped in veils, with great dark eyes. There were princes and slaves and every rank between; and above them

all one in a tall crown, whom they worshiped on their faces
as if he had been a god.

All dead. All gone. He saw that in the dark before dawn,
when his soul was at the ebb and his prayers were lost in
silence: the silken people fled, the demons in bronze hur-
tling in, and the flames leaping up, soaring to heaven.

It was terrible, it was beautiful, a sacrifice of fire. The
one who led it was fire himself, hot-gold armor, hot-gold
hair, and he laughed as he ran, streaming flame through
the gilded passages. Sometimes Hasan fancied that he met
the conqueror's eyes, and they were odd, mismatched, one
dark, one light; and he was more truly alive than any man
who walked the living earth.

Dreams. Hasan lay on his back. He had no memory of
falling. The sun hung low, casting the shadows of pillars
across the broad stone floor.

He was old in fasting and in abstinence. From youth he
had belonged to God; in his manhood he knew what he
was in the world, and that was one of the great who walked
in shadows. But this time maybe he had gone too far. His
bones were as light as reeds, his flesh thin parchment
stretched over them. The tent he had pitched in the shade
of a great carved stair, the water he had fetched from the
spring to which God had guided him, were a world's width
away.

It was Ramadan. He could not drink till after sunset.
He would be dreaming again before that; then the dead
would take his soul away. They were hungry, the dead,
with their ghostly wine and their strengthless fire.

He sighed. He did not want to die; but if Allah willed
it, then he must accept.

"That is nonsense," said the air.

He was far gone indeed. He neither started nor went for
his knife.

The air had a clear voice, sharp and rather cold, and
hands that took him up with effortless strength. It had no
substance that he could see.

"Are you a demon?" he asked it.

It returned no answer. He was flying: wind on his
cheeks, sun in his eyes, a blur of pillars, sand, sky.

"Do you know the name of Allah?" he demanded. That
was bold to foolhardiness, as high up as he was, and far

to fall if the demon dropped him and fled shrieking from the Name.

The hands held fast. The air, it seemed, had fallen mute.

He sighed. "Ifrit," he said. "Spirit of air." The thread of his soul stretched thin. He slid down it into the dark.

Water murmured. Leaves whispered. Hasan woke slowly.

If this was paradise, then paradise was a subtler thing than any book told of. A single tree, a spring bubbling from its roots, a little sward of grass and flowers, and beyond it a darkness that was a cave's mouth.

He was stiff, but when he rose, his knees did not buckle. The light upon him was moonlight. Full moon: half of Ramadan gone, half still to endure. He stooped to drink from the spring. The water was cold and clean. There was something beside it. A cloth, and on it a loaf of bread.

He blessed the bread in Allah's name. It did not crumble into dust but remained bread, fresh and still warm from the baking. He ate sparingly, with the restraint of one who has fasted often and long. He drank again from the spring. Then he prayed, blessing the God who kept him from fear.

This was not the ruined city that the people round about called Jamshîd's Throne and the learned sages named Persepolis. It was nowhere that he knew of. The sky was the sky he remembered, the air was desert air, sweetened with the scents of the oasis. The cavern sheltered nothing but silence.

Hasan returned to the tree and the grass and the spring. "Spirit!" he called. "Ifrit!"

The air did not stir. The moon stared down.

"Ifrit," said Hasan, "in Allah's name, show yourself to me."

"What is your Allah?"

Hasan whirled about. Shadow stirred beneath the tree. He could discern no shape, but in it was a faint green gleam of eyes. "You know not Allah?"

"I know nothing," the shadow said. "I am nothing. I am air and empty words."

"And hands," he said, "and wings to carry us through the air."

"No wings," said the shadow.

He essayed a step toward it. It melted into the tree trunk.
"Ifrit?" he asked.

It was gone. No call or command could bring it back.

Water from the spring and bread from the air brought
back his strength. When day came, he searched out the
cavern. It was threefold, and the innermost was a wonder:
a pool of warm and ever-flowing water, in which, giving
thanks to God, he washed his body clean. By night he slept
in the outer cavern, which presented him with his own
blankets and his meager belongings and a single lamp that
never emptied of oil. Bread appeared again, with dates and
figs and one sweet fragrant apple from the gardens of Damascus. There was no mistaking it; such apples grew nowhere else.

But he was not in or near Damascus. When on the third
day he mustered strength to climb the crag that rose beyond the cave and to take the path that wound down from
it, he found himself on a hillock over the ruined city, and
the court of the pillars before him, where he had thought
that he would die. And when he went down, it was as it
had been when he left it; and when he went back, the cave
was undisturbed, the spring flowing as it always had, and
the tree whispering in the wind off the crag.

There was no such crag behind Jamshîd's Throne. And
yet, when he walked upon it, it was as real as his own
flesh, as solid as the stones of the fallen city. Neither prayer
nor the name of Allah altered it.

One must accept; one must not question. Allah had preserved the least of his servants through a spirit who pro-
fessed not to know his name. The least of his servants
offered due thanks and pursued his prayers in peace, undisturbed by man or beast or spirit of the air.

Yet at times he thought that he felt eyes on him; sensed
a movement just out of sight, a breath drawn where no
breath should be. It frightened him no more now than it
ever had. Fear was the enmity of a prince, the hatred of a
caliph, the malice of a sultan in the courts of Cairo or
Damascus or Baghdad. Fear was a thing of men and cities.
Here in the clean desert, there was nothing to fear but
death; and death was an old friend.

"Death is my servant," he said of a night, when the

lamp burned bright and the stars burned cold. "I shall teach men to bow to him."

"And through him to you?"

This time he did not try to pursue the shadow. It hovered out of the lamp's reach. It had a shape, maybe. A gleam that might have been eyes. A curve that might possibly have been a shoulder.

"No," he said to it. "I do nothing for myself."

"But," said the shadow, "I hear you thinking. You think that many men come to you and call you master. You ran away from them. But you will go back. You have found a place for them, a mountain and a garden, and you will take it and be lord of it and forge knives for the ones who follow you. Then they will use those knives in the name of your Faith."

He shivered. But he said calmly, "You are a perceptive spirit."

"There is nothing else for me to be," said the ifrit.

"Are you bound here?" he asked it.

"No," said the ifrit, but slowly.

"Then why do you stay here?"

"I do not remember," the ifrit said.

Hasan opened his mouth, but shut it again. The shadow wavered, but it did not flee, not yet.

"I am empty," it said.

"Of course," said Hasan. "You do not know Allah."

"Is he someone I should know?"

Hasan settled more comfortably. Here was a gift from the All-Merciful: a spirit to bring to the truth.

The ifrit being deathless and, it seemed, unburdened with flesh, seemed content to listen nightlong. Hasan's voice gave out toward morning; he had by then intoned nine-and-twenty *Sûrah*s of the Koran, and begun another, and he finished it in a whisper. Then perforce he fell silent.

"That is very interesting," the ifrit said. And went away.

That day he was alone. He prayed, silently. He pondered what he had come to this place to ponder: the world and its follies, and the nations of infidels, and the revelation that was taking shape here in his stony solitude.

Faith alone was not enough. In pure spirits—in the ifrit

that attended him—it might suffice. But men were dross as well as spirit, and they lacked eyes to see and ears to hear. Even where they had both, still they resisted. Then they turned against the Faith and its faithful, and thwarted it with clear will and malice. For them, one punishment was fitting, and that was death.

The Sword of Allah he would not be. A sword was too bright a thing. He would be a knife in the dark, a whisper in the shadows. Where sweet reason had failed and true faith had fallen, he would teach through fear. Men—and princes above all—would learn then the truth of God, and serve it in firm conviction, for if they fell short of it, they would die.

It was a pure thing, a simple thing, a truth and a certainty. It filled him with joy. Had he had voice he would have sung.

In the evening the ifrit came back. He had been expecting it. The lamp was lit, his supper eaten. There had been honey for the bread, which soothed his throat remarkably.

The ifrit sat closer to the light this time. Yes, that was a shoulder, and that an arm, and that, perhaps, a knee. It seemed almost to have substance, as moonlight will; and it was as white as the moon's light, and nigh as bright.

He had begun to cherish a suspicion. He did not try to confirm it. It was shy still, this spirit. When he made an unwise motion, reaching too suddenly for the water in its flask, the ifrit flickered out of his sight. It came back in a little while, when he had begun to think that it would not, but it was wary, like a wild thing, and like a wild thing it watched him, eyes gleaming green. He kept very still except for his voice, which God or the pause had given new strength.

As before, when his voice failed, the ifrit went away. And as before, at evening it came back. There was honey again with the bread, and apples, and a decoction of herbs and sweetness that soothed his throat. This time once more the spirit moved closer. It had a body, shaped in moonlight, and it wore a cloak, unless that were its hair: a wonderful color, dark red like the wine that was forbidden the Faithful, through which shone the white glimmer of its limbs. As he chanted the holy verses, he darted glances, seeking to pierce the veil of shadow and of red-dark cloak.

Almost, at length, he faltered.

Ifrit, no. But ifritah certainly, she-spirit of the people of air. Once he was sure of it, there was no mistaking it; her voice though low was sweet, and the shape of her was never a male's.

He said nothing of it, not then and not after she had gone wherever she went in the dark before dawn. And when she came back, he was able at last to see what face she wore. She was almost in the light, almost close enough to touch. He heard her breathe. He saw the curve of her cheek, the arch of her brow. She was not beautiful as mortal women were. Her face was carved clean and carved fierce, like a knife in the sheath or like the moon in Ramadan. It was beauty as spirits knew it, nothing human in it at all. And that was her hair, that wonderful cloak, and she was naked under it, as unaware of herself as an animal.

He would not vex that innocence. Not this night. He sang the last *Sûrah,* and spoke the words of Faith to seal it, the Name of God and the name of his Prophet. And then he fell silent.

The ifritah waited with the patience of the deathless. At length, when still he said nothing, she said, "You may go on."

"That is the end of it," he said.

She frowned. Her eyes were as green as ever, and as inhuman as a cat's. "Is there no more at all?"

"There are," he said, "the prayers that one should say."

"Teach them," said the ifritah.

He taught her the prayers and the prostrations, five for each day that passed under the eye of Allah. And then he must teach her why it was that one bowed toward Mecca—once she had understood what that was, and where—and from that it was inevitable that she ask who was this Muhammad whose book he had given her and whose prayers he had taught her. She was an apt pupil. She did not fidget, she did not lose patience; and she did not forget.

He realized with somewhat of a shock that it was well past sunrise, and she was still with him; she had not melted into the air. She seemed a firm and solid creature in the light of day that came in the cavemouth, a white-skinned slender woman in a cloak of wine-red hair. But her eyes were alien, and her face did not take expression as a human woman's might. It was as immobile as an animal's, yet as transparent as glass. He could see clear through it to—what?

Not emptiness, for all that she might say. There was a soul in her, wrought of fire as the souls of her kind were. It was clean. No weight of memory, no burden of mortality. She might have come into existence on that day when he lay dying in Persepolis. He had dreamed her, maybe, and dreamed her still, face-to-face over a lamp that, at last, guttered and went out.

She vanished with it, as swift as the flame, and more complete.

That day he did not go down to Persepolis. He bathed in the innermost cave, in darkness perforce for there was no lamp nor candle; he washed his garments and his turban and spread them in the sun to dry. He swept the outer cave and made it tidy. He prayed when it was time. He kept firm rein on apprehension. If the ifritah did not return with the night, she might not come back at all. He would go back to the ruined city; and after that, to the world from which he had come. His people were waiting. His Mission was ready to begin. And he knew where he would begin it: where she had seen, walking the paths of his thought. There was a castle in the mountains of Persia, far and far indeed from here, though hardly as far as Baghdad or Cairo. The people who had built it called it the Eagles' Nest: in their tongue, Alamut. With Allah at his right hand and the faithful at his back, he would take it. Then he would win the world for the Faith.

Dressed in clean clothes against his clean skin, he watched the darkness fall. No ifritah took shape in it. No lamp lit itself in the cave. No bread came, no fruit of paradise. He slaked his thirst with water as always, and rebuked his stomach for protesting that he had not fed it, and settled again to prayer. In the morning he would gather his belongings and go. Tonight he would pray, fasting, and strengthen his will for what he must do.

The ifritah would only have been a distraction. He told himself that, and sternly. But he found himself tensing at the whisper of wind in the tree's branches, starting at the shifting of shadows as the moon rose.

What brought him out, he did not know. Restlessness, maybe. He did not love this place. He owed its owner nothing, if owner the ifritah was. She had preserved his life, but he had taught her the Truth. They were fairly acquitted of debt.

The moon was waning, but his eyes were sharpened to its light. He climbed easily to the top of the crag and then down, upon the narrow way. The moon marked it with silver. He was not a man for fancies, but he found himself imagining that he walked not on earth and stone but on light. It was solid beneath him, both warm and cool, and smooth as a road of the old Romans; but they would have been startled to walk such a way as this.

Persepolis waited for him. He came down the last steep slope, on a road that no longer even pretended to touch mere earth, and walked between the pillars, and stood on the floor of stone. The ghosts seemed to have fled at his coming, but as he paused, they crept back into the light. None touched him or threatened him. The moon was his shield and his guard. Allah was his protection.

He saw the fire as it came, the golden king, the men in strange armor with their empty eyes, whirling in a drunken dance. There were women too; he had not seen those before. Shameless, gauze-robed, rouge-cheeked women, their eyes as empty as their men's, as all the ghosts' but that one who was their lord.

"Sikandar," said the air.

Hasan stiffened but did not, would not turn.

"That is Sikandar," the ifritah said behind him. "Al-exander, that he was then. Every night he comes. Every night he dances."

"Is he an ifrit also?" Hasan asked her.

"No," she said. "Oh, no. He was a man once; a king. Now he is dead. But he is one of the strong ones, the mortals whose spirit is fire. It was too strong for his flesh; it consumed him."

Hasan stood still. A great thing had come to him, not precisely with the force of revelation, but close to it, and part of it. "I have heard," he said at length, "that if a man have power, if he be bold beyond the measure of his kind . . . he might master such as this. Yes, even a mortal man, with mortal will, can rule the mighty dead."

"They have a word for that, these dead," the ifritah

said. "They call it hubris. The arrogance that mocks the gods. It fails, mortal man. It destroys the one who suffers it."

"But if a man is strong, if he acts in Allah's name— might he not prevail? Even against the dead?"

"The dead have no power," said the ifritah, "except to take a fool into their realm. As they will take you, man, if you approach them. See, they hunger. They drink life; they capture souls."

He knew. He felt it. His flesh was cold even in the moon's armor, its warmth stolen by the crowding ghosts. But he said, "If a living soul could capture them, he could wield them against the world."

"They can be captured," she said, "but no one can wield them. Even I; and I am powerful, O mortal man. I have looked the dead king in the eyes, and he has fallen back before me."

"I have not," said Hasan.

"You have never met me face-to-face."

Nor would he, if he had wisdom; but he did not say it. "I know what you can do, spirit. You can fly through air. You can alter your shape and substance as you will. You can feed a man in the wilderness. What terror is in that, that great Alexander, even dead, should bow to you?"

"My spirit is fire," she said, "and my soul is stronger than his. He was dross as well as spirit. I am spirit wholly."

"Yet you wear flesh."

"Immortal flesh." She was in front of him who had been behind, with no sound of movement, no flicker of it in his straining eye. She spread her white arms wide. "Go back," she said. "Go away from this place, lest it consume you."

"Why do you care for that?" he demanded of her.

She did not answer. Her face, lacking the taint of humanity, yielded nothing.

He went back. The road was plain stone now, and hard, both steep and stony. He hardly noticed it; or the hours it took him to traverse it, into the dawn and beyond, under a pitiless sun.

He had it now. The Mission—that was solid in his mind, as real as if it were accomplished, his people gathered, his stronghold won, his life's work truly, at last, begun. But Allah had given him more.

Why bind the mere and mortal dead to his service? Why, when he had true power and true fire all but laid in his hand?

He was no mage nor sorcerer, but he had studied widely in his youth. He had read enough to know what it was that he needed. There had been elaborate rites, he remembered; preparations that consumed months, years, decades. But the heart of them was simple.

The floor of the outer cavern was of earth over stone. A sharpened stick, gift of the tree by the spring, marked it well enough. He did not remember all of the words that were to be written; but surely holy Koran would suffice, first *Sûrah* and last, and verses that spoke of the binding of the djinn. He sealed them with the name and seal of Suleiman, but he left it unfinished, a gate to be shut when the prey was within.

His heart was beating. The sun hung low, casting a long spear of light across his working. He made no effort to disguise it. She who knew not the name of Allah might well know the name of Suleiman who bound all her kind, but he had cast his wager with fate, that she would walk into his trap.

He baited it well. He set himself in the center of it as the sun sank toward the hour of prayer. He called, "Ifritah! Would you pray with me?"

He did not wait, or tremble, or betray his eagerness. He began the prayer as if he had no care but that. When he rose from the first prostration, he had a shadow, wine-dark hair, moon-white body, praying as he prayed. Being spirit and not mortal, she prayed with all that she was. She shone like a lamp in the gloom.

"I could wish," he murmured between prayer and prayer, "that there were light."

And there was light: great banks and torrents of it. He did not even need calculation: he had bolted from the circle, blinded, astonished, and stood outside of it, before it came to him what she had done. She had filled the cave with light. Lamps, lamps, everywhere, lamps hung on chains from the ceiling, lamps banked on stands, lamps scattered across the floor like stars in the naked heaven. Only the circle was empty of them.

With the last of his self-possession, he drew the line

that shut the door, and wrote the words that sealed it, the name and titles of Suleiman ibn Daoud, king in Jerusalem, master of the spirits of earth and air.

She rose slowly. She did not look frightened, nor—and this he had feared more—was she angry. She turned in her prison. It was wider than both arms' stretch, broader than the length of her body if she lay down. She approached the edge that had been the gate. He held his breath. Just as she reached it, she shied. Her eyes went wide; for the first time her face held an expression. Astonishment.

"It burns," she said.

He did not allow triumph to swell in him. This was the gift of Allah. Allah's was the glory of it.

"Would you serve God?" he asked the ifritah.

She had retreated to the center of the circle. She crouched there, arms wrapped about knees and chin upon them, green eyes fixed on him.

When she did not answer, he said, "Your spirit is stronger than mine. But Suleiman was stronger than you."

"Suleiman is dead." She rocked on the pivot of her haunches. "You are afraid of me. You think that I could burst these bonds, turn all to fire, and sear you to ash for the crime of taking me captive."

So he had been thinking, but deep, where consciousness was a dim and distant thing. "Would you do it?"

"So full of fear," she said, "and yet so fearless. So much you trust your Allah."

"Not mine alone," he said. "Yours, too, and every earthly creature's."

"But he protects you. He let you trap me."

"So that you might serve him."

She shivered. It was not with cold: she never felt it. "I am nothing."

"You are Allah's."

"Can nothing belong to Allah?"

"Everything," he said, "and nothing."

Her lips curved. It was less like a smile than the arc of a sickle. "Will I serve Allah if I am bound here?"

"You will not be bound here," he said, "If you will be bound in another fashion."

"If I will be bound to you." She rocked, back and forth, smiling her terrible, ifritah smile. "You could have asked me."

That was so human, and so female, that he laughed before he thought.

That sound like bells in the Christians' churches, clear and cold, was laughter that echoed his. When it died, he said, "Would you have consented?"

"You have not asked."

Woman to the bone, whatever else she was. "Will you serve Allah in my service?"

"Will you keep me near you always?"

"Do you wish that?"

"Yes," she said.

He let his breath out slowly. This, he was beginning to think, was not the simple art that he had taken it for. A sorcerer drew the circle; he bound the spirit in it; he bent the spirit to his will. That the spirit might have will of its own, and that not to escape, but to bind itself and the man who would have bound it—there was nothing like this in any philosophy that he knew.

Nor was there anything like her. "What is your name?" he asked her.

She blinked once. "I am I. What need have I of a name?"

"Every creature has a name," he said.

Her brows drew together. "I am—I—" She stopped. "I have no name."

"You must."

"I have no name!"

Her anguish rocked him. He steeled himself against it. He bent, poised his hand over the gate. "If I freed you to discover your name—would you go?"

"No," she said.

There was a silence. The lamps burned in their constellations.

He measured the words carefully, lest they escape too soon. "You do not wish to be free?"

"No."

"You will stay here until the sky falls?"

"Until you leave," she said. "Then I follow you."

"Why?"

"Insh'allah," she said.

Allah wills.

"I will serve you," she said, "in Allah's name."

"And in your own."

"I have no name," she said.

"Then I give you one," he said. "In Allah's name, I name you Morgiana."

There was a tale, a cavern full of thieves, a clever slave, a dance with daggers; no spirits of air, no magic such as this one had, but magic enough, and blood of those who broke faith. The name shaped itself from that. Or perhaps the name shaped the tale.

"Morgiana," she said, as if she tried the shape and the taste of it, turning it on her tongue. "Morgiana." She rose. She looked down at herself; she ran hands down her sides. She turned about. "I am . . . something. I have a name. I am myself, a self. Morgiana." She laughed. "Morgiana!"

She stopped. He remembered to breathe again. She was not human nor mortal nor even true flesh, but the shape of her was woman entirely. He would not have been a man if he had been immune to it.

"And you," she said, "Hasan-i Sabbah. You gave me myself. I give you what I am. I serve you. I serve Allah, for that you serve him."

"You must," he said, "serve Allah for himself."

"I shall learn," she said. "I will dance for you, bring light for you, protect your life and take the lives of others in your name—do all your bidding, for my name's sake." She bowed low in a sweep of wine-dark hair. "My lord, I am your servant."

As he, in truth, was hers. She, whose power was so great, whose presence in his following would make him feared wherever men were, had chosen to belong to him. What she did, she did for him; if she did ill, on his head it would fall. And if she did well—then it was Allah's gift, and Allah's will, and Hasan's the merit in the courts of paradise.

It was a terrible thing, to be so bound. Terrible, and wonderful.

He swept his hand across the line of the gate. It parted with a sound like a lutestring breaking. He waited, hand still outstretched.

After a moment that stretched to endlessness, her hand met his. Her clasp was warm and solid and very strong. He drew her out into the light.

"Now," he said, "we begin."

It is said that it is the ability to learn that separates man from the animals.

I have had long discussions with my genie about this. He is of the opinion that it is the inability to learn that separates men from genies, and makes him one with the animals. And sooner or later, to prove his point, he usually recites this story. . . .

BUGS

by Rick Katze

"There are sufficient facts to find you guilty of driving while intoxicated," said Judge Horton, looking sternly at Robert Jenson. "This being your second conviction within three years, you are sentenced to sixty days at Lakeville State Hospital for treatment of your drinking problem, your license to drive is suspended for three years, and you will do one hundred hours of community service after you are released from treatment. You have a right of appeal. Will you exercise it?"

After conferring briefly with his defense counsel, Jenson softly said "No."

If only Judge Stephenson had heard the case rather than "No Sympathy" Horton, he would have avoided Lakeville. It wasn't as if anybody or anything had been hurt. Higgins was only giving him a warning about driving faster than the posted speed limit until he saw the empty beer cans in the car.

"You are released on the same bail pending your appearance at Lakeville on July 12, 1993."

It was a bright, warm, early summer day when Bob left the Plymouth District Court and casually strolled up Russell Street, past the police station and down the hill until he reached his car several blocks away. After starting the engine and fixing his seatbelt, he drove directly to Horseneck Beach, having decided that it was still too early for lunch. Tomorrow would be soon enough to call Graphic Software and give them the bad news.

He wandered aimlessly about the beach until he found a secluded section, stretched out on the sand, and opened a beer while watching the tide beginning to recede. After eating a corned beef sandwich and drinking five more beers, he shut his eyes.

"Drinking again, Mr. Jenson!" roared Judge Horton. "*This* will not do."

Bob suddenly found himself strapped to a chair that was slowly being lowered into the pond by four grim-faced men dressed in Puritan garb, then raised, and lowered again. He gasped for air, choking as water poured down his nose and throat. "Please stop!" he screamed as he again sank into the water.

Judge Horton directed that the dunking be quickened, gleefully smiling each time Bob emerged, gasping for air.

Suddenly Bob awoke to a darkened sky with the tide surging over him as it raced farther up the beach. As he arose, an object floated toward him. Instinctively he grabbed it and then walked toward the dry sand. The object reminded him of the bottle which Larry Hagman found on that deserted beach and from which Barbara Eden appeared. The TV show may not have been great but, in her genie costume, *she* sure was.

Pretending that he was Larry Hagman, he pried loose the stopper and called forth the genie. A dark cloud emerged from the bottle and began coalescing into a humanoid form. It didn't seem so funny anymore. He hoped that he was still dreaming.

From the swirling cloud, a booming voice said, "I am CXS. I will do three reality transformations for you. Be wise in their use."

Listening to CXS, whose conversation began with jumbled terms like "alternative reality perception, time loops, and forbidden transformations," Bob realized that CXS couldn't grant him the three wishes genies normally gave, but could change the present reality by inserting people wherever and whenever he specified.

"What happens if you send me to a time before I was alive?" asked Bob.

"If you were not yet in existence, you would simply appear. If it was during your lifetime, you would merge with your existing self but would retain the memory of what was to happen unless you directed otherwise. Many people have decided not to have foreknowledge when they make their third request and simply accept what will happen,'' said CXS.

"What other choice do they have after the third wish?'' asked Bob, thinking that he had obviously missed something.

"If you don't like the results, you can cancel it. I will appear and give you an opportunity to change your mind. Once you make your decision, your memories of this will disappear and the changes that have occurred will seem as they have always been.''

Time—CXS almost spoke of it as a living organism—didn't like to have its events changed. For reasons he could not follow—the jargon used by CXS was far worse than what he used in explaining the programming problems to the illiterates who paid so well for his services—no matter how major the shift, CXS would stay with him until his three requests had been made.

He had enough money and liked playing around with computer problems. There was no way that he wanted to change that part of his life. Could CXS affect the drunk driving rap? Bob decided to ask CXS some more questions.

"If I ask you to send me three weeks into the past, one day before Higgins stopped me for speeding, will I have the free will to avoid it?'' he asked CXS.

"Yes, but be warned,'' said CXS in a tone that might be used by a parent to a wayward child, "that even if you avoid *that* accident, another incident could occur on a day that was otherwise uneventful. The farther back in time you travel to avoid something, the greater the likelihood of other events happening to recreate the time stream. Time will fight to maintain what has been.''

"I'll take that risk.'' After swigging another beer, Bob said, "Do it.''

Three days without a beer, thought Bob. *One beer ought to be safe; maybe even two.*

Ten beers later, Juanita called. "Bob. Surprise! I'm at the bus station. Please come and get me.''

Thinking about Juanita changed his driving plans. He would slowly drive to the bus station, find Juanita, and carefully drive home. Arriving safely, he found Juanita and they walked back to the car.

Officer Higgins was watching the red Maserratti slowly wending its way through the Plymouth Streets. *Jenson never drove that slowly,* thought Higgins. After following him for about a mile, he started the patrol car's flashing lights, and pulled Bob over.

Higgins carefully walked to the driver's side of the car, and after Johnson rolled down his window and began to speak, he knew he had hit paydirt. "Would you please get out?"

Bob attempted to act normally but, when he responded to Higgins' questions, his speech was slightly slurred due to the beers.

"You are under arrest," said Higgins. "You have the right . . ."

"There are sufficient facts to find you guilty of driving while intoxicated," said Judge Horton looking sternly at Robert Jenson. "This being your second conviction within three years, you are hereby sentenced to sixty days at Lakeville State Hospital for treatment of your drinking problem, your license to drive is suspended for three years, and you will do one hundred hours of community service after you are released from treatment. You have a right of appeal. Will you exercise it?"

"*That* sure didn't help. Cancel that wish," said Bob to CXS. He found himself back on the beach with two wishes left.

"I warned you to be careful," noted CXS, "but you foolishly drove after drinking. You must be very careful not to give Time the opportunity to mend itself."

"Can you somehow get Horton to be lenient with me or, failing that, remove him from my case?" asked Bob.

"I cannot affect the punishment that you will suffer, but circumstances could be altered to have another judge sentence you," suggested CXS. "Tell me what you want changed."

"I want Judge Stephenson to hear my case. On the morning of the day my case is to be heard, send Horton, totally naked, to Salem Common at high noon on January 20, 1692. Let him spend fifteen days there before returning him to the present, fifteen days after he left. That should teach him to have sympathy for others," Bob said with a grin, wondering if Horton would like the Salem witch trials. If this didn't work out, he still had another request.

It was just like a beta test of new software to find the bugs the programmers had missed.

"So let it be said, so let it be done," said CXS with a flourish.

At 4:30 P.M. Friday afternoon Judge Stephenson had just finished hearing the Jenson matter and still had three more cases to hear before court would be adjourned. His plans to leave early for a long weekend on the Cape were frustrated when Judge Horton had not appeared that morning and there was no other judge available to replace him.

"There are sufficient facts to find you guilty of driving while intoxicated," said Judge Stephenson looking harshly at Robert Jenson. "This being your second conviction within three years, I sentence you to sixty days at Lakeville State Hospital for treatment of your drinking problem, your license to drive is suspended for three years, and you will do one hundred hours of community service after you are released from treatment. You have a right of appeal. Will you exercise it?"

After conferring briefly with his defense counsel, Jenson surprised everyone, including his defense counsel, by saying "Yes." He left the courtroom, spoke to the probation officer, and again strolled back to where his car was parked—all the while in deep thought about his next request to CXS if the appeal was unsuccessful.

The appeal was denied. Bob said, apparently to the wall, "CXS, cancel that request."

Back at the beach, Bob asked CXS, "Did you know this would happen?"

"No," came the reply. "But I told you that circumstances were not easily changed. Unless carefully stated, Time will try to maintain those facts that previously happened." CXS paused. "You have one final request. You can alter reality, but because of the time paradox restriction, you can never have more than three requests no matter how cleverly you phrase your desires. If you craft an exception within the general rules, Time will cheat and change the rules to avoid it."

"What happens if you send me into the future immediately after completion of my sentence?"

"You would merge with yourself assuming you are still alive. It's just like going into the past."

"I have no desire to remember what's going to happen to me at Lakeville," Bob said, cringing at the thought of spending sixty days with the do-gooders at the hospital.

"Do you want your memories edited? The actual events will still happen, but you will not remember them."

"Yes. Send me forward to September 14, 1993, but without those memories."

CXS merely waved his hand this time as Bob vanished from the beach. The cloudlike form slowly evaporated, wondering how Time would frustrate Bob in this instance.

Bob found himself at home. He went to the refrigerator, grabbed a beer, and started drinking it as he sorted out his memories of the past sixty days. He remembered leaving Lakeville on July 20, 1993, after being treated by some doctor.

Suddenly, he felt sick and vomited. The beer looked and smelled okay. What was wrong?

On the kitchen table he found a thick packet of papers dated July 20, 1993, that contained documents from the Plymouth District Court reinstating his driver's license and sealing his criminal record, and from Dr. McKenzie of Lakeville Hospital, advising him that he should avoid all alcohol consumption since the Uvinedon would make him vomit if he ingested any alcohol. Dr. McKenzie also congratulated him for volunteering. He felt sick again.

Damn that coward! He couldn't even take sixty days of Lakeville, thought Bob.

Dr. Summers gave him the bad news. "It's permanent. You'll never be able to drink liquor again."

"Cancel that request, CXS!" yelled Bob, fearful of what the future held but thankful that he would not remember it.

Pretending that he was Larry Hagman, he pried loose the stopper. It was empty. If only there had been a genie, he could have wished away Lakeville.

Bob decided to have another beer.

I do so love stories about myself!
Here I am again. Although, in truth, I view this
particular adventure as a learning experience. . . .

BINDING

by Patrick Nielsen Hayden

"It hath reached me, O King of the Age, that
there dwelt in a city of the cities of *China* a man
which was a tailor, withal a pauper, and he had
one son, Aladdin hight."
—Burton, *Supplemental Nights, Volume 3*

Know ye, O prince, that upon a time the djinn came forth
from his lamp to grant Aladdin three wishes, and Aladdin
wished:

To live in interesting times. And no sooner had the words
left Aladdin's mouth than a great wind arose, and the
sounds and sights of the everyday world left him, and he
was borne away as on a zephyr for an age. And there came
to him sights like those seen in lightning on a moonless
night, flash of steel, crash of arms, urgent shouts by strong
men, and before he could fully regain his senses or ask
the djinn what had transpired he was on a street both
known and unknown, the street of his childhood yet studded with buildings vast and strange.

"Here," said the djinn. "No time is more interesting
than this. From this crucible will come the Leap, in a
generation or less. Listen. See."

And Aladdin listened and saw, and it came to him that
the street swarmed with thousands, the greater part young,
all moving at a great rate. And some wore clothes almost
like Aladdin's, and some wore strange garments of fibers
unknown to him, and some shouted and some bore large
signs and some were silent. And all of them moved in the

same direction, toward the center of the town. And Aladdin looked in that direction and saw spires that scratched Heaven itself rising hundreds of feet into the air. And then Heaven, wounded, responded with a downward shaft of light that rang like a sword of finest steel, and where there had been a rushing mass of people not a hundred feet away there now rose only curls of dust from a pit, and blood ran over the edge of the pit. And those left on the street stood still with the horror of it, and gazed upward to blue emptiness, and their rage was terrible to see.

And Aladdin clutched his lamp and looked about for his djinn, and saw no djinn, and he cried out, and no sooner had he done so than a huge cart rolled up next to him and opened a door from behind which came a command to enter, and Aladdin entered. And after the door had closed him inside but before his dazed eyes could see, Aladdin dimly realized that the sign on the back of the cart had read WISH 2.

To come to the attention of those in high places. Moira's nose wrinkled. The child smelled, but then fresh pickups usually did. The first order of business was always to calm them, and a quick look at this one's pupils confirmed he could use some calming. "It's terrible, what you just saw," she said. "We won't let you be hurt; we're here to take you to a better place. Have you eaten recently? Can we offer you anything?"

Huddled at the end of the stretch limo's facing seat, the child stared at her wide-eyed, trembling like a fever victim. Okay, okay, don't push it, Moira thought to herself. Time enough.

"Out of range," the driver announced. "We're going up."

"Mikos, wait," Moira called back. "This one isn't from the twenty-oughts. He's not even sure what a car is, much less a flyer."

"Well, that's a surprise. I thought this was a routine job."

"It was, until the call came in just before we hit the site. I didn't have time to explain and navigate us past the ought-seven powersat strikes at the same time. 2007 isn't the easiest year to drop into Canton, after all."

"Fair enough. So who's the passenger? Wildjumper, out of his depth?"

"I assume so. All the call said was 'special'; that's usually the code for a lost pre-Leap wild talent stuck in a cusp futureward of their own time. Still, this one's odd. Chinese face, understands English, but I could swear he looks . . . How's your Arabic?"

"Good enough. But we may as well scoot." He reached behind the steering wheel and began flicking switches, tossing a glance up at his rearview mirror. "First, because it's *really* starting to smell in here now. And second, because now that your charge is done retching, he's passed out." Gold enveloped them, wind consumed them, a million stars surrounded them, and they went up.

To be given his heart's desire. No one must know. All of them, the happy billions, depend upon the Leap. Our gift from the shining ones uptime, energy from nowhere, poverty abolished, the stars within reach at last. The universe turned upside down, its only cost the minor effort of patrolling the string along which we have come.

I had hoped to forget these scenes, not live them again through different eyes. No one must know.

I don't pretend to understand the physics. I merely administer that which was, that we may continue as what we are. As I'm instructed by those who shall be: as uptime, so before.

The past is ours, the future forbidden.

But the child is not from our past. Or anyone's.

(Almost anyone's.)

He shifts and flickers, overtly Chinese, responds to English and several other languages, but what he speaks is undeniably Arabic. He clutches his battered oil lamp, and when I ask to see it he flinches and asks if I am his uncle.

"I am not. Nor need you fear us; we will force nothing from you," I say.

"Then you are my third wish," he says, and is silent.

His fingers leave no prints. Our scans and probes draw blanks, as I knew they would. Will my own staff betray me, teasing his true identity out with impossible, post-Leap skill? I think not.

Only I know what the Leap did to us. We live in a storybook now, awakening from history to an endless, powerful happily-ever-after. What wonder, then, that when the world becomes a storybook, Story leaks into the world?

But in Story, chapters may be skipped, pages read out of order, wild lies made true. Anything is possible, up to the edges of the binding.

The past is ours, the future forbidden. By the uptimers. Who grant our fondest wishes, and live in light.

I slouch back to my office, slam the door, grab my lamp, and angrily summon my djinn.

And Aladdin reigned in justice and mercy for an age of the world.

Genies are not the most sophisticated creatures in Cre-
ation. Especially not my genie: he has so many problems
adjusting to the pace of your modern life. Every time he
gets a new master I worry about him.

But just as I learned from my wishes, so, too,
does my genie. Eventually.

IF WISHES WERE GENIE'S
by Terry McGarry and Austin Dridge

In the convolution of space that was his universe, he
waited. Perhaps it was a kind of cabin fever; perhaps it
was too many centuries alone, too much time to brood on
perceived injustices; perhaps it was some quirk of his el-
emental nature, some streak of impudence that grew and
mutated as he flitted about in the confines of his own mind.
Whatever it was, something had driven the genie mad. "I
wish," he muttered to himself, savoring the symmetry of
long and short vowels, the sibilance of desire. "Transformed, by me, from the contrary-to-fact subjunctive to
the indicative, even the imperative. . . ." He let slip a
maniacal giggle. "I can do it, I know I can!" And he
repeated, again and again, "I wish . . ."

1

Borden and Kara Kendall lived in a luxury co-op on the
Upper East Side of Manhattan. He took cabs to his
investment-banking firm downtown; she preferred to walk
to her publishing offices on 59th Street. Their signature
wardrobe was Stanley Black; they worked off their intake
of fine cuisine at exclusive health clubs. With Borden's
end-of-year bonus they had purchased a new bright-red
Miata for him and a silver-fox stole for her, as well as
completing their annual upgrade of audiovisual compo-
nents, and hiring workers to put an addition on the house

at Fire Island. Although their reading consisted of trade magazines and *The Wall Street Journal*, their motto was literary, a phrase from an Anouilh play Kara had read at Princeton in the late seventies: "I want everything of life, I do; and I want it now!"

When Kara brought the tarnished oil lamp home, Borden scoffed at her flea-market taste in antiques. When she said "Well, check *this* out," and rubbed it with a custom-embroidered napkin, he chided her for soiling an heirloom. When the genie appeared, he said, "Hey, you didn't tell me this was high-tech! What's the deal—holographs?"

The genie quickly put him straight, and offered them three wishes, although he grumbled that by rights it should be two, what with the recession and all. Borden attempted to negotiate for three wishes apiece, but the genie was adamant that they wish as a pair. It required surprisingly little arguing for them to come up with youth and money, but they haggled over fame and power a bit before settling on the latter.

"Those are your choices?" the genie said, a strange twinkle in his eye.

"Yes," they replied together, and closed their eyes. Their motto was coming true!

When they opened their eyes again, they found themselves in a palatial mansion overlooking the Hudson. They had to wave away servants bearing champagne and canapés, and secretaries announcing phone calls from Donald Trump and Brandon Tartikoff. They sank down on a twelve-foot white couch and looked at each other. Kara saw Borden as he had looked at Princeton: the forelock of brown hair that had not yet receded, the unlined eyes bright with eagerness. He had wanted to change the world. . . . And Borden saw Kara as the willowy, artistic girl she had been then, hair long and straight, no makeup, baggy sweatshirt. They embraced joyfully, crowing, "We've made it! We've *really* made it!"

For two days they enjoyed their young bodies, their influential friends, their bulging, diverse portfolios. But it all began, inexplicably, to wear thin; Kara found herself buying books instead of stocks, and Borden found his limousine rides harrowed by an obsession with the homeless they passed. The third day, Kara came home and told a maid to get rid of all her furs, that she couldn't help seeing dead animal carcasses when she looked at them; Borden came home and announced that he had sold off three chemical companies at a resounding loss, because they had been accused of polluting the environment.

"What's the *matter* with us?" Kara cried. "I have an unbearable desire to wear stone-washed jeans, and today I hired a new publisher to turn *Design Innovations* into a political-protest journal!"

Borden nodded, a pained expression on his youthful face. "I just made plans to renovate half the South Bronx for decent low-income housing. I couldn't help myself . . . I had to do it. . . ."

Kara sighed. "I guess what we wanted at twenty-one isn't what we wanted as aging yuppies. What do you think will happen to us?"

Borden shook his head in despair. "I don't know, Kara . . . I just don't know."

Before the month was out they were bankrupt and friendless, sleeping on cardboard boxes in Grand Central. The lamp was the only possession they'd saved. Kara tried several times to invoke the genie and get him to restore their former lifestyle. But he said he couldn't do it, and he enraged her with his continual pleas to be released from his bondage, now that he'd granted their wishes.

Borden continued to give away any food he scrounged to those even worse off, and Kara, when she wasn't ranting on street corners about the city's homeless policies, was risking her life to put the lamp under bus wheels, to do anything she could to destroy it utterly.

"No, no, no," said the genie irritably, inside his tarnished (now dangerous) prison. "This wasn't what I meant at all. . . ."

2

When Paige Johnson brought the filthy oil lamp home to the Upper East Side co-op she shared with her husband, Garrett, she was somewhat embarrassed to admit that she had bought it from a crazy homeless woman down the street from the Harvard Club. But Garrett stopped his scoffing when the genie appeared and convinced them he was real. They had a little trouble deciding what to wish for, but quickly boiled it down to youth, money, and power. Paige would later tell herself that she should have noted the lunatic gleam in the genie's eye as he asked them if they were sure that's what they wanted. For when they opened their eyes, expecting to see all the appurtenances of wealth and influence, they found themselves seated on a monstrous Harley-Davidson motorcycle, surrounded by hairy, leather-clad bikers asking them where to go next. Garrett's hair was pulled back in a ponytail, and his incipient spare tire had turned to muscle where Paige gripped him from behind. When he turned to look at her, Garrett saw an eighteen-year-old girl with wind-whipped hair, and the beginnings of a look of excitement he had never before seen on her face.

"I don't know," Garrett said in response to the nudging of his gang members. He could tell them to ride into the depths of hell, and they would, for him. "Let's just cruise."

On the first day, they rode high on the adrenaline of the wild life. Garrett had apparently hit Pennsylvania Lotto last week for two thousand dollars, so they had plenty of bucks to play with. They did everything they'd ever dreamed of at eighteen—took off when the mood hit them, zigged and zagged through highway traffic playing chicken at top speed, reveled in the lack of responsibilities or ties. It was a rush. But on the second day they began to feel grungy; money was already running low, and the chopper had broken down on the way to New England. Garrett and Paige began to complain; they missed their comfortable apartment, their old jobs; they didn't even have college degrees, and they didn't know what to do with themselves.

"I guess being eighteen again isn't all it's cracked up to be," Garrett—banged up from losing a dominance fistfight to his former second-in-command—said on the third day, as they watched their gang ride away without them.

"Yeah," Paige agreed, trying to adjust her metal bustier so it would stop pinching. "And money and power are sure relative things in this world. I guess what we wanted at eighteen just isn't good enough for the aging yuppies that are still inside us."

They pulled the old lamp from Paige's travel bag and invoked the genie. But he refused to give them any more wishes, and he kept asking them to set him free.

"Set you free?" Garrett finally burst out in a rage. "After you've put us in this crazy situation? I'll set you free, all right. . . ."

At his threatening tone the genie retreated into the lamp, and Garrett hurled it into the road before him and revved his engine deafeningly. As he prepared to run the lamp over, Paige cheered.

"Blast it," the genie muttered, as his universe was sent spinning head-over-heels and left in the roadside dirt. "This is simply not what I had in mind, not one little bit. . . ."

3

"This is great!" said Fletcher Monroe to his wife, Ashley, as the genie hovered in their Upper East Side co-op. Fletcher set down his Martini and brie. "Where did you say you found it?"

"At a roadside flea market," Ashley replied, "on my way home from that Yale trustees meeting in New Haven."

"I would like to be freed," the genie said. "It might be wiser for you to do it now; my powers have been a bit erratic lately."

"What, and give up our three wishes?" Fletcher exclaimed. "No way, Jose! What is it we always say, Ash?"

"I want it all, and I want it now!" she crowed cheerfully. "Now, what shall we wish?"

They quickly settled on youth, money, and power. In moments they were staring at each other over a lemonade stand. There was a pile of nickels on the makeshift counter, and a crowd of clamoring kids around them. Ashley was in braids, and Fletcher had a baseball cap on. They were eight years old.

Although they found it difficult at first to adjust to having parents, bedtimes, and homework again, their former grownup lives soon seemed like a dream, and they would giggle about it over the phone until their parents yelled that they were running the bill up. Then they began to argue. One evening about three days later, Ashley pulled the lamp out of her toy box and rubbed it with the sleeve of her pajamas.

"See?" she said to the genie who appeared. "Fletch said it never happened, that we made it all up! But you *are* real, aren't you?"

"Yes," said the genie, and his eyes took on an excited gleam. "And, Ashley, it's very lonely inside my lamp. Do you think you could just say, 'I set you free, my genie'? Then I could stay out here and play with you and Fletch forever."

"Sure," Ashley said with a shrug, and opened her mouth to say the words.

Soaring up into the ether, reveling in the wind rushing past, looking down to see the lights of New York growing smaller and dimmer below him, the genie cackled madly to himself. " 'I wish I were free'!" he said. "It took three tries, but I got it right. I certainly did get it right!"

"All's well that ends well." You've heard that a million times. (And why shouldn't you have? I was the first one to say it, and I was born millennia ago.)

But did you ever stop to think about it? Have you ever asked yourself why things end well?

Consider the story of Tonie and Rich, for example . . .

A DREAM IS A WISH THE HEART MAKES

by Marie Parsons

"Hey, Tonie, quit fiddling with that ring. Your tea is getting cold."

Tonie looked up dazedly to see Richard eyeing her over his coffee cup as he drained the last dregs. The remains of his chicken salad were still on his desk, crumbs dotted around his mouth like light freckles on his brown face and sprinkled over the latest draft of his dissertation on the future of nanotechnology.

A sudden pain in her finger reminded Tonie that she had indeed been twisting her ring too hard. *Oh, rats! Has Rich caught me staring off into space again? I know he's going to ask me about Professor Kendall. He probably thinks I sat here all day daydreaming again.* She looked down at her desk. Sure enough, the encyclopedia was still open at the beginning of the reference on "Carpets as Decoration" and the screen on her laptop computer was still blank.

To cover her embarrassment, Tonie pretended to check her watch and ran her long fingers through her short brown curls. She was about to ask Rich if he'd bought her lunch, when she noticed a mug and sandwich sitting on a magazine in a corner of the desk, covering the article "Ancient Carpets of Persia." She lifted the teacup to her lips. Rich was right. The tea was tepid and just about undrinkable.

"Thanks anyway, Rich. Guess I got so busy I wasn't paying attention." *Right, like he'll believe that.*

"Honestly, Tonie, you'd think that ring was some magic talisman, the way you fiddle with it. Just because you bought it from some swami in a sheik's outfit doesn't mean it will make all your wishes come true. *You* have to make things happen for yourself."

Richard may have been a scientific genius, but he couldn't seem to comprehend that swamis were part of the Hindu religion and had nothing to do with Islam. Tonie always told him about upcoming cultural events, especially the Middle Eastern ones, but he wouldn't come with her to the Egyptian Festival, the Moroccan Street Bazaar, or to the library's prose readings from the Abbasid period. If Rich had only heard Abou al-Muhad's mellifluous English rendition of fables from the *Kalilah wa Dimnah,* he would have understood her fascination. Tonie had bought the ring at a small curio booth in the bazaar just before she went to the library. Okay, so the figure etched into the stone looked like a djinn, but Richard didn't have to keep teasing her about magic and wishes.

"So how is the dissertation coming, Rich?" Tonie threw out the last bit of her sandwich, took a sip of tea, and pulled her laptop closer on the desk.

"Don't sidetrack me. I want to hear about your conversation with Kendall at the museum." Richard tossed his chicken salad remnants in the trash after the coffee cup, finished wiping his mouth, and inserted a clean sheet into his typewriter. He looked over at Tonie, who was busily leafing through the Encyclopedia of Near Eastern Textiles. "Tonie, you *did* talk to Kendall, didn't you?"

Tonie shrugged. "There was an exhibition of Mamluk period rugs, and I wanted to check it out." She pulled a Museum Shop bag out from under her desk. "And I bought the most beautiful copper-colored lamp."

Richard groaned. "What is it with you? Last month you were bent on interning at some Turkish Museum so you could research Moslem art. You said it could inspire you for writing the great Arabian historical novel. Did you get there? No, you got sidetracked by reading the Arabian version of the Crusades, so you never applied." He paused for breath. "Then last week you said you wanted to go work on some archaeological dig in Arabia. And now it seems that you've been sidetracked again with this research on Persian textiles, though what it all has to do with writing a story about flying carpets is beyond me. Anyway, you've always wanted to see real archaeologists at work, claimed you could make a book out of it, so I figure, we've been friends since junior high, I'll help you out. I make the appointment with the man in charge of volunteer applications for the dig, and what happens? You don't even show up! And the deadline for application was today." He shook his head and raised his hands imploringly. "She's hopeless."

"Look, I remembered to call and make my apologies. But Rich, you just have to look at this lamp. It's a beauty, and I know just where to hang it in the apartment."

Richard sighed, walked over, and picked up the lamp. It was rather unremarkable, plain and unadorned. About 14 inches tall, it had a solid circular top, eight inches in diameter, with a small hole in the center. The sides curved inward like a woman's torso, then widened into a bowl shape, and sat on a narrow pedestal. There were two rings on each side of the bowl through which a suspension chain could run. The lamp's color was dull and brassy.

"So what are you going to do with it? A little polishing wouldn't hurt, but don't expect a genie to pop out and grant you a thousand wishes."

"I am going to hang it in that corner near the plants. And just because I did my senior Lit paper on *A Thousand and One Nights* and got my MA in Eastern Literature doesn't mean I believe in magical lamps or wishes that come true."

Richard chuckled. "*That's* a relief! The way you told that Aladdin story to my brother's kindergarten class, I half thought you believed in all that stuff."

Tonie rewrapped the lamp and placed it gently back in its bag. "A good storyteller doesn't have to believe in her story just to make it seem real." She turned haughtily aside and said, "Now shoo. We both have papers to finish."

"Right." He suddenly snapped his fingers. "Damn! I forgot I have to return a book to the library today. Catch you later."

He fished a book out of his desk drawer, grabbed his jacket, and ran out of the room. Tonie looked after him fondly, then with annoyance as she remembered his mocking references to her countless unfinished attempts to become "famous" in the literary world. She began twirling the ring on her finger again, but stopped as the stone cut into her palm. *What is it with me? Is Rich right after all? Do I just like the idea of having a project, rather than actually finishing something?* She angrily shook her head. *Tonie Masia, you quit this. Rich is your friend, not your conscience. You have something to do right now. So hop to it.*

Realizing that she was only going to waste more time if she allowed this self-absorption, she quickly inserted a fresh batch of paper into the printer and typed the proper PRINT command into her laptop. Reading her work in hardcopy always helped clear her mind and suggested new avenues in her thought processes.

As the printed pages rolled out, Tonie examined her hands. The slight bruise she had given herself from playing with the ring had lessened. She considered removing the ring altogether, but decided against it. It was beautiful, and suited her small hands as no other ring ever had. The stone was a large blue lapis set in a wide silver band. Wearing the ring seemed somehow to be a positive affirmation that *this* time she would really finish something she started.

The last page shot out from the printer. She picked up the pile of papers and sat back at her desk. As she prepared to begin reading, she rubbed her hands front and back. She felt a shock as her fingers brushed against the lapis stone. *Friction, that's all.* She rubbed the stone again to reassure herself. As she did so, suddenly a cloud of faint blue smoke wafted from the ring and formed a growing pillar in the middle of the room. Within the cloud a shape began to form. *Oh, brother, this is too weird!* The shape was that of a tall, well-formed black man—Tonie hated artificial color labels, but, well, his skin *was* darker than Richard's—wearing . . . Tonie suppressed a giggle. *He* would *be wearing a loincloth and nothing more. And he has a, what is that called, a topknot? I gotta stop watching old movies. Next thing I know, Sabu will be dropping in on a carpet.*

The djinn's—Tonie was willing for now to concede her vision might be such—muscular arms were folded across his broad chest. He stared at her for a second, and then in a booming voice said, "Your slave is at your service. Ask me what you will, for I am the slave of whomever wears the ring."

Tonie didn't know whether to pinch herself, slap her cheeks, or run out for espresso. Maybe she *was* taking this Middle Eastern study too seriously. Trying to educate the Western world about its desert neighbors was noble indeed, but not at the price of her sanity. She settled for rubbing at her eyes, then looked up. No, he was still patiently standing there. She decided to take another tack.

"You know, this *is* the twentieth century. Uh, *late* twentieth century. TV doesn't even run 'I Dream of Jeannie' anymore. I might love a good fantasy yarn now and then, but it's okay. I don't need any djinn, thanks all the same."

But the djinn didn't disappear back into a puff of smoke. He just stood there looking at her with his soulful brown eyes and repeated "Ask me what you will, mistress of the ring."

Tonie muttered under her breath. "I wish I had a good strong cup of coffee."

The djinn waved his hand and pointed. "Behold, mistress. As you have wished, so it is done." And there on the corner of her desk stood a mug with black coffee.

This was just too much. Wishful thinking was all well and good, but she was taking wish fulfillment just a bit far. Richard had been trying to instill the virtues of coffee in her for weeks without success, and he continually planted cups of the (to Tonie's taste) bitter beverage virtually under her nose. He had probably left this one as well, and she'd just gotten around to noticing it. No djinn was necessary to explain this. But then again . . .

"Okay, Djinn, how about a real wish to make come true? Let's see now." Tonie pulled out her latest copy of *Archaeology Magazine* and opened to the listing of regional expeditions. She held the page up to the djinn and said "I want to be an assistant on the Kendall dig."

Seconds ticked by. No flash of light, no thunder, no change of scenery. Tonie didn't expect anything, but she was somehow disappointed. She had always figured her imagination was capable of more than this. But there was the djinn, just standing there actually looking a bit forlorn.

"A thousand apologies, mistress, but this is beyond my

small powers. You must consult the djinn of the lamp.''
And with that, the djinn disappeared.

Oh thanks a lot, Rich. You just had to remind me about that Aladdin story, didn't you?

Well, what the heck. She wasn't accomplishing anything else right now anyway. Tonie pulled the lamp gently out of its bag and unwrapped it. She took a tissue from her purse and proceeded to polish the lamp. Suddenly a wisp of faintly copper smoke began to rise out from the top of the lamp, and as it grew it billowed into the middle of the room.

A shape began to form within the smoke. Tonie stared at the apparition before her. The djinn of the lamp was tall and muscular, with swarthy skin and a thin goatee. His head was wrapped in a gold turban with blue embroidery. He wore a gold vest and blue . . . were those harem pants? On a *guy*? His feet were encased in gold slippers with turned-up toes. Like his predecessor, his arms—Tonie was convinced that all djinns must have belonged to the equivalent of a good health club—were folded across his chest, and he glared at her before her spoke.

''What is your will, O mistress of the lamp?''

Tonie decided to go for broke. That's what fantasy is all about, right? Letting your imagination run wild? She opened a drawer and rummaged until she found the material from the Topkapi Suray in Istanbul. ''See this?'' She waved it at the djinn. ''Wish Number One: I want to go to Turkey to do research at this Museum. Say, in the fall.''

Now, where was that issue of *Archaeology Magazine*? Ah, lying under the Museum bag. Tonie showed the regional listings to the djinn. ''Now for Wish Number Two: I want to assist Professor Kendall in Arabia come spring.''

The djinn had remained silent through all this. Tonie wasn't sure if he was overwhelmed, amused, or simply patiently awaiting the end of her requests. ''Uh, Djinn whatever-your-name is, I have just one more wish, but I don't want to go over my limits.''

At that, the djinn almost smiled. ''Mistress, ask me what you will.''

''Okay then, I have this manuscript for a fantasy novel. Set in Moorish Spain, with a Moslem prince and a Castilian princess . . . oh, you don't need the details. I want this manuscript to be published.'' Tonie sighed and sat back. ''That's it. Three wishes. Can you handle it?''

The djinn closed his eyes. He breathed in deeply, muttered something Tonie couldn't catch, then opened his eyes and studied Tonie with a penetrating stare. ''Here are your wishes fulfilled, little mistress of the lamp. You will attend the Topkapi. Professor Kendall will accept you as a volunteer, and your book will be published.'' With that, the djinn disappeared.

Tonie jumped up and grabbed the lamp. She shouted into the hole, ''That's it? That's all? And I'm supposed to believe you, with no time frame, no dates, nothing except your word?'' Suddenly the absurdity and impossibility of the last few minutes struck her, and she burst out laughing. ''Well, what did I expect? He said I'd get my wishes, so I'll just have to wait and see.''

But how will I ever explain this to Rich. Guess I'll just have to mail in the application to the Turkish Consulate, plead with Kendall, and submit my manuscript. Then when everything happens, I can just say ''The djinn did it for me.''

Tonie was watering the plans about two months later when Rich yelled out from the front hall. ''Hey, Tonie, there's a letter here from Imagining Books. Their editor wants to meet with you and your agent to talk about publishing your Arabian romance.'' He came into the living room. ''Good thing I bugged you to finally submit that manuscript.''

Before Tonie could say a word, Rich added, ''Oh, by the way, I have a little confession to make. You know that letter you got from the Consulate, inviting you to stay in Turkey as a museum researcher for three months? I filled out all the paperwork for you and sent it off. Sorry if I interfered, but just once I wanted to see you *do* something instead of simply dream about it.'' He dropped the rest of the mail on the table. ''Gotta get back to the library and finish my dissertation.'' At the door Rich turned to her. ''Oh, and you'll have to tell me what you said to Kendall that made him waive the deadline. He's always been a stickler for procedure. But at least you'll be going on the dig. Good going! I knew you could do anything you wanted.'' Rich whistled as he closed the door behind him.

Tonie sighed. Well, that explained the Topkapi. Now she knew she could never tell Rich about the djinn. She had tried a few times, but started to disbelieve it had ever really happened. When she got Professor Kendall's letter, she had been convinced that Rich had gone to see him, and since volunteers were always being sought, thought nothing more about it.

But Rich thought *she* had talked to Kendall. And how could she ever explain that Imagining Books was going to publish a novel that, as far as she knew, they had never seen. The envelope had been in her mailbox a few days after she had sent it, marked ''Returned To Sender'' for ''Insufficient Postage.'' Tonie had forgotten to add stamps and remail it. It was still sitting buried on her desk.

Tonie looked at the lamp swinging gently on its chain. Finally she took a tissue out of her pocket.

Okay, I've got this great idea for a screenplay.

By now you know that things are not always what they appear to be.

The corollary is that wishes are not always what they appear to be either. I have seen subsequent masters of my lamp make the most thoughtful wishes and have them turn to dust, or make the silliest wishes and get exactly what they want.

Take, for example, the case of Carter Waymon. . . .

DJINN & TONIC
by Susan Casper

Noise from all over the office seeped into the cubicle that Carter Waymon used for an office. Typewriter bells jangled, voices, undecipherable and therefore all the more annoying, were a constant buzz. And the computers. The computers were the worst. Subject to strange fits and capable of going down at the most inopportune moment, leaving him stranded just when a fifteen page report was due. How could anyone concentrate in a madhouse like that?

The copier ground out the pages of his report with a high-pitched whine, then the telephone joined the cacophony. He resisted an urge to throw the damn thing across the room. "Hello," he said as he picked up the receiver, trying to keep the irritation out of his voice.

"Waymon!" It was Zasloff. Carter sank into his swivel chair, defeated, then had to make a quick grab for the desk to keep himself from going over backward. In the process he dropped the phone. He could still hear Zasloff burbling from somewhere on the floor. "I want that report and I want it now!"

Carter brought the phone back up to his ear. "Yes, Mr. Zasloff. Right away, Mr. Zasloff," he said, keeping just enough composure to hang the receiver up gently. He took his jacket from the back of the chair, paused to straighten his tie in the vague reflection cast by the glass upper half of the walls that cordoned off his little cubicle from all the others that lined the vast room. The last sheet of paper was just now coming out of the copier and he grabbed at the page, tearing the corner. He had to paper clip the whole set together a little closer to the center than was strictly office norm. "Two demerits," he told himself wryly.

Zasloff's office was one of the few that was actually a room. It sat just inside the public entrance to Liss, Blvatsky and Shore with a pebbled glass window that announced Orinkov Zasloff, Director. Carter knocked on the door, then opened it without waiting for a summons. Zasloff was on the phone. He was always on the phone, and never so happy as when he was able to blast somebody. At the moment his vocal cords were getting an excellent workout and Carter was very glad that he was not on the other end of the line. He took a seat, perched on the edge for an easy exit should Zasloff take offense, but the paunchy old man never even seemed to notice him as he hurled epithets off into the ether.

For a full twenty minutes Carter half-sat, every muscle tensed, and when Zasloff finally looked up, there was no kindness in his beady eyes, no friendship in his voice. "Waymon, where the hell have you been?" he bellowed unfairly. Not knowing what to say, Carter handed him the report and Zasloff looked it over, shaking his head. "Late and sloppy," he said.

Carter looked up at the large prison clock that hung on the wall behind him. The report had been due at the end of the day, still fifteen minutes away. "You are going to have to do better than this if you want to keep working here," Zasloff continued. He kept him sitting, listening to a litany of his flaws, until the bell finally rang, announcing the end of the working day.

Carter was the last one out of the parking lot. He would have thought that the traffic, at least, would be somewhat lighter, but instead it was worse than ever. His mail lay just inside the door, a huge stack, all bills and advertisements. He picked them up and threw them disgustedly onto the catch-all table beside his favorite chair. There was barely time to straighten up and order a pizza before the game came on. Now he would finally be able to sit back and just relax. It was something he didn't get to do all that often. If it wasn't a report due in the morning, it was his ex-wife Alice calling to say she needed something, or his mother, telling him how lonely life was in California, and what a good boy his brother Michael was for taking care of her, but how much happier she'd be back on the good old East Coast. He turned off the bell and turned on the TV.

The game was just getting under way. Carter took a slice of pizza and leaned back in his easy chair. An ice cold brew would have been lovely, but it was strictly diet soda until he lost a bit of that gut he'd put on lately. He popped the can absently, hearing the satisfying hiss as the trapped air escaped. His eyes never left the television. That had clearly been an incomplete pass, but the referee had made an icing call. The good old green and purple was having a hard time keeping track of the puck. It was obviously going to be one of those games where the team just couldn't get it together. "Geez, I wish you guys had a better offense," he said.

"Done!" a deep voice boomed in his ear.

Carter jumped in his seat, missing the beautiful relays that were suddenly coming together on the ice. There was a man in the room with him. A big man. Perhaps the biggest man he had ever seen. Dark curls framed a face that was dwarfed by a veritable eighteen-wheeler of a body. But if the man himself was strange, it was his clothing that really caught Carter's attention. Those massive, double-Schwarzenegger shoulders bore a vest of lemon gelatin yellow. What there was of it was satin shiny, trimmed in colorful jewels, but it might well have been borrowed from a rather scrawny five-year-old. It was open in the front, exposing more than a foot of smooth, tight bronze skin, and came down only inches below his armpits. The material itself was splotched and streaked with what appeared to be cola stains.

His trousers were pale yellow gauze, obviously meant to balloon around his massive legs, but damp enough to cling in hideous lumps. His feet were bare, and toes the size of sausage links were encircled by rings of beautiful craftsmanship, sometimes several on a single toe. The creature laughed with a resonance that made the windows hum and shook the improbable turban on his head.

"Who the hell are you?" Carter asked, his voice a high-pitched squeak that cracked mid-sentence. He cleared his throat and tried again, this time managing to put some indignant authority behind his words. After all, Carter himself was not a small man. A college athlete, he had been working out recently to take a ten-year layer of fat off of his wiry ex-jock frame. The TV droned on, unheeded in the background, ignored despite the announcer's astonished cries of "Score!" which came much more frequently than was usual.

The stranger looked at him benignly. He had a pleasant face and a truly friendly smile. Mollified, Carter noticed for the first time that soda was dribbling down his arm and banged the can down firmly on the table, knocking the rest of the pizza onto the floor.

"I am a djinn," the stranger said at last. "Abu el Mahdi, to be precise."

Carter looked at him warily. "A . . . what did you say, a gin?" he asked.

"Perhaps the word genie would be more familiar, kind master," the spirit said with a flourish of his arm.

"Right! Just like Barbara Eden. I was just noticing the resemblance. In fact I was just saying to myself, that man . . ."

"Please, master. I have come to grant you wishes. You have two left," Abu said.

"Well, if you're a genie, where the hell did you come from? I didn't rub any lamps or open any spirit bottles," Carter said. The genie waved an arm, indicating the can that Carter had dropped on his table. Carter's eyes grew wide and his jaw dropped to his chest. "You came in a can of soda? A *can* of soda? Diet soda? And store brand, at that!"

Abu shook his head sadly. "Ah, yes. Even *we* have been forced to modernize. Now please, kind master, if you would just make your wishes. I would like to go home and change my clothing. This is quite uncomfortable," he indicated his damp and sagging pants. "They did not used to put us in with liquids."

Carter sighed. It was all too much. He bent to pick up the pizza and noticed that some of the mail had fallen into the box. He pulled out a come-on from the stamp of the month club, and another from Wrestler's Guide magazine, both liberally covered with pepperoni and olives. The pizza was ruined. Angrily he wheeled around. "You want me to make a wish. Okay. Here goes. I wish that you and all these other assholes would just stop giving me a hard time," he said.

"Done!" the genie bellowed.

"Oh, go away," Carter said, pettishly.

"You wish me to go away?" Abu asked.

Carter did not understand why the man sounded puzzled. It was lucky for Abu that he wasn't calling the police that very moment. "Of course I do," Carter said. "What do you think this is? Open house or someth—"

The genie didn't simply vanish. Slowly, feet first, he began to transform into a column of smoke. A slender gray column that twisted like a miniature whirlwind, winding its way across the floor and into the soda can. In less time than it takes to tell the column was sucked inside the can like a vacuum cleaner ad, where it disappeared with a final, wet pop.

Carter sank back into his chair, hands shaking. Perhaps he really *had* been a genie. The magnitude of what he had done began to sink in. Two wishes. A genie had offered two wishes and he had just pissed them away in a fit of pique. Why, he might have asked for anything. Fame, wealth, Sigourney Weaver, anything. Worse, he had made a wish. He tried to think about how he had worded his request and what the ultimate ramifications might be, but the images that came to his mind were so horrible that he soon gave up. Mouth dry, he reached for a drink. "Ah, you took the can!" he whined.

A shout of "Scored again!" caught his attention and he looked at the game. At least his team would be playing well for a while. He wondered how long it would last.

Carter got little sleep. He spent the night thinking of missed opportunities and kicking himself again and again.

Next morning the alarm failed to go off. Carter rushed into his clothing and raced down to the car. Fortunately, traffic wasn't so bad. The cars almost seemed to get out of his way as he rushed to work. It was late when he got to the office. Worse than that, Zasloff stood by the door, certain to see him when he arrived. He thought about turning around and calling in sick for the day, but that would only make things worse. Sheepishly, he pushed through the doors.

"Waymon," Zasloff said, before he had even taken two steps across the room. Carter braced himself. "I read through your report last night. Great work!" he said, slapping him lightly on the back. Amazed, Carter walked to his desk. The office was strangely quiet. Almost peaceful. The usual hubbub of morning activity had slowed to a dull, pleasant roar. For a wonder, the phone wasn't ringing. He poured himself a cup of coffee, then took off his jacket and hung it over the back of his chair. There was an envelope on his desk.

The envelope contained one sheet of paper. A tax exclusion form? It seemed to say that he no longer had to pay the IRS. He'd never heard of such a thing, but a quick call to personnel confirmed it. Carter eased back into his chair and a slow smile spread over his face.

Perhaps he had not made such a bad wish after all.

There are lamps, and then there are lamps, and not all of them are magic.

On the other hand, not all of them aren't.

This is the story about a husband and wife who try to recreate my life, and of the difference a lamp makes. . . .

THE GENIE OF P.S. #32

by Karen Haber

Aladdin sat on the damp floor of the dark and gloomy cave, straining to see by the light of his one guttering candle. Around him were piles of gold and jewels, fantastic wealth: several kings' ransoms. But he ignored them all, oddly fascinated by the ancient lamp which he held in his hands.

"What should I do with this dirty old thing?" he mused. "It doesn't even look like it has a wick, much less any oil."

"Clean it!" screamed several childish voices.

"Maybe I'll use it to pry open the slab with which that evil magician locked me into this cave."

"No! Rub it!" the voices screeched.

"If I can't escape, what good is all the treasure of the world to me?" And Aladdin hung his head in woe. Tears coursed down his cheeks. He blew his nose loudly and long in the sleeve of his homespun robe. As he did so, he inadvertently rubbed the thick fabric against the tarnished side of the brass lamp.

"Kaboom!"

The sound was that of a dozen brass cymbals crashing together.

Aladdin fell backward in surprise and alarm.

"What is your wish?" asked a deep, mournful voice.

Aladdin grabbed hold of his purple turban and looked

all around him, once, twice, three times. "Who's there?" he said. "Who called?"

"It's the genie!" yelled the voices once more.

But Aladdin didn't seem to hear them. Instead, he stood, trembling with terror, the lamp nearly falling from his nerveless fingers.

A tall and magnificent bearded genie in green harem pants, golden slippers with turned-up toes, a mirror-embroidered vest, and a scarlet turban strode into view and turned, arms crossed upon his mighty chest, to face the audience. "I am the genie of the lamp," he thundered. "Your every wish is my command."

The children of Germantown Public Grammar School #32, grades 1–3, cheered and pounded their feet against the floor of the auditorium. One little girl in the front row tried to grab the great ballooning side of the genie's pants, but her teacher pulled her back into her seat by the straps of her pink corduroy overalls.

The genie set Aladdin free, as he did at every performance of Shores' Rolling Players' spring show. The children clapped and yelled and giggled as they had in every elementary school from Philadelphia to the Lehigh Valley.

And after the show, the genie and Aladdin removed their makeup and resumed their offstage roles as brown-haired, clean-shaven Glen and blonde-haired, green-eyed Linda Shore.

"What's for lunch?" Linda said.

"Peanut butter. Again."

"Oh, goodie. What a surprise." She bit into the slightly limp sandwich and chewed thoughtfully. "I suppose we could be eating soggy ravioli in the cafeteria with the eight-year-olds."

"Thank you, no."

The Shores had managed not to starve or to take day jobs. But they were getting tired of the meager rations they could afford on the proceeds of their traveling show. Not that they were complaining, of course. At least they were working. But it took every cent to keep the Rolling Players on wheels. The Pennsylvania State Educational budget had a smaller piece of the financial pie to serve up each year while gas—and peanut butter—were not getting less expensive.

After sandwiches and warm iced tea, Linda and Glen

packed up and stowed their kit in the van. They had designed the set and costumes for durability and simplicity rather than aesthetics. Packing took them minutes and they prided themselves on their speed.

"Did you get the check?" Glen asked.

"Right here." She waved the white envelope at him.

"Great. Want to splurge on a motel tonight?" He grinned lecherously. "I've almost forgotten what it's like to make love in an actual bed."

Linda shook her head in mock severity. "Don't be such a spendthrift."

"You mean you want to do something boring with it, like buy groceries."

"Something like that."

They climbed into the battered white van, Linda behind the wheel.

"How far is it to Allentown?" she said.

"I should think you'd have it memorized by now."

"You know I forget it."

"Forty-five miles or fifty minutes."

Linda set the mirror and peered out the window. "Okay, buckle up." She started the motor and backed the van out of its space, shifted, and pulled forward out of the school parking lot and onto the road leading to the freeway approach.

"Yes, Mom."

"Fine, go ahead and be a macho jerk. I'm sure I can find another genie on short notice."

"Not with my pecs." He flexed his biceps, took a deep breath, and exhaled noisily.

"At any gym."

"You planning on having an accident?"

"Not me. The other idiots on the road." She turned the wheel sharply, the van swerved, and a red Toyota swept past them, horn blaring. "Like them, for example."

"I see your point." He buckled up. They always had this mock argument and he always gave in, eventually, and always would. He leaned back in his seat and closed his eyes. "Wake me when we get to the far side of Bethlehem."

Andrea Robinson was six years old with sleek black hair in neat braids and big blue eyes. She was extremely bright and precocious and she knew it because her mother had told her so on several occasions.

. Right now she was crouched behind the door of the cloakroom with a bundle hidden in a brown paper sack from her lunch. She waited, scarcely breathing, until the bell had rung for recess and she could hear her classmates laughing and yelling from the schoolyard. She knew she would be safe until math, next period, when Mrs. Stanley would count heads and miss hers. But that gave her twenty minutes: an enormous chunk of her lifetime.

Her heart pounded as she reached into the bag and grabbed the object within. It was cool and metallic. In a moment she was staring at the lamp of the genie. Its surface was embossed with elaborate scrollwork and it smelled faintly of ammonia, a scent which reminded her of her cousin Billy's diapers. Andrea wrinkled her nose. Her precocious logic told her to stop being a baby, it was only a lamp. A prop. But Andrea was only six years old and she had seen the genie. She knew the lamp was magic. And now it was hers.

It had been easy to hide in the bathroom, lingering until she knew that the auditorium was empty. Then she crept backstage and peered through the curtain. There the lamp was, gleaming, on a scarlet pillow. Aladdin and the genie were nowhere to be seen. Maybe they were eating lunch. She darted forward, grabbed the lamp, and raced out of the auditorium and back to the safety of her homeroom.

She examined the lamp carefully. She had expected it to weigh a ton: how could so lightweight a lamp hold such a big genie? Should she rub it? Would the genie appear? What if he did? Would he make a lot of noise? Would the teacher find out? Better not to take chances. She would wait until she was alone, at night, in bed.

So she bundled it back into the paper bag and tucked it carefully into her knapsack.

That night, after her mother had kissed her on the forehead and turned off the light, Andrea waited under her pink down comforter, heart pounding, until the sound of footsteps receded downstairs. She waited another five minutes, growing more excited with each passing second. When she could wait no longer, she threw back the covers and hung, upside down, from her mattress, foraging under the four-poster canopy bed for the bag she had hidden behind a stack of board games.

Her fingers brushed something and paper rustled. There. She grabbed the bag and pulled it up, swung herself into a sitting position, and pulled the lamp out of the bag.

It was cool and light in her hands. Andrea didn't hesitate for a second, not even to savor the moment. She had waited too long already. With trembling fingers she rubbed the lamp, back and forth, and whispered, "Bring Daddy back home. Bring Daddy back home."

She paused, waiting.

Nothing happened. There was no clash of thunder. No great echoing voice. Not even a golden shoe with rolled toe.

Well, maybe the genie was busy. Maybe he had more than one lamp, the way Andrea's mother had more than one phone. Maybe the genie had call waiting, too. She tried again and this time, for good measure, she squeezed her eyes shut.

"Please bring Daddy home. Make him want to live with us again."

Again, nothing.

Andrea's throat felt terribly full and tears welled up in her eyes. There was no genie. There never had been and never would be. Her father was gone for good.

She shoved the lamp back into the bag, wadded the whole thing into a lumpy ball, and dropped it in the pink wastebasket next to the bed. She decided that she didn't believe in Santa Claus either. Then she curled onto her side under the covers and cried herself to sleep.

Glen and Linda had splurged on a motel room in Allentown. They slept soundly on the rented mattress and awoke rested and refreshed. It wasn't until ten minutes before they were scheduled to perform for the first four grades of Saucon Heights Elementary that they discovered their loss.

"Where's the lamp?" Linda said.

"I thought you had it."

"No."

"Oh, it must be in here with the costumes. I just grabbed everything and threw it in the bag."

"If you're not more careful, we'll have to replace the

costumes before the season's over," she said sharply.
"And we can't afford to do that."

"I know, I know." He grabbed the duffel bag which
held their props and rummaged inside of it. "I don't feel
it here."

"My God, we can't go on without the lamp."

"Sure we can," he said. "We'll pantomime."

"No, I've got to have an object to concentrate on. I
can't just Zen it the way you can. Go look under the seats
in the van."

Glen gave her an exasperated glare. "I'm in full makeup.
Do you want the kids to see me? You go look."

"All right, dammit."

She was back in a minute, her face pale with two livid
spots on her cheeks. "It wasn't there, either. Oh, God,
this is awful. We'll have to cancel. I can't do it without
the lamp."

Glen put his arm around her. "Calm down, honey. Of
course you can do it without the lamp."

"Excuse me, can I be of any help?" A short, balding
man in horn-rimmed glasses and a red beret was at their
elbows. "I'm Walt Gansky. I head up the art department
here. And you must be the thespians." He looked at Linda
and then at Glen. "Is there a problem?"

"We've lost our magic lamp," Linda said.

"Hmmm. That is a conundrum," said Mr. Gansky.
"Especially for Aladdin. Well, how about a sketch of one
on posterboard, cut out? Would that do?"

"What do you think, Lin?" Glen said. "Can you work
with a two-dimensional object?"

"I don't know."

"Would it help if I spray-painted it gold?"

"That would be great," Glen said. "Can you do it and
have it ready in about five minutes?"

Mr. Gansky beamed. "Of course."

"We'll hold the curtain."

"I'll hurry. I quite understand. You know, I wanted to
be in the theater when I was young." With a conspiratorial
wink Mr. Gansky scurried away.

He was back in five minutes with the cardboard cutout,
still sticky from the gold spray paint. He held it out with
obvious pride.

"What do you think?"

Linda gazed at it dubiously.

"It's perfect," Glen said. "Terrific. Can't thank you enough." He pumped the man's hand while waving the cardboard lamp in the air to dry. "Come on, Lin. We've got a show to put on!"

Somehow they struggled through the performance. The children stamped and screamed and didn't seem to mind in the slightest that the lamp was a cardboard cutout.

As they packed their stage kit in the van, Glen let out a slow whistle.

"What a relief," he said. "I never thought we'd get that one done."

"You fink!" Linda threw her turban and caught him in the nose with it. "You said we could do it. You told me so!"

He smiled mischievously. "I was afraid you'd pull a Sarah Bernhardt on me and faint. But you didn't. You came through like a trouper."

She pretended to be put out and, turning away, began to toss props into the duffel bag.

"Hey, look out," Glen said. "You'll put a fold in the lamp."

Linda stared at him, aghast. "You don't expect to keep using this thing, do you?"

"Why not?"

"First off, it won't last."

"We'll make another."

"We'll FIND another," she said. "I've got to have an actual lamp, Glen. I need it."

"Okay. Okay. Let's stop on Eleventh Street and check out the junk stores. Maybe we'll see something there we can use."

Linda brightened. "Great."

After a half an hour of serious browsing they discovered a suitable lamp in a dark, dusty little shop whose faded sign read: "Ye Olde Junke Shoppe." The proprietor, a plump woman wearing a bright red wig, wanted $12.50 for it, but Glen charmed her down to $9.00.

As they left the shop Glen practically popped the buttons from his faded shirt as he preened. "Pretty good, huh? Nine bucks for a terrific old lamp."

Linda squinted at their prize. "It looks like part of a hookah to me. I'll bet old men in Cairo used to smoke hashish in this thing. I wish I could read the hallmark on the bottom of this thing. I'll bet it says Egypt. Or maybe Taiwan.''

"And I'll bet it lit the interior of a small bejeweled mosque belonging to a pasha's beautiful daughter.''

"You would. Boy, it's heavier than the last lamp.''

"And prettier, too.''

"If you like this sort of elaborate metalwork.''

"You don't like it?'' Glen clutched his chest melodramatically.

"I don't have to like it. I just have to use it.''

Glen and Linda had finished the second show of the day at Emmaus Day School and were wearily packing their props.

Linda said, "Y'know, honey, when I was young I always thought I'd want to be a traveling actor. But now—''

"You'd rather be a legal secretary?''

"Don't tease. Can't I complain in peace?''

"Nope. Not to me, anyway.'' Glen stowed their gear in the back of the van and locked the door. His tone was light, but when he turned to face her he looked somber, almost grim. "What would you prefer, Linda? A white picket fence? I thought you liked the boho life, being free and unencumbered.''

"I didn't realize it would mean being so poor.'' She toyed with the frayed black tape which covered the disintegrating upholstery of the van's front seat.

"What do we need money for?''

She glared at him, green eyes blazing. "Aside from the obvious, like food and rent and van repairs, I'd like to put something aside for the future. Remember the future? Someday I want to settle down and, I don't know, maybe have a kids' theater. In an old barn somewhere or a storefront. Something like that.''

"Yeah, yeah, I know.'' Glen patted her shoulder sympathetically. "Keeping the theater tradition alive. Well, baby, maybe someday we will. But right now, we're due in Schuykill.''

Their performance that day was lackluster but efficient. The children screamed and cheered as always, but even that failed to raise the Shores' spirits.

As they removed their makeup, Linda began to cry.

Glen stared at her in dismay. "Honey, what is it?"

"I'm sorry," she sobbed. "I just don't think I can keep doing this. We never have enough money. All we do is ride around and put on silly little plays at schools where the children won't remember us for five minutes after we're gone."

"That's not true. You're just tired."

"Don't you want anything more?"

The genie embraced Aladdin. "As long as I'm with you, I'm happy. You know that."

Linda wept for a moment longer. Then she raised her head, dried her eyes, and blew her nose in a tissue.

"I'm okay," she said. "No, don't look at me that way. I just had to get it out."

"Sure, I understand." He kissed her on the forehead. "Come on, let's get moving or we'll disappoint our next audience."

"Where are we going?"

"Lehighton. And you'd better give me that role of plastic tape. The front seat is starting to go."

"Again?"

Three miles outside of Lehighton the van's engine began hiccuping. Half a mile later it stalled dead. Linda steered them off the road and onto the shoulder. For five minutes she pumped the gas and turned the key in the ignition, over and over. But the engine groaned, growled, and refused to start.

"What's wrong?" Glen said.

Linda gazed, frowning, at the dashboard and its blinking yellow idiot lights. "I don't know. We have enough gas and oil. I checked when we headed out."

"Maybe the engine's flooded."

"Don't be ridiculous. You can't flood an engine while you're driving."

"Can't you get it started again?"

Linda tried once more. The engine coughed weakly but didn't catch. "No."

"Then I guess we hoof it into town."

The sun played hide and seek behind the clouds as they slogged down the road. Halfway into town they flagged down a ride and were taken to the nearest service station. A truck was dispatched and within the hour, the van, on two wheels, was towed into the gas station's malodorous bay.

"It's the alternator," said Joe the mechanic after rummaging under the hood. "She's not charging the battery."

"How much?" Linda asked.

"Rebuilt, a hundred and fifty. New, three hundred."

Glen and Linda exchanged horrified looks. The cost of the rebuilt alternator was ninety dollars more than they had. "Will you take something in trade?"

"I don't know. Whatcha got?"

"How about a lamp?" Linda said, suddenly inspired by desperation.

"A lamp?" Joe squinted at her and wiped his hands on his stained gray coveralls. "No. I don't think I can use that. I meant tools or tires or something."

"No, sorry."

He pointed at a store halfway down the block. "Well, there's Graham's pawn. They might be interested in your lamp."

"Thanks."

The door of the pawnshop tinkled with bells as Glen pushed it open. A dark-haired woman in a cowboy hat sat behind the scratched glass display case reading a magazine. She didn't even look up until Glen had placed the lamp on the counter.

"Afternoon," Glen said.

Without a word she pulled out a loupe and gazed through it at the lamp, tapped its surface, shook it gently.

Linda held her breath.

The woman pursed her lips in irritation. "No. We can't take it."

"Why not?" Linda said, a mite defensively.

"It's not worth anything. For a minute I thought your lamp was a piece of Russian inlay—it's getting very popular, you know."

"But it isn't Russian?" Linda said.

"No. To tell you the truth, I'm not really sure what it is. And we've already got too much junk collecting dust around this place. Sorry." She handed the lamp to Linda and went back to her magazine.

"Damn," said Glen.

"I guess we'll just have to call my brother," Linda said. Her brother, Ron, had bailed them out before. And he was none too eager to do it again. But Linda pleaded and promised him outlandish things, and finally, grumpily, he agreed to wire the money to their checking account.

"For God's sake, you're thirty years old," he said. "When are you going to get your life together?" Then he hung up.

Joe the mechanic was waiting for them, looking both pleased and puzzled. "All set," he said. "That'll be twenty-five bucks for labor."

"Only twenty-five? What do you mean?" Linda asked.

"Well, I installed the perfectly good alternator that you had in your trunk. Why didn't you tell me you had an extra? I've heard of being prepared, but you folks are something special."

"Are you saying you found an extra alternator in our trunk?" Glen asked.

"Yeah. Don't you remember putting it there?"

"Yes," Linda said quickly. "Of course. Now I do." She turned to Glen and whispered, "Settle up with this guy while I go call Ron and cancel the loan. We might make it to the school in time for the show after all." She tucked the lamp under her arm and hurried back to the phonebooth.

The wind was behind them as they sped down the street with Glen behind the wheel.

"Hey, this old bomb is really moving," he said. "That new alternator must be super-powerful. Where the hell did that thing come from anyway?"

"Oh, don't be silly," Linda said. Her tone was more than a little superior. "Don't you see that Joe was giving us a break? He must have felt sorry for us, two broke actors down on their luck, and found some old alternator he had laying around. What a sweet guy. I hope his business doubles."

"I don't know," said Glen. "I've never met a charitable mechanic before."

"You're just too cynical."

"Maybe."

"Definitely."

With minutes to spare they pulled into the parking lot of Lehighton's Paul S. Harding School. Their show was flawless, in fact, more spirited than it had been in some time.

Backstage, Glen hugged Linda and said, "Not too shabby."

"We outdid ourselves," Linda chortled. "We deserve an Oscar."

"Madame Bernhardt." He handed her the lamp.

She was all graciousness as she accepted. "Lord Olivier."

"Pardon me," said a high, thin nasal voice. "I don't mean to break in, but I wonder if I could talk to you?"

The speaker was a woman with brassy golden hair, a face embalmed in makeup, and bloodshot brown eyes. She wore a red suit and carried a black purse on a golden chain. "My card." She handed Glen a gold-embossed card that read: Carol Mandis, Talent Representative.

"You're an agent?" Linda said.

Carol Mandis beamed. "Well, sort of. I do scouting for my sister-in-law, Lorraine. She's got an office in New York. Anyway, I saw your show: my little grandson Joey is in the fourth grade here. I just lo-o-o-ved it. I know you two would be just right for some commercials Lorraine is trying to cast. Have you got photos and bio sheets?"

"Uh, yes, of course," Linda said. "But they're a little bit out of date."

Carol waved away that small consideration. "Don't worry about it, honey. After I rave to Lorraine, you won't need a bio sheet to get an audition. In fact, I'll bet you get the job." She winked stagily. "Just give me your info, and an address where I can reach you."

Later, in the van, Linda shook her head. "Do you think anything will come from this?"

"Nah. She's just a restless grandma," Glen said. "Probably makes a nuisance of herself to her sister-in-law."

"I don't know. She seemed pretty certain."

"All agents are certain. At first."

"I guess you're right."

The letter from Lorraine Mandis came a week later. Linda found it waiting in their P.O. box. In stunned disbelief she tore it open and read it aloud to Glen.

"She wants us to come to New York! To audition. But

she says that's just a formality. She's looking for actors who can not only sell products but amuse children and thinks we sound very promising.''

Glen fidgeted with an old faded piece of silk from the rag bag. ''Linda, I thought we were interested in live theater.''

''Think of how much money this would mean!'' Linda's eyes twinkled, twin emeralds. ''Oh, Glen, we could finally afford to stop touring. We might even be able to buy that little community theater.''

''Oh, I see. It's all right to sell out as long as it's a means to an end? How would we make time to go to New York? We can't afford to cancel any shows. And the van is on its last set of tires.''

''Why do you have to call it selling out? It would be just another gig.''

Glen refused to argue. ''Speaking of gigs, we've got to get going for our next one, remember? Let's talk about this later.''

They made the trip to Allentown in absolute silence, passing green fields where cows were grazing and stone houses with quaint signs in front which advertised cheese, meat, even ducklings. Usually, Linda exclaimed happily over each new sign but not on this trip. She drove quickly, almost grimly, and her eyes never strayed from the road.

As she carried the lamp into the auditorium, Linda slipped and nearly fell, catching herself only at the last moment. She gazed down and saw what had tripped her: a blank folded manila envelope with its flap open. Inside it were two round trip tickets by train from Philadelphia to New York, good any time between now and the end of the month.

''Glen, I don't believe this.''

He put down the duffel bag filled with props and gave her a one-sided smile. ''Oh, so now you're talking to me?''

''Look. Train passes. To New York. It's fate. Now we can get to that audition.''

''Lin, those belong to somebody else. We've got to turn them in at the school office. Whoever dropped them will be looking for them.''

''I don't think so. I think these were meant for us.''

''Are you crazy?''

''No, of course not.''

"I'm not so sure. Give me those passes, Lin."

"No." She tucked them into her purse. "I want them."

He stared at her as though he had never seen her before. "You're really beginning to worry me."

"I don't care. One of us has to think about the future. If you won't, I will."

By the time the curtain went up, Aladdin and the genie were barely speaking to one another. Some of their stiffness spilled over into the performance, and the children watching them were unusually subdued. They clapped obediently at the end, but there were no whistles or cheers.

Backstage, Linda pulled off her turban and threw it to the ground.

"Why did you tell their light crew to throw a red spot on the lamp?" she snapped. "Is that your idea of a joke?"

"Why would I do something like that?" said Glen. He tore off his fake beard. "I thought YOU told them to do it."

"Why would I?"

"Beats me. But I'm having a hard time understanding you lately."

Linda glared at him. Then she turned away and dressed in silence.

"Oh, come on, honey," Glen said. "Wasn't the performance bad enough? Say something. Anything."

"What do you want me to say?"

"Don't be that way, Lin. There's no reason. You want to go to New York? Okay, okay, I give up. We'll go to New York."

She smiled wanly. "All right. But now I feel like a bully."

"Good. You should. Now c'mon, the van's all packed. Let's get on the road. I'll drive."

It was late in the afternoon and overcast. The street was slick with drizzle and the dark clouds looked ready to dump their contents at any moment.

Glen and Linda had just passed the city limits when they saw the police checkpoint. A squad car sat in the middle of the road, red lights blinking, reflecting red on the wet road. A red-haired policeman in a blue uniform motioned them over to the shoulder.

"Now what?" Glen muttered. "The last thing we need is a ticket."

"Our insurance forms are in the glove compartment," Linda said. "Don't forget to be polite."

Glen killed the motor and rolled down his window. "Afternoon, officer."

The policeman peered through mirrored sunglasses at them. "You the Shores?"

"That's right." Glen stared at him in surprise.

"Out of the van, please."

"But—"

"Out, please. Both of you."

"Don't argue with him," Linda said.

They scrambled onto the gravel-strewn pavement. The cop scarcely looked at them.

"Open the back of the van, please."

"Why are you searching us?" Glen said. "How did you know our name?"

"Got a report on you. Was told you might be transporting hot merchandise."

"Hot? You mean stolen? Now wait just a minute!"

"Open the back, please."

"Do you have a warrant?"

"This is a legal checkpoint. I don't need a warrant."

Linda sighed and unlocked the van. The interior reflected the squad car's red lights with an eerie pink glow.

"Please empty the contents."

"Onto the road? But everything will get wet."

"Now, please."

Dutifully, Linda and Glen pulled all they owned out of the back of the van: sleeping bags, picnic coolers, the jack, the spare tire, the duffel bag filled with costumes, and the duffel bag which held the props.

The policeman prodded the bags with the tip of one well-polished black shoe. "Please empty these as well."

Scarlet satin and homespun wool spilled out onto the damp asphalt along with the gray and white papier-mâché boulders, the golden slippers with curling toes, and the enamel and brass lamp. The lamp glowed strangely with each rotation of the police car's light.

The officer bent and picked up the lamp. "So," he said. "Our reports were correct. I'm afraid I'm going to have to confiscate this."

"Why?" Linda said. "It's just a cheap old lamp."

"Those are my orders."

"Now wait just a minute," Linda said. She stared at the cop. "Why would you be instructed to take this lamp? It's not stolen. And it's not worth a cent, either. Who told you we had it, anyway? And how did you know who we are?"

"Damn. You ask too many questions."

The cop scowled at her and, as Linda watched, he seemed to waver as though struck by some strong breeze. But there was no wind. In fact, the air was dead calm. The policeman wavered, blurred, and became so transparent that the outline of the squad car could be seen through him. Soon he was nothing more than dust motes sparkling in the red light.

"What the hell?" Glen said.

The motes coalesced, turned dark, filled out into form and shape once again. Linda and Glen stared, mouths gaping, at a woman in a red diaphanous harem outfit. Her dark red hair was braided and curled around her head under a small red veil.

"I was afraid it wouldn't work," the houri said. She sounded both chagrined and amused. "But it was worth a try. I thought I would at least get your attention by masquerading as one of your recognized authority figures."

"Who are you? How did you do that?" Glen cried. "What's going on here?"

"That's not important," the houri replied. "But for the sake of simplicity, you can call me Anne. What is important is that I've found the interpolator."

"The what?"

"What you call the lamp. It belongs to my mistress. She nearly blew a gasket when it came up missing. We've been searching for it for quite some time. Damned if I know how it got here." She held the lamp up and admired its pulsing red glow. "Very nice, even in this limited dimension."

"The lamp?" Linda's voice nearly stuck in her throat. "I don't believe this. You can't be saying that that lamp is enchanted!"

Anne's smile was frankly condescending. "That's one way to interpret its function," she said. "Probably the easiest for you to understand. Let's just say that it provides for a wide variety of needs."

"But we bought it," Glen said. "It belongs to *us*."

The houri laughed. "You don't want this. You don't even know how to use it properly. It would soon cause you endless grief."

"Is that where the spare alternator came from?" Linda demanded. "The New York talent scout? The train tickets?"

"Yes."

"Well," said Glen. "I wouldn't exactly call *that* trouble."

"Nevertheless, soon you would be at each other's throats over its use. Trust me."

Linda and Glen exchanged startled, embarrassed glances.

"But you can't just take it," Glen said weakly.

"Of course I can." Anne the houri smiled sunnily. "Oh, don't worry, you'll soon find another prop for your theatricals."

"We paid good money for that thing," Linda said.

Anne reached into her harem pants and pulled out a hundred dollar bill. "Will that cover it?"

"Uh, yeah, I think so."

"What about the lamp's miracles?" Glen demanded. "The alternator? The audition? Will those vanish when you do?"

"No. And, just between us, if I were you I'd make time for that audition, know what I mean?" For a moment, her voice sounded high, thin, even nasal. "Now I've got to go. So long." She faded, faded, faded on the nonexistent breeze and was gone.

"I don't believe it." Glen sank down onto the roadbed and rubbed his eyes. "Did I just see what I think I saw?"

"Get up," Linda said. "You'll get run over."

"Have you even seen a car since we stopped?"

"No, but that doesn't mean one won't come buzzing along. Besides, your pants are getting wet."

"Linda, I don't believe you. You're acting like this happens every day. Policemen pull us over, turn into harem girls, and vanish."

She tugged him toward the van. "Let's be practical, honey."

"Huh?"

"Come on, help me pack up our stuff. We've got an audition to get to."

Glen sighed and began to stow their gear in the duffel bags. He threw the bags into the back of the van, locked the double doors, and, shaking his head, climbed into the passenger seat, taking care to ease himself over the patched leather. "Two in one month," he said. "I don't believe it."

"What are you talking about?"

"We lose more lamps in this business." He smiled a half smile.

"Yeah," Linda said, and happy tears began to trickle down her cheeks. "But I've got a hunch that one was our last. Know what I mean?" She pumped the accelerator, turned the key in the ignition, and turned the van out onto the road, heading north to New York.

My genie was not always kind, but he was un-failingly honest.

Under some circumstances this is considered a virtue; under others, it is merely a hazard to be overcome. . . .

LAST WISH
by Martha Soukup

"Do not wish for wealth beyond compare," said the genie.

"Wealth beyond compare sounds pretty good," said Derek. He slid his thumbnail along the raised filigree of the battered oil lamp, marveling. The lamp had cost twenty dollars at the Goodwill. Two or three impulse purchases like that in a month, and he wouldn't make the rent. Wealth beyond compare would be a fine return on a twenty-dollar investment.

The genie towered above Derek. Derek did not understand how that was possible, since they were in his cramped, low-ceilinged basement apartment. He could jump and brush the ceiling with the palm of his hand, and he was not athletic.

"Why wouldn't I wish for that?" he asked the genie, craning his neck. Especially with two more wishes to follow.

The genie sighed, a deep sound that echoed in the water pipes along Derek's ceiling. "Over the eons, many have asked me for wealth. None have had joy of it."

"Why not?" Derek asked.

"Early, I destroyed them simply," said the genie. "I gave them wealth in gold and jewels. It filled their rooms and crushed them to death."

Derek felt the blood leave his face. This genie was, after all, a monster: ancient, powerful, and incomprehensible. His high spirits vanished.

"I was less cruel then," said the genie. "Later, I did not allow the wealth to kill them immediately. I gave riches to peasants, who spent freely until robbers cut their simple throats. Others realized that wealth made them lords; but they did not know the ways of rule and self-preservation. They were overrun by enemies and destroyed, along with their entire families."

Throat dry, Derek asked, "What if they only spent the money as they needed?"

The genie nodded. "The cautious lived, at least the span of a mortal. Some lived high, but in a manner that would not attract attention. They died young when their livers gave out, or they lived long lives of trivial pleasures, berating themselves on their deathbeds with thoughts of how trivial those pleasures had been. Others hoarded their riches against discovery or waste, shriveling up and becoming sour. These misers lived a long time. But they took no joy of it."

"Are you saying money destroys people?" Derek asked. He wanted to say it with heavy sarcasm, but an acute sense of the genie's might made the words come out in an appeasing squeak.

The genie's eyes were deep and dark. "I speak only of genie riches. I do not know what mortal wealth would be to your life. I know what I would give you. Do not ask for it."

Derek thought about why he wished for money. "Women," he said.

"Do not wish for women," said the genie.

"What," said Derek, "you'll fill the room with them and crush me?" Instantly he wished he hadn't said it, but the genie only shook its head.

"Early," it said, "I destroyed men quickly with women. Men who wished to unfailingly draw women could not walk on the street without women hanging on their arms, their backs, their necks, pleading, promising, begging. Some were lucky, trampled to death by women who later could hardly comprehend or remember the strange dream that had come over them."

"I wouldn't need *all* women," Derek said.

"Some asked for one woman," the genie said. "She would be the woman of another man, who would slay them both in their bed. Or she would be a woman the wisher despised."

"They must not have asked very carefully." He thought of Lisa, who worked in a different department at Woolworth's. She was short and dark and curvy and she told the best dirty jokes of anyone in the store. He had been thinking of asking her to a movie, except he didn't know if she'd say yes, and if she did, he didn't know if he should invite her for coffee after, and if he did, his apartment was a mess.

"Later, I grew crueler. She would be the woman he dreamed of, but she would change over the years, becoming lazy or angry or ugly, still never leaving, inextricably enchanted to him. Or he would ask for her to never change to him, to be the same girl who besotted his adolescent eyes. He would become, as the years passed, a changed, matured man with a naive wife whose simple, girlish love cloyed on him. Some of these killed themselves; others cheated on these lovers who had become strangers, and who would forgive them anything; but these never found happiness elsewhere. They had asked for the love of only one woman."

"But love doesn't have to be like that," Derek said, troubled.

"I speak of genie-given love. The lives that humans make with each other, I do not know. I know what I would give you. Do not ask for it."

Derek had passed his thirtieth summer. As time slipped away, he was no longer confident of his ability to make a good life for himself. When he was sixteen, there had been all the time in the world. Nearly another sixteen years had run away with his life. "Then," he said—

"Do not wish for immortality!" thundered the genie.

Derek fell back into his battered sofa, clutching the cushions. The lamp rattled on the floor.

"Early," the genie said, its voice rumbling deeper than a jackhammer, "I gave men who wished for immortality endless life, but I did not give them youth and health. They ached, they shriveled, they blew away. They cursed me with ruined voices.

"Later, I grew crueler. I grew much crueler. I gave them eternal life, with eternal health and youth."

And the genie stopped.

Derek waited. Finally he took a deep breath. "What is wrong with life?"

In a distant voice, the genie said, "I do not know what humans can make of their lives. Those I gave immortality found eternity to be of no meaning. They might acquire money, harems, power. They might give it up and spend centuries in contemplation. They contemplated how to live, when all they loved died around them. None found an answer. I do not know human life. I know genie immortality. Do not ask for it." Derek could not see the genie's face. There seemed to be an oppressive air in the room; it grew darker.

Derek picked up the lamp and put it carefully on the table by the sofa. It had looked old when he felt the whim to spend everything in his wallet on it at the Goodwill; now he felt it must be the oldest thing in the world. "What should I wish?" he said quietly.

The genie's voice was a murmur. "Ask for things a genie cannot foul," it said. "Ask for human things."

"What?"

"Ask," said the genie, "for these two things. Ask that you always find work which satisfies and interests you, for which you are justly compensated."

It was not riches beyond compare, but Derek had been thinking lately he would like to leave Woolworth's and teach music to children. Only the fear he wouldn't make enough to live on had stopped him. Justly compensated. Always find work that would satisfy. He nodded. "And?"

"Ask for the wisdom to know and appreciate your friends. I have noticed," said the genie, "that humans seem to have a large capacity for enjoying each other, when they are not too frightened or blind to accept it, or too greedy to think their happiness lies elsewhere. You are social creatures, you humans. You die without other humans."

Derek thought about Lisa again. He though about the gang he argued about baseball with after work, at the diner.

"I thought you wanted to trick me," he said. "But I don't see the trick. Anything else? Health?"

"I am a powerful spirit," said the genie. "I would not have you ask me for something I do not need to do. I see that you will have a long life, as human lives go, and that you will be as comfortable as a human may expect to be."

"But why?" said Derek. "Why should I trust you? You've described terrible things. I don't understand why you did all of them. I don't understand why you'd change now."

"You cannot," said the genie. "It takes millennia to become truly cruel. It takes power to act on ancient bitterness. But, over the eons, even spirits can change again. You are a human. You will never understand. Be grateful."

"I wish, then," said Derek, "for the two things you suggested, exactly as you suggested them."

"As you command," said the genie.

Nothing happened.

Derek remembered Lisa mentioning that her cousin was on the school board, and that he'd told her they'd had a contribution to expand the arts program. He'd brushed it off, figuring he couldn't get the job. But Lisa liked him— she liked him a lot: she wouldn't have mentioned it if she hadn't thought he had a shot. He reached for the phone.

"As cruel as I was, I was never wholly cruel."

Derek dropped his hand. Somehow phoning Lisa had suddenly seemed more important than the genie that filled his apartment. He didn't know how that could be.

He did know.

"You are so powerful," he said, slowly. "Yet you say you've been released from that lamp over and over. What could trap you, so often?"

"The eons are long. My power cannot transcend itself. All the things I have done to mortals: what consequence are they?"

"A lot of consequence, to them," said Derek. "How many people did you destroy? Is that what you've lived for?"

"Be glad you cannot understand a genie's bitterness. But I say again: in my cruelest wishes granted, I was never wholly cruel."

"I don't understand."

"When I granted the worst wish, I always made sure the human saved one wish. That was my kindness. None of the immortal ever failed to use that wish, after a time. After enough time."

"That wish?"

"You know that wish."

To die, Derek thought.

The genie watched him.

"Whatever your reasons, you have been good to me," Derek said slowly. "You've left me one wish."

The genie was silent.

"I grant my last wish to you."

The apartment was empty. The lamp lay on its side on the table. Its great age and strange beauty seemed to have left it. It was a cheap-looking piece of tin.

Derek thought for a long time, before he was ready to pick up the phone.

Then he picked it up, called Lisa, and lived the rest of his human life.

I like to think of my genie as being the only one of his kind, but of course there are many of them. And, like any other group, they have their own goals, their own needs, and their own agenda.

In fact, I often wondered why they didn't hold a convention to decide exactly how to behave toward their masters. . . .

GENIECON
by Deborah J. Wunder

"They don't need or want us anymore." Yonan ibn Andur shook his head angrily. "Ask for their three wishes, and all you get is nonsense about their stock not crashing, or a better grade of cocaine." He glared about the large conference room, noting the long table at its front. A portable lectern, hotel logo emblazoned on the front in gold, with a microphone attached, sat centered on the table. The room was painted in pale, schoolroom colors, designed to keep minds from wandering. The increasing buzz of individual conversations, mostly uneasy, provided both background and context for the coming panel, as people streamed in from the crowded hallways.

"When I was a lad," Kaliq ibn Daoud agreed dolefully, running a hand through his snow-white hair, "their dreams were grander." His elegant clothes and bearing and his quaint turns of phrase attested to his years serving various minor members of English royalty.

"Well, I certainly don't have that problem. What men want when they see me is pretty universal," argued Layla Kalari, shaking her waist-long, glossy, reddish-black hair.

"Yes, well, maybe if you'd stop wearing those see-through clothes; I mean, you don't give 'em much chance to want anything else," Yonan grumbled, half to himself. They chose seats near the front and moved toward them, passing djinni in every costume imaginable, from harem outfits to business suits. The panel, entitled "What Do We Do Now?" promised to be a crowded one. "Damned female rights movement. Weren't djinna once supposed to listen to us?"

The older djinn tried to deflect Yonan's argument. "That, my friend, is neither here nor there. We have assembled to handle a different problem today. After all, if—as you claim—Men no longer need or desire our services, what then? Who will we serve? Or shall we, perhaps, sail to the West, as the Celtic divinities did?"

"True enough, I suppose." As Yonan settled sulkily into his chair, the moderator, Coman ibn Dabir, walked to the lectern, poured a glass of water from the pitcher beneath it, cleared his throat, and called the group to order. "Welcome, djinna and djinni. Our purpose today is to define relationships between humans and djinns, with emphasis on the problems therein." Several djinns started talking at once. "Please, wait. We will attempt to hear everyone in turn. We have a lot to discuss today, so kindly settle down. Our first speaker is Yonan ibn Andur, who has clearly defined the problem for us." Yonan rose, and walked confidently to the lectern.

"Gentlefolk, we are here today because things are going exceptionally poorly for us. Our masters and mistresses no longer have any sense of the grandeur of life. Their wishes have shrunk in scope and size, and they no longer have any real use for us . . ." He spoke for about ten minutes, occasionally moving a stray lock of hair out of his fiery, chocolate-colored eyes. He silenced several side conversations, one of which almost became a fistfight. Most of the djinns were concentrating on his words, however; only leaving their seats to get beverages from the white thermal pitchers spread along a small back table. As Yonan returned to his seat, Coman again stepped up to the lectern.

"Why don't we throw the floor open for discussion of Mr. ibn Andur's hypothesis? Why don't you begin, Sir?" Coman pointed to an elderly djinn.

It had been a boring day, and Yonan was glad to return to his room before dinner. The bulk of the two sessions had been devoted to various djinns outlining their problems with Men. Mercifully, the moderator had declared a moratorium on experiences occurring before any djinn's

last two periods of service. Still, after six hours all that
had been accomplished was a lot of spleen-venting. He
had agreed to attend the convention reluctantly, and without consulting his Master. After all, it meant leaving his
Master's New York condominium, and being unavailable
to serve; an unheard of thing for a djinn. Further, among
djinns his own age, Yonan was well-known, but the group
here was so diverse that he was one of its lesser lights; a
new and disagreeable position.

He glanced around the room, noting the bed that had
been slept in too many times, the vase with the tired daf-
fodils, the way the sun would enter the room full blast in
the morning unless the heavy drapes were drawn, and
sighed. "Perhaps," he thought "I'll read for a bit before
meeting Kaliq and Layla for dinner." Although he had
agreed to meet them after they had shared a quick lunch
during the session break, he now debated whether to cancel out and dine alone. Deciding against it, he made himself presentable, then tried to get comfortable on the hotel
bed. After ten minutes of constantly rearranging pillows,
he realized that, even for a djinn, finding a comfortable
position to read or sleep in was a task of the same magnitude as cleaning out the Augean stables with a used
toothbrush.

Layla had gone shopping with several other djinna. They
discussed many things, including the convention's purpose, and the attitude of the djinni they had met. Most
djinna were much better than average-looking, and used
to reactions of pleasure from human men, and resentment
from the younger djinni. Not that they weren't resented by
the older ones, but that was veiled by courtliness and pa-
ternalism, rather than rudeness. Since the djinna had become more independent—a process requiring at least three
centuries—the younger djinni had become even worse.
Some of them made no effort to conceal their contempt.
Others still thought that being male was enough to give
them dominion over the djinna. "Well," Layla and her
friends agreed among themselves, "they would learn—
some sooner, some later—just how foolish they were."

In actuality, Layla and her friends had a much clearer
picture of the way things stood between djinns and humans
than Yonan and his friends. Informal discussions had

shown that the bulk of elder djinni agreed with their analysis. Their problem was finding ways to implement their solution without creating more resentment. Layla was spokeswoman for her generation of djinna, as Kaliq and Yonan were for theirs, and she knew her dinner with them would only be one of the hurdles she had to clear to accomplish that implementation.

Although the food and its preparation were excellent, and the seating and decor of the hotel's French restaurant were opulent, dinner was tense. Kaliq's courtliness, and Layla's seeming obliviousness to Yonan's cynicism made Yonan even more uncomfortable. As the sommelier poured their wine, a fine rosé, they discussed their current situations, and their relevance to the problem at hand.

Layla was serving an older man, who considered himself lucky to have found her. He greatly appreciated her granting him a comfortable old age, and accepted her advice as though she was his equal. He delighted in his only granddaughter, who adored him, and he'd shown the child how to summon Layla, who had agreed to serve and advise the child after he passed on.

Kaliq's current mistress was a peeress, and his major duties were escorting her around the world and advising her on financial matters. Her friends were enthralled by her "gentleman companion," and his wonderful stories, and he had become quite attached to her, an unusual thing for a djinn. She was gentle and refined, which pleased Kaliq's sense of propriety, and she was one of those women that time is physically kind to. She had encouraged Kaliq to attend the conference, on the grounds that his wisdom and patience would be invaluable in any discussion.

Yonan's master was a Manhattan stockbroker in his early thirties, who lived a high-profile life, with all the accoutrements thereof. His cynicism, honed to a fine point, was ardently copied by Yonan. His outlook on life was selfish and self-protective. He kept Yonan, although the djinn often angered him, because Yonan smoothed over much in his life, seeing that whatever he wanted was there when he wanted it. Kaliq and Layla were hopeful for the future, while Yonan predicted gloom and doom. "They have absolutely no conception of what we could do for them," he groused.

"Have you made an effort to show them," Layla's voice was musical and sweet. "Or have you spent your whole time wallowing in self-pity?"

"Wallowing in self-pity? Really, Layla, you can't expect me to . . ."

"Now, Yonan, I'm not at all sure that you grasp the enormity of your accusations; although I know many of the younger djinni agree with you." Kaliq offered gently. "Perhaps you and your friends have changed. After all, many of us are happy with our lots in life. Mine, for example, is hardly insufferable, and Layla has even chosen her next mistress."

"But not all of us are so fortunate. That's part of the problem. These humans have no idea of how powerful we are. Why can't they wish for world peace, or something on that scale?"

"Because they haven't done so until now is no guarantee that they won't in future," Kaliq explained patiently. "Besides, our mode of service does not include standing in judgment over them."

"But how can we not do so? They defy any sensible ideals."

"Do they really? Or have you, perhaps, encountered a situation you are unequipped to handle, and blown it out of proportion to the point where no solution is possible?" Layla queried. "I don't mean to offend you, but it seems to me that your perspective is based on several bad incidents, rather than analysis of the whole."

"I try to be objective, Layla. I don't claim to hold the answers but, surely, the question must be raised. If not, we may perish from their abandonment."

The argument continued, each holding his or her own viewpoint. By the time they parted, Yonan was, however, thoroughly confused. Although Kaliq's and Layla's composure had rocked him, he could put his finger on neither how nor why. He was not given to questioning his own motives, but certain thoughts began to nag at him.

"Could Kaliq be right? Were their problems with Man caused by some quirk in their makeup, rather than that of the humans they served? Could it be? Well . . ." He decided that a walk would help clear his mind and, adjusting his body temperature so that he would be comfortable in the crisp fall air, left the room.

"Yonan!" It was Fadil, one of his closest friends. "Yonan! Are you quite well? You look a bit—off—somehow. Jamila and I are having a small get-together later. Will you join us?"

"I'm not sure. Do you need an answer immediately?" He avoided looking at Fadil's eyes.

"What's wrong, Yonan? You usually can't wait to party."

"Nothing, Fadil. I just have a lot on my mind. I need to be able to argue correctly tomorrow."

"Correctly? What do you mean? Most of us know what your views are and agree with them."

"But are they accurate, Fadil? Some of the older djinns apparently think I'm overstating the case."

"They are old and dried out, Yonan. What do they know of living passionately? What can they know of how we chafe at our Masters' reins?"

"Well, I would've agreed with you about that until as recently as dinner."

"What happened there?"

"I ate with Layla Kalari and Kaliq ibn Daoud. He seemed to have had a pretty passionate life. To judge from his stories, he has experienced all our questions, and more."

"But he's only one djinn. Many of us are dissatisfied."

"He and many others maintain that our own cynicism is our undoing."

"And if he's right, Yonan? How can we change what we are?"

"Fadil, I don't know. I'm not even sure what the right questions are yet. I have a lot to sort out before tomorrow. That's why I'm not up to partying tonight. Perhaps the three of us can meet for dinner after tomorrow's sessions."

"I'll ask Jamila what her plans are. What room are you in? I'll leave a message for you."

"Room 723. Thanks. See you tomorrow." Yonan continued to head toward the elevators, adding Fadil's remarks to his own questions. As the elevator door opened, he turned to enter, nearly slamming into Layla as she exited.

"Sorry! Are you all right? I didn't . . ."

"Fine, Yonan. Did I hurt you?"

"Layla? Are you on this floor? I was just going out for a walk. Um, would you care to walk with me?"

"Sure. Can you wait till I change my shoes? These are pretty, but not made for walking."

"No problem. See you in a few." His eyes followed her along the hallway, noting that her room was two doors beyond his. "Hmm," he smiled to himself, "when she's covered, she's a fine looking djinna."

"Hi, Donia! Is it important? I was on my way out." Layla answered the phone on the third ring.

"Catch your breath, Layla. I just wondered what you were doing this evening."

"Well, Yonan ibn Andur just invited me to go for a walk with him."

"Did you tell him to get stuffed?"

"No. I told him I'd be happy to."

"Layla!"

"Now, Donia, don't condemn him out of hand. He may be arrogant, but he seems to have been thinking about what we discussed at dinner. I want to hear what he has to say." She fished under the bed for her walking shoes.

"Know your opposition, right?" Layla could almost see Donia wink at her through the phone.

"Nope. Getting to know a very complicated djinn. He really intrigues me, for some reason. I keep thinking that if we could just talk, without a million djinni telling us what our stances should be, we could probably get along quite well." She found the shoes, sat on the bed's edge, and slipped them on.

"Get along? With Yonan? Have you lost your mind?" Donia was horrified. "Layla, he's one of our most dangerous opponents!"

"I know that he's been very outspoken, which could be all to the good if he really examines the issues."

"Well, I don't envy you your evening."

"I have to go. Don't want to keep him waiting too long."

"Good luck, Layla. And don't let your emotions carry you away." Layla hung up the phone gently, and tied her laces. She knew Donia meant well, but was amused by her overprotectiveness. "After all," she mused, "I am a

grown djinna. I can take care of myself.'' She grabbed her
bag, adjusted her sweater, and left her room.

"Hi! Sorry to take so long, but someone called.''

"That's okay. Pretty color.'' Yonan nodded at the plum-
colored, fisherman-knit sweater. They left the hotel and
walked along city streets, all but oblivious to the sounds
of life that rose around them. Yonan questioned Layla, and
was surprised by the acuity of her answers. "This is one
djinna who's much, much more than just a fair face and
form,'' he thought. "Her answers make at least as much
sense as mine do; some of them more.'' Eventually, their
steps brought them back to the hotel. They parted at Layla's door, after agreeing to meet at breakfast the next
morning.

The meeting room filled quickly. Djinni and djinna alike
wore serious looks, knowing that they had two sessions
left to come to some agreement among themselves about
how to solve the problem raised yesterday. Many of the
assembled djinns had no reason to wish to leave their current masters, and worried about how such a thing could
be accomplished. Would they be able to finish out their
terms of service? Would they have to bid their owners farewell and vanish in a mist? Would they be able to stay until
their owners either passed on or released them?

Coman ibn Dabir again approached the lectern. "My
friends, there has been a slight change of plans. Yonan ibn
Andur and Layla Kalari have combined their presentation
to save time, since they feel there will be ample discussion
of their proposal. I give you Yonan and Layla.''

The two djinns rose, broad smiles on their faces. "Many
of you would not have believed a rapprochement possible
between our positions as stated yesterday, myself among
you,'' Yonan began. "However, I have had a long discussion with Ms. Kalari, and she has many valid points. We
have, perhaps, created this predicament ourselves, since
our stance has always been passive. Ms. Kalari's position
is that the relationships will change if we become more
actively involved. Both she and Kaliq ibn Daoud spent a
great deal of last evening pointing out djinns who were
happy in their relationships with humans. Under examination, well . . . would you take the floor, Ms. Kalari?''

"Certainly. Under examination, as Mr. ibn Andur began, we found that the common thread in the 'happy' relationships was invariably that the djinns had taken a more interactive stance than usual.'' Confused murmurs rose quickly. ''Therefore, we propose the following: For the balance of your current service, and your next one, take a more active stance with your Masters. If what they propose strikes you as arrant nonsense, try explaining why. We need to raise our level of service to where humans feel we are truly looking out for their best interests, not just their momentary desires. It's both that simple and that complicated. We will now take questions.'' The discussion period covered another three hours, as the assembly sought ways to implement Yonan's and Layla's plan.

Yonan settled back in his favorite chair. It had taken about an hour to calm his Master when he had arrived home, but it was worth it, to Yonan's way of thinking. ''I wonder how he'll react when he finds that I have feelings on what 'good' and 'moral' are,'' Yonan mused, ''Or how he will adapt when I request time to visit Layla? After all, even a djinn deserves a day of rest once in a while.''

Have you ever thought—I mean, really thought— about the consequences of a life with genies?

Let me give you an example. What if you wish to spend the night with my wife, and I wish her never to share her unquestioned charms with anyone but me?

Or what if you bet on one racehorse and I bet on another, and we each spend a wish to insure that we win?

Well, you can imagine the red tape involved. Surely the Congress would attempt to regulate wishes, and Las Vegas would have to take them into account when setting the morning line on sporting events, and the genies themselves would have a powerful lobby to make sure that they could not be held responsible for illegal wishes.

Which doesn't mean that people still wouldn't tamper with the system. . . .

BLACK ICE
by Barbara Delaplace

Sept. 14th - Got us a new winger, a kid named Jason Barber. He's supposed to be Hot Stuff—at least *he* thinks he's pretty Hot Stuff. Idolizes Gretsky. Even wears his jersey out on one side. Give me a break.

Oct. 21st - Another loss, 7-zip. Poor Boisvert, he must have felt like it was open season on goalies, he took so many shots.

Oct. 24th - Road trip was a disaster (as usual). 0 and 5. I'd have settled for a lousy tie, for God's sake. Felt bad for Richelieu—the guy just keeps trying, even when it's hopelcss. Never gives up, never lets up, always encourages everyone. He deserves to be captain of a better team.

* * *

Operation Twist-Tie
Surveillance tape #2-438-65
Excerpt of phone call between Joey Giotta and Mike Durning:

Giotta: "Look, we'll clean up. Start it early enough and nobody'll ever figure out what's going on."

Durning: "I dunno, Joey. If it's that easy, how come nobody's ever tried it before? It's so obvious."

Giotta: "How do you know they haven't? Maybe they did and it worked so well no one ever figured it out. But maybe nobody ever has. I mean, how long have the lamps been around? Not very. We're in on the ground floor on this thing, Mike. We gotta do it now before anyone else figures it out."

Durning: "I hear the genies have some sort of council or something. Regulations they gotta follow."

Giotta: "Nah, that's just about how many wishes they can grant and stuff like that. They don't give a [expletive deleted] about 'mortal law' or whatever the hell they call it. They're too high and mighty to bother themselves about that."

Durning: "Yeah? So why don't we just get our hands on a lamp and wish for a billion dollars each?"

Giotta: "Geez, don't you know *anything*, Mike? The *federales* already thought of that one years ago. The banks gotta to report anyone with cash deposits over $10,000. How're you gonna explain your sudden wealth to 'em, huh?"

Durning: "So my second wish is that no one finds out."

Giotta: "Forget it. That's one of the regulations genies hafta follow. They can't grant wishes that conceal the results of a previously granted wish."

Durning: "I thought you said we'd be in on the ground floor, Joey. This sounds like it's all regulated tighter than a [expletive deleted]."

Giotta: "Look, Mike, why don't I just look into it, okay? I know a broad at the State Lamp Lucky Lotto. I'll see what I can get from her, okay?"

Durning: "Well, okay. But don't you go starting anything, Joey. I know you—you go off with another one of those [expletive deleted] ideas of yours and we'll wind up in the slammer for sure."

Giotta: "I'll just *talk* to her, I promise."

* * *

Nov. 18th - Groin pull. I'm out for 3 weeks. I *hate* this! My body's turning into a traitor. Ain't being the Grand Old Man of the team wonderful? You betcha.

Dec. 16th - The wins, how they do trickle in. We're still in the cellar, of course, but we played okay tonight. I was even able to stop Javert on a breakaway in the third period.

Operation Twist-Tie
Surveillance tape #2-871-89
Excerpt of phone call between Joey Giotta and Mike Durning:

Durning: "So what's happening?"

Giotta: "Mike, I think I found one. They had a Lamp Lucky Lotto winner who doesn't want the lamp."

Durning: *"What?* What kind of idiot wouldn't want a chance at three wishes?"

Giotta: "This one's a religious nut. Something about wishes being a form of magic and magic is forbidden in the Bible or something. The only reason his name was drawn was because the draw's based on Social Security Numbers—everyone in the state is automatically entered. So he won, and said no."

Durning: "You're kidding, right?"

Giotta: "No, really. He honestly doesn't want the lamp."

Durning: "So if he doesn't want it, how come they haven't taken it back?"

Giotta: "There's a thirty-day cooling-off period. Sally told me they'd run into a few cases where someone would say it was against their principles to use a magic lamp, and they'd take the lamp back, only to have the guy change his mind after a while and say he found a way to live with his principles after all. Only by then the lamp would have been passed on to someone else, so the first guy would sue."

Durning: "Sue? Sue for what—loss of wishes? You're putting me on."

Giotta: "My mother's grave, Mike. Breach of promise. The state had promised them possession and use of a lamp and hadn't given them sufficient time to make 'an informed decision.' 'Informed' my [expletive deleted]. Anyhow, after a couple of these, they passed a law saying there had to be a thirty-day period so the possessor of the lamp could search his soul. And make peace with his conscience, I guess.''

Durning: ''So how do we know this guy you found won't be like everyone else and go for the wishes? Sounds like a bust to me, Joey.''

Giotta: ''Mike, Mike, I'm working on it, okay? I just found out about this guy last night, and I had to give Sally what she wanted, right? I called as soon as I could. She just left the apartment.''

Durning: ''It's a rotten job, but somebody's gotta do it, eh? You'd better give me what *I* want, Joey.''

Giotta: ''I'm going to check it out right away, okay? I'll get back to you.''

Jan. 10th - So much for our winning streak, all 2 games of it.

Operation Twist-Tie
Surveillance tape #2-899-23
Excerpt of phone call between Joey Giotta and Mike Durning:

Giotta: ''He's really on the level, Mike. I checked around. Long-time churchgoer, elder in the church, charity work, the whole bit.''

Durning: ''So if he's so honest, how're you gonna get the lamp from him?''

Giotta: ''Look, I got it all figured out. I'll tell him I'm from some charity. . . .''

Official Hearing
Deposition of Joel Lamb:

Q: ''Mr. Lamb, could you tell us when you first met Joseph Giotta?''

A: ''I first met him about a week or ten days after the January lottery drawing.''

Q: ''That being the Lucky Lamp Lotto drawing held on January 5th of this year?''

A: ''That's right.''

Q: ''And what were the circumstances of your meeting?''

A: ''He phoned me up. He said he'd gotten my name from the state lottery officials, that he represented the Charity of Mercy.''

Q: "Did you realize that lottery officials are not permitted to give out the names and other information about winners without the express permission of the person involved?"

A: "I know that now, but I didn't then."

Q: "And what was his explanation?"

A: "I don't follow your question, I'm afraid."

Q: "What was Mr. Giotta's explanation as to why the officials had given him your name and phone number?"

A: "Oh, I see. Well, he said that his charity was in constant communication with the lottery officials, in case there was a winner who didn't want to accept the lamp and make three wishes. He said the Charity of Mercy would ask such a winner if he'd be willing to donate the lamp to the charity, so that it could be given to someone less fortunate who could make good use of the wishes. He said that after the three wishes had been made, the charity would return the lamp to the lottery officials."

Q: "And you believed him?"

A: "Yes. I know it looks pretty stupid of me, but it just didn't occur to me that it wasn't on the up-and-up. I mean, how would he know that I was going to return the lamp without making any wishes? The lottery people told me not to mention it to anyone, so that I wouldn't be harassed by cranks or have my house broken into, or anything like that."

Q: "So you assumed he represented a legitimate charity?"

A: "Yes, I did. He offered me a Lamp Transfer Tax Credit receipt to use on my income tax, so it seemed perfectly proper. And I figured the wishes would be going to a good cause."

Q: "And when did you actually give Mr. Giotta the lamp?"

A: "I asked him to give me a day to think it over. When he phoned the next day, I told him I would agree to give the lamp to his charity. He came by and picked it up that afternoon."

Q: "When did you discover that you had in fact been deceived?"

A: "Not until the end of the month, when the lottery people called me to ask when I was planning to return the lamp."

Q: "And you told them about Mr. Giotta."

A: "Yes. You see, I assumed he'd be in touch with them, that I was out of the loop. When I showed them my tax credit receipt, they told me it was fraudulent, that I'd been had. They were pretty upset. I can understand why, now."

Feb 8th - The suits offered me a job in the front office today. The G.M. talked it up, but we both know what it's really about—they don't plan to pick up my contract. My last year as a player. I know it's something any pro athlete has to face, but. . . .

I just wish I—no, make that *we*—every guy on the team works bloody hard, they deserve it, too—had a *chance* at the championship. Not to win, even, just a chance to play.

Official Hearing
Deposition by Joseph Giotta

Q: "Mr. Giotta, you've agreed to answer questions here today with the understanding that no legal action will be taken against you as a result of what you might reveal about your activities, is that right?"

A: "You got it."

Q: "Very well, Mr. Giotta. We've already established how you came into unauthorized possession of a magic lamp. What were you planning to do with it?"

A: "You kiddin' me? What do you *think* I was planning to do with it?"

Q: "Just answer the question for the record, please, Mr. Giotta."

A: "Call me Joey. Okay, I was planning to give it to a player on a team that had no chance to make the play-offs, let alone win the Cup. Then I'd get him to use a wish to make his team the champions. My pals and I would spread our bets around without calling any attention to them and clean up when they won. Is that clear enough for you?"

Q: "Perfectly, Mr. Giotta. You must have realized the Magic Lamp Act controlled what kind of wish could be fulfilled, of course? The player involved couldn't simply wish his team would win the Cup."

A: "Sure I did. I read the rules, you know. A wish like that wouldn't work, since the genies only grant wishes that directly affect the guy making the wish. But they *could* grant a wish that the guy be on a Cup-winning team. The catch is, it'd hafta be a player in his last year, so this year would be the only year the wish could be granted.''

Q: ''So you went looking for an aging player on a losing team, did you, Mr. Giotta?''

A: ''Call me Joey. Right. What kind of odds you gonna get on a favorite?''

Q: ''Didn't you think it would be a bit obvious if a losing team suddenly started to play like champions in the middle of the play-offs?''

A: ''Sure, I knew it had to be subtle. That's why I went hunting *before* the play-offs. Nothing suspicious about a team that just squeaks into the play-offs after a hot streak at the end of the season—happens all the time. The sportswriters love it, gives them a chance to write about a Cinderella team, how hockey history's being made, all that [expletive deleted].''

Q: ''And you found exactly the player you were looking for, on exactly the sort of team you were looking for, is that right?''

A: ''Right. Matter of fact, I had the guy in mind when I came up with thc scam. Paul Cardinal, an old pal of mine from school. We keep in touch, which is how I knew he was down on his luck—team in the basement, last year of his contract. Everything fit. So I went and paid him a visit.''

Q: ''Wasn't Mr. Cardinal concerned about being seen in the company of a criminal with ties to Vegas?''

A: ''Hey, don't talk about me like that, buddy. I ain't never served any time. My record's clean. So I have business interests in Vegas? So what? So do lotsa guys.''

Q: ''I'll rephrase the question, Mr. Giotta. Don't hockey players have to be careful about who they're seen with in public? Wouldn't your association with Mr. Cardinal have caused comment?''

A: ''I told you, he and I were pals. We always got together for a couple of drinks when I was in town. Folks were used to that. And with the team record, there's no chance I could have been asking him to throw a game—I mean, they tripped over their own skates enough as it was.''

Q: ''So you approached him. Was he receptive to the idea?''

A: "I wouldn't call him enthusiastic. But he was pretty depressed about how his career had turned out. . . ."

Feb. 22nd - Joey blew into town, so we went out for a few beers. I guess maybe I had one too many, and anyway, he's a good listener. He knew about our lousy season, and I told him about *my* lousy season—my lousy last few seasons. He said he'd have a proposition for me, one that might make the season worthwhile.

Mar. 3rd - Joey gave me the lamp today. I held it in my hands for a long time. A Cup win, just for the wishing.

I couldn't do it.

I wished instead that I'd play to the very best of my ability for the rest of the season, no matter how long it lasts.

From *The Intelligence-Picayune, March 28th:*

In a surprise upset, the second place Orcas were defeated by the suddenly hot Glaciers on Sunday night, in a 3–2 overtime squeaker. Rookie winger Jason Barber finally lived up to his predraft promise when he fired a slap shot from the blue line at the 3:22 mark. With several of their star players on the sidelines, the Orcas were not at their best, and the Glaciers played like men inspired. The win puts them fourth in the division, and they're now headed for the playoffs for the first time in five years.

WSR (Sports Radio) "Play-off Preview" program, April 2nd:

. . . a team to watch in the play-offs could be the Glaciers, who were 6-1-2 over their last 9 games of the season. However, they're slated to play the division champion Skimmers in the opening round. The Skimmers had the league's second-best overall record . . .

From *The Intelligence-Picayune, May 12th:*

The Glaciers came onto the ice last night and rolled right over the Lumberjacks, who played as if *they* were the ones frozen solid. Their 5–3 victory makes them conference winners, one of the biggest upsets in hockey history.

The Big Blue Iceberg became the Cinderella story of the season when, overcoming an 18-point deficit, they squeezed into the play-offs to the delight of their long-suffering fans. And those fans were nearly hysterical last night as they watched their team win the 6th game of the series. The noise level in Memorial Arena was so high it could be heard all the way down to the waterfront . . .

MEMO
Fr: Jim Haney, Chairperson, Senate Committee on Regulation and Control of Wishes
To: Mûktar, Mortal Sphere Liaison, Interdimensional Brotherhood of Discorporeal Beings
Re: Possibility of improper conduct
Our office has received copies of Racketeering Squad surveillance tapes which indicate that a Spirit of the Lamp may have improperly granted a wish requested by a person unauthorized to possess a Lamp. I have enclosed transcripts of the relevant portions of the tapes so the Brotherhood may investigate, and if necessary take measures to discipline the Spirit involved.

MEMO
Fr: Mûktar, Mortal Sphere Liaison, Interdimensional Brotherhood of Discorporeal Beings
To: Jim Haney, Chairperson, Senate Committee on Regulation and Control of Wishes
Re: Possibility of improper conduct
We have investigated the claim of improper wish fulfillment as reported to our office in your recent memo #215567. Findings indicate that the Spirit of the Lamp involved acted at all times in accordance with regulations laid down in the current contract agreed to by your government and our Brotherhood.

MEMO
Fr: Jim Haney, Chairperson, Senate Committee on Regulation and Control of Wishes
To: Mûktar, Mortal Sphere Liaison, Interdimensional Brotherhood of Discorporeal Beings
Re: Possibility of improper conduct
The Spirit involved may have acted according to regulations, but it must have realized the wish could have been in potential violation of the law, and should have declined to fulfill it.

MEMO
*Fr: Mûktar, Mortal Sphere Liaison, Interdimensional
Brotherhood of Discorporeal Beings*
To: Jim Haney, Chairperson, Senate Committee on Regulation and Control of Wishes
Re: Possibility of improper conduct

Whether or not the wish was in violation of *mortal* laws governing appropriate use of wishes is outside our sphere of concern.

MEMO
Fr: Jim Haney, Chairperson, Senate Committee on Regulation and Control of Wishes
*To: Mûktar, Mortal Sphere Liaison, Interdimensional
Brotherhood of Discorporeal Beings*
Re: Possibility of improper conduct

Genies have an obligation to adhere to the spirit as well as the letter of the law, at least insofar as they are familiar with the statutes. And the ordinance that applies here is among the most important of all those governing Wish Fulfillment. The government feels it is not unreasonable to expect that the Spirit involved in this case would have a working knowledge of what are, and are not, legally approved wishes.

Personal memo: Look, Mûktar, the Spirit really should have *understood* this, you know. *Jim.*

From The Intelligence-Picayune, May 30th
GLACIERS WIN CUP!!!

The Big Blue Iceberg proved unstoppable last night as they defeated the favored Thunderclouds 2–1 to win the series in the 7th game. Forward Jean Richelieu slammed the puck into the net with only 20 seconds remaining in the final period, to the cheers of a noisy contingent of blue-scarf-waving-fans who flew to the Coliseum in hopes of seeing their team win.

And win the Glaciers did, in a hard-fought game that saw brilliant work by goalie Michel Boisvert and defensemen Paul Cardinal and Bob Kelmchuk, who held the dangerous Thundercloud "Lightning Line" to a single goal. Said a grinning, champagne-drenched Cardinal, "It's a dream come true for me, for us to win the Cup!"

MEMO
*Fr: Mûktar, Mortal Sphere Liaison, Interdimensional
Brotherhood of Discorporeal Beings*
To: Jim Haney, Chairperson, Senate Committee on Regulation and Control of Wishes
Re: Possibility of improper conduct

The Brotherhood's position is that while every effort is made to familiarize the Spirits of the Lamps with mortal law, it can't be expected to be aware of all the minutiae of every wish situation's legality.

Personal memo: Nice try, Jim. You don't really want me to bring in the Grievance Committee on this one, do you? *Mûktar.*

From *The Intelligence-Picayune*, June 10th:

Rumors are flying that the Cup-winning Glaciers may have won their championship with the aid of magical help. It is alleged that one of the players may have been in possession of a magic lamp at the time of the play-offs.

The Wish Regulation and Control Statutes (informally known as the "Wishful Thinking Rules") don't expressly forbid an athlete from possessing a lamp. However, the Magic Lamp Act sets down controls on what wishes genies may fulfill, and the Act indicates wishes can only be of direct benefit to the person making the wish. Since wishes cannot be made on behalf of a group, it is alleged that the player wished for a Cup victory for himself and thus, of course, the team he was playing for.

The Glacier front office is angrily denying the rumors. General manager Jack Stevenson said, "Our players have the very highest standards of conduct, and we stand one hundred percent behind them. These scurrilous allegations must be stopped, and I'm demanding an immediate investigation to clear the good name of the Glaciers."

Coach Tom Blackmore added, "It's a pretty sad state of affairs when it's assumed a team like ours can't possibly win without the help of a genie. My guys have played their hearts out all year, and it finally paid off. Can you imagine how they feel now?"

MEMO
Fr: Jim Haney, Chairperson, Senate Committee on Regulation and Control of Wishes

To: Mûktar, Mortal Sphere Liaison, Interdimensional Brotherhood of Discorporeal Beings
Re: Possibility of improper conduct

Personal memo: Come on, a *sports* team? Alarms should have been going off in the Spirit's mind. Anything to do with sports is a quagmire, you know that. Please interview the Spirit involved. Of course I can't expect exact details, but at least you can let me know what was wished for in general terms. *Jim.*

MEMO
Fr: Mûktar, Mortal Sphere Liaison, Interdimensional Brotherhood of Discorporeal Beings
To: Jim Haney, Chairperson, Senate Committee on Regulation and Control of Wishes
Re: Possibility of improper conduct

Personal memo: I checked the standard Post Wish Report filed by the Spirit involved, and it was a real borderline situation. This particular Spirit is new to Lamp Service, inexperienced in probability extrapolation, and didn't realize all the ramifications. It was a simple wish to enable the mortal to perform at his personal best, which is an entirely legitimate request. *Mûktar.*

MEMO
Fr: Jim Haney, Chairperson, Senate Committee on Regulation and Control of Wishes
To: Mûktar, Mortal Sphere Liaison, Interdimensional Brotherhood of Discorporeal Beings
Re: Possibility of improper conduct

Personal memo: Oh, brother! Yes, that does sound like a legitimate wish—but look at the results. The League Commissioner is on our case, looking for complete exoneration for the team; the Racketeering Squad is on our case, saying they've got jurisdiction over us and want the two mobsters involved; and the Vegas bookies are on our case yelling about pay-offs on a rigged game. We have to get this cleared up or there'll be a bill on the floor to get the whole batch of lamp use regulations revoked. *Jim.*

MEMO
Fr: Mûktar, Mortal Sphere Liaison, Interdimensional Brotherhood of Discorporeal Beings

To: Jim Haney, Chairperson, Senate Committee on Regulation and Control of Wishes
Re: Possibility of improper conduct
Personal memo: Revoked? Hallelujah, then I could go get my karma realigned. Go on a vacation. Enjoy a little peace and serenity. *Mûktar.*

MEMO
Fr: Jim Haney, Chairperson, Senate Committee on Regulation and Control of Wishes
To: Mûktar, Mortal Sphere Liaison, Interdimensional Brotherhood of Discorporeal Beings
Re: Possibility of improper conduct
Personal memo: Sure you could. Remember what things were like *before* the Act was passed? More and more lamps showing up on the market from that archaeological find in Losan. Robbery rates going through the roof from folks trying to get their hands on a lamp. Spirits being invoked half a dozen times in a day. Multiple wishing causing energy drains from the mystic spheres. Conflicting wishes creating harmonic disturbances on the astral plane. I'll bet the Brotherhood would just *love* to have those days back, wouldn't they? *Jim.*

From The Intelligence-Picayune, June 13th
League Commissioner Darcy Longstreet released a statement today in which he indicated a full investigation would be made into the claims that the Glaciers won their Cup victory with the alleged use of a magic lamp. "We are pleased to report that the government officials involved with wish regulation have offered to fully cooperate with us in our efforts to find out the truth of these allegations . . ."

Official statement issued by the Senate Committee on Regulation and Control of Wishes, Jim Haney, Chairperson:
I have been in contact with the Mortal Sphere Liaison of the Interdimensional Brotherhood of Discorporeal Beings, and while the Code forbids the Spirits from revealing specific details of any particular wish, I have been informed that Paul Cardinal's wish did not involve any mention at all of the league championship or the Cup.

Official Hearing
Deposition by Jean Richelieu:

Q: "Now, Mr. Richelieu, as team captain of the Glaciers, and appreciating that I'm asking about intangibles here, would you say the team played beyond its abilities during the play-offs?"

A: "You don't want much, do you? Yes, the team played its best. But many teams do at play-off time—it's not uncommon at all."

Q: "It sounds as though it was uncommon for the Glaciers, though. When did the team last make the play-offs?"

A: "Five years ago."

Q: "And the team's record since that time has not been outstanding."

A: "No, it has not. Look, I know what's going on here—you're trying to make a case that we couldn't have won except because of a wish. And that's not fair. The team played hard, played its best. Sometimes you win games that way."

Q: "Mr. Richelieu, we're not trying to make a case about anything, we're simply trying to get at the truth."

A: "No, you're not. You're looking for a scapegoat, and Paul Cardinal's a convenient target, since he had a lamp."

Q: "An *illegally-obtained* lamp, I remind you, Mr. Richelieu. And shortly thereafter, the team with the worst record in the league started winning crucial games."

A: "Yes, we started winning. Because the team started working together. Paul played the best I've ever seen him play in six years, and the guys started doing the same."

Q: "The best you've ever seen him play. Conveniently, in time for the play-offs."

A: "You bastards. Paul's an honest, up-front guy, and a hard-working hockey player. He wouldn't take unfair advantage—"

Q: "That's enough, Mr. Richelieu . . ."

From *The Intelligence-Picayune, September 17th:*
The league hearing into the Glaciers affair released its findings today. It concluded that the Glaciers, through the actions of defenseman Paul Cardinal, obtained an unfair advantage against opposing teams through the means of a magic lamp. The findings made it clear that Cardinal's teammates were unwitting accomplices, and attached no

blame to them. Cardinal has been removed from the team roster and will never be permitted to play in the league again.

The Cup has been awarded to the Thunderclouds. Thunderclouds captain Les Coombs said, "I don't condone what Cardinal did. But every player knows what it feels like to want to be on a championship team. And when you don't make it you tell yourself there's always next year. But the years keep going by, and soon there's no time left at all. Maybe if I were in Cardinal's place, I might have done the same thing." Asked how he felt about winning the Cup by default, he said, "I don't feel it should have been given to us. It shouldn't have been awarded at all this year."

Cardinal could not be reached for comment.

MEMO
Fr: Jim Haney, Chairperson, Senate Committee on Regulation and Control of Wishes
To: Mûktar, Mortal Sphere Liaison, Interdimensional Brotherhood of Discorporeal Beings
Re: New regulations

This is to officially notify you of the new regulations regarding who may legally possess a lamp. As of now, *any* athlete competing at *any* level of *any* competition, professional or amateur, may not possess a lamp for any reason while he or she is active in competition. Please pass this along to the membership of the Brotherhood, so that they are aware of the change.

Personal memo: Well, that's another loophole plugged. *Jim.*

MEMO
Fr: Mûktar, Mortal Sphere Liaison, Interdimensional Brotherhood of Discorporeal Beings
To: Jim Haney, Chairperson, Senate Committee on Regulation and Control of Wishes
Re: New regulations

The Brotherhood has been notified of the change in regulations.

Personal memo: I'm sure there'll be another loophole

turning up any time now—you mortals are so ingenious at finding them. Thanks be to the Powers that I'm a spirit. Lacking the ability to subvert natural law makes existence *so* much simpler. *Mûktar.*

We have come to the end of the book, and I think it is only proper that we should conclude as we began: with a story about me, Aladdin, the Master of the Lamp.

And since you have seen me in my many incarnations, and at the height of my powers, I think it is fitting to show you that I, too, was once young and innocent and hopeful. . . .

ALADDIN AND THE LOST CITY

by Jack C. Haldeman II

A great sandstorm raged continuously around the walled city in the desert, isolating it. If there were any roads leading in or out of the city, they were not visible in the swirling grit. Strangely, the air directly above the city was always clear. The sun beat down on tightly packed buildings the color of sand even as the savage winds raged outside. It had always been this way.

The market was loud and crowded. A vendor, wearing a flowing caftan, was arguing with a potential customer about the price of the fine fruits and vegetables stacked on his makeshift table. The customer insisted the price was too high for such bruised and damaged produce.

While the vendor was distracted, Aladdin reached up and stole two figs and a date from his table. Although he had not been seen, Aladdin ran away from the stall out of habit, dodging harried people and bleating animals in the dusty square until he reached the dark, narrow alleyway that would take him to his secret hiding place.

Aladdin was young, and alone in the city. This did not particularly bother him, for he had to answer to no one and could live as he pleased. And it pleased him to live an easygoing life with no responsibilities and no obligations.

The secret hiding place that served as his home was an abandoned shed behind the house belonging to Reza Bah-Hein, a blind storyteller. It was an ideal situation. The old man was gone most of the day, sitting on his precious carpet in one courtyard or another, telling pointless tales and speaking in riddles for people who would sometimes give him a coin or two or a morsel of food. While he was gone, Aladdin would help himself to the old man's water, which had to be carried from the well on the far side of the city. He had looked upon the storyteller's carpet with envy, for his own carpet was threadbare, but as yet had found no way to trick the blind man out of it.

Aladdin took a long drink from Reza's earthenware jug. It was cool and delicious, all the more so because it had cost him no effort.

"Aladdin."

The voice startled the young boy. He turned and saw a figure standing in the doorway dressed in the rags and old clothes of a calender, a member of the begging order of dervishes.

"Who's there?" asked Aladdin.

"Alms? Alms?"

They both laughed.

Aladdin recognized the voice of the Second Calender. It was said that he had once been the son of a king, but he would never confirm nor deny that, just as he would admit to no given name and was simply called Second Calender. He wore a patch over his right eye.

There were two other calenders in the city, though Aladdin had not seen First Calender in some time. Third Calender, who claimed to be a king by name of Agib, was kind of a snob, at least as far as Aladdin was concerned. Second Calender was an okay guy, though.

"What brings you here?" asked Aladdin, trying not to stare at the patch.

"I seek Sinbad. We had an arrangement."

"Sinbad comes and goes," said Aladdin. "The Cyclops—"

"His third voyage," sighed Second Calendar. "I am tired and bored of hearing about it. As if there was anything unusual in having only one eye. Humph! Now *three*, that would indeed be a story.''

''What do you have there?'' asked Aladdin, eyeballing the coarse muslin bag Second Calender was carrying.

''This and that,'' he said. ''Things and stuff.''

Aladdin rubbed his hands together. ''May I look?''

Without waiting for a reply, he took the bag from Second Calender's hands and opened it. It was full of junk; a few pots, some chipped cups, a frayed scarf. Down at the bottom something gleamed. A lamp. He dug it out and held it so it caught the light.

''Ahh,'' he said, thinking about how dark his room was at night. ''This is just what Reza Bah-Hein has been looking for.''

''A lamp?''

''Certainly. He himself asked me to find him one.''

''What would a blind man want with a lamp?''

''Am I not in his house?'' asked Aladdin. ''It is not for me to understand the man, but to do his bidding. He will gladly pay you for this tomorrow.''

''This is not another trick, is it?'' asked Second Calender. ''You have tricked me before.''

''All mistakes,'' said Aladdin quickly. ''A failure to properly communicate. This is different. He really wants this lamp.''

Second Calender looked at him carefully. ''I will believe you this time,'' he said, ''for it is in my nature that all men deserve a second chance. I will come back tomorrow for my payment.''

''Good,'' said Aladdin, pushing Second Calender out the door. ''He will be quite generous.''

''I hope so,'' said Second Calender, shouldering his bag and turning. ''I hope so.''

Aladdin could not contain his glee when the beggar had left. It was a fine lantern. A little dented perhaps, and not as shiny as it might be, but better than the darkness. He placed it in a pouch of his tunic, left the house of the blind storyteller and started wandering the streets. Perhaps he could find someone to trick out of some oil.

It was his misfortune to turn left at the corner by the baker of sweet breads, for he wandered into a courtyard where Reza Bah-Hein sat cross-legged on his carpet.

"Aladdin," he said. "Come sit with me. And don't try to turn away again, for I know it is you."

"I—"

"Come sit," he said, patting the carpet beside him. "We will talk now, for I do not have much time."

Aladdin sat in front of the blind man, shifting his tunic so the lantern was behind him. "Are you sick?" he asked. "Can I have your carpet when you die?"

Reza laughed. "You know so much for one so young," he said. "But you know so little. Tell me of your father."

"My father?" asked Aladdin. "He was a humble tailor. We lived in China."

"Tell me of him. Tell me what he looked like. What did he like to eat? What habits did he have? What kind of thread did he use? Were his needles curved or straight? Tell me the color of his hair, his eyes. Details. Tell me details."

"He looked like me, I guess," said Aladdin. "He was older, but I'm pretty sure he looked like me."

"You don't remember?"

"Sure, I . . ."

"Tell me the truth, child."

"Well, sometimes I don't remember too good."

"And what of your memories of China? Was it at all like this city? Was it a place of grass and mountains and rain, or was it all dust and sand like here?"

"I think it was different."

"And I think you should return the lamp."

"What?" asked Aladdin.

"It is not time yet. It is best you return it. I will explain. Do you know Ali Baba?"

"Of course. All of us know him."

"Have you seen him lately? Or his brother Cassim?"

"No. They must have gone somewhere."

"And where is there to go, Aladdin? Have you ever seen anyone leave this city?"

"No."

"Or return?"

"Sinbad returns. He leaves and comes back with many tales."

"Ah, Sinbad the Sailor. There are seven voyages in his life; future and past. Seven is a magic number."

"Seven?"

"Take a coin. Place other coins around it. Seven coins are strong, they form a circle. They cannot be pushed apart. More coins, or less coins and the circle is weak."

"Is this another of your riddles?"

"Perhaps," said the blind storyteller. "But, on the other hand, perhaps all life is a riddle, and we are but pawns in someone else's games of chance. Does the name Scheherazade mean anything to you?"

"No."

"A storyteller," he said. "From the present, the future, the past. Makes no difference. Tell me about the band of thugs."

"What?" asked Aladdin, confused. "They left with Ali Baba and his brother."

"It was their time," said Reza, a little sadly. "As all our times will come. Soon this city will be deserted and covered with sand. It will exist no more. All the stories will have been told."

"But—"

"Wait!" said Reza as his carpet shimmered. "You must get off the carpet now."

Aladdin stumbled to his feet and backed off. The edges of the carpet flexed and waved. Reza Bah-Hein started to rise into the air.

"Remember the lamp," he said as he cleared the wall, riding on his magic carpet. "It is not your time." Then he was gone, disappearing into the swirling dust that constantly surrounded the city.

"What was that?" asked Second Calender, who had just arrived.

"It was the blind storyteller," he said, feeling the pull of the lamp and the even more powerful magic of Reza Bah-Hein. "He said he won't be needing his lamp. He won't be coming back."

Aladdin reluctantly returned the lamp to Second Calender and ran back home, stopping only to grab a few olives from an unguarded table on his way.